Forever and Always

Sonni Lagodinski

authorHOUSE®

AuthorHouse™
1663 Liberty Drive
Bloomington, IN 47403
www.authorhouse.com
Phone: 1-800-839-8640

First published by AuthorHouse 3/18/2010

ISBN: 978-1-4490-8263-5 (e)
ISBN: 978-1-4490-8261-1 (sc)
ISBN: 978-1-4490-8262-8 (hc)

Library of Congress Control Number: 2010923978

Printed in the United States of America
Bloomington, Indiana

This book is printed on acid-free paper.

Acknowledgements

A special thanks to my wonderful editor and
English teacher, Mrs. Weigel. Thank you.
To my parents, Mom and Doug, who stood behind
me throughout the whole process. Love you two!
My amazing family who supported my want to
write this book and the many others to come.

Contents

preface

I never thought I would be the girl on the milk carton or the face on a t-shirt saying "We Believe." Nor posters with "Have you seen me?" on them with my hair color, height, weight, age, DOB, and date missing. It never crossed my mind.

"Are you ready for your big audition?"

My father's voice was cheery, ready for the big moment. Two days after my ninth birthday, I had an audition for a movie. My feelings were indescribable. I was bouncy in the seat of our old Dodge pickup. My dad's smile was more than convincing.

"You know it, Daddy."

"I love you, Bug. You'll do gr..."

A horn beeping.

The look on my dad's face.

A loud crash.

Pain.

Screaming.

Black.

A painful memory that will never leave my thoughts. I have to think about the drunk driver smashing into us every day.

I just didn't know that he would be angry. I mean, it wasn't my fault! I couldn't stop him, though. He wanted to kill me and there was nothing I could do to stop him.

Home sweet home never seemed so sweet!

CHAPTER ONE

new beginnings

Lili sighed, "I can't believe you're leaving."

My mom, Cadie Young, got a promotion with her job. She was an oncologist, one of the best in her field. That job, in particular, was in need all over. She was currently told by her bosses they needed her expertise somewhere else.

"I won't be far," I said.

She was transferred to Jeffersontown, North Dakota. Mom searched around for the best school. She had heard of a little town forty minutes away from Jeffersontown, named Edgemont, with a school said to set high educational standards.

"Sara," she whined.

Topanga Beach, California, was my home. Leaving the sun, heat, ocean, beach, and, most importantly, my friends behind wasn't on my recent "to do" list. Moving away from this paradise was actually the last thing I ever expected to do.

I shrugged, "Only a phone call away."

I sighed and laughed. The August wind blew through my open window. If I wasn't moving, I'd be out running along the beach with Lili enjoying the last days of summer vacation. Late August was the best for swimming.

"I promise we'll call and text and everything possible. Promise." All I wanted was for her to smile, to see that smile on her face.

Her short, dark, curly hair was blowing from the breeze coming in the window. The tears in her brown eyes were real. I threw more clothes into a suitcase that was nearly filled. My room was bare, everything in labeled boxes in the moving truck outside.

She took a picture from the floor. It was one of us together. Just a random photo of the crazy Lili and Sara together. Lili looked at me and smiled. I had to look away to avoid a major breakdown. I was weak, a true softy.

"I don't want to think about not seeing this house again. Like the way you guys have it." She stopped and looked around. "Or, *had* it."

"Are you trying to make me cry?"

She shook her head with a smile. I took the picture and put it in my purse.

"Remember when we had a sleepover here?" She started to laugh. "And, your mom said we couldn't leave or have boys."

I laughed, remembering. "Mom gave me strict orders."

"We sneaked out the window and had boys come over."

She sighed, "Good times. Cute boys."

"Very cute boys who have now turned into jerks."

"Yeah." She paused and looked around. "Remember our trip to see Nadir Remerez?"

"Man. What a hottie!" I giggled.

Our favorite actor was Nadir Remerez. He was in Hollywood for a movie he had just been in. He acted weird when we got to the table. He was nervous, somehow. It was like he was speechless. He *was,* actually. Words never came out of his mouth, he just nodded. He just stared with the pencil busily moving. The piece of paper he handed us was full of scribbles, no sign of an autograph.

"When we asked for a picture"—Lili stopped to catch a breath of air in between laughing—"and he just nodded!"

"His hand was literally shaking behind my back!"

She breathed calmly now, "Where's that picture at?"

"You have it, don't you?"

"I'd have to look."

I thought about his green eyes. As I stared into them at his signing table, they were amazing. I will never forget eyes like those. Green as emeralds.

Mom's voice echoed as she hollered up the stairs that it was time to leave. Lili and I looked at each other with a sigh.

One final look in my room, I walked down the stairs for the last time. My hand slid against the wall I touched every day. I looked at the dust squares left on the wall by pictures that have been there since we've redecorated years ago.

I walked through all the halls and rooms. I had one last time to remember all the memories that happened here. This house was my home. But I had to leave it to go to North Dakota.

"Please promise me you'll never forget me?" Lili asked as we had packed everything in the car and were ready to leave.

"I promise." My only reaction was to run to her arms for the last hug of a long time.

Lili was doing a half-smile, half-cry thing. "I love you, Sara."

"I love you, too, Lili. I will never find a friend in anyone like I did in you."

By this time, we were both crying.

"Forever..." she sniffled. Her smile never left that beautiful face of hers.

I smiled, "...and always!"

Watching Lili wave good-bye from our front door step was agonizing. We'd been neighbors since I've known her. I looked back one last time at our house in California with my best friend waving good bye in our driveway.

At Cali North High, I wasn't what you say "popular." Your typical girl was tall, tan, and dark haired. I have blonde hair and blue eyes, and I'm short. I'm not a stick, I have curves. I wouldn't classify myself as overweight, though. Wearing dark, thick rimmed glasses didn't help me much, either. And, on top of that, I had metal braces on both my top and bottom teeth. I was perfectly happy with who I was.

But the boys in my school didn't think so. Braces and glasses defined my life; I was mocked by everybody. Lili told me I looked good in glasses; I didn't object. In my mind, glasses were stylish. And I didn't mind the braces, they'd be gone soon.

I'll never forget the time a big-shot jock shoved me out of the way.

"Get lost, freak," he'd said. "Oh, and by the way" - he nudged his friends and laughed - "you got something in your braces. Might want to, uh, clean that up." As each one of his buddies passed me, they all gave me a shove.

All he did was smile and walk away.

"Someday, we're going to kick that guy right in the..." Lili had said, but I stopped her.

"Lili, calm it." I had forgotten about it within minutes.

I wiped away a falling tear that rolled down my face before my twin brother Cole would notice.

Before we'd left California, I'd gotten my braces off. And, I *accidentally* stepped on my glasses. I begged Mom to let me get contacts. I wasn't going to a new school with my *old* image.

"There is a new Sara Young coming to Edgemont Public School," Lili had said to me when I'd got them off. "Everybody beware!"

California had been my home since I was born. I lived and breathed the ocean breeze at night and the warm sun every morning. The sand between my toes told me everything was perfect. But, one mistake changed that. Luke, my father, was killed in a car accident involving a drunk driver. So, I could say, getting away from California is leaving that memory behind.

My grandmother Joanie, Dad's mom, lived close by. I saw tears stream down her face that I've never seen before. She'd become my best friend as I had grown older. The good-bye from her was truly the hardest. I was extremely close to both of my grandmothers, since my grandfathers had died long ago. She waved goodbye from her window as our car passed her house.

Granny Marion is my mom's mother. She lives in Edgemont, something which made my mom happy about moving there. Edgemont was Mom's hometown growing up. That was an option that influenced why we planned to live there. I would talk to Gran Marion for hours on the phone catching up on things that she'd missed.

State after state rolled by as we crossed the United States. I stared out the window in a daze. Leaving Lili behind was depressing.

We've been best friends since kindergarten when I shared my snacks with her.

"Sara." Cole, my brother said, startling me. I looked up. "Need to stop?"

I shook my head and went back into my daze.

Cole is my twin brother. His brown eyes are so deep, they almost look black. He's been there for me for everything. I can always rely on him. The smile that he puts on his face can immediately put a smile on mine.

Cameron, my older brother, is your average boy, looking just like Cole. He's tall and muscular with dark hair and blue eyes. Cameron has a smile that would melt your heart if you looked too long. He's a big man, but with a big heart.

Cole and I are sixteen and our birthday is on September 22. When the leaves are falling off the trees and the air turns to a cool, crisp temperature every morning, you know it's almost time for our birthdays. Cameron is seventeen and his birthday is on November 23.

My mind wouldn't stop shooting horrible thoughts of how badly this transition could be. Then again, it could be very helpful and exciting. I just had to believe and everything would be good.

Traveling into North Dakota, I was astonished to see all the open land, going on for miles. In one field, I saw a big, red machine that looked as if it were cutting down stalks of something. Semis lined the edge of the road. All along the road were these machines, each cutting something different.

As the sun was setting we rolled into our new beginning. The sign welcoming us to Edgemont told me that this wasn't California anymore. Edgemont was a small town, about 650 people.

Moving from California with all the stuff we had was impractical. Cameron drove Mom's Intrepid along with Mom. Cole drove his pickup with me accompanying him. He pulled a trailer with my car in it.

I sighed as we saw the house down the street.

"Come on, Bug," Cole said. "You've been fogging up the windows since we've left."

I looked at him with my eyes puffy from the crying.

"I can't help it."

He cocked his head and smiled.

"Cheer up!"

I tried not to get my spirits down again.

As we got out of the car in the driveway, Mom encouraged, "Wow, what'd I tell you guys? This isn't so bad!"

"It's nice, Mom," Cole said enthusiastically.

It *was* a beautiful house. The house was black and big. Although I wasn't in the mood for excitement, I managed to give her a convincing smile.

The house was breathtaking inside. I was speechless. Even with nothing up decorated, it was nice.

We unloaded the things from the car and waited until the moving truck got here. I claimed my room and a bathroom, the only two on the top floor. There was no way I was sharing with two boys!

From the car, I brought some important boxes, containing necessities such as a few pillows and my suitcase. In the moving truck were my decorations.

My mind began to wonder as I sat alone in my bare room with two boxes. What if I wasn't accepted into the school? I was worried. All the possibilities ran through my head. Was it possible to be let down in a school you've only been in for a day?

No.

I couldn't let my mind control me. But then again, what about Mom? Why was she so eager to move? She was almost excited to get out of the house. Wouldn't she miss Dad? Of course, Dad wasn't at the house technically, but I had the feeling he was watching over us the whole time.

Then again, she probably couldn't say no to the job. If Mom liked the job, Mom could have the job. And it was a nice job.

Just a big transition.

Glancing near the window where my purse was, I saw the picture of Lili and me. It made me think back to all the moments we've had together. For us, nothing was wrong. It all just seemed to fall right into place. I sighed and looked out the window when I heard the sound of a car door slamming. Outside was the moving truck containing our possessions. I dragged myself out of the bedroom door halfheartedly and slugged down each stair.

Of course, throughout the process of moving everything in, Mom kept the smile on her face. She was happy that everything was here and that it would finally feel like home. So in order to keep her happy, I had to put on the phony smile that was supposed to make her believe I was happy.

In ways, I was.

In others, it wasn't what I wanted to do. I wanted to stay near to Lili. I wanted to be near to Dad. I wanted to stay in my home. I guess wanting isn't as important as needing because Mom needed that job.

After all the lifting and hauling and lifting and hauling, we finally sat down for supper. The hardness of the floor was gone with the help of the couch cushions we sat on, and since there wasn't anything to cook the food with, we ordered pizza.

Mom explained with the hint of enthusiasm about our new school.

"You start school on Tuesday. It's called Edgemont Public High, home of the Wolves. Scary, huh?" she laughed. Her laugh was soft, but beautiful.

"What about football, Ma?" Cole asked impatiently with a smile.

She returned her answer with a smile, "Well, I did ask Mr. Field, your principal, about you guys joining late, and he said that is fine, you just won't play in the first game."

"Okay, so when's practice?" Cam asked.

"Nine o'clock sharp." She nodded her head making it official.

Taking a bite of my slice of pizza, which was way over greased, Mom interrupted me by saying, "Also, you guys need shots." Her statement made me drop my pizza. Cole laughed and grabbed it.

Needles were, in my mind, enemies. The way they slide through your skin and poke you each time. Or, how it's a stinging pain. I've never had blood drawn and I sure don't think I ever will. I've never needed an IV or anything. Just shots, each time ending with me running out of the room.

"No." It wasn't a statement or a question, it was a demand. "No way. Never."

Cameron snickered, "What? Little Miss Perfect afraid of a little needle?"

I shook my head, "No, I was just..." I bit my tongue, knowing I've been caught. I sighed, "Uh." I quivered as I thought of the needle going into my arm. "The needle, ugh, going into my arm just, just makes me want to..."

"Puke?" Cameron finished.

I nodded, suddenly losing my appetite.

"I've made an appointment for you on Monday," Mom instructed. "I can be there if you want me to."

I shook my head, "I'm not a baby. I can handle it. I won't *like* it, but I'll do it."

"Okay."

Mom wasn't like your ordinary mom; she was more like the sister that I never got. Maybe she's making up for it. I love her more than ever. Ever since my dad died when I was nine, we have been really close. She's my best girl friend. She's also young.

My dad and I got into an accident involving a drunk driver. I came out of it with a broken arm and a concussion. But my dad wasn't so lucky. He died about an hour after the accident. The drunk driver, however, got out from his car and walked away with a headache. We had, though sued him. He was sentenced to ten years in prison, with two suspended if all the fines were paid. This year, my seventeenth birthday, would be the eighth year anniversary.

My mom has held strong ever since, dating occasionally. She said that none of them were the right guy. She promised that if she planned on remarrying, she'd ask us first.

"Wow, I'm full." Cameron said letting out a huge burp.

"That's disgusting, Cam! You're a pig!" I said.

"'Better out than in, I always say,'" he quoted from Shrek.

"Well, I'm going upstairs to start unpacking. What are your plans for tomorrow, Mom?" I asked.

"I wanted to go uptown to get groceries, so if you have a hunger issue, let me know. I also want to just cruise around and see the town. I want to check out and see if they have any little stores or something."

"Can I go with, shopping, I mean? Then, you can drop me off and I'll unload everything while you 'check out' the town." I had to laugh.

She smiled at me, "Sure, Sara."

"Okay, what time?"

"I'm thinking noon? Is that all right?"

"Yeah, it's fine, Mom."

My room was a mess. Boxes were everywhere. I had no idea where to start. I started to rummage around for my bed. I looked at the pieces and gave up.

"Cole!" I hollered at the top of my lungs. I knew this bugged him, but I sat on my empty floor with a smug smile and waited for his answer.

"What?" He walked in.

"Will you help me put my bed together?" I ask in the sweet voice with the puppy dog lip.

"Yeah."

He put it together like he would a preschool puzzle. It would have taken me a half hour just to figure out how to get it right. With all the bolts and pieces, it's confusing just talking about it.

"Cole, are you worried about Mom?"

Surprised by my questioned, he answered, "No, why? Should I be?"

I just shrugged, "Well, no, but she's really happy lately. I've never seen her this happy. In California, she'd scare me sometimes because I didn't know whether or not she was happy. Even since, well you know, dad, she doesn't really talk about him. I just wonder if it's all building up inside, ready to explode at any minute."

He reassured me with a smile, "She's happy. I think this new job will be perfect for her. I think every day she was reminded of him by our house. This is a new beginning for her. We'll all be fine, I promise."

He winked with that smile and gave me a huge hug. It was nice to have him here, knowing all my needs

"Night, Bug."

I smiled, "Night, Cole! I love you!"

He turned around and smiled. "Yeah, I know you do," he joked as he left the room.

I dreamed that night of my dad. The picture was fuzzy; I couldn't see what we were doing. It was all so real, as if he was really here.

The sun on my face woke me up that morning. It was Saturday, a busy day.

The upstairs consists of my room and bathroom, an office, and a game room. From the downstairs, you go up seventeen stairs, I counted them, and then you have two choices; either turn right to go up eight curvy stairs to my room and bathroom, or turn left and go up eight curvy steps to the office and game room. Either way of taking them, they wind up leading you to the same hallway.

The main floor is unique. When you walk in the front door, you see in front of you the stairs to upstairs. To the left of you, you see the kitchen. From the kitchen, you can go into the dining room and from there, into the living room. To the right, you can go walk into the living room, so it's a bit of a circle. Mom's room is also on the main floor along with two bathrooms. The boys have the downstairs to themselves. They have one bathroom, but they each have their own bedroom.

I went down the stairs into the kitchen where Mom was making breakfast. I could see in the living room that they had set the TV up along with the couch.

"Good morning! How did you sleep?" she said, welcoming me with a smile.

"Morning, Mom. Good, and you?"

"I slept soundly through the night. You hungry?"

"Yeah, a little."

"Okay, well, there's fresh coffee and the pancakes are almost done," she said, continuing to flip Mickey Mouse pancakes on the stove.

I always drink coffee in the morning. It was going to be a bad day if I didn't get my coffee. Milk and sugar were a perfect combination which made it just sweet enough. My dad got me into drinking coffee. I grabbed a mug, added the milk and sugar, and went to watch TV. Cameron woke up soon after, joining me on the coach.

"Morning," he said, in a crabby tone. He's not a morning person.

"Morning, crabby," I replied.

"What's Mom cooking in there?" he asked sniffing the air.

"Pancakes. Want coffee?"

"Nah, not this morning. I'm cutting back. *What* are you watching?" he asked.

I laughed; he never liked the things I watched. "Here, you can have the remote, I'm going to eat." I threw the remote towards him.

"Pancakes are done," mom yelled from the kitchen. My stomach rumbled at the smell coming from the kitchen.

"Where is your other brother?" Mom asked. "That boy can sleep for hours. Please, go wake him up."

"Cole, let's go! Wake up!" I screamed at the top of my lungs, right where I was sitting.

Mom gave me a dirty look.

"Sara, just go down stairs, please," she instructed.

I tumbled off the chair and made my way down to his bedroom. I jumped onto his bed, right on top of him. "Wake up, sleepy head!"

His eyes shot opened and his lips curved into a smile.

"Ah, Bug, get off of me! Yeah, you're light, but get off!" he hollered, shoving me off. "What time is it?"

I gave him a smile, "It's 10:30. Mom has breakfast ready, you coming?"

He jumped up, threw me over his shoulders, and ran up the stairs.

"Put me down!"

I couldn't help but laugh as I bounced on his shoulder up the stairs. Wasn't I too old for this?

"Morning, Mom!" he said as he plopped me on the coach.

I went upstairs to keep unpacking. I had most of my clothes unpacked and in their place. Everything else was unpacked; it just needed to be arranged. We went shopping in Cali before we came for decorations for our rooms and bathrooms.

"I'm ready, Mom," I called down the stairs ready for grocery shopping.

"Great. Me, too. Let's go. Boys, we'll be back in an hour. I expect you guys to have your rooms fully unpacked when I get back," Mom demanded. "Do you guys need anything special?"

"No, just get enough to stock everything. We're boys, we got to eat," Cam said.

"Okay, be ready to help unload when we get back."

We drove through the town of Edgemont. It wasn't as small as you think. While we were shopping, we had a lot of people come up and talk to us. They introduced themselves and their families. They knew who Mom was because she was talked about in town. They couldn't wait for a top doctor to come into this little town.

I tried to put on a convincing smile to each face that had something to say to us. All were nice although after the twentieth person who came up to us, it did start to get on my nerves.

A couple, looking young but standing out, introduced themselves. Mom had bumped into the man, making a stack a toilet paper fall.

"Oh!" Mom said, "I'm sorry!"

He just smiled, "It's okay. Probably my fault."

He started to pick up the toilet paper with Mom and his wife helping. I couldn't help but the notice a figure behind them, disappearing and reappearing around the aisle continually. It was a boy, maybe my age, almost 17. But, I couldn't get a good look at him. He had copper-colored skin and pitch black hair.

"I'm Robert Pierce."

I looked at the man smiling at me, holding his hand out.

"Sara."

"Cadie Young." My mom's voice was welcoming, almost proud.

The woman stepped up, "I'm his wife, Melanie. And this is our son, Caleb..."—she turned around searching—"well, I do have a son, just not with us at the moment."

The two also had copper-colored skin and black hair. Both stunning. Melanie was beautiful in more ways than one.

I tuned out the rest of the conversation, looking for their son. Unfortunately, the aisle was empty and no longer did his body come from behind the other aisle.

"Nice to meet you," my mom said, pushing on my back.

"Nice couple," she whispered as we walked out of the grocery store.

Cute boy, I thought with a smile.

We got home, unloaded the groceries, and relaxed. The rest of the day was just rearranging things. We got all the boxes unpacked and things in their proper place. I sat in my new room looking at the new features. Sitting on my bed reminded me that I wasn't in California. My thoughts took me back to my dad and the accident.

My accident with my dad was long ago, almost eight years now. We were on our way to auditions for me. I wanted to audition for a movie that looked like it could be fun. Dad encouraged me to go. My mom called the studio and asked about it and the people seemed interested in me. Mom had to work that day, so Dad took me.

The auditions were two days after my birthday, the auditions being my birthday present. We were almost there, but it was a red light. When it turned green, my dad went, but so did a drunk driver from the side lane, which had a red light. He ran the red light and crashed right into my dad's driver door. Luckily, we both got out alive.

They separated us, but we met again at the hospital. The last words he said to me were, "Never give up. Please promise me you'll never quit." And I know he heard me, "Oh, I love you, Daddy! We all do. Stay strong." He didn't stay strong, he died minutes later. Mom, Cole, and Cam got there just in time to hear him say I love you to them.

The crash went by fast. I couldn't remember what happened exactly. When the doctors asked me questions, I just held my head and said I didn't know. But, knowing that I came out alive without my dad didn't help the matter.

I never gave thought to the guy who killed my dad. Most days I just stopped thinking about him and concentrated on my dad. When I saw his face in the back of the police car, it was awful. His hair was messed up and his eyes were droopy. He was definitely drunk. Who is that stupid that they get drunk?

Shaking off the memory, I got off my bed and made up my mind to go drive around.

"Mom," I said when I got into the kitchen where she was, "I'm going to drive around. Be back later."

I own a Dodge Avenger and the thermometer read seventy-nine degrees. It was definitely colder in North Dakota than it was in California. The houses in Edgemont were all different, each having their own look. In California, each house was built in almost the same way. I saw the individual look to each house, wondering which of my classmates would live in each one.

I decided to drive out to the town Cenex to burn some time. I didn't feel like going back to the new house quite yet.

As I pulled up, there was a group of people, looking about my age, standing by the door. I was nervous to get out of the car. I didn't know why I came. What would I buy? Reaching into my pocket, I made sure I had money.

I took a breath and stepped out.

"...new doctor in town." I wanted to turn around when I heard it.

"I heard about that," another girl said. "I hear she's got kids. Three. A girl, I think she's like seventeen or something. Two boys."

Then, there were hushes going around in the group.

"Shh."

I walked by without looking at the group. I heard snickers and whispered but kept walking. As I rounded the corner and made sure I was out of sight, I heard more talking.

"That's her!" I heard a girl voice say.

"Man, she's hot," a guy's voice spoke.

"Oh, Josh!"

I smiled and walked in. I rummaged around to find something to buy. Cappuccino caught my eye. With a cup in my hand, I braced the whispers as I stepped out the door. They were still standing there when I walked out.

I planned on just walking by but had to stop when one guy spoke, "Hey, you."

I turned around and gave him the "are you talking to me" face.

"Yeah. Are you the doctor's daughter?"

I nodded, "Yeah."

"I'm Josh."

"Sara."

His face was humorous, like this was all a joke. "Are you going to school?"

"Yeah."

He was cute. I could see me being friends with him. Tall. He was surrounded by a group of girls. A boy in the background wasn't very noticeable and I couldn't see him clearly.

"What grade are you in?"

I had to answer his question without being completely humiliated, "Junior. You?"

"Junior."

Awkward silence. I couldn't handle it anymore.

I mumbled, "I better go."

"See you in school." As I turned around I could hear the crude laughter.

"Knock it off, Josh," I heard a boy say. He sounded absolutely dreamy.

"I just introduced myself, Caleb."

Josh, I thought. *Cute. Rude.*

When I woke up on Monday morning, the boys were already gone for football practice. I groaned realizing what lay ahead of me today.

As I was getting my breakfast, I heard my phone go off. It was Lili's ringtone. I ran to it.

"Hello?"

"Hey girl!" she said.

"Hey! How are you?"

I could hear the excitement in her voice. Man, did I miss her. "I'm good, it's nice and hot here. How are you?"

I sighed, "I'm all right. It's hard to adjust. You know?"

"Yeah. Have you met anyone?" She laughed. I knew she was talking about boys.

My mouth curved into a smile as I remembered the kids at the Cenex, "A few said hello."

"Oh, well," she giggled, "you still have school, tomorrow. There outta be a cute boy in every school."

I laughed and paused. "I miss you."

I heard her sniff, "I know. I miss you, too. I wish you were here."

"Oh, I do, too." I choked back tears. "I miss the sun."

There was an awkward moment of silence. I wanted to pour my heart out and tell her how badly I wanted to see her face, but I couldn't. I said the first thing that came to my mind.

"What if I'm not accepted?"

She groaned, "Please. Look at yourself in the mirror."

"That's not what I mean." That's exactly what I meant, though.

Her voice sounded confident, "Then, what do you mean?"

I sighed, "I don't know."

"Exactly." I could picture her smiling in victory.

"You know, if you ever get a chance, you should come visit me here. You'd be amazed."

"Nothing like California?"

I shook my head. As if Lili could actually see me. "Nothing. It's different."

"I will have to then."

A long pause. Again, it was awkward. I haven't even been gone for a week and I can't make a simple conversation with Lili productive. Once again, I just blurted out a random thought.

"You'll never guess what I have to do today."

"What's that?" she asked with a chuckle.

I sighed, "Get a shot."

I could hear her burst into laughter, catching air whenever possible. I couldn't help but smile.

"Are you done?" I asked, slightly annoyed at my dreadful upcoming.

She breathed, "I think so." She let out one more giggle. "Okay. I'm guessing you're scared?"

"Well," I started, "yeah! Give me blood and anything internal, just don't poke me with anything sharp!" I screamed into the phone for more emphasis.

More laughing, "Sorry. I know how much you hate needles. Good luck."

"Thanks. Well, I better go get ready for the doctor."

"Okay. Be sure to send a picture of your house. I can only imagine what it's like. And," she chuckled, "have fun at the doctor."

"I will. If only you could see my face glaring at you." I giggled. "Later, Lili."

"Later."

I dressed in sweats and my hair was a mess. The doctor's office smelled funny and there was a sneezing woman sitting next to me. I didn't think I could take it much longer before my stomach would burst. The urge to get up and walked away was in my head. The only thing keeping me from getting up was the woman sitting at the counter eyeing me the whole time.

I flipped through People magazine but didn't even read the pages.

Shot.

Shot.

I couldn't get the word shot out of my head.

"Sara?" a nurse called finally.

I stood up, uneasy, and made my way following the nurse. Each door I looked through somebody was being poked by needles. Nausea quickly swept over me like a cool breeze on a stormy day.

"Now," she said, startling me, "your mother told us that you aren't very good with shots." I nodded, speechless. "Okay, you'll be fine." She gave me a convincing smile and scribbled down something on paper. "Billy?" When she said the name, an old man came walking in with a smile on.

"Good morning, Miss Young." His voice was low and very welcoming, but, no matter how welcome a voice is, I just don't want a stupid shot.

"Morning," I mumbled.

"Have a seat." He paused and dug through a closet. "Okay, I want you to ease everything from your mind."

Oh, sure, easy for you to say, I thought.

As he said this, he took the syringe in his hand and squirted out liquid. I heard a scream and a loud bang. The room started spinning and there wasn't light.

Darkness and pain. Bad combination.

"Sara?" Someone was shaking my body.

"Sara. This is Dr. Leeds. Are you okay?" No, *I* was shaking my body.

Dr. Leeds was smiling when I opened my eyes. I felt uncomfortable with his arms around me. I had moved from the chair to the bed in the room. I wasn't shaking when my eyes opened.

"We quickly gave you the shot while you were passed out, so it's all over with. How do you feel?"

"Fine," I murmured while rubbing my head.

"Okay, just stay lying down. We are in no hurry. Just rest."

I sat up quickly and wanted to get off the bed. "No, really, I should go."

"Do you feel well enough?" His tone was the voice that doctors use when they care a little too much after they just done something that you didn't want them to do in the first place.

I wanted to glare at him. He just didn't understand I didn't want to be there. "I feel fine."

I slowly climbed down from the bed with Dr. Leed's arm around my waist all the way. He never let go, even in the waiting room. All the eyes once reading the paper were now on the doctor and sick girl walking out the door arm in arm. As much as I wanted to, I couldn't tell him to let me go.

He, also, had no problem helping me to the car in his white robe. I was unsteady getting to the car, but by the time I was home, I felt fine.

I slumped over my bed and grabbed my guitar and started to sing. The guitar belonged to my dad which encouraged me to teach myself how to play. I didn't think anyone cared if I played or not, so I just kept my guitar—playing to myself.

All memories ran through my head as I sat on the ground with my guitar. Why did my dad, big and strong, have to leave? Why couldn't it have been someone else's dad, and not mine? I shook my head.

No, that's selfish, I thought.

As soon as I heard the front door slam, I immediately placed the guitar under my bed where it always sat.

Deciding to be lazy the rest of the night, I just sat in my room and read. Occasionally one of the boys would knock at my door and bug me about something bizarre, but they would leave me alone after I gave them the annoyed and tired look.

During the best part of my favorite book, my phone vibrated telling me I had one new message from an unknown number.

'Sara. I'm out and I'm not happy. I don't know where you went, but I'll find you. I'll find you!'

Without thinking, I deleted the message immediately, assuming it was from someone being dumb. Just trying to play a trick.

Little did I know.

I needed to get all the sleep I could get for the next day. Tomorrow was an important day. I was excited but still really nervous. I was ready to experience the feeling of starting a new school. It was a good feeling, too, to know that nobody knows your past. I want to keep what's in the past, in the past.

But, I tossed and turned in my bed. My head was full of memories. There were nights that I remembered everything from the accident. It wasn't a blur or just something that was faintly in my mind.

I could almost hear his voice. Almost...

CHAPTER TWO

edgemont public high school

"Are you ready, Bug?" my dad asked.

I nervously nodded my head. I was nine years old. Getting ready for the audition of a lifetime. My seat belt felt too tight.

"Daddy, do you think I'll do good?"

His smile went wide across his face, "Of course I do."

"And if I don't?"

He smiled wide. "You'll still be my number one."

"Thanks, Daddy."

"I love you, bug. You'll do gr..."

At the hospital, I leaped off the gurney and ran through the hallways looking for my dad's room. My hopes were low when I couldn't find him. After realizing what just happened, tears were streaming down my face. We were in an accident. The doctors were running after me trying to catch me. My head hurt but I ignored it. There was piercing pain in my right arm but it didn't faze me. I wanted my daddy.

As I slowed down, arms came around me. I had hoped they were my dad's. My hopes were high but were crushed when it was the doctor scooping me up in his arms.

"Your dad is this way. Please relax."

How could I relax when I couldn't find my dad? I didn't know if he was alive or dead. Disgusting thoughts ran through my head. The doctor's arm weren't comforting; I wanted him to set me down so I could walk.

He walked into a dark room. I could hear the monitor's beeping. I could see my dad lying on the bed, with a white sheet over him, blood spots everywhere.

"Set me down!" I whispered in a holler jumping out of his arms.

In the bed, Dad was surprisingly smiling.

"Oh, Daddy."

He coughed and his voice was hazy. "Bug, are you all right?"

I sighed, to hear his voice was amazing. "I'm fine, Daddy. How are you?"

He coughed, "I'm good. Your mother is on her way."

"I don't want to leave." My voice cracked as I spoke.

"Bug, you don't want to be here. It's not fun."

I could see scratches on his face, more than one. And, yet, I couldn't look away from his face. I tried my hardest not to cry in front of him. It didn't work too well.

"Bug," he began with a worried tone, "this crash didn't end well." I shook my head not wanting to believe him. "I don't think I'm..." he coughed with a painful sound.

I had to cut him off, "Daddy."

"Shh, it's okay, Bug. I don't know how it's all going to end. But you know that you're my princess. I love you."

"I love you, Daddy." I sniffled and gave my dad a big hug.

As I was hugging him he said, "Listen to me, Bug. Never give up. Please promise me you'll never quit."

I got up and looked Dad in the eyes, his blue eyes full of fear, knowing that my eyes were, too, full of fear.

"Promise?"

I nodded, "I promise you, Daddy."

"I love you, Bug."

I cried, "I love you, too, Daddy. Hang in there."

"I will."

We sat in silence. The monitor told me he was still alive. What was wrong with him? Why were they worried? Why didn't he think he was going to live?

The doctors came and went, checking on both Dad and me. They offered me a bed, but I refused. They wanted to check me over, but I still refused. I wasn't going to leave my daddy's side. No way!

Mom came rushing into the room an hour later, her face soaked with tears. Cole and Cameron followed behind crying, too.

Mom told us to leave the room. Cameron's face was more than worried. He looked at me confused, but suddenly rushed over to hug me.

Then, doctors came rushing by. I could hear Mom screaming in the room.

"Get in here!" I heard her say. "Luke!"

As we rushed in, Dad spoke only once more.

"I love you, Cadie. I love you, Cole." He took a deep breath and the machine went wild. "I love you, Cameron. I love you, Sara. I love you all."

"I love you, Dad," Cole said crying.

"I love you, too, Dad," Cameron said.

"I love you, Daddy." Being last was hard.

"Luke! I love you!"

The monitor beeped no more, just one long steady sound. Mom was screaming. Doctors rushed beside us, hollering numbers and commands. I couldn't understand anything they were saying.

"We need to do CPR. Stat!"

"There's nothing we can do. He's gone."

Mom's frantic cries were heard throughout the hospital.

The white sheet covered his whole body.

I ran out the room.

The rest, it's history.

I shook my head. Why did I let that memory come back? It wasn't a memory, it was a nightmare. I tossed and turned until I couldn't stand it anymore. I went down the stairs and popped two Tylenol PM's in my mouth. I wiped my red face with a Kleenex and laid in bed staring at my dad's picture on my night stand.

Good night, Dad. I love you, I said in my head as I drifted off to sleep. The clock read 4:00 am.

School.

Uh.

Three hours of sleep wasn't good. Although when I started to get ready, I perked up somewhat. We took my car to school, arriving early enough to meet the principal and find our way around. Edgemont's school had a grand total of 190, now 193, students in both elementary and high school. It also wasn't hard to find because it was at the edge of the town. The building was located on a long street. It was a one-story building, a block long.

We walked into the main doors and saw black and gold everywhere.

I wanted to see what I looked like one more time before I went and met all the new people.

"I'll be there in a bit, I have to use the bathroom," I told my brothers before running off to the bathrooms. My eyes wandered to the notes posted on the bulletin board and the signs hanging on every wall.

I saw all the past class pictures hanging up from the start of the school all the way to the current year. The doors to the math and English room were in my view. This transition to the new school was going to be hard.

Unthinkably hard.

Then, I tripped. My face was inches away from the floor. I stood up quick hoping no one saw that. But, with my luck, there was one bystander.

The hands of this person were collecting the notebooks and books that were once in my hand.

Then, he spoke with such serenity. "You'll have to watch that carpet. It'll get you." His laugh echoed in my ear. I didn't look up.

"Thank you," I said as he handed the books to me.

And, he was gone before I could see who he was. He disappeared into one of the nearest rooms. A glimpse of dark hair caught my eye. And, the scent he left behind was mouthwatering. Cologne and linen mixed together. Perfect combination.

Cole and Cameron were laughing as I came back to them. I skipped the bathroom part. I didn't feel the need for anything else embarrassing to happen. When we walked into the office, there were shirts, pants, coats, sweatshirts, and anything else you could thing of for sale. A short, dark haired lady with a name tag, reading Lorii, was at the counter to greet us.

"Good morning. You must be the doctor's kids. Welcome to Edgemont! I truly hope you like it here. I'm Lorii, and I'm the school's secretary. You can come to me if you have a question, are sick, need Tylenol, anything, just come to me," she explained, with a smile. She seemed friendly and in a good mood. We'll see how long that lasts.

"I have arranged students of your own grade to show you around the school and help you get from class to class. Mr. Field is our principal and he'll be giving a lecture right after you take role for first hour. Then, you'll go to your homeroom, and so on. This is your schedule for the year. The students I've chosen will explain it more. Okay, enough of me talking, which of you are the twins?"

Cole and I raise our hands. "I'm Sara and this is Cole, my twin. And, that is Cameron." Cameron nodded. Lorii smiled and called the students who were going to show us around. The first to come in was a short-cut, dark-haired girl, taller than me. She had light copper-colored, perfect skin.

She walked in with a beaming smile on her face. "Good morning, Lorii. Oh hey, everybody, I'm Penny. You must be Sara!" she spoke with such an excitement as she looked at me. "I've been waiting all weekend to meet you! Lorii called me on Friday and told me I'd be the lucky one to show you around. Follow me, please!"

She was a cute, lively little thing. She had dark eyes, almost black, and I couldn't help but stare at them. "This is going to be so exciting," she continued. "Everyone's been talking about it. I mean, a professional doctor moving into a small town. Who knew? We are so lucky to have your family here, especially your mom. Have you met anyone, yet?"

"Nope, you're the first," I mentioned, trying to convince her I was just as excited as she was. She led me to our lockers down the hall, talking the whole way.

24

I could honestly say I was looking for Josh and trying to find the similar features I saw last night. He was appealing and maybe he'd remember me and help me out.

I saw Josh standing with a group of guys looking as good as he did last night.

That's when I first saw him.

There were a lot of guys around him, so I don't know why I picked him out first. He had black hair and copper skin, too, almost looking identical to Penny. There was something strange about him. He looked so familiar. The black hair...

"Who is *that*?" I asked, with a little too much curiosity in my voice.

"My brother, Caleb," she sighed, obviously annoyed at how much attention he got. "All the girls want him."

I asked with hesitation, "Have any of them been lucky enough?"

She shrugged her shoulders, "A couple. He's not what you call a player. He's so busy with acting..." she quickly stopped.

"Acting?" I asked confused.

"Um"—she stuttered and played with her hair for a second before continuing—"I mean with his work."

"Where does he work?"

She seemed to be getting flustered and I have no idea why. She stuttered again, "Children's library." She paused and smiled, "Any other boys?"

Nodding, I smiled, "What about Josh?"

She shrugged her shoulders, "All right. You know, typical teenage boy."

I moaned, "Have a lot of those in California."

Penny laughed, "Did you say California?" Her voice wasn't what you'd say convincing of the way she was so intrigued about California, but it did sound like she wanted to change the subject.

"Yeah, why?"

"Oh my gosh! I love California!"

I questioned the tone, "You've been there?"

Her face turned to a worried look. She quickly thought, "Well, no." She breathed. "Not exactly. But someday, yeah, hopefully."

I shrugged, "Maybe you could come with me sometime. We plan on going back there occasionally. You should come, it'll be fun."

"That would be awesome, Sara!" she screamed, grabbing my arm, "I'm so excited! Here, I'll introduce you to my brother."

"Woah, wait, what?" I said, pulling back. "No way, oh my, no way. I can't! It'd be too nerve-racking. I'll meet him some other time."

"Okay, calm down," she laughed, gesturing with her hands. "Just tell me when you're ready. Let's go, we are going to be late for first hour. My brother will be in there," she said winking at me, "he's a junior, too."

"You are twins?" I asked. "Cole and I are twins. Cool."

"Yeah, and we are adopted," she explained, while getting into first hour. "Our parents found us on their doorstep alone when we were just babies. I guess we were lying side by side in a basket, with our older sister sitting next to us, wrapped up in blankets.

"There was a note that said, and I quote, 'We're sorry we can't take care of our children. Whoever finds them, please take care of them.' They took us in and waited a year. When no one claimed us, they adopted us. Our older sister is graduated and getting married, though. And, in college. She's nineteen. We are seventeen."

"Already?"

"They held us back. Instead of making us the youngest in our class, we are the oldest."

I nodded and continued, "Tell me about Josh."

She smiled, "Josh. Man. What to say? He's a player, you could say."

"Does he have a girlfriend?"

Penny shook her head.

I contemplated that as we walked into the room. She showed me where to sit. I could see Cole with group of guys, including Caleb, over in the corner of the room. First hour was math, something I dreaded. If there's one thing I absolutely hate about school, it'd be math.

I don't understand it at all. I've never had a good enough teacher to teach it to me. I'm hoping that this year will be different. I believe that if you plan on involving math in your future, then you have to take it. If you don't plan on it, you don't have to. Simple enough.

Mr. Reynolds, our math teacher, walked in whistling. "Good morning, class. Ready for another great year?"

"Morning, Mr. Shorty. Yes, I am," a boy from the back of the class said.

I can understand why they called him Mr. Shorty. I guessed he was about 5'4", maybe. He seemed in his mid-thirties.

Penny tapped my shoulder and whispered, "He's really funny and smart. You'll learn a lot from him. He's never once yelled at us."

"Good morning, Michael. I see you're already off to a good start with the name calling," he said, but jokingly. "My name is Mr. John Reynolds, and I'm saying that due to the fact I see two new faces with us. You must be Cole and Sara Young. Welcome!" he blurted.

I could feel my cheeks getting five different shades of red, fast. How could everyone know?

"The freshman and sophomores may be dismissed at this time," Lorii said over the intercom.

Saved by the bell. I'm not much of a person to speak in front of people or to be talked about, so hearing the dismissal saved the embarrassment. I blush very easily.

"Now, the juniors and seniors, also," she added.

Penny walked beside me, along with girls named Courtney and Sonya.

"We have a lot of cliques in our school," Sonya explained. "We are the girls who aren't in those cliques and we plan not to be in them. We have been friends since the first grade. But, you seem like you'd fit right in. Just watch out for Kali and Kory, the meanest girls you will meet. They are your first-class bullies."

"Yeah, you're better off with us," Courtney warned me, with a wink.

I smiled.

I noticed Josh walking with the group of guys. He was laughing and talking, everything a boy *would* do.

Mr. Field talked about safety, rules, requirements, sports, and all the things that you needed to know. I wasn't paying attention. I scanned the bleachers and saw Cameron, sitting with a bunch of guys. Cole was still with the group of boys that he was sitting with in math.

I looked to see Josh smiling at me. I tried to look away without smiling but failed as I grinned while blushing.

I turned my head the other way, and my heart skipped a beat. He was looking right at me. Caleb Pierce. I blinked and then reacted with a smile. He smiled back. His teeth were perfect, white and straight. His black hair wasn't gelled back; it was free to do what it wished. It was very chic and natural. He was close enough for me to see that his eyes were a bright green. I couldn't look away.

I wanted to look away for a boy *that* great wouldn't want someone like me. I wouldn't think twice about dating him.

Some way or another, he looked familiar, like I've seen him before. I couldn't think, though. He took my breath away.

Those eyes.

"All right, Sara," Penny said, breaking the trance I was in, "let's go to Mrs. Hoffi's room. She's our English teacher. Beware, she's kind of mean, but just get on her good side," she laughed.

I was guessing that Mr. Field had ended the lecture and told us to go to our homerooms.

The first half of the morning went by so fast. Penny and I had all the same classes. I saw Josh in math, English, and history. Too shy and nervous, I didn't get the courage to go up to him and talk. He wasn't in my Chemistry class. Luckily, Penny and I have the same schedules. Caleb was also in most of my classes. He was being loud and obnoxious in all the classes just like all the boys in his group.

In English, Caleb sat directly in front of me with our assigned seats. His hair wasn't long, but yet it wasn't short. It was dark black. He turned around and smiled while handing back papers that Mrs. Hoffi passed out. He still hadn't seen me throughout the day.

"No talking unless I allow it," Mrs. Hoffi said. She continued something else but I wasn't paying attention. "You guys know the drill. Nothing new."

Then, Penny tapped my shoulder from behind, "Talk to him," she whispered. Although, she said it too loud.

Caleb turned around and when I thought he was going to talk to me, his green eyes turned towards Penny. "What are you doing after school?"

"I don't know, why?" she answered.

He shrugged and turned around, "Just wondering."

"Caleb," she said catching him before he turned back around, "this is my friend Sa..." But, the bell rang and he jumped out of his seat.

Walking out of the room, "Forget it, Penny. Caleb's got higher standards than me."

Penny just smiled and walked out of the room.

Chemistry was slow. Science was not my thing. My lab partner was quiet, never talked. In fact, I don't recall his name ever being mentioned. He sat far away from me. He wore glasses and his blonde hair was in a mess. He wore a button up shirt, buttoned all the way up to the collar. It was tucked in. He needed a fashion makeover. Majorly.

"Get used to your partners. You'll have them for the rest of the semester." Mr. Schulz was going to get annoying. He was smart, but cocky.

I sighed and looked at the back of my partner.

Mr. Schulz assigned a problem out of the book to do with our partners. He just moved farther away and turned his back towards me. Obviously, he never talked to girls. I would change that.

"Hello."

His back remained turned towards me.

"I'm Sara."

I wanted nothing but for him to turn around.

"I think I need help on this problem." I knew the answer, though. "I think the answer is radon, but I'm not sure."

"That's wrong." His voice was low, but friendly.

"Then, what is it?"

He huffed and scribbled on his paper. "Hydrogen."

"Okay."

He never turned towards me. I gave up when the bell rang.

At lunch, Penny introduced me to more people. I met Hannah and Lisa, seniors who played basketball. We quickly got into the subject of basketball while waiting in line for our food.

"Are you any good?" Hannah asked.

"Well, I've been starting since I was a freshman back at Cali."

"Wow, you must be good then," Lisa answered.

"Yeah, I guess I'm all right. I really like it. My dad had me shooting hoops ever since I was little."

We sat down at a long table, filled with students. Some guys talked to me, introducing themselves. It was awkward, but exciting. I could be who I wanted to be. But, I would be myself.

"I'm Sam. I saw you in English class. This is my friend, Rob." The guy next to him smiled and stuck out his hand.

"I'm Sara. Nice to meet you guys. And you are?" I asked, gesturing to a shy looking guy next to Rob.

"Brandon. We have math together."

Penny sat down at the table, stopping the conversation between the guys and me. I looked around the room and saw Caleb, he was sitting with Cameron, Cole, and other guys, and they were laughing. All of a sudden, Caleb turned his head and looked right at me. He smiled, flashing his pearly whites.

Penny smiled, "I tried to introduce you two in English."

"Don't make a fuss. I'm not good enough."

"You two would be a cute couple!" Penny said encouragingly, interrupting our gazes at each other. I blushed, guessing it was obvious that he and I were looking at each other. "I've never seen him look at a girl like that before. He's in love with basketball and baseball. That's probably why no girl is good enough, because they don't like sports. You like any sports?"

I shrugged as I ate a spoonful of chicken noodle soup."Yeah. Baseball, basketball, track, and volleyball. Sports are my life. I'm a huge Twins fan."

With a shocked look on her face, she questioned me, "You are? He's like a major Twins fan. Okay, now I'm convinced. Go talk to him. No, better yet, make him come to you." She laughed.

"Penny, I need to focus on school here." I took a breath. "So, Penny, do you have a boyfriend?" I asked, changing the subject. I knew I've been blushing the whole time.

"Yeah. Didn't I introduce you to James? Sara, James. James, Sara."

A guy sitting next to her, who was turned the other way, turned toward us and smiled. She seemed a bit nervous to introduce me to him. For some reason or other, she was trying to avoid the introduction.

James was tall, muscular, and tan. He had short blonde hair. He was your average boy, cute.

"Hey," he spoke with a Spanish accent, "I think our moms work together. You're Dr. Young's daughter, right?"

"Yeah. Your mom a nurse or something?" I asked, curious how he already knew me. Another person who *already* knew me, great.

"Yeah, your mom's assistant."

"Oh, okay," I said remembering, "Gloria, right?"

"That'd be her."

"Okay, yeah. We went to go meet everybody the day before Mom started working. Your mom seems really nice. She was actually the nicest one there."

"I'll tell her you said that, she'll like it," he joked.

I laughed, "Well, it's true." I could tell by Penny's expression that she wasn't liking the immediate connection that James and I had. I tried to get Penny in the conversation by asking, "Okay, so where next?"

"Spanish III. Excited?" she asked. The mood got lighter and happier. James slipped his arm around her stomach, and started whispering in her ear. She completely ignored my reply which was simply, "Oh, yeah." They were laughing and flirting like crazy.

I *was* jealous in a way, that I didn't have that guy to resort to and laugh with. I'm sixteen and I've never been kissed. It's embarrassing to admit, but I've never had a boyfriend. I haven't tried very hard to get one, though.

Of course, Cameron and Cole are way over protective. I had a date one time, and my brothers chased him off even before I got down the stairs. I didn't talk to them for a week. Cole was the first to apologize, so I forgave him first.

"All right," Penny said, focusing on the time, "we better go before we're late. I'll talk to you after Spanish, James. See ya!" She watched him walk out the cafeteria and sighed, looking at me with a defeated smile. "Sorry about that, he's been so nice to me, he's perfect." We got up and emptied our trays and headed for Spanish.

"I'm happy for you. You two look cute."

She just smiled and kept walking. "Caleb's in Spanish with us. May be he'll make his move then," she pointed out.

"What move?" I asked smiling. "Anyways, I've only been here for one day."

She shrugged, "Are you good at Spanish?"

I shrugged, "A little, you know, the usual."

"Yeah, me too, except," she paused. I turned my head to see Caleb standing next to her. A whiff of his cologne caught up with us; it smelled phenomenal.

"Hey, Sis, how's it going?" His voice was dreamy and perfect; not too low or high. He spoke with such ease. It was a familiar tone. "Who's your friend?" He never stopped smiling. Those greens eyes were as bright as a lime. His face was flawless, mesmerizing.

"Hey, Caleb," she said, winking at me, "this is Sara. Sara, this is my brother Caleb."

He threw out his hand for me to shake. I'm sure I was already shaking when I shook it. His hand wasn't rough, it was smooth and warm. When I touched his skin, he smiled wide.

When I look at boys, I notice their eyebrows. It just one of the things that matter to me. Bushy eyebrows, no thank you! The way his eyebrows were reminded me of something, weren't bushy at all. I shook my head, knowing it wasn't possible that I've seen him before.

"Nice to meet you, Sara," he said smiling. "Hopefully Penny hasn't said too many embarrassing things about me. You're Cole and Cameron's sister, right?"

Not even a day, and I have a younger sister reputation.

Great.

I nodded, speechless.

"So, Penny, are you willing to share this lovely friend of yours? I'd be glad to show you around town after school, maybe get a smoothie at Nelli's?" he asked.

"What's Nelli's?" I asked, catching on to their conversation.

"Best hang out place around, especially for a date," Penny answered, her face promising. "And"—she nudged me—"I'd love to share her."

Caleb switched from Penny's side to my side, slipping his arm gently across my shoulder, "So, what you think? You up for it?"

If my heart were wearing a heart monitor, it'd make no noise, for my heart literally stopped.

"Yeah, sure." I could feel my nerves finally kicking into gear. I couldn't believe it; I was talking to Caleb Pierce.

"Great. It's a date." I could only smile and nod when he spoke. "All right, I'll be at your locker after school. We'll take my vehicle," he said, taking his arm away and disappearing in the room.

The scent of his cologne brushed by me as he walked by. Why is he so perfect? Can it be real? Can *he* be real?

From behind us, I heard, "Jeez, new girl. Move that big butt of yours." I turned around and just as I did, Kali bumped into my side, hard, ramming me into Penny. "You should watch where you're going next time, new girl."

They laughed in unison.

My mind couldn't create any harsh comments for a comeback; I was too furious.

Being a savior, Mr. Field walked out and said, "Kali. Kori. My office. Now!"

I saw the look on Kali and Kori's face. It made me smile when they looked embarrassed that they were caught. Good. They deserve it.

"Don't worry, her butt is way bigger than yours," Penny whispered encouragingly with a smile. "Yours is tiny. She's just jealous because Caleb likes you and not her."

I just nodded and could only think about one thing. Those green eyes.

"Penny. Does Caleb wear contacts?"

She nodded her head.

"Colored?"

She shook her head, "Aren't his green eyes amazing? I wish I had them."

I could have sworn I've seen those eyes before. My thoughts subsided when we entered Spanish.

"Hola, clase!" our teacher greeted us.

Spanish was my favorite class; the language came naturally to me. There were only five students in Spanish III; Caleb, Penny, Jordan, Cole, and me.

Senora Garcia had no problem assigning homework the first night. Our assignment was to write an essay on why we liked Spanish. If we wrote it in Spanish, we got extra credit. We could judge how long it could be.

I'm probably what you'd call an over achiever. I like to make sure I do things right. I don't like to make people mad. I've gotten good grades in school since I was young. But, I've never been the teacher's pet.

Caleb kept to the boys in Spanish. It would have been too nerve-racking to talk to him again.

Sixth hour was my study hall with some of the juniors. Caleb wasn't there, I was hoping he was. But, I could use this time to actually focus on my homework. I signed out of study hall to go get more books from the library. The school was small enough not to get lost, so I decided to go by myself.

Josh was walking down the hall as I walked out of the door. He stopped and smiled.

"Well, well, well. Look who we have here."

"Trying to rhyme, are we?" I laughed.

Josh just shrugged his shoulders like he was the coolest guy in the school, "Yeah. Where you headed to?"

I didn't want to sound like a nerd so I lied, "Cruising around. Exploring."

Josh laughed and smiled, "Need help?"

I shook my head, "I think I got it."

He shrugged, "See you later."

I was deep in thought with a book that looked interesting in the school's library. I found it appealing with the cover, a prince and a princess.

"Fancy meeting you here," a familiar voice behind me spoke.

I turned around just enough to meet the fascinating gaze of Caleb. His green eyes were luscious and his smile was wide.

I couldn't speak. I couldn't remember what I was going to say, so I just smiled.

34

"Find anything good?" his dreamy voice asked.

I held up my book, not realizing I still hadn't spoke.

"Ah," he said, smiling, "The Prince and Princess. Sounds interesting."

I nodded and placed the book back on the shelf. It *was* interesting, but he obviously didn't think so.

He was dressed in clean-cut, torn-up dark washed jeans with a polo shirt. The cologne wasn't strong, but enough for you to smell it as a breeze came through. His dark black hair was shaggy, free to do what it wanted.

"Are you ready for our date tonight?"

Speechless, I just nodded. Why couldn't I talk?

You dumb fool! Talk!, I thought.

"Are you ready?" I asked as evenly as I could.

"Sure am." He paused but smiled, "I am just hoping I get a *little* more out of you."

"Yeah," my voice cracked and I had to look down.

"Did the carpet catch your feet again?" He chuckled as he asked the question. So, it was *him* who saw me and helped. Oh boy, this topped the embarrassment chart.

I shook my head and smiled and looked down, sure of the fact blood was quickly flowing through my cheeks.

He chuckled making my cheeks turn ten more shades of red, "I think it's a turn-on when girls blush." He moved just inches away from my ear and whispered, "It's hot."

I looked up at him and him down on me. He smiled and turned around and headed towards the door, only to look back and wave with a smile and walk out the door. I quickly grabbed the book and checked it out after hearing the bell for next hour.

Replaying the day was easy. First, I made a fool of myself by tripping in front of some boy. Then, I realized it was Caleb who I tripped in front of. Then, everybody knew me and who I was. Josh turned out to be on the list of interesting guys. And, finally, I was a total idiot while speaking with Caleb. What a day! And, I had to somehow pull it together in our date tonight.

I was hoping that by seventh hour, gym, that my cheeks were normal color. None of the people I've met so far were in gym. Our gym teacher had us play basketball. I was excited to get my hands on a basketball.

One boy came up to me while we were in a time out. "Hey-y," he said, breathless.

"Hello."

"I'm Chris. Chris Baker. You new?" he asked regaining his breath.

I nodded. In a way, I was shocked that he didn't notice me. Everyone I've talked to had known me already. I smiled.

Chris was cute. He had curly, blond hair and was, of course, taller than me. Who wasn't? When he smiled, he had little dimples. He did seem big and brawny. Not as big as Cameron, though.

I stuck out my hand, "Sara. Nice to meet you."

"You, also. I was watching you play. You're..."–he paused to catch his breath—"well...amazing."

I chuckled, "Thank you. You're quite good yourself." In all honesty, I didn't even notice him play.

He huffed, "Yeah. I'm all right."

"I haven't seen you all day. Are you a senior?"

"No." He looked down. "Sophomore."

"Even better. I'm a junior." I tried to smile when I said that, hoping he'd take it the right way.

He just nodded.

"So, I guess we'll see each other all year here, huh?"

His head shot straight up with a smile. "Uh-huh. Lucky us."

I laughed, "Well, at least I have one friend in gym. I was afraid I wouldn't have any."

"Well, you can count on me."

I'm usually nervous with talking to boys, but with Chris, it just fell into place.

Before more conversation, Mr. Hansen blew the whistle for us to shower. I was sure to shower thoroughly, for I didn't want to stink for my date. Chris quickly left my mind and it was focused on Caleb.

I met some new girls while we were in the locker room. There was one that stood out, Giselle. She was gorgeous, tall and skinny, with long brunette hair. I recognized her because of her basketball skills.

She played post, while I played point guard, and she was excellent. She moved with such grace.

"Hey," I said, approaching her with a smile, "I'm Sara. I noticed you were really good at basketball today."

I was skeptical about talking to her; she was wrapped in only a towel.

"Giselle, and thank you. You're quite awesome yourself." She was putting on makeup. "You're the new doctor's daughter, right? The one who just moved into town?" She seemed interested.

"Yeah, that's my mom. Gosh, news travels fast doesn't it," I laughed.

She giggled, "Sorry, but small town, big news. You'll learn."

She turned around and slipped off her towel, making me more uncomfortable.

"Uh, yeah, I guess I will. Are you a junior?"

"Sure am. I saw you in math this morning. How was your first day in Edgemont?"

Looking around, I finally saw all the girls dressed making it more comfortable to talk to her.

I sighed, "It was all right, really stressful, though." I laughed, thinking about what I had coming up after school. It really hadn't been a stressful day, but what else was there to say. "I've meet really nice people. But, it's funny; they all seem to know who I am already."

She laughed, "Like I said, small town. Interested in any cute boys?" she asked with curiosity in her tone.

"Well," I started, "there is this guy I'm kind of looking at, but it's only the first day. I don't want to get carried away."

She started laughing, "Yeah. Who is this guy?"

"Caleb Pierce."

She nodded, "I thought I saw you with him today. Lucky. Everybody wants him. Except for me," she winked. "But, there's something strange about him."

Curious, I urged her to go on, "What do you mean?"

"Well, he's only flirted with a few girls. He sticks with his sports buddies. He's really quiet, I guess. Only really talks with certain guys, like Josh, Jordan, Jake, and Tyler. They have this "group" thing going on. I don't know really. He just seems weird. Like this one time," she continued, roping me in with curiosity, "he was gone from school for three months. Didn't tell a soul where he was. Penny was gone, too. She came back saying they were both sick. Come on, sick, for three months."

In her tone, it was disbelief. It was hard to imagine someone being sick for three months, without telling anyone. Then the bell rang.

"School's out. We'll talk later. I'll give you more details." She smiled and walked out the door before popping her head back through, "Oh, I'm having a party this weekend at my place, the rentals will be gone. Want to come?"

"Sure, sounds fun."

"Great! I'll give you directions for my house later this week. See you tomorrow!"

She trotted out the door. I didn't even realize that I wasn't close to being ready for Caleb.

I scrunched my hair with mousse. My hair was naturally curly, and naturally a pain in the butt. I straightened it every day, easiest thing to do. Because of that, it was frizzy, and nothing but. But, whenever I did have it curly, I got good comments on it.

I threw some make-up on, not very much, though. I always thought over-bearing make-up looked ugly. I put a little body spray on, and headed out the door with a plan to talk more on the date.

I was hoping my luck would be better after school.

CHAPTER THREE

twenty questions

Caleb, just as he had said, was leaning against my locker. His legs were crossed and his arms were folded and he had a smile on his face. My heart started to beat faster when I saw that he had flowers in his hand.

When he smiled, it showed in his eyes. You could tell he was happy. As I approached, he took the flowers and said, "Beautiful flowers for a beautiful girl." Corny, I know, but sweet.

"Thank you, they're beautiful. You've been waiting long?" I asked, acting as calmly as I could.

"Nah, just got here. Ready to go?"

"Yep." I grabbed my homework.

"Oh, and by the way, you've already said more words than you did in the library." He laughed.

I blushed again, "Do you like to make me blush, because, gosh, you sure are good at it."

Again, he laughed and led the way to his car.

He had a bright red Challenger with white strips down the hood. It stood out. "Nice car," I pointed out.

"Birthday gift. You like cars?"

My head nodded without any words coming out. I could start to feel myself getting more comfortable with every second. I wasn't afraid to talk to him, just still nervous as can be.

He pulled out of the school's parking lot and headed down the street. "All right, let's be creepers and ask each other questions. I'm too lazy to find out any other way." He smiled then winked.

I laughed, "Okay, you first, then."

"First off," he began with a smile, "aren't you scared about riding with someone you've never met before?"

I shrugged my shoulders, "I trust you."

"What's your full name?" he asked running his fingers through his stunning hair.

I answered, "Sara Raquel Young. Yours?"

"Caleb Robert Pierce. Favorite food, not including a salad." He winked.

"Chicken. I love chicken. I don't eat any other meat, really, except for chicken."

He smiled," I like chicken, too. But deer meat, man, that's my weakness. My family and I are hunters: deer, goose, you name it. Big outdoorsmen."

"Really?"

He smiled with a hint of humor, "Yeah. Have you been hunting?"

"No."

He laughed but quickly turned his face into a humorous shocked looked.

I continued, "I think it's mean to kill animals, even though I eat meat. If I ever watched something get killed, I'd be scarred for life." I shivered at the thought of it.

"But you still like hunters, right," he asked with a smile.

"Yeah, still like hunters."

He smiled, and I couldn't look away. Something about his smile reminded me of someone. How could I have possibly seen him before, I had moved half-way across the country?

He pulled to the edge of a building with Nelli's on the side of it. He got out and came around my door and opened it for me. When we walked in, I noticed some of the faces sitting inside. He led me to a table, told me to wait, and took off. He came back with two smoothies in his hand.

"Banana Berry Smoothie, my favorite. Hope you like it."

I took a sip, "It's good."

"All right, your turn to ask the questions for a little while," he suggested.

I sat there for a split second gazing into those green eyes. Something about them was so breathtaking. Those eyes couldn't have been real. I wanted to think of a question that wasn't idiotic or too boring for Caleb to answer.

"Favorite color?"

He smiled, "Green. Yours?"

"Lime green and pink. Favorite music?"

"Country. And yourself?"

"I love country. When's your birthday?"

Caleb chuckled and answered, "June 24. Yours?"

"September 22. How old are you?

"17. You?" He took a sip from his smoothie with a hint of a smile.

I blushed, "16." I needed to get my cheeks a different color and fast. "Are you Catholic?"

"Sure am. You?"

I nodded. I couldn't help but smile. Somehow, he made me feel all bubbly inside. He had that personality that was so wonderful, you couldn't describe it. He was perfect. Well, I'm sure he wasn't *perfect* by any means, but he sure put on the perfect face around me.

We sat at Nelli's for three hours. We talked about all about favorites. We got to personal subjects, like family. When he talked, I couldn't focus. His lips synchronized with his words. His eyes sparkled when he would laugh. His hair would blow when the late August breeze blew.

"What's your mom and dad's name?" he asked.

"Cadie and Luke. Yours?"

"Melanie and Robert. And you have two brothers, is that it?"

"Mhm, Cole and Cameron."

"O boy, I better watch out then tonight, huh? They might hunt me down if I bring you back too late. Your dad would be right along with them, too," he joked.

I laughed, "Yeah, they probably would." I didn't want to tell Caleb about my dad until it was necessary.

I hated having to explain his death over and over again. Knowing that I came out of it just fine made me mad. I often asked myself if it was my fault. With my dad dead in the ground, how could I not feel guilty?

"Okay, so, do you like baseball?" he questioned me.

"Are you kidding? You're looking at the biggest Minnesota Twins fan!" I shouted for excitement.

"Prove it. First base?" he questioned me like I was on a game show.

"Justin Morneau."

He looked at me with a puzzling face, "Catcher?"

"Joe Mauer, my favorite."

He raised his eyebrows, "Closer?"

I laughed, "Joe Nathan, my favorite closer!"

He clapped his hands in a sarcastic way, "Wow. We just might have to go to a game some time. Have you ever been to one?" He sounded surprised at how much I knew. Little did he know, I knew much more.

"No, I've really want to though," I sighed. "Your sister said you were into sports, what else do you like?" I asked, trying to avoid the whole subject of my dad.

He answered quickly, "Basketball, that's my favorite. I feel free, like I can do what I want. The only person who is stopping me is my coach."

I was in awe. "Basketball is my passion. I feel the same way. Do you start?"

"Yeah, usually. Did you play back at California?"

Shocked, I asked, "How did you know I moved from California?"

He had to think of an answer. "Uh, my sister told me. Besides, everybody knows who your family is. You aren't a secret, Sara. You're famous and you don't even know it," he replied with a smile on his face.

I laughed, "I guess you're right. It seems like everybody knows who I am already. In a way it's a little freaky, having everybody know. It's kind of funny, too, though."

He winked and smiled. When he smiled, my heart melted. He's got the way to make my heart jump. "You didn't answer my question. Did you play in California?"

"Yeah. I've been starting since I was a freshman."

"Impressive," he said with a little too much sarcasm. He sniffed the air, "I smell a challenge coming on. You and me play one-on-one. What you say?"

"Okay," I giggled, "but, you don't have a chance."

"I honestly don't think I do, against a 5'5" point guard, that is." He laughed.

"Hey now, you making fun of my height? I happen to like it," I chimed.

"Nope," he said defending himself, "just saying I'm going to get circles run around me. I'm pushing 6'3". We have a bit of a height difference."

I blushed, "That's okay. So you're a whole head and a half taller than me, who cares."

He laughed, "Yeah. So, we going to play basketball or what?"

"Where is there a court? I'd love to run circles around you." I smiled.

"At the armory," he chuckled. "It's a good gym, little smoky, but a big court. Sometimes we have to practice there for basketball."

"Okay, when do you want to play?"

"Now, let's go." He got up, waited for me, and led me out the door. I was about to get into his car, but he caught me by the arm, "It's this way. We can walk." He let go as I turned toward him.

"What about a basketball?" I asked.

"We already have some there. We play there a lot," he smiled. "Cole seems cool. Does he play basketball?" he asked. We were walking closer than I thought we would. We weren't touching but he obviously wasn't scared to walk close.

"Yeah, he does. But he's more into baseball and football, though. You can probably say that my whole family is sporty."

We walked in silence for about a half a block. The smile on Caleb's face never left and he kept his hands in his pockets of his dark, faded jeans. What a stud!

"Here we are. What you think?" he asked. It was a big building with army trucks all around it. The firehouse was attached to it.

"Looks like soldiers are going to come out anytime and attack us," I joked.

He laughed, "Nah, they're all off duty, but we better be out of here before dark, that's when they attack the most." He smiled.

The gym was big and smoky, just like Caleb said. Caleb grabbed a basketball from a room and passed me the ball. I took off my high heels and shot a three.

Swish.

The sound of a basketball dribbling is like my dad humming my favorite song. The swish of the net after a beautiful shot was mesmerizing. It was so natural. Basketball was my year-round sport. I touched the ball every chance I got. Thirty-two minutes. It's the time that I loved.

We played one-on-one for a little while. Caleb talked, but never forgot to get me to talk. We played and talked so long, we lost track of time.

"I better get you home," Caleb said, looking at his phone. "Your men will attack me, remember?" he mocked.

I smiled and looked down to avoid *more* blushing.

When we got to the house, he walked me to the door. "I know I've only known you for a day, but it feels like I've known you longer. Are we continuing 20 questions tomorrow?"

I smiled, "Of course."

He had this way of smiling that I was beginning to like. It was a big smile that flashed all his teeth, perfect in every way. "So, do you have a cell?"

"Yeah, want my number?" I asked, as if I didn't know already.

He let out a chuckled as if laughing at my absurd question. Wasn't he catching on that he made me nervous sometimes?

"I'll see you tomorrow, Sara. "

"Yeah." I smiled as Caleb stepped towards me inching closer and closer to my face. My heart began to thump faster than it has ever has before. Then the door flew open. It was Cole and Cameron.

"Sara, where have you been, young lady?" Cole said in firm, but pathetic voice. Cameron was trying to hide his smile.

I wanted to give them the worst profane word that I could think of for ruining this moment but I settled for a glare, "Oh, grow up you two. Good night Caleb, see you tomorrow."

"'Night."

"Bye," Cole and Cam said in unison, laughing. I wasn't mad, because I saw Caleb smiling as he drove away.

As we walked through the door, I stormed, "You jerks. You couldn't leave me out there alone could you? You know how close we were to kissing!" I screamed all the way up the stairs.

I looked at my phone when I got into my room. Text message! It read, 'C told u, men bout to attack me!:)'

I replied, 'they're jerks.'

His reply, 'nite Sara.'

I went to bed smiling. Did this guy really exist? And what was this secret that Giselle was explaining to me earlier? It didn't matter, though.

I dreamt of Josh that night; it was a good dream, too. It was getting really good when this noise started going off. I awoke to realize it was my alarm clock. The good part is always ruined before you have a chance to see it. But then I wondered why it was about Josh.

When I woke up, I looked at my phone. Two new messages, both from Caleb.

'Good Morning!'

'See you at school.' There were these butterflies that came in my stomach whenever he did something by surprise.

"So, Sara, how was the date last night?" Cameron asked as we driving to school.

I gave both of them a malicious look. "Could've been better if it wouldn't have been interrupted," I snickered. "You two couldn't just let me have fun, could you?" Cameron and Cole just sat there and smiled. "It was funny, he was just telling me that if he didn't get me home soon enough that my men of the house would be mad," I laughed.

"We just prevented you from going too far on the first date. It was the first time you've met this guy," Cole chimed in.

"Yeah, whatever. We played 20 questions to get to know each other more. Actually, it was more like 50 questions." I could tell I was rambling on about Caleb with my "in love" voice, but I didn't care.

Cole and Cameron looked at each other laughed. I just ignored them.

Mr. Reynolds came walking in with papers in his hand. "Okay, so your first assignment for today is, drum roll please! Just kidding, no assignment. Caleb, would you pass out the books for me please? And, Sara, is it?" Oh no, second day and he already picks on me.

"Yeah?"

"Will you hand out the workbooks? Caleb will show you which ones."

"Back here, California," Caleb said, smiling. A few people started to snicker, laughing at his nickname for me.

At the table where the books were at, Caleb whispered, "Like the nickname?"

"Fits just right. Should I call you North Dakota, then?" He smiled.

We handed out the books to each person. We were in Algebra II, the hardest of them so far.

Mr. Reynolds didn't waste any time by assigning seating partnerships. Three to a group. Maybe it was fate, but it was Caleb, Wade, and I. But, I could tell that Wade would get really annoying... really fast. Mr. Reynolds taught the lesson and gave us the rest of the hour to work in our groups. With Wade and Caleb's brilliance, we finished first.

The rest of the morning went by fast, each subject adding a little more homework than before. I was happy to finally get to lunch and relax.

"Good afternoon, students," Lorii said over the intercom. "There will be a short boy's and girl's basketball meeting for 5 minutes in the science lab after school. All planning to join basketball are asked to attend. Also, all planning on joining pre-season practice are expected to attend. Pre-season practice begins Monday, September 13. Thank you."

I was sort of excited to get to Chemistry to talk to my mystery partner. I wanted to know his name. Again, with the outfit, the button up shirt wasn't working. His back was against me. I was determined to know his name!

"I'm Sara."

Silence.

"And, you are?"

Silence. I fiddled with my pencil trying to think of what to say.

"Well, we are going to be partners until Christmas. You have to talk to me sometime."

He turned around. It was the first time I've seen his face. He had acne, not a lot, but it was noticeable. He didn't smile.

"Toby."

"Sara."

He moaned, "I think that's the fiftieth time you've said that."

"Sorry."

He continued his work and remained silent. I didn't like the silence.

"Are you just going to ignore me all the time?"

"If I have to." His monotone was getting on my last nerve.

I sighed and kicked the table with my foot.

I think I heard Toby laugh, "You don't have to kill the table."

The bell rang and off Toby ran without another word.

Penny greeted me in the lunch line. "It's been a busy day. How's it going for you?"

"Homework in every class, but I think it'll be easy. And, I know practically everybody in the junior and senior classes," I said, proudly.

She started laughing.

"What? It's nice to know everybody. In Cali, I only have four good friends, the rest were strangers." I meant for that to sound sarcastic.

"I suppose, but still it's funny to see your reaction to this," she added one last time, giggling. "So...how was the date last night?"

"It was good." It seemed like we left it at that and continued a different conversation at the dinner table with the rest of the crew.

Again, in gym, Chris was friendly and talking. It wasn't the annoyance that was bugging me; it was how I felt when we talked. I wasn't nervous, and yet I still felt intimidated. The way he smiled sent shivers up my back. The way he was "cool" about talking to me.

I wasn't expecting it, but Caleb was leaning against my locker, just like yesterday. I smiled, as I approached him. I didn't see it this time, but he had a single rose that he handed me.

The way he dressed impressed me. It was just plain, jeans and a T-shirt, but it was the way he wore it. His muscles that made the shirt too tight around the arms. When the shirt would catch a breeze and blow against his abs, need I mention the six-pack of abs? No, it was an eight-pack; the other two were just hidden.

He had a smirk on his face. "Ready for round two of 20 questions?" How could I decline that stunning tone of voice?

"Round two?"

He nodded.

"Sure." I paused while putting the books into my locker, "Should I tell my men or do you want to?"

He rolled his eyes mockingly and smiled, "You're funny. I'll meet you out here when you're done with the meeting," he said smiling.

We drove separately because I needed to take my car home. I had a black Dodge Avenger. It was warm out today, showing 74 degrees on the thermometer. The temperature back in California would be much warmer and I'd be wearing shorts with a tank instead of jeans and a tee.

"Mom?" I screamed as I got into the house. "Are you home?"

"No," Cole answered from the couch, "she's still at work. She'll be home at nine. What do you need?"

"Caleb and I are going to hang out for a little while. I'll be back before nine."

"Where are you going?" he demanded.

"I don't really know, yet. I'll text you when I know. I'll talk to you later!"

"9:00 sharp!"

I was out the door before he could say more. Caleb was waiting patiently beside the passenger door, "Hop on in," he said as he opened the door for me.

"Thank you, sir," I complimented. As he got in, I asked, "So, where to today?"

"Now, that's a surprise. I won't keep you long; I know how much homework you have. Besides, I have the same."

We drove for about 10 minutes, him jabbering on about hunting. I didn't even realize that we were heading out of town. I tried to pay attention, but he was so distracting.

"Here we are," his words startled me. He parked the car outside of a big house, almost like a mansion. It was bigger than my house.

"Is this your house?" I asked.

"Sure is, come on. My parents won't home until dark and Penny is shopping with Courtney and Sonya. So, we're home alone. Let's go." He jumped out, came over to my door and waited for me to get out. "I don't have any pets, so you don't have to be worried." He chuckled.

We walked up to vast doors, leading into an incredible house. The deer heads and antlers weren't shocking but were scattered all through the house. Every corner held some species of animal that they had killed.

I winced at a grizzly bear, actual size, at the edge of one room. I had to stop in my tracks to make sure it wasn't alive. My heart skipped a beat. I grimaced at the teeth that stood out.

"Stuffed. Don't worry, Fuzzy Bear won't hurt you." He grinned.

I laughed he walked over to the bear and started to pet it. He just smiled. Caleb grabbed my hand and led me up stairs, down a hallway and into a room.

"This is my room. Sorry about the mess." It looked like an ordinary boy's room, messy but normal. He hopped on the bed.

"It's not messy at all," I said. He had a collection of books, something you don't see in every teenage boy's room. I even

49

recognized most of the books, most of which I enjoyed myself. "You read a lot?"

"Yeah, in my spare time. It's not something to be proud of, if you know what I mean." He went over to the window and looked outside. "Let's go down stairs," he proposed. He led me to the living room.

We sat on the couch and continued our game while watching *The Grinch*.

"This is my favorite movie!" I exclaimed.

He started laughing at me.

"What?" His laugh was almost a fake laugh like the kind you make to seem like you're laughing. In another way though, Caleb was truly laughing at me. "Humor me, what are you laughing at?"

"The totally seriousness in your voice and the expression on your face. The way you said it," he snickered, obviously amused by me.

I threw the nearest coach pillow at him, "So, you're telling me that you don't have a favorite little kid's movie?"

"Nope, I never said that. I just as a matter of fact happen to like *Bambi*." He threw the pillow back at me.

"But that is just a sad show. Bambi's mom gets killed!"

He shook his head and smiled, "Yes, but he also gets a girl and big antlers."

"True, but what's a girl and antlers compared to a parent?" I protested.

"Absolutely nothing. Are you going to shoot down my favorite movie all night?" he asked smiling wide.

I smiled with a shrug of my shoulders, "If I have to."

"Moving on. Favorite subject in school?"

I thought a moment, "Spanish. You?"

"All school subjects are against me. But, science seems to be the nicest."

"Oh man, that kills me. Science plus Sara equals injury," I said.

He laughed, "Need help?"

"Most definitely." I paused and added with a giggle, "Can I rely on you?"

"Most definitely." The smile on his face couldn't get any bigger. It made me wonder. As I studied it more, it became familiar. "Favorite TV show?" he asked, breaking my trance.

"SpongeBob."

He questioned me by squinting his eyes and moving his eyebrows in disbelief. "Shut up, for real."

"SpongeBob," I repeated. I tried not to laugh.

"Okay," he said, dragging it on as if to be saying yeah, you're crazy, "favorite grown-up TV show, then?"

I shrugged my shoulders and didn't answer his question of a "grown-up" TV show. Instead, I tried to use a comeback, "I'm guessing yours is the hunting channel?"

"No, very funny," he said shaking his head with a smile, "hunting network." He flashed his teeth, beaming my favorite smile. I felt weak. He thought a moment, "If there was one thing in the world that you wanted, what would it be?"

My dad, of course, but that was unrealistic, and Caleb didn't know about him.

"Can I think a minute?"

"Go for it."

I thought about it carefully. It was hard to want something that I can't have. And, I have everything I *need*. Nothing came to mind that I *wanted*.

"I would love to get a puppy," I blurted out. "I've never had a pet before. A puppy would be amazing. But since the big city, Mom didn't think it would be good for it. It wouldn't have any room."

"A puppy? I gave you the whole world and you want a puppy. Now, that's deep." He smirked.

"I've always wanted one. Okay, consider this? Minnesota Twins tickets?"

He smiled, "Better."

"What would you want?"

"Pizza." He laughed, "Just kidding." He looked down but looked up with serious eyes. "Well, you know I'm adopted, right?" I nodded. "I'd like to use all the money I have to find my parents. But that's almost impossible. So, I'd take one of those expensive watches." He smiled and paused. "So, if you got this puppy, what would you name it?"

"Depends what it looks like."

51

He gleamed, "So, if it looked like me, you'd name if after me?" Somehow, he always made me laugh.

Again, we got caught up in the moment, asking more questions. I looked at the clock and realized how late it was. "I should probably go—lots of homework."

"Okay, I'll take you home. Penny will be back soon anyways."

The car ride home was the same, us finding more about each other. We pulled up into my driveway and he shut the car off.

"I had fun, again. I hope I didn't keep you too long. If any of your men get mad, make sure to blame Penny," he teased. It was dark, but I could still see his white teeth smiling.

Once again, Cameron and Cole stepped through the front door with a blow horn. Cole held his finger on it for at least 30 seconds.

"Well, I better go." We both laughed. "Thank you for showing me your house. See you tomorrow."

"Bye, California. See ya." I slid out of the car and glanced back for one last look at Caleb. He was smiling, of course. I shut the door and headed up to my brothers.

Stomping up each step, I roared at them, "You two are *the* lowest brothers." I screamed. "Two nights in a row. Come on! A blow horn? Are you nuts?"

"Sorry, Sara. Just doing my job," Cole apologized.

"Let this be the last time, please?" I begged.

"We'll see," Cameron put in.

The mysterious number had sent me another text message again after I'd gotten home. It read, 'Man, you guys are hard to find! Watch out!' I just deleted it and let it slip my mind from anything else.

I took a shower and headed to bed. I couldn't fall asleep until midnight, just thinking about the past days.

Chemistry got easier with Toby making an effort to sit facing forward instead of his back to me. I could actually concentrate on the lesson and not if Toby thought I was a freak or something.

"Do you like Edgemont?" His voice surprised me.

Startled, I answered, "Yeah. I'm meeting good people. Lots of friends."

"That's good." His nose was planted in a book. His busily turned the pages. I wanted to talk to him more today.

"Where do you live?"

Keeping his nose in the book, "At the edge of town. You?"

"Edge of town," I replied quickly.

He looked up with his eyebrows raised, "Where?"

I answered puzzled, "5th street."

"Weird." He continued in his book.

I asked still confused, "What's weird?"

He smiled, "That's where I live." He winked at me and then looked back down on his book again.

"5th street?"

He nodded.

"What does your house look like?" I questioned.

"It's white," he mumbled humorously. His face didn't leave the book.

"Right next to one with bricks?" I asked.

"Yeah."

His house was the one next to mine, "We're neighbors."

He shrugged and nodded putting no enthusiasm in his voice, "I've seen you before."

"Ah."

It did, honestly, make me mad that he didn't tell me. He knew this whole time that I was his neighbor and he didn't tell me! I let it go when the bell rang.

Giselle met me one day at lunch during the week before her party and told me the directions to her house, also telling me to bring a date.

Penny caught up with me at lunch as usual and asked me if I wanted to spend the night at her house after the party. I was glad to accept the invitation. The need to mingle was exceptional right now. An added bonus was that Caleb would be there.

All week long Caleb would just sporadically smile or nod or do some gesture of a hello. He'd pass me in the hallways like we were just friends. I guess that's all we were, but still I was shocked he was as quiet as he was.

Finally, there was a group of people hanging out. Caleb was in that group. We were sitting at Nelli's on Friday, the day of the party. My heart was pounding through my chest for I wanted to ask him so badly to come to the party with me! It was when we were about to leave that I asked him, "Are you going to Giselle's party tonight?"

"I was thinking about it, but I don't really have anyone to go with." Then, he smiled. "Would you like to go with me? I hear it's going to be fun," he urged.

"I would love to. What time?"

"How about I pick you up early, so we can hang and then we head to the party?"

"All right. You might have to watch out for Cameron and Cole. They were invited, too."

He smiled, "Oh no. I better bring a shield and a lot of towels."

I laughed and questioned, "Towels?"

"For you to wipe up my blood when they murder me for taking you tonight," he joked.

Caleb dropped me off at my house with plans to meet up soon again.

Mom was cooking supper when I walked in. She was humming the song that was playing on the radio. Of course, she was dancing her dance. Mom's way of dancing is snapping her fingers and moving her hips. It made me laugh.

Hearing my laughing, she turned around and asked, "How was your day?"

"They're getting better and better," I sighed in relief with a smile.

"Only 'cause of Caleb," Cole chimed in as he came up the stairs.

Mom paused, "Caleb?" She sounded concerned. Not in the "what's wrong" voice, but the "a boy?" voice. Almost as if she was excited to hear about a boy.

"You're such an eavesdropper, Cole." I flashed him an annoyed looked and looked back at Mom. "Nobody, Mom. Just this boy I met in school. He's in my grade. He's Penny's brother, remember Penny? Oh and speaking of Penny, she asked me to spend the night tonight, is that okay? I already told her I would."

"Is Caleb going to be there?" she questioned. Boy, she catches on fast.

"No, he's hanging with his friends."

She shrugged and went back to cooking, "Fine, only if he's not there. What time are you going over there?"

"Later."

"Okay. Dinner's ready. Let's eat."

I quickly did the dishes, rushing through in order to have enough time to get ready for my date. I'm sure some food would be left on the plate, but it'd get washed off later. Caleb was waiting outside my door at the exact time he'd told me.

"What's with the bag?" he asked as I climbed in.

"Campout at your house tonight, with Penny."

"Oh, okay." He smiled.

Before the party, Caleb took me to the city park. It was big, surrounding the outer edge of the city. A path was in the middle, being almost a mile long.

Side by side, we walked through the moonlit park.

Caleb spoke looking up to the sky, "What a night."

He never seemed to be fazed by anything. His perfection seemed unreal. Maybe it was just the way I fell so hard for him that nothing seemed wrong.

"Yeah, it's nice."

He stopped walking and grabbed my hand and slid his fingers through mine.

"You're amazing, Sara."

Shocked by his words, I mumbled, "What?"

He smiled and looked around but then meeting my gaze. He chuckled, "You know, you're beautiful."

I looked down and was sure I was blushing.

He only laughed, "I love it when you blush."

"It's your lifelong dream to make me blush, isn't it?"

"Sure is. I told you, it's hot."

I looked up at the sky. Half of me wanted to pour out my heart and tell my story. I bit my tongue. It wasn't time. I pulled away from him, smiling, and kept walking.

He sneaked up behind me, grabbed me by the waist, and threw me to the ground, gently. He pinned my hands above my head. His strength was showing.

"Want to wrestle?"

Laughing, I tried to speak, tried to defend myself. I managed to let out a scream.

"Was that a yes?"

"No!" My attempt not to smile didn't work.

He was inches away from my face, "Oh, I think it was."

"Caleb!"

He flipped me around and put me into a position that I couldn't move.

I wanted to scream from the little pain that I had shooting in my back, "Can I say I surrender!"

He laughed and let his grip go. He stuck his hand down for me to grab. Just as I stood up, he captured my arms again, tightly behind my back.

"You're under arrest."

"Says who?"

He chuckled, "Me."

Releasing me, he walked further up the path, but stopped and looked around and smiled.

"On a serious note?"

I stopped laughing and paused to look at his serious face. He calmed down and kept walking throughout the park.

"I've never met someone like you before." He paused. "Well, *I* have, but then she disappeared. She was amazing. Her smile would bright up the world."

I looked down; I didn't want to hear about past girls that he knew. It made me, well, jealous.

You're not jealous. You're in love, I thought.

I smiled.

I could feel my phone vibrating noisily in my pocket. I held up my finger to Caleb urging a second to read it.

It was the same mysterious number reading, 'I'm getting really frustrated, Sara. where the hell are you?'

I tried to think of the number just in case it would be familiar, but nothing came to mind. I let it go and looked at Caleb with a smile.

"Just a forward," I lied. "We better go."

He nodded and we continued through the park. It was beautiful, flowers and trees lining the pathway. Here and there were fountains with lights.

When we got out of the park, it was close to midnight.

"We better get to the party," I suggested.

"Right. But, it's better to be fashionably late than on-time, right?" He winked as he spoke.

I nodded as my heart fluttered with a million butterflies at his wink. It was a *perfect* wink. Sure, okay, yes, everything *is* perfect about Caleb Pierce!

When we got to the party, it was packed. I noticed Giselle surrounded by people. Everybody looked as though they were completely wasted. I didn't see Cam or Cole, though; I was just guessing they never came.

The music was too loud and it was crowded. It wasn't fun to me. Caleb didn't seem to like it, either.

"Want to leave?" he whispered in my ear.

"Most definitely," I told him.

Just as we were leaving, someone started screaming, "Cops! Cops! Everybody run!"

Caleb grabbed and pushed me to run a certain direction. We ran out of the house, into the backyard, through some trees, and into a corn field.

"Get down and stay down if you want to play basketball!" he whispered throwing his arm around me. "Don't move!" Just as he said that, a flashlight came swooping over top of us. I heard a cop yell, "Clear over here, let's go inside."

I tried my hardest not to panic, yet alone burst out laughing. I could feel Caleb's arm around me, keeping me tied to the ground. In a strange way, I felt protected.

As we were lying on the bottom of the corn field, I heard something move. At first, I thought it was Caleb, so I just ignored it. But then it kept getting closer and closer. Then, I felt it.

"Caleb, there is something crawling by me," I screamed in a whisper, as quietly as I could.

"Stay calm, and don't scream!" he whispered.

All the sudden, a snake came right in front of my face. I couldn't help but scream. Caleb, gently, but with force, put his hand over my month. I could hear him snickering, trying to hold back the laughter. The snake slithered away from us. Snakes are my biggest fear and to have one that close gave me a heart attack. It was too dark to see where the snake had gone.

Then, more flashlights, "I heard a scream. They're out there."

More cops. The corn stalks ruffled in front of us.

"Leave them, we'll never find them in the dark. Besides, I didn't hear anything," another cop said.

We lay in the corn field for what felt like hours. "I think we can go." Caleb's words startled me making me jump. He picked me up and led me out of the corn field.

He drove to his house. I looked at the clock and it showed 4:30a.m. I was cold, but far from complaining.

Caleb was sitting in the seat next to me trying to focus on the road. I'd never thought I'd be sitting with Caleb. It was the way he smiled that made my heart leap, the sound of his laughter that made butterflies creep up. I really hadn't changed since I got my braces off, so how could this, wonderful, handsome, nice, guy want *me?*

"Where have you two been?" Penny shouted as we came through the door. "I've been worried sick. Did you get lost after running from the cops? James showed me an escape route and we came straight here."

Caleb took the blame, "We had to hide in a corn field. Then, I think we fell asleep. But let's get Sara a nice, warm shower and a bed. We don't want our basketball star getting sick." He looked at me and winked. "Good night, you two. Have fun." He smiled as he headed up the stairs to his room.

Penny showed me where to go and I took a shower.

She crawled into the bed and I sacked out on the floor right beside the bed. I explained to her what happened with my last bit of energy.

"It was a blast," I mumbled.

She chuckled, "Sounds like it."

"Yeah." I was close to falling asleep, my eyes slowly drifting shut.

"Sara?"

"Mhm?"

"I'm really glad I met you."

My eyes shot open as I searched for the best of words, "Me, too. I never thought I'd meet someone like you so fast. You remind me so much of my friend in California."

"I just hope we can stay friends."

"Of course."

She sighed, "Even if things between you and Caleb don't work. Or, even if they *do* work?"

It was too dark to see her face. "Always."

My mind wandered farther away from sleep, only thinking about Caleb. All I knew was that I was falling in love after a week of knowing someone. Was love at first sight *real*?

CHAPTER FOUR

utter confusion

Penny woke me up telling me it was past noon. I sat up, yawning and stretching. Then I remembered morning breath, and Caleb.

"Bathroom?" I asked, forgetting where it was since last night.

"Down the hall," she said.

I grabbed my bag and headed to the bathroom. I took a long, hot shower, brushed my teeth and put my makeup on. I ran a comb through my hair and added a little mousse. Penny was dressed when I came back into the room.

"So, do we need to talk about last night anymore?" she begged me to tell.

"Um, I do believe I told you everything." Her face turned to sadness, as if wishing for more.

"How'd you guys get into a corn field?"

"When the guy came running in, Caleb pushed me through the door, telling me where to go. We started running and got into the corn. He told me to duck down and stay down. Then, we heard a cop yell it was clear over here, but Caleb didn't think he was being serious so he said be quiet and stay still. That's when I think I, or we, fell asleep."

"Nothing happened, then?" she asked in a shocked voice.

"No, like what?"

"Never mind." I could tell what she was getting at, but I tried to switch the conversation around.

I remembered the snake, "But, there was a snake. Scared me. I screamed and the cops came back, but they quit looking. *Then*, we fell asleep, er, I fell asleep."

She just nodded.

"Where is Caleb this afternoon?" I asked, noticing Caleb wasn't around.

"Work. He works with children at a library. Private place. Only workers and members are allowed," she answered. It sounded phony, though, as if she were lying. I tried my hardest to keep a straight face of acceptance and not disbelief. "When does basketball start?"

I thought a moment, "Next Monday, I think. I'm nervous, too. The coach said that my old coach informed him of me. At the meeting the other day, I was the center of attention. It was so embarrassing," I said.

"Ugh. I know. I'm not excited at all for practice."

I looked at the time. "Gosh golly, I better go." Then, I thought a moment, "Shoot."

"What?" she asked.

"How exactly do I get home?" I laughed.

"Caleb will be done soon if you can hold off for about an hour. Need to call your mom?"

"Yeah, I'll wait. No, she's working," I said. "Besides, I'm not five." I smiled.

"Coffee?" she offered.

"Of course, never turn that down. I'm addicted."

She laughed, "Oh man, me, too. It's so hard to stop. I love milk and sugar in mine, how about you?"

"Same," I said, giggling. We headed down the stairs and to the kitchen. She poured me a cup of coffee and we watched TV.

"So, how is Caleb working out for you?" she asked.

I grinned, "He's good. I have to admit it. Is that okay? I feel bad that I like your brother."

She giggled, "Don't even worry about it. Just as long as we can be friends. I really like you. I think we'd be perfect friends. Sonya

61

really likes you, too. She's always talking about your hair and how much she likes it."

"That's really funny. I love Sonya, she's hilarious."

"You haven't seen anything, though. You just wait. Are you hungry?"

"No, not at all. But, thank you," I lied. I wasn't the kind to eat in front of people. It was just a pet peeve and somewhat uncomfortable.

"So," she began, "your brother seems almost protective."

I laughed, "He sure is. Ever since my dad..." I stopped, biting my tongue.

"Ever since your dad what?" she asked.

"Ever since he realized I was into boys, he has wanted the boys to protect me from them." That was the lamest save ever, but it worked.

"Oh. Yeah my dad is tough like that, too."

"Where are your parents at?"

"Work."

"So, are you in any sports?" I asked, trying to avoid any more questions about my dad. My heart was beating fast. Man, the Pierces sure make my heart go wild!

She nodded, "Of course basketball, and track."

I just nodded and pretended to watch TV.

How would I tell Penny or even Caleb about my dad? How could I possibly manage to keep it a secret? I can't *lie* to them for the rest of my life. The accident is my secret.

My life.

My story.

His death.

As the door slammed, I jumped. I turned to see Caleb walking through the door with a wig on. It had blonde, short, shaggy hair. He looked completely different in some way. I couldn't put my finger on it, but he looked like a movie star I knew. I just couldn't remember the name.

His face turned ghostly.

"Hey there, California," he stuttered. "How'd yo-o-o-u sleep?" he asked, grinning.

"Soundly and you?"

"Like a baby. Ready for home? I suppose you're sort of stuck out here until one of us gives you a ride, right?"

While he was talking, Penny was pointing to her hair, obviously gesturing to Caleb to warn him that he still had his wig on. When he noticed, he quickly grabbed the wig off and threw it on the ground.

"Oops, left my wig on. We were playing dress-up today at the school where I work."

"Penny told me you work at a library." I was confused. Penny looked confused, also.

"Well, the library is in the school. I work in the library that's in the school," he quickly corrected himself.

"Oh," I simply said, trying not to fuss about it.

"We better get going. I'll be back later, Penny," he said.

"Bye you two! See you in school on Monday, Sara."

"You, too. Thanks for letting me sleep over," I added.

"Anytime."

Caleb pushed me out the door before Penny or me could say anything else.

"So, how was work?" I asked, starting the conversation once we got into the car.

"Really fun, I love working with little kids. You should come with me some day in the future."

"It's a plan."

With a moment of silence, it was the first uncomfortable moment with Caleb.

"What's your biggest pet peeve?" he asked breaking the silence just in time.

"That's a hard one."

"Why?"

"Well, there are a few things that annoy me."

"And they would be?"

"Can I think?"

He nodded.

"Well definitely cocky people." He nodded. "Bushy eyebrows." He cocked his head to one side with a questioned face.

"Bushy eyebrows?"

I laughed, "They are just weird."

63

"Okay, what are some more?"

"Hmm, well I hate it when couples hold hands in public."

He nodded, "I don't like that either. Too gross." It was too much sarcasm to be the truth. He smiled a crooked smile, and looked at me.

"Are you *mocking* me?"

He smiled, "Nope, just stating a fact."

"Yes you are!"

He shook his head and flashed me a smile.

"Fine. What's your pet peeve?"

"Girls who don't eat anything because they're too scared it'll make them fat."

Shoot, I might lose him over my fetish over eating.

I tried to act like I agreed, "Yeah."

He looked at me with his head crooked and smiled, "Are *you* one of those girls?"

I shook my head with a smiled, "No." He'll find out anyways. "Not exactly."

He smiled, "I knew it."

"How?"

"Look at you. What do you weigh, 55 pounds."

"Humph, aren't you nice."

"Well."

"Have you know I do eat. I just don't like to eat in front of other people. I feel it'll look like I'm a p..." He laughed before I could finish.

"Well, then I guess you'll easily get over that." He smiled wide.

Never once was it awkward silence in the car. He always had something to talk about and never was it something boring. We said good bye as we pulled up the driveway. He drove out from the driveway and out of sight.

Cameron and Cole were sitting in the kitchen when I walked in. I walked straight past them, ignoring their comments and questions. I hollered down the stairs, "Please do NOT enter my room until I come down these stairs." I slammed the door behind me to make it official.

I threw my bag on the floor and turned my TV on. I slumped over the bed, and, soon, I was drifting off to sleep.

Caleb was in the dream. But, yet, it wasn't him. It was the famous movie star that I've seen in movies before. He was acting like the normal Caleb I knew. I was running towards him, away from something behind me. As the faster I tried to run, the slower my legs would go. Finally, when I reached him, I woke up. The clock read five in the afternoon.

Caleb Pierce completely took over my heart at that moment.

The alarm for school on Monday went off more than once. Again, each day Caleb brought me a single flower, adding each one to my collection. We walked to classes together and sat by each other at lunch. I found it easier to talk to him every day. I took a little extra effort with my wardrobe and hair each day for Caleb.

Toby was surprisingly warming up to me. We worked through the problems together. I cracked jokes and he laughed. I hadn't noticed his teeth, but they were perfect. White as freshly fallen snow. Straight. I didn't see that coming.

It made be worried when Caleb wouldn't put all his focus on me during that next week. It seemed as if we were just friends. Caleb hadn't talked to me all week in school. Just an occasional smile and "hello." I was worried he wasn't as into me as I thought he was. Maybe Giselle was right, maybe he just didn't care about girls. Only sports. But why would he be so nice then not talk at all?

"So, California, you busy tomorrow?" Caleb asked me in Spanish class on Friday. My heart finally was smiling since he talked to me.

"Not that I know of, but I'm just guessing that I am now," I smirked trying to make him continue to flirt with me.

He smiled, "You'd be guessing right. I'll pick you up at noon?"

"Sure." He leaned back the other way, talking to Cole and Josh. Those butterflies were sneaking up on me again. One thing's for sure, Caleb sure didn't make too much of an effort to talk to me.

Mr. Hansen blew the whistle for partner shooting in gym. Chris came up to me, assuming that we were partners. I didn't decline. It was nice to talk to him.

"How is your day going?"

I sighed, "Long."

He laughed, "Every day is long for you."

"Yeah. Junior year is long."

"Oh, great. That makes me ready for next year."

I was used to the drive home from school every day. The familiar road was burned into my brain from taking it day after day. Mom was cooking dinner when I walked through the door. The aroma of the food swept over my body.

"What are you doing home so early?"

"The office let me off early," she sighed. "How was your day?"

I sighed with a smile, "They get better and better. Can we talk about Caleb?"

"Sure, hon. What about?"

"Well, he wants to hang out tomorrow afternoon. I was wondering if that was okay."

Her face got serious, but calmed, "Of course. Can I finally meet this boy that takes up your morning, noon, and nights?"

I laughed, "Yeah, I suppose you can."

"Okay. Supper will be ready by five. Your brothers ran to Jeffersontown to get some things for me, they left their 7th hour classes. They'll be back by then," she told me as I headed up the stairs. "Oh, and clean your room. It's beginning to look like your brothers'!"

I walked into my room. It wasn't that messy. I pushed all the folded clothes into my closet, hiding them from her view.

At five, I headed down the stairs for supper. "Are they home, yet, Mom?" I asked.

"No, not yet. And they haven't called yet either," she sounded worried. "Supper's ready if you want to eat, but I'll wait for them."

"I'll wait, too," I insisted.

We sat in the kitchen until 7 o'clock. Mom called frequently, staying as calm as she could. Mom didn't move, as if she was frozen to the chair. The food on the stove stayed on the stove.

"Sara, go ahead and eat. It'll go to waste."

I didn't decline, I was starving. When 8 o'clock rolled around, we both got antsy. I looked at the clock often, each second that ticked by the feeling was stronger. The feeling that something wasn't right.

Lili called me at nine.

"Hello?"

"Hey, Sara. How's it going?"

"Oh. Hey, Lili. It's all right. You?"

"You sound anxious. What's wrong?"

I sighed, "Cam and Cole went to Jeffersontown and haven't come home, yet alone call. We're worried."

She gasped, "Anything I can do? I suppose not."

"Well, I don't know. We are just waiting."

"Are you going to call the cops?"

I shook my head in disbelief, "I don't think that's crossed Mom's mind." I couldn't imagine having to call the cops for Cameron and Cole. *No*, I thought in my head, *not going to happen. They'll be fine.*

"Oh. Sara, it'll be okay."

"I sure hope so. I'm just guessing their phones are dead and they just forgot about supper."

"Yeah. Call me when you hear, okay?"

"Okay."

"I'll talk to you later."

"Wait, Lili. Did you call for something special?"

"Just to check up on you, see how you like your new home."

"It's nice."

Silence.

"Okay, well call me when things change. I suppose you want to keep the line open. It'll be good. It'll be good. Don't worry! Just pray. Love you!"

"Bye, Lili, love you!"

I walked back over to Mom.

"Mom, where are they?" I asked, breaking the silence.

"Maybe their cell phones are dead. They'll be here soon. Just, um, go into the living room and watch TV." I did as I was told. I didn't watch, just turned it on. Where were my brothers? I was praying that they'd just forgotten that Mom had supper ready.

It became dark and 10 o'clock rolled around; five hours late. The more the clock ticked the more worried I got.

When the doorbell rang at a quarter to eleven, Mom and I both jumped. Mom answered it to three policemen. I rushed over to her side just in time to hear them say, "Your sons have been into an accident. It involved a drunk driver." Then, a loud bang and a huge headache pierced my head.

I don't remember what happened after that until I woke up. The three policemen and my mom were standing over me. And I had realized that the huge bang came from my head hitting the floor.

"Sara, are you okay?" Mom asked.

"You took a hard fall," the first policeman said.

"Yeah. I'm fine. How about my brothers?"

"Are you sure you're okay, you've been out for awhile. Sit up slowly," the second policeman insisted, helping me up.

"Enough about me. Where is Cole and Cam?"

"They're in the hospital. Cole has a broken leg and, Cameron just a concussion," Mom answered. "Once you've relax, we'll head up there. Are you feeling faint, light-headed, anything?"

"Guys, I'm fine, really. Let's go see my brothers." Just as I said that, I stood up too fast and fell right back down. One of the policemen caught me and carried me to the couch.

"Now, you just relax." I rejected and tried to sit up. "Relax!" the cop commanded. I did as I was told, for I didn't feel well the way it was. I found myself drifting even before the officer left the room.

"Sara?" The room was spinning and it was loud, what's that noise?

"Sara." Who was talking? I just wanted to sleep.

"Sara." He said my name gently, trying to wake me up. Why was he here? Was I dreaming? This was a weird dream. "Sara?" At that moment, I opened my eyes to see Caleb. Nope, no dream. "Hey there, sleepy head. Finally good to see those blue eyes."

"Where's my mom?" I asked, startled.

"It's two in the morning. She went to the hospital. She called me to come stay with you 'til you felt better, and then we are going to go up when you're ready. She called a little bit ago and told me the boys are doing fine. Although the drunk driver isn't doing so well." I held up my hand motioning him to stop.

"Can we leave now?" I pleaded, jumping up, once again too soon. Caleb caught me by the waist, setting me gently back down on the couch.

"How about we wait a few minutes? You don't look so good." He got me a drink of water and turned on the TV. I got restless and stood up.

"Let's go," I commanded.

"How about I carry you out to the car?" he insisted.

"I'll be fine, I just got to..." and before I could finish my sentence, Caleb had me in his arms and headed the door."Grab my shoes!" I demanded.

"Already in the car," he replied. "Your mom packed everything you would need."

Then, it truly hit me. My brothers almost died in an accident. The tears started coming. I couldn't hold back anymore. Caleb held me tighter letting me ruin his shirt with my watery makeup stained on his shirt. I was wishing he wouldn't let go. I cried in his arms all the way down the front stairs and into his car. He set me down on the seat, and there was a pillow and blanket waiting for me. He covered me up in the blanket and shut the door.

I couldn't focus straight.

I didn't realize that Caleb was carrying me to *his* car. Caleb Pierce.

On the way there, he put his arm around me and I leaned on it for support. My head was spinning with hundreds of thoughts. What was I going to tell them? What would Cameron and Cole say? Could I face the drunken person alone?

I didn't even realize the darkness outside. I didn't care, though. Caleb found my hand and held it. For once, my heart didn't mind that we touched. I was finally getting used to him. His fingers between mine made me a little happier. The ride to Jeffersontown was long, seeming like we've been on the road forever. We held hands the whole way.

"It'll be fine," he said, squeezing my hand.

"Caleb," I sighed.

He looked at me puzzled by the sigh.

"Why are you being so nice to me?"

He wasn't smiling anymore; he was truly confused.

"What do you mean?" he asked with a perplexed tone.

"You're so nice. You treat me like," I paused looking for the right word, "like royalty. Like I matter."

"You do."

I shook my head, "You barely know me and now, you're driving in the middle of the morning or night or whatever time it is, so that I can see my brothers."

He nodded.

"Why?"

He stared out onto the road for a moment and his lips curved into a smile.

"I like you, Sara." He paused and squeezed my hand again. "There's something about you. It's different than most girls."

"Caleb, if you only knew what I was like before I came."

"You couldn't have been different."

I did a full nod. I didn't want to admit it, but I guess I was in the mood. "I had braces and glasses. People looked at me like I was a freak."

He chuckled, sounding like relief, "I thought you were going to say something else." He laughed again. "Like your personality is different. That you're just putting on a..."—he paused—"never mind." He smiled.

"Oh, gosh no," I said sniffling.

"Well, you don't have braces, now. And, if you did, I wouldn't care."

I smiled and closed my eyes and listened to the car making its way to Jeffersontown.

When we reached the hospital, Caleb told me to wait in the car. He ran around the front side of the car and opened my door. He reached in to pick me up, but I pushed him away, "I'll be fine, just help me walk." Caleb found out their room number and we headed toward the elevator.

"Caleb, I have to tell you something when we get out of here and once we're alone."

"Sure thing, California," he said, grabbing my waist and hugging me. "How are you feeling now?"

"Well, I have the biggest headache I've ever had, my arm hurts, and I can't stop thinking of my brothers. Add it up and I feel pretty crummy."

"That was a rhetorical question, I guess. But don't worry. The guys are fine and alive. Don't worry."

His advice was comforting. The doors of the elevator opened and we headed to their room. I paused outside the door, trying to hold back the tears that were coming again.

"What's wrong?"

I sighed, "Nothing. Let's go." I knocked on the door.

"Come in!" It was Cole's voice.

Then, the anxiety came in full gear. I pushed open the door and ran to Cole's arms. I gave him the biggest hug I could possibly give him. I ran over to Cameron to do the same.

"Hey there, Bug," Cole said.

"If you two ever do this to me again, I swear. I can't take another accident after the last one and this one. If I ever lose you two like Dad, what would we do?"

Cameron got out of bed and headed over to me to give me a hug, "Sara, it's okay. We won't leave you. We're both fine. Sorry we didn't call. We were fine," he chuckled. I gave him a harsh look. "Sorry! It's going to be okay." He noticed Caleb, "Hey there, Caleb. Thanks for taking care of our bug. This must be a hard time for her." Cam shook his hand, and then headed over to his bed. I went over to sit by mom on the couch, motioning Caleb to do the same.

"When are you two coming home?" I asked with my eyes drooping.

"This morning if things go well," Cole answered. I looked at the clock. It didn't even seem like it but it was four in the morning. No sleep suddenly dawned on me.

"You guys better go, Sara doesn't look so good. Jeez, what happened to you?"

"Just a faint accident," Caleb chuckled. "I'll take her home right now."

"Thanks, Caleb," my mom said. "I'll stay with these guys until they get released tomorrow and bring them home. Caleb, you are more than welcome to stay with Sara if she needs you or if you want."

"Thanks for the invite, Cadie," Caleb said helping me up. "See you guys later, get better."

On the way home, he reached for my hand again. How could I refuse? His warm hands made me forget everything. Well, almost.

All the memories of our crash ran through my head. My dad's facial expression when the car hit his side. The way he wasn't panicked, he somewhat smiled. I remembered the horn beeping as we were hit. The bright lights.

"Favorite flower?" his question startled me, escaping me from the nightmare.

I had to blink to focus, "What? Sorry."

"Favorite flower," he repeated.

"Tiger lily. Yours?" I laughed at the odd question, but I started getting used to the random questions.

"Nice to hear you laugh. Well, if I had to choose, my choice would be carnations. They're cheap." He smiled.

I laughed, "Caleb, thank you for this. I don't know what I would do if I was alone."

"Sara, I would do anything for you. We'll cancel tomorrow as of now, just so you can be with Cameron and Cole."

That surprised me, "No, it's okay. I *want* to hang out with you. Can I still see you, please?"

Squeezing my hand, he said, "Of course you can still see me. Do you want me to stay the night?"

"Please? I don't want to be alone tonight."

"I sure will. Anything you need."

I could feel my eyelids closing, "Thank you," I mumbled.

The door slamming woke me up, but only enough to realize we were home. I was too groggy to comprehend that Caleb was carrying me. Confused, I thought I was dreaming, flying at that. Caleb set me down on the couch.

"The couch is very comfortable," I mumbled, "and if it's not, you are more than welcome to sleep in Cole or Cameron's room."

He just laughed, "Don't worry about me. You sleep."

72

And I did. As soon as my head hit the pillow, I slept, long and hard.

The afternoon sun woke me up, along with the smell of bacon. I smiled, thinking Mom and the boys were home and she was cooking breakfast. I got up slowly, remembering what happens when I get up too fast. As I walked into the kitchen, I saw Caleb over the stove.

He looked when he heard me and smiled, "Good afternoon, beautiful. How are you?" he asked.

"I'm good. What time is it? Where's my mom?"

"It's 2:30. Still in Jeffersontown. She called at noon saying that they wanted to do some last tests on Cameron to make sure it's a small concussion. They should be back by 5 or so. Hungry?"

"Starving." I glanced at myself in the microwave. My hair was in knots and my makeup ran down my face. "Actually, er, I'm going to go shower."

He laughed, but didn't object.

The hot shower felt nice against my oily sink. I dressed in comfy clothes, but did my hair and make-up for Caleb.

We watched TV on the couch, Caleb sitting right by me with his arm around me. I could only stare at him in amazement. There was just something about his eyes that were breathtaking.

"First crush?" Caleb asked.

"That's a hard one. I've really only been interested in basketball. I've never had time for boys. But, there was this boy that moved to our town when I was in sixth grade. He was an eighth grader. I fell so hard for him. Then, he dated my worst enemy, a girl in my class."

I could see his lips refusing to curl up into a smile. "I had braces then, so he probably thought I was a brace face. I was crushed. I ate ice cream every night for a month." Caleb started laughing at me, "What? It was so depressing. He turned out to be jerk in the end. He shoved me out his way whenever he saw me. All right, then, who was your first crush?"

He smiled, "You know Giselle? Back in second grade, we were a thing. But, she got a better grade on a spelling test and I dumped her. She really hasn't liked me since."

"Are you serious? Giselle? She's gorgeous." I giggled, "A spelling test?" I had to laugh even harder.

"And you aren't?" he gleamed.

"Do I have to answer that?"

"My point exactly," he smirked, flashing my favorite smile.

"My turn. Where was your first kiss?" I asked.

"I was over at this girl's house. We were watching TV and laughing and talking on her couch. She wasn't feeling good and wasn't having the best morning. Then, I leaned in and kissed her."

In all honesty, I thought he was going to say he'd never had one. I didn't want to ask him for the fact that I thought he hadn't. My heart seemed to sink when he began, but fluttered when he stopped urgently.

Caleb turned his head and smiled. As he leaned his head in, my heart began to beat fast. He gently touched his lips on mine. His kiss was perfect. I couldn't believe he kissed me. My first kiss!

I thought for a moment.

"Wait a minute," I realized, pulling back, "this was your first kiss?"

"You catch on fast, don't you?" He leaned over for another kiss. His lips were warm and soft against mine. "So, when was your first kiss?"

I looked down. Caleb lifted my chin. He pointed at himself with a shocked look and smirked. Caleb just had the way of making a serious moment a funny moment. It wasn't an awkward moment which I liked.

I nodded. We sat in silence for a second or two before the phone rang. I jumped up to grab it.

"Hello?"

"Hey, Bug," Cole answered back.

"Cole. Gosh, it's good to hear your voice." Even after knowing he was going to be okay, I couldn't keep my voice even.

"Oh, Bug, don't start crying. Everything's okay. We're on our way home. Is Caleb there?"

I choked the tears back, "I'm not. Yeah, he stayed with me."

"Okay, good. Mom was worried you'd be alone. Never mind, though. She also wants to know the supper plans for tonight. Cameron wants to go to the restaurant, is that okay? Caleb can come, too."

"Yeah, that sounds good. Then Mom won't have to cook."

"Exactly my thought." He laughed.

"How far away are you guys?"

"We just left."

"Okay, well thanks for calling and be safe. We have lots to talk about when you get home and when we get alone. You owe me an explanation."

"I know I do. I promise, once everything settles down, it'll be just me and you, one-on-one."

"Okay. See you soon, Cole."

"Later, Bug." I stayed on the phone until I heard the other line was dead. Caleb was by my side in a second, giving me a hug from behind.

"Favorite lotion?"

"You and your wacky questions. Love Spell from Victoria's Secret."

He sniffed me with a chuckle. "I knew it! I smelled something so good, but I couldn't figure out what it was. I just realized it was you."

When I asked if he wanted to come with us to the restaurant, he shook his head no. It did surprise me. I thought he'd stay with me. I couldn't make him go though.

With Caleb's arms still around me, the front door flung open. "Come jump in these arms!" Cameron exclaimed. Mom and Cole followed him, Cole on crutches. I ran over to Cameron and leaped into his brawny arms. Cole hopped over to the couch.

"I'm starving, let's go eat," Cameron pleaded.

"We'll go soon. Don't you want to clean up?" Mom asked.

Cameron sighed, "I suppose. I'll be done soon, and when I'm done, let's go." He went downstairs and showered. It wasn't 10 minutes before he came back up. "All right, let's roll."

I said a quick goodbye to Caleb as we headed to Fred's, the town's restaurant. Everybody stared at us. I'm sure they all knew about the accident and Cole on crutches didn't help much.

After we got our food, Mom looked at me, "Sara, we were wondering if you would like to speak to the driver of the other car. He's still in the hospital and he'll be there for awhile."

I thought a moment. "I don't know if I could handle it. What if I were to break down and cry right in front of him? What if I would totally freak out on him?"

"It was just a thought. But, you could help us, even him. I can't even begin to count how many times he apologized. It was a bad mistake and he feels horrible."

Cole nodded, "How about it, Bug? I'll go with you if you want me to."

"When could we go?" I choked back the tears as well as I could.

"Tonight, if you wanted," Mom answered. "But he'll be there awhile. His name is Jeremy Jacobs. He got banged up bad."

I shook my head. "I don't want to go tonight. And I'm making a run for it if one thing goes bad." I winced at the thought of things going bad.

We finished up our food and set plans for going to the hospital tomorrow afternoon.

When I got home, I texted Caleb about the planned trip to the hospital and to see if he would take me.

It read, 'caleb, want to do a favor for me?'

He replied, 'depends :)'

I replied, 'well, we still have our date for tomorrow right?'

He replied, 'yup'

Caleb was making this more and more difficult to ask. It felt like I was asking a lot.

I replied, 'care to go up early and visit a person I don't want to?'

He replied, 'who?'

I replied, 'the drunk who slammed into the boys.'

He replied, 'of course. pick you up.'

"Cole, can we talk?" I asked as I walked down the stairs. It was late but I didn't care.

He nodded and hopped over to the couch with his crutches. "Are you ready for the story?"

I nodded.

"Okay"—he breathed—"well, Cameron and I were almost there. Almost! We were laughing and listening to music. What's scary is that we were at an intersection. Cam stopped at the red light. On

green, he went, and that's where it stops. The room kept spinning."
I was so caught up in it, I didn't even realized why he stopped. Tears
were streaming down my face. Cole scooted closer and hugged me.
"Is this too much for you?"

I shook my head, "I'm a crybaby. Keep going."

He chuckled while shaking his head, "Honestly, I can't remember
the actual crash. You'll have to ask Cameron."

"Which side got hit?" I mumbled. Those words were the hardest
to get out.

"Mine."

I gasped, trying not to overly panic.

"Bug." He smiled wide enough to make me laugh. "Bug, please
don't worry. It's all over."

"Yeah," I nodded, "it's all over."

Cole hugged me and hopped down the stairs to his room.

I took a long, hot shower. Different questions for the driver ran
through my head. I let the steaming hot water burn my skin. How
could I face someone who almost killed the only two men left in my
family? How could I forgive and forget? How could I forget that this
was the same thing that happened to my dad, only it killed him?
What would I do? What would the driver say to me? How could I
forgive? So many questions and so little time.

CHAPTER FIVE

my life story

I slammed my fist down on the snooze button just one more time. I'm not a morning person; therefore 7 o'clock is just too early. My bedroom door flew open and Cameron came walking in.

"Bug, I've heard that alarm go off five times. Please wake up before *I* wake you up." I reached for my pillow and chucked it at him. Cameron came over, cradled me up, and carried me up the stairs. He set me down on the couch. He made me coffee, exactly how I love it.

Afterwards, I jumped in the shower, letting the hot water run off of me. Not for long, though. I stared at myself in the mirror. I looked long and hard. The questions kept running through my head that I was going to ask the driver. Did I even want to know his name?

My cell phone rang Lili's tone, I ran over to it, forgetting that I was supposed to call her.

"Hello?"

"Sara! Are they okay? I tried to wait for you, but..." She sounded more than panicked.

I cut her off, "Lili. Lili, it's okay. They're fine. It's a bad thing, though."

"I have time. Please."

"Okay. Well, they didn't come home. And, then, some policemen came to the door."

She gasped.

"It's okay." I could hear her start to cry. "I got to the door, hearing the police officer say they'd been hit by a drunk driver."

She started to cry, loud. This made me start, too.

"And I fainted. I hit my head. Hard. The policeman carried me over to the couch and made me sit there. I fell asleep right away."

This was truly hard to explain to Lili. It just didn't seem real. And, yet it was.

She questioned, "Are they home?" I could picture how her face looked.

"Yeah."

She sighed, "Good. I'm sorry. Oh, gosh, I'm so happy that they are okay."

I sighed in relief and agreement, "You have no idea."

"I'm really happy that they are okay."

"I better go, Lili. Talk to you later."

She quickly added a quick "Bye!" before I heard the line go dead.

Caleb told me he'd come pick me up at nine. I quickly threw some clothes on, scrunched my hair, and put some makeup on. I ate a bowl of cereal. By the time I was done, it was nine. I looked out the window, and sure enough, Caleb was waiting for me. I hollered good bye and ran out the door.

Caleb was leaning against the passenger door when I stepped outside the door. "Good morning, California. You're looking lovely this morning. Are you ready for an adventure?" Caleb always greeted me with the biggest smile, one I've come to love. He opened the door and I slid in the seat.

"Morning," I said as he got in, "I'm always ready for an adventure." He drove out the driveway and we were on our way to Jeffersontown.

"Are you scared?" he asked.

"About the driver?" He nodded and I continued, "Definitely. More than you know."

He paused a minute, "Want me to come in with you?"

79

"You know I would love that, but I think I have to do this myself. If I need you, don't worry, I'll let you know. Thanks for doing all this."

"I'll do anything for you, Sara." He paused a moment and concentrated hard on something. "Okay, so after the hospital, if you're still in the mood, I want to take you somewhere."

I smiled, "Of course I'll be in the mood. Can you tell me where we're going?"

He laughed, "Never, it'll ruin the surprise." He grabbed my hand and held on tight. "So," he continued, "tomorrow basketball starts. Excited?"

"Ehh, don't want to think about it. First week of basketball sucks. Literally. The coach seems nice, though. When does your practice start?"

"Tomorrow."

There was silence, but it wasn't uncomfortable.

"So," I began, "have I mentioned my best friend?"

"Penny?" He sounded confused.

"No. The one from California."

He didn't seem to be paying too much attention on me. More so on the road so he only replied, "I don't believe so."

"Well, her name is Lili. We are like sisters. She called right before you picked me up. She was really worried about Cam and Cole."

"Will I meet this Lili?"

I smiled, hoping I would get to see her soon. "In time."

"Biggest fear?" he asked after a moment of silence.

"Easy. Needles." I shivered at the word.

"Needles?"

I nodded.

"You're scared of a little thing poking you."

He laughed softly.

I punched him in his biceps.

"Hey, don't punch the driver"—he turned the wheel to make it seem like we lost control—"if you want to stay alive."

I frowned jokingly, "Well, I thought that maybe you'd be a little more sincere about it."

"Well, I'm sorry. I will—no, I promise—never to get you near needles." He smiled. "I'll make it go by fast when you land on the bed of needles falling from the top of a mountain." His smile was wider than anything else, and it was a smile of victory.

I turned up the music as if I was mad, so loud it hurt my ears. Out of the corner of my eye I witnessed a smirk on his face when he turned it down.

I turned the music up a little more and we listened to music the rest of the way. I couldn't stop picturing what the driver would look like. I never did ask Mom how old he was, and she never told me.

When my dad died, I asked not to see the driver, although I do regret it. I wished I could've punched him in the mouth. Mom told me I shouldn't see him for it might traumatize me.

As we pulled up, I asked, "Will you come in with me as far as I need you to?"

"Of course," he said with a smile.

I asked the front desk for his room. "Room 5550, hon," the nurse instructed. "You must be Sara Young." I nodded. She flashed me a huge smile. "Your mother told me you were coming. Mr. Jacobs also knows. Use the elevator to the 3rd floor and turn to your left and you're there. Good luck. If you need me, you know where to find me."

The beep of the elevator door startled me as we reached the 3rd floor. I walked out the door and turned left. Room 5550, Jeremy Jacobs.

The time was now.

"You all right?" I felt Caleb's arms wrap around my waist, with his head resting on my shoulder. His light breathing soothed me.

I turned around. "I'll be fine. Just stay with me, please." It was definitely harder than I thought it was going to be. I felt my knees getting weak.

He nodded.

"Be strong," I heard Caleb whisper. He opened the door, one arm still around my waist. Inside was a teenage boy, not much older than Caleb or me. He looked strong, tall and muscular. Yet, he had a huge bandage on his head and one leg was in a full length cast. He had IV's all over his arms and a heart monitor was beeping loudly.

"Good morning, Jeremy?" I asked, beginning the conversation, trying to hold back the tears. I couldn't help but notice that handcuffs strapped his arms to the bed.

"'Mornin'." He spoke in a southern, high accent. "You must be Sara. And the guy behind you, your brother?"

I shook my head, "N..."

"No," Caleb answered before I could, "her boyfriend." I was shocked when I heard those words come out of his mouth. He let go of my waist and grabbed my hand.

"Sorry, my mistake. Listen, Sara, I'm truly sorry about the accident. I promise I'll never do it again. I have a feeling I won't have a chance to do it again." I held my hand in the air.

"Please, let me talk. I'm not going to take your apology. Not even close. I will not consider listening to it, anyways. You made a dumb decision that could've easily been prevented. You know, I haven't touched alcohol my whole life and I don't plan on it. I will not let my life end like that," I stopped to catch my breath.

The expression on Jeremy's face went from sarcasm to fearful. It felt good to get all this off my chest. I was surprised I could keep calm and yell at him without raising my voice.

"Little do you know my father died of an accident caused by a drunk driver. A drunk driver!" The tears began to stream down my face. I saw him try and sneak a word in, but I wouldn't let him. "I'm scarred for life since that accident."

I looked over at Caleb's surprised expression. I felt bad that he had to learn about my life this way. But, I wasn't worried about Caleb, more so Jeremy. Tears were in his eyes, which only made my tears worse. He looked down and never looked back up. I went and sat down on the chair in the corner of the room.

"Jeremy, I didn't mean to make that sound harsh, but I couldn't handle losing more family from something as stupid as drunk driving. Drunk driving just shows how people have don't have feelings for other people. They only care about themselves."

He sat there silently, playing with the cord on the IV. I felt queasy just looking at the insertion point. "Don't apologize. I should be the one apologizing," he pleaded after a short time. "I'm truly and respectfully sorry. I know I can't bring your dad back, but..." he stopped short.

"But what?" I asked.

"But I don't really know. I shouldn't have used your dad like that. I don't know what happened to him. I'm truly sorry. I'm honestly happy that your brothers are okay. I feel horrible. Want to know the story?" He sounded as though he was being serious. Like maybe he wanted me to know how he got drunk.

"Sure, why not?"

I rolled my eyes.

Caleb moved over to where I was sitting. I stood up, letting him sit in the chair. After he sat down, he gently grabbed me by the waist and pulled me down to sit on his lap.

Jeremy began, "There was this huge birthday party down at a friend's house that everybody was going to be at. So, I went. Before I knew it, it was three in the morning. We kept drinking, though. We went to bed, hung over like crazy the next morning. He wanted to keep celebrating. We kept drinking. I finally decided to quit and go home. I suppose that's when it happened."

"I suppose," I sneered. I wasn't in the mood for him feeling sorry for himself. He wasn't getting off the hook for this. "Listen, Jeremy. Promise me you'll never do it again."

He looked down. "I'm not going to promise I won't drink, but I promise I won't drive after drinking."

"That's not good enough, but I'll take it. Do you know how long you'll be in here?"

"They said up to two weeks. It's going to be long. But, I guess I deserve it."

Damn right, I thought. "Well, I hope we can be somewhat friends."

He smiled, "You're not mad at me?"

"Oh, hell yeah I'm mad at you, but my dad always taught me to forgive and forget. I will never forget but in time, yes, I will forgive you." I paused. "Well, we better go. I'm glad I got to meet you."

He nodded, "It was good to meet you, too. Once again, I'm sorry. I truly am. I do hope they recover fully. Cade, was it?"

"Caleb," Caleb corrected him. Caleb held out his hand to shake Jeremy's.

"Caleb. I'm sorry."

"It's all right, man. Don't be apologizing to me. Save it for her."

"Right, Sara, I'm sorry."

I tried to smile, "Stop apologizing, you're going to wear it out. I'll talk to you later."

"Bye."

I looked back one last time and saw his face. The tears where still in his eyes as I waved good bye.

Caleb didn't talk to me the whole way down in the elevator, or all throughout the way to the car. His firm grasp on my hand was painful, but I wasn't going to let him go. He couldn't have been too terribly angry with me. The front desk nurse waved good bye as we walked out the doors. We walked fast, trying to avoid another long conversation.

He opened the car door for me, without saying a word. He grabbed my hand and concentrated on the road. We drove in silence, winding all over Jeffersontown. Caleb drove out of city limits and to a gravel road. He kept driving for at least an hour.

Finally, he pulled onto a prairie road, driving up a steep hill.

"This is my place I go to help clear my mind and just be myself. I've never brought anyone here with me before. My dad owns this lake and everything around it. No one else is allowed up here." He didn't talk with his sweet, loving voice.

The hilltop was in sight. As we drove over it, a huge lake came in view. It was a beautiful scene. The water looked crystal clear, there was a sandy beach surrounding it, beautiful flowers, and trees. It was also deserted in a way, no one was there. Caleb pulled up and parked the car.

It was a nice day, hot and sunny. The thermometer read 79 degrees in Caleb's car. It was September 12; our birthdays were coming up.

He wrapped his arm around my shoulder and led me over to the beach area. He took off his shirt, shoes and socks and ran into the water. I threw my sandals and watched him splash in the water. Watching his amazing six pack of abs made me forget about everything for a minute. He came back, the bottom half of him soaked. He sat down on the sand, plopping myself beside him.

We stared into the lake for awhile, just enjoying the view. I looked at him; his perfect complexion. He was smiling, still slightly confused and angry. His hair was blowing gently in the wind.

Perfection in my mind.

"I was nine," I began, "when my dad died." He turned to look at me with confusion in his eyes. "I was into the whole singing thing and acting. He always told me one day I'd be famous, thanks to him. He came back one day after driving to San Francisco telling me that he'd found auditions for me," I stopped just to see his face. It was smooth, full of curiosity.

"It was part of my birthday present. Two days after my birthday we went. My mom had to work that day of auditions, so my dad took me. He told me how proud he was of me over and over again." I could feel the tears starting to come. I sniffled, "We were at an intersection, and our light was red. He was explaining to me how many opportunities this was bringing me. As soon as the light turned green, he went. Last thing I remember is my dad saying, 'You'll do great'.

"My dad was pinned in the car since the driver slammed into his side. The door, steering wheel, and console trapped him in. They said, if we wouldn't have been wearing our seat belts, we would've died instantly from flying out the window. They told us that the driver was drunk and ran his red light. I only had a broken arm, concussion, and a few cuts on my face. I couldn't breathe. The doctors had put an air mask on me, but I kept ripping it off." He just nodded, but his face remained serious.

"They hauled us away in separate ambulances. As soon as they got me into the hospital, I jumped off the bed and ran into my dad's room. They couldn't stop me," I cried. My face was soaked with tears. So much for the makeup. As I told Caleb, it was as if I replayed it again, just like it happened eight years ago.

"He was still alive when I got into the room. I grabbed his hand. He looked me straight in the eye and said, 'Bug, I'm so sorry.' I kept telling him it wasn't his fault. 'I love you so much. Never give up. Please promise me you'll never quit.' I promised him, and I'm going to keep that promise. My mom and brothers got there in time to see him smile one last time and to hear him say 'I Love You', but that's all." I sniffled as I finished my life story.

"And, I'm sorry I didn't tell you sooner. I didn't want people to know."

He scooted closer, grabbing my hand and wiping a tear from my face. "Why didn't you tell me sooner? I mean, now, I feel horrible about making the comments about your dad being mad if I brought you home late. I feel...just horrible."

I shook my head. "Caleb, don't feel horrible. I didn't want to have to explain. It's like I have to live it over and over every time I tell it to someone. I'm sorry I haven't told you. I just never found the right time. And since the accident..."

Caleb interrupted me, "Don't apologize. It's okay. It just shocked me when you told that to Jeremy. I almost thought you were lying, but the seriousness on your face made me believe you. I just can't believe you had to go through something like that."

I wiped my face, "It's over and done with and I'm doing all right. I don't dwell on it."

"No, you surely don't. You wouldn't even be able to tell. You're so happy and bubbly." He smiled my favorite smile.

"Yeah. Well, I promised my dad I wouldn't give up."

"Is he buried in California?"

His questioned shocked me, "Yeah, why?"

"Well, do you guys not want to see his grave every day?"

I thought a moment. I've never thought of that before. I went to his grave almost every day that I could, just to talk to him. Now that we're in North Dakota and he's in California, I don't get to. "I think Mom was thinking about that, moving him to North Dakota with us. That would cost a lot of money, though. Besides, it's not his hometown."

"Is it *your* hometown?" He scooted closer to me, wrapping his arm behind me.

"No," I stopped short and thought a moment. "But, I guess, yeah, it is." I turned my head to look at him. His eyes were a beautiful shade of green. He smiled, leaned and kissed me. He started laughing. I pulled back, "What's so funny?"

"I was just thinking, you're a good liar. Anything else you want to tell me?"

"Hmm, nope, I think I just spilled my life out. Anything *you* want to tell me?" His expression changed. He got restless. What was his big secret?

"Nope, you know me." I kept it at that. He didn't urge my story, why should I urge his?

"Hold on, did you say you were on your way to audition for a movie?"

"Yeah. I used to act and sing all over the house."

"Didn't you ever try to audition again?"

I looked away, "I couldn't. It was too sad. It reminded me of my dad. I couldn't even go onto the street that the accident happened on. There were marks, from the accident, that were noticeable and brought back all the memories."

"Well, do you still sing?"

"Singing is my passion, along with basketball. I sing every once in a while, but I don't know if I'm any good. I get so nervous, and on top of that I don't know if I'm good. My mom tells me I have a gorgeous voice, I just don't believe her."

"Will I ever get to hear this amazing voice?"

"In time, probably."

We left it at that. We just sat there, sitting close, looking at the beautiful lake. It was something I've never seen before. Back in Cali, the ocean is our beautiful lake.

"So, since you're from California, you've probably never seen snow."

"In movies and stuff, never in real life. What's it like?"

"Cold," he smirked, "you'll like it." I blushed and looked away, hoping he didn't see it. "You'll have to learn that North Dakota is unpredictable. It can snow one day and rain the next." He paused, but quickly added, "Ever seen a combine?"

"A what?" I've never heard of that so I was completely confused.

He chuckled, "A combine. Come ride with me sometime. You'll like it."

"Ride where?" Once again, he laughed. I couldn't figure out why.

"We are big farmers; we harvest wheat, barley, beans, corn, and sunflowers. If you're planning on staying, you've got to learn this stuff." He winked at me. "We ride Case IH, no John Deere." As if I knew what any of that meant. "Don't worry, you'll catch on."

"Are they red?"

"Sure are. Seen one?"

I nodded, "On our way from California. I saw them, had no idea what it was. I felt so dumb. This is totally different than California."

"Most definitely. But, better."

"Caleb, why do you like *me?*"

He chuckled, "How can I not? You're gorgeous."

"You don't think you moved too fast before you really knew me?"

"Sara," he began, "I didn't need to know you. I fell for you. Your personality and your smile were amazing. Your looks"—he winked— "were a bonus."

I laughed, "It's weird."

"What's that?"

"You look so familiar, but I know it's impossible."

His expression turned blank, "Impossible." He mumbled it too much.

He jumped up and lifted me to my feet. Explaining my story to Caleb lifted a large weight off my shoulders. Caleb was way more supportive than I'd thought he'd be. I'd just hope it would stay like this. We walked hand in hand for a while down the beach, but my feet were sore and it was getting late.

Cole and Cameron were sitting on the couch when we walked through the door. Cole had his leg up on the chair.

"Will you guys be okay for a little bit while I go shower?"

They all nodded and instantly began to talk about sports. I walked around the corner, but stopped to hear if they'd change their conversation, but they didn't.

The shower felt wonderful. The heat fogged up the mirror when I got out of the shower. I threw on sweats. I stared at myself in the mirror. My damp hair was dangling with droplets of water falling off. My face was beet red from the heat of the shower.

I heard the laughing going on downstairs and I blocked it out. My life was going good in my new beginning. Everything was put into place. I couldn't believe it.

As I rounded the corner of the living room, I paused, overhearing their current conversation.

"...about your dad. Sara had told me today." Caleb's voice sounded sincere.

"It's all right, it's been almost eight years now," Cole said. "It'll be eight years two days after our birthday. The guy that killed him is getting out of jail, too."

I gasped, remembering now that it'd be eight years and the drunk would be free. I choked back tears. I couldn't let them know I was listening.

"Really?"

"Yeah," Cameron said. "You'll treat her good, right?"

"Of course."

I walked into the room before they could talk anymore.

"You smell good," Cole said.

"Really?" I just shrugged.

When Cole and Cameron left us alone, Caleb and I sat on the couch. Caleb threw his arm over my shoulder and kissed my neck.

"Caleb," I said evenly.

"Mhm," he answered continuing to kiss my neck, slowly moving up my cheeks which sent shivers down my back.

"My mom's upstairs."

"I know." He pulled back and smiled. "I better go."

"Eh, school." I made a face.

His smile grew wider, "We can skip if you know what I mean."

"Um, no." I laughed reaching in for one more kiss.

He laughed, "It'll be fun!" He continued to kiss my neck, making me speechless.

I sighed, "It would. Not tomorrow, though."

He moved up to my lips and continued. His hand slipped around my back pulling me closer to him. He sure seemed to know a lot about kissing for never kissing a girl before me.

I knew my mom would be down any minute.

"Caleb," I said stopping him again.

He just wouldn't stop. It was pleasurable, but not with my mom listening or possibly coming down the stairs at any moment. She could easily hear us.

"My mom."

He sighed and got up quickly.

"What's wrong?" I tried to ask innocently so he wouldn't be too mad at me.

Too late.

"You don't want to, do you?"

I shook my head in defense, "Not with my mother sitting up there."

He sighed again, "I like you, Sara. A lot. You always stop me at my finest!"

I laughed which made Caleb smile.

"Fine. Sorry, babe. I'll let you go. See you tomorrow in school."

His perfect lips touched mine one more time before Caleb left with the hint of the aroma of his cologne still in the room.

CHAPTER SIX

one bright star

Beeeeep.

Beep. Beep. Beep. Beep. Beep.

Mornings. A bad word for me. Particularly, it was the first day of pre-season practice. I would be dreading it all day.

I dragged myself out of bed and into the shower. Hot water washing over my body woke me up. I threw my hair up into the towel and went down stairs to eat breakfast.

I turned on the TV with my bowl of Frosted Flakes in hand, watching SpongeBob, the only thing good on. At the commercial, I made my way up to my bathroom to get ready. I scrunched my hair, making it a curly mess, and put on makeup. I put on a nice pair of jeans and my favorite T-shirt and sweatshirt. I rummaged around the house for my duffle bag. I threw my shoes and all the necessities of basketball practice in it.

When I went down stairs again, Cole and Cameron were up and ready for school. They had the choice to stay home from school since the accident, but they didn't want to cause attention. Cameron had headaches occasionally from the concussion and Cole, just minor aches and pains.

I drove us to school, since they were obviously incapable of it. When I walked into the hallway of my locker, Caleb was leaning against my locker, with a tiger lily in his hand. He had a huge grin planted on his face.

I glared, "You."

"Good morning to you, too," he said handing me the flower.

"By the time I'm out of school, my room will be full of flowers," I stated, accepting it.

"You keep them all?"

"Of course I do."

He laughed, "I thought you'd just throw them away, but never mind. All right, so if we both survive basketball practices, what should we do?"

"Throw a party?"

"Nah, I was thinking more on the line of a back massage."

I sighed, "That'd be great."

He chuckled, "I meant me."

"Oh." I slammed my locker and turned away from him.

I could just imagine the look on his face as he said with a chuckle, "I was just kidding. Back massage for Miss California and how about a kiss for the North Dakotan?"

I turned around, "If there weren't cameras in this school, you'd get yours right now."

He smiled playfully, "What's a little detention?" His perfect teeth were perfectly straight in the most perfect way.

"My basketball career. After practice, that'll keep you motivated." I winked at him.

He ran his fingers through his hair and pouted, "I can't wait that long!"

"Oh, yes you can."

We walked to math together. Mr. Field had a strict policy of no contact in school, even if it's two girls, best friends at that, hugging. It's a dumb rule, everybody hates it.

Mr. Reynolds sped through two lessons in order to have a test this week. Great, exactly what I needed during basketball. In our partnership, Wade worked fast. His favorite subject was math. We were finished with the assignment way before anybody else.

"How's the homework coming?" Wade asked me.

"Man, how is this so easy for you?"

He shrugged with a smile, "Comes natural. I can be your tutor sometime if you'd like?"

"That would be great!" I pleaded. "We can study at my house."

The smile on Wade's face couldn't have possibly gotten bigger, "I'd love that."

"Great. Next chapter looks like a killer. I'll tell you when I need you."

I couldn't help but notice the expression planted on Caleb's face. His attempt to hide the smirk from overhearing our conversation was failing. I tried to kick him underneath the table but missed and kicked Wade.

"Oh! I'm sorry, Wade!" I exclaimed, trying not to laugh. "I didn't mean to. My foot slipped."

"Nah, it's okay," he said rubbing his shin.

Caleb was trying his hardest not to laugh and was saved by the bell. Wade ran out the room as usual, just to get to the next class on time.

"Whew," he said, bursting out laughing, "now, that was close. Nice job kicking him, though."

"I meant to kick you."

He smiled, "You missed."

I tried to kick him, but he moved and I totally missed.

"Missed me, missed me, now you have to kiss me," Caleb chanted.

I just smiled and stormed off to English.

The English, history, and chemistry teachers didn't have a problem piling on the homework. By lunch, I was exhausted.

Penny came walking up behind me, "What's up?"

I sighed, "Mucho tarea."

She laughed, "Mi no hablo español."

"You know what I mean. Lots of homework. You have it, too, though, don't you?"

"Yeah. You're lucky you have Wade in your group for math."

"I most certainly am. Math is like my enemy, it's worthless." I smiled, "I told him he could be my tutor for it."

She gasped, "You didn't!"

I nodded, "Bad decision?"

"Horrible!" she screamed.

Caleb came up along with the great smell from his cologne, "What's the loudness about?" It made my heart flutter.

Penny laughed with sarcasm, "You let Sara tell Wade he can go over to her house, *alone*?"

"It was quite amusing actually." He laughed again.

I tried to change the subject, "Ready for basketball?"

She chuckled, "Are you nuts? Never."

School went by faster than I wanted it to, time for practice. I quickly changed into my practice clothes and headed to the gym where we would run and run and run for the next hour and a half.

Caleb's car already sitting in the driveway when I pulled up to the house after practice; he wasn't in it, though. I stepped through the door, and there he was, grinning my favorite smile.

"I'm ready for my reward," he beamed.

I tried to stall, "In a minute, I'm thirsty." I walked right past him, smiling, and grabbed a glass of water and headed in the living room.

He grabbed me from behind around my waist, "Oh, no, you don't. You promised." I turned around, still in his arms, and kissed him on the cheek and turned around. His didn't loosen his grasp, he held on tighter.

"You never said where specifically," I smiled.

"Oh, but you know what I meant."

I turned, only to meet his face inches away. He kissed me gently a few times, "Now, that's what I meant. I didn't suffer through basketball practice for nothing." He let go, just as the door flew open and in walked my mom. My heart was thumping and not from my mom walking in and seeing us, but from the butterflies creeping up. I spilled my water, which startled me.

As Mom walked in, the phone rang.

"Hello?" I answered. I saw Caleb wiping up after my mess with my water glass.

"Hi. Is this Sara?" The voice sounded familiar, a boy's voice I couldn't quite remember.

"Yes."

Silence.

"Hi." It was very quiet and anxious sounding.

I asked, "Who is this?"

"Jeremy Jacobs."

Anger rushed over me faster than it has ever before. I hung up the phone. I wasn't in the mood to talk to him.

"Who was it?" Caleb was at my side when I put the phone down.

"Jeremy Jacobs. Drunk dumb donkey who almost..." Caleb cut me off before I exploded.

We had learned that Jeremy had been released from the hospital and had to go to rehab, pay fines, and go to court. I didn't want to have anything to do with Jeremy. I couldn't go through the hell I went through eight years ago. I'm sure he'd keep bugging us until we replied, but I didn't care.

"Well, Sara, you can't be that mean," Mom sounded disappointed. I shrugged and focused on Caleb.

Surprisingly, the week went by fast, each school day ending with basketball practice and each basketball practice ending with Caleb coming over. Each day started off, of course, with Caleb handing me a single flower. I couldn't figure out how he did it.

Wade had bugged me in every day in math to come and help me with my math.

"Need help today?" he asked.

I shook my head, "I understand it, actually."

His head fell, "Okay."

"But, thanks for the invitation."

He shrugged and slid off his seat when the bell rang.

"Do you can Caleb have plans for tomorrow night?" Penny asked me in practice on Thursday.

"Probably just hang out. I never know with him, though. Why?"

"Well, James and I are going to a movie, it'd be nice to double date. How about it?"

"Yeah, that sounds fun, something different. What movie?"

"It's this new comedy that James's been talking about. It should be funny. Caleb would like it if James does."

I texted Caleb right after practice, 'movies? tmro nite? double date with yur sis and dev?'

His reply, 'absolutely. only if i can sit by u:)'

My reply, 'that can be arranged.'

His reply, 'good night, california. sweet dreams.'

My reply, 'nite. you also'

I smiled and set the phone down. I went to bed with my phone in my hand, knowing Caleb would wake me up in the morning, like always.

School the next day went by fast. Coach said he'd go easy on us if we worked hard throughout practice. Afterwards, I quickly jumped into the car and drove home as fast as I could. Worrying I was going to be late for the movie date tonight, my shower was less than five minutes.

The vibrations from my phone were annoying, telling me I'd gotten a new message. Once again, the ID said the number I didn't recognize. I grabbed a piece of paper and wrote down the number.

The message read, 'You know how hard you are to find? She hid you good! I'm free, free like the bird. I've paid my debt, now, you have to pay yours.'

That message sent shivers up my back and I pressed the erase button on my phone. I could hardly breathe with my heart racing. I jumped when I heard a noise outside my bedroom window but calmed my breathing down as well as I could.

I realized the noise was Caleb picking me up for the movie. But, what was that text message about? Who would send something like that? Who was free? What debt?

Peeking out the window, I saw Caleb's shiny red car. I couldn't see all of him in the driver side but enough to see him smiling.

James and Penny were at the movie theatre by the time we got there. Penny was dressed in a cute knee length black dress and James in jeans and a polo shirt. Compared to Caleb and me, they looked like they were really on a date.

I don't know how long it's been since I've laughed that hard at a movie. It was nice to just hang with friends. To know that I had good friends just after a few weeks. We laughed and talked. Unbelievable.

"Hey, California, ever seen stars at night? Ever stopped and looked at them for a long time?" Caleb asked on the way home.

I smiled and laughed, "Of course I have."

"Let's go, then, find a spot and lay out for awhile. I know just the place." He smiled and sped up.

He pulled into his house. We walked up the stairs that lead to his bedroom. We went into his bedroom and he opened up the window, "Follow me." He helped me out the window. The cool air felt nice. He climbed up a ladder, leading to the roof. The roof was flat, just right for laying and looking at the stars. There was already a blanket and some pillows up there.

Caleb lay down and pulled me down with him. He kissed me on the forehead, and snuggled me closer to him, wrapping his arms around me. He smelled like fresh linen just getting out of the dryer.

"I've never seen anything as beautiful as this," I exclaimed.

Caleb said winking, "Neither have I." He kissed my cheek.

"I'm really happy I met you," I said after a while of silence.

I wish I could have seen his face, but it was too dark. The fall air was crisp, but soothing.

He sighed, "My life was consumed by sports. I didn't make time for anybody or anything else. Penny told me one day I was a worthless athlete. That woke me up. Then, I saw you, again, finally, walking with Penny. I couldn't resist. You were gorgeous." I was sure I was blushing.

Caleb said the words "again" and "finally" as if he's seen me before I even moved here and met him the first time. Even with the similarities that I saw in Caleb, I don't believe that I've ever seen him before.

"What do you mean again and finally?"

He cleared he throat, "When you tripped on the rug."

I nodded reluctantly knowing the fakeness in his voice.

"You were like a tidal wave coming in. Your long, blonde hair and your bright blue eyes. You're like a shot of numbing medication."

I laughed, "Numbing medication?"

He shrugged, "It's the best I could come up with. "

In the sky, my eyes focused only on a bright, single star. I knew for a fact it wasn't the North Star. I believed it was my dad. I smiled at the thought of him always being there, guiding and protecting me through my life.

It wasn't a chilly night, it was just right for star watching. The wind wasn't blowing and there wasn't a cloud in the sky.

"What's your biggest fear?" I asked remembered I forgot to ask him earlier.

He hummed a little. I got nervous, thinking I shouldn't have asked that.

He answered after a moment of silence, "To be lost, and not know where I am. To have the feeling of not knowing. Not know where you are, where your family is, and why you got there. That'd be my biggest fear." He paused. "Maybe more than that, that if someone I knew got lost and I didn't know where they were. It'd just be awful."

I nodded in agreement and remained silent and closed my eyes just for a second...

A feeling shook me from a light sleep. I couldn't respond right away. It was a constant buzzing that was beyond annoying. I realized it was my phone vibrating. I looked at the phone and it read 4:37a.m., and I had just missed a call from "Home."

"Crap!" I jumped up, startling Caleb, who was also asleep. "Caleb, we feel asleep. Shoot, I'm dead."

He jumped up and helped me down the ladder. I called Cole as soon as I got into the car. The phone rang and rang.

"Hello?" Cole answered.

"Is mom awake?" I asked.

"No, she told me to wait up for you. Where are you?"

My heart stopped beating fast and calmed down. I almost had to laugh.

"We were looking at the stars on Caleb's roof and we fell asleep. I promise I'll be home in 15 minutes."

"You better be."

"We're on our way now. Please, don't wake Mom up. Does she have her fan on so she doesn't hear me?"

"Yeah, she has it on. Be careful. See you in a bit." The line went dead before I said good bye.

Cole wasn't in the best mood when I got home. He told me I was lucky that Mom had gone to bed and that he was the only one up. I just ignored him. So, it wasn't the best ending of the perfect night. Who cares? I crawled into bed, forgetting about everything, just thinking about sleep.

"Sara?"

"Sara?" Mom was knocking on my door, loudly.

"Let's go, it's past noon."

I rolled out of bed and onto the floor creating a bang. My alarm read twelve thirty. I slipped into my slippers and climbed down the stairs. My hair was a mess and my makeup was smeared across my face.

"My, my, my. Don't you look beautiful," Cameron mumbled. "You look like you've been through hell and back."

"Gee, thanks," I uttered. With hearing that, I turned right around and headed for the shower.

Caleb texted me all day, distracting me in everything I was doing. I tried to clean my room, but failed whenever I'd hear his ringtone. Then, I'd figure I'd call Lili, but Caleb, again, called me and I forgot all about calling Lili.

September was my favorite month. Not only was it my birthday, but also it was fall. When I was younger, I couldn't wait for fall to be with my dad. He had a job that made him work during the summer months. When fall came around, I'd run home from the bus stop just to play catch or shoot hoops. A girl's father is her role model. But, I had lost mine.

Sometimes, when I see girls with dads, I get a tear in my eye. I ask God a million times why he took mine away. Why do girls have their dads and don't even care? If only they knew what it was like without them. If only they knew.

On Sunday morning, Caleb picked me up for church. It was nice to have a boyfriend who was the same religion. It was also nice to call him my boyfriend. Caleb and I've only known each other for a short time, but we were happy. Mom didn't like the fact we moved fast, but we didn't move as *fast* as she thinks. Mom's getting used to seeing us together. She trusts him to take care of me and to keep me safe. Cole and Cameron are getting used to him, too. They don't try to scare him off like when they first met him.

Penny has become my best friend. She doesn't let her brother and my relationship get in the way. She will never be a "Lili," but she has a special place in my heart.

After church on Sunday, she came over to my house.

"What color is better for my nails? The pink or black?" she asked fluttering her nails in my face.

"Black is totally in." We were painting our nails, while talking about the latest gossip.

"Penny? Giselle was telling me, when I first starting talking to her, that you and Caleb got sick for three months. What happened?"

She paused, and looked up at me funny. It took her a few seconds to answer. "Caleb got a high fever one night." She was stuttering as she spoke. "We rushed him up to the hospital right away. Not two hours later, I caught the fever, too. It was contagious, anybody could catch it. They kept us in isolation until we were completely cured."

"Oh, that sucks. Did the school know?"

"Yeah, our mom called them and told them. I guess they didn't want to scare the students by telling them what we had."

"Yeah."

"Did you hear about Brandon?" she asked, quickly changing the subject.

"No. What?"

She smiled and almost shouted, "He and Giselle are going out."

"No way!"

She nodded, "Way!"

"Are you sure?"

She shrugged, "That's what Sonya told me. I don't know if it's true." She paused and fidgeted with her nails. "Sara. Where's your dad at? I never see him when I'm over here. And, you never talk about him."

I looked down. I just wasn't ready to reveal that portion, yet, to Penny. "He's, uh," I stuttered, "at work, I think."

"This late?"

"It's not that late. He's usually back by ten or eleven."

"Where does he work?"

"At an office, with loans and stuff." I was hoping she wouldn't urge me on, but knowing her, she did.

"What's his name?"

I coughed out his name, "Luke."

She nodded her head, "Is Cameron or Cole named after him.

I nodded, "Cameron Luke. Cole James."

"I see." She looked at her nails. "Good choice with black."

Penny left at nine. I packed my bag for practice, grabbed a cup of hot chocolate and went to my room. I'd really hoped she hadn't been smart and asked Caleb about my dad. In thinking of that, I texted Caleb, immediately.

'Caleb.'

He replied, 'yes.'

I replied, 'tonight, penny asked me about my dad. and i still havent told her about him. promise me you wont?'

He replied, 'why haven't you?'

I replied, 'I didn't want to have to explain it. i will, soon. i promise.' As I typed those words, I could feel my throat getting tight and water swelling up in my eyes.

I grabbed an old scrapbook that I made after my dad had been killed. I blinked twice to make a single tear fall down my face, soon followed by more. He was a handsome guy; I can see why Mom fell in love and married him.

I turned to a page of Dad with me on his lap. It was my birthday party, the one before he'd been killed. I used to love my birthdays. But after my dad died, I celebrated them differently. As I'm getting older, though, I'm less and less enthused. They remind me of him so much. On all my birthdays, he'd greet me with "Bappy Birthday, Bug!"

After Dad had died, Cole promised to take his role. Cole started to call me bug and has since. When Cole says bug, it makes me smile.

This week in school was homecoming week. The big football game was Friday night against our rival team, the LaVont Rebels. Of course, Cameron and Cole were nervous wrecks. Here in Edgemont, they have Homecoming King and Queen, and Prince and Princess. King and Queen were chosen seniors, as voted by students. Prince

101

and Princess were juniors. They were crowned on Wednesday, which was mine and Cole's birthday.

Every day was repetition; going from class to class. Caleb sat by me in all the classes that didn't have assigned seats. Overall, I was adjusting well to Edgemont. I got good grades, had great friends, and was surprisingly, somewhat popular. Everybody knew me, which wasn't a surprise, considering how small it was.

Caleb's friends accepted me into their group, finally. At lunch on Monday, they started randomly talking to me.

"So, how's basketball going?" Jordan asked. Jordan was the loudest of them all, the friendliest, and the nicest to me. He seemed to be the better of friends with Caleb. They all were extremely tall, Jake towering over 6' 6".

"It's all right," I sighed. "It's still a long ways from the real season, though."

Jake put in, "You'll be the best one out there, though. You and Penny, I mean." He winked at Penny. Jake was usually quiet. He just sat there and laughed at funny things, winced at nasty things, and followed the rest of the crew.

Josh and Tyler are weird, plain and simple. They are your typical teenage boys. They don't think; they do dumb stuff.

"What number do you want to be?" Josh asked as he continued to make his mashed potato tower.

I mumbled concentrating on the tower, "I'm hoping four."

Caleb stood up and held out his hand, "If you don't mind, I'd like to steal my Cinderella. My lady?"

I waved goodbye as I took Caleb's hand. "What's this about?" I asked as we were leaving the cafeteria.

"I just wanted to be alone with you for a little while."

I laughed, "We're always alone."

"One more second wouldn't hurt." He led me behind a wall, away from sight, and kissed me. Then the bell rang. I pulled away, "We better go. You, Mister, are going to make us late."

Caleb gave me the annoyed looked but reluctantly went to class with me.

In gym, Chris continued to make me laugh. He spit out jokes like nothing, each making me burst. Coach Hansen warned us and gave a stern look. Chris seemed to just click with me.

"This stuff is stupid," Caleb complained, throwing the papers down in English class and making me laugh. English wasn't Caleb's strongest class.

"It's not that hard. Just focus," I suggested, trying to hide my urge to laugh.

He fixed his perfect, black hair by running his fingers through it, "How can I focus with you sitting here laughing at me?" His confused faced made me chuckle.

I laughed, "I'm not laughing at you. I'm laughing at your anger."

He seemed frustrated with me, "Why don't you shut your mouth?"

I gave him a stern look, "Caleb, I'm sorry I didn't mean to..."

He shook his head, "Sorry, I just get annoyed when you say stuff like that. I know you're great at English. I'm not, though."

"I'm sorry."

He shrugged and continued to shake his head, "It's my fault. I'm sorry I yelled at you."

When the bell rang, I shot up without talking another word to Caleb. He didn't have to get that worked up about it. I didn't look back either as I headed to my next class without him.

Caleb caught me as soon as the bell rang the next class.

"Sara, I'm sorry."

I shook my head, "I just need to be away from you for a little bit. You can't get mad like that."

He took a deep breath in and let it out slowly, "Sorry."

I had to smile, "I forgive you. You can shut up now. Leave me alone 'til lunch, though." I gave him a wink and walked to class without him.

Tuesday was the day that all the students would vote for Homecoming Royalty. Wednesday they'd crown them. I wasn't expecting to win princess since I had only been in Edgemont a month. Caleb was sure to get prince, though. He was the one that was the star of everything: academics, sports, and girls.

Practice on Tuesday was easy. I wasn't even paying attention to half of it. When Coach blew the whistle for practice to be over, it startled me.

Mom was home when I got back from practice. She was cooking dinner. "How was your day, Sara?"

"Oh, Mom, it was just wonderful," I said with too much sarcasm.

Her face turned evil-looking, "I just asked. Mine was good, too, thank you."

"Sorry, I'm just exhausted from everything. I have loads of homework and practice is a killer. I'm stressed."

She laughed, "You're 16, you can't be stressed."

"Oh, but I am. Where are the boys?"

"Downstairs. Go get them, supper's ready."

I was way too sore to make a trip down the stairs and back up. I picked my cell up and called Cole. He answered, confused, but laughed once I told him to come upstairs and eat. I told him to get Cameron, too.

I went straight up to my room after supper to study *Romeo and Juliet*. I read it in my freshman year at California. This was all review for me.

My phone beeped; text message from Caleb.

It read, '"O, she doth teach the torches to burn bright." that's all I got.'

I replied, 'now aren't you smart. did you learn that yourself?'

His reply, 'sure did, did you like it?'

I replied, 'that's one of my fav quotes from that play.'

His reply, 'AND i know what it means. it means Sara is the most beautiful girl i've seen in a long time and she's shown how my heart to love.'

I couldn't reply; my fingers couldn't move. I was speechless and breathless.

I replied, 'well thank you:)'.

His reply, 'no, thank you! i love you. Tomorrow night, you're in for a surprise. Be ready.'

I replied, 'i love you, too. Good night'. Why would he want to surprise me?

His reply, "good night. good night. parting is such sweet sorrow that i shall say good night 'til it be morrow. night beautiful.'

I tossed and turned in my bed. I couldn't sleep because of that text message. I think I finally fell asleep after midnight. My dream was a replay of my ninth birthday morning. That morning my dad woke me up by playing and singing happy birthday with his guitar. Why did he have to go? Why did my daddy, big, strong, and healthy, have to die?

CHAPTER SEVEN

bappy birthday

"Happy Birthday to you."

Who was singing?

"Happy Birthday to you!"

Why are they singing?

"Happy Birthday dear, Sara."

What's with all the noise?

"Happy Birthday to you!"

Cole.

My birthday.

I opened my eyes, remembering that today was my birthday. Cole's, too. Cole came in my room that morning singing, like he did every year since Dad died.

"Bappy Birthday, Bug!" Cole said.

"Uh, too early for singing," I winced.

"Aren't you going to say something else?"

"Let me think. Nope." I rolled over smiling.

"Oh, come on, bug. We're twins. Today's your birthday, it's also someone else's."

"Happy birthday, Cole," I mumbled.

He jumped right on top of me in my bed. I screamed. He grabbed me and threw me over his shoulder. His doctor let him get his cast off and the crutches were gone. The break wasn't as bad as they thought. Cole had begged and begged them to take the cast off for his birthday.

Mom had a big birthday cake on the kitchen counter when we came down the stairs, with presents around it. Cameron was putting up balloons around kitchen and living room.

"Good morning, birthday girl! Happy Birthday. We'll save the cake and presents for you after practice," Mom said. "I'll have supper ready."

Cole cleared his throat as set me down.

Mom laughed, "Happy birthday, birthday boy."

Cameron added, "Sara, your present isn't wrapped, as you can probably tell. It's the only thing without wrapping paper. You know me, I'm not good at wrapping." I looked around and saw a jewelry box lying on the counter. He nodded when I pointed to it. Inside was a beautiful sapphire necklace, my birthstone.

"Thank you! I love it! It's gorgeous, Cameron. Thank you!" I turned around to let him put it around my neck. "I better go get ready. Here's your gift, Cole."

I had bought him a nice shirt with a necklace to match. I think it's hot when boys wear a masculine necklace. Cole got me a box of different colors of nail polish; I picked it out.

In my room, there was a big box, at least five feet tall, with a huge bow on top. It wasn't there when I left my room. On the card attached, it read,

'Open for a big surprise. Happy Birthday, California!'
Caleb.

The box moved and a noise came from inside. It made me jump. I stood back.

I knocked on the box. "Who's there?" Caleb's voice came from inside.

He plunged through the side of the box with a huge grin on his face. "Happy Birthday, my love."

"You scared the crap out of me," I screamed with a sigh.

"Sorry, hon. Didn't mean to." He wrapped his arms around me and gave me a hug. "Happy Birthday." He kissed me. "So, I've been thinking." He paused and kissed me, again. "Since you're now seventeen years of age, I believe you should get seventeen kisses. Am I right?"

I smiled, "Correct. Did that one count?"

"Nope. Just a tester." He kissed me, again. "That one didn't either."

"So, when do they?" I jumped up on my tiptoes to reach in for a kiss.

He shrugged, "When I feel like ending at seventeen."

"Let me go shower and get ready for school. Does my mom know you're in here?"

"Yeah, I was downstairs when you were sleeping. I hid in the office while Cole carried you down. Then, I sneaked in here and climbed in the box." He squeezed me as tight as he could and touched his lips against mine one more time.

"I have to go shower. I'll be back."

I quickly jumped into the shower, turning it on hot to wake me up. I shaved my legs for ultimate smoother legs. I wasn't one to let the hair grow for two days then shave; I shaved every night. I combed through my hair and brushed my teeth. I put on a pair of jeans and my favorite t-shirt and headed down the stairs.

My phone was beeping with a new message. I couldn't figure out who it could be.

It read, 'Happy birthday, there, miss Sara. Watch your back. I'm out. I'm free. I'm coming for you. Oh, and happy anniversary, eight years of your precious daddy being gone.'

I gasped, *who would send me something like that?* I thought. I pushed it aside, knowing I had handsome men waiting for me downstairs.

Cole, Cameron, and Caleb were sitting on the couch, laughing at something on TV. Mom was just leaving for work. She wished Cole and me one last happy birthday and headed out the door.

I was excited to look out the window and see the bright red vehicle sitting in the driveway. Over the past few weeks, Caleb's Challenger quickly became my ride to school. I was overwhelmed in the school's parking lot where I received plenty of happy birthdays.

Penny was just as enthused as she was the first time I'd met her. She bounced around all bubbly and handed me a gift while I sat blushing in math class.

"Penny, I told you. No presents!" I argued.

"It's something little. It's from my parents and me. It's nothing really." I opened it up; it was a gift card to my favorite clothing store for $100.

"Wow. Penny. You guys! That's way too much."

"It's just something you can treat yourself with. I'm a girl, trust me. It's not that much when you go into a store." She laughed. "Continue."

"There's more?" I exclaimed. I dug deeper and found a jewelry box. Inside were sapphire earrings, matching my necklace. I had to laugh at the anxious expression on Penny's face. "They're beautiful. They match my necklace that Cameron gave to me. Thank you so much. I'll be sure to tell your parents thank you, too. You guys didn't have to buy me anything."

"Oh! You hush. It's our pleasure. I heard Caleb scared you with him in the present idea," she giggled.

"Yeah. I think he accidentally bumped the box and then started laughing. Scared me half to death. It was funny."

"Did he give you a present yet?" she asked, urging me to tell her.

"No, but I think my present is seventeen kisses, which according to him haven't started yet."

She laughed, "Don't worry. It's coming. The present, not the kisses." She smiled.

Mr. Reynolds came waltzing in whistling. "First things first," Mr. Reynolds said as he came through the room, "happy birthday, Cole and Sara."

"Thanks," I said quietly not wanting the attention.

He rushed through the lesson and gave us our homework to work on. Wade and Caleb talked about hunting. I blocked them out and finished my work, easily.

Mrs. Hoffi wasn't going to go easy on the homework, though. As I looked at her, I realized how pretty she really was. She wasn't old or young. She was middle age. But beautiful. Her smile, rarely seen, though, was radiant. And, her brains! She was smart! She knew what to say, the correct answer, and if she didn't, she'd find the right one. She wore nice clothes. Always dressed up. Her nails were brightly painted a color, never showing wear and tear.

"...but only if you have a direct object."

I couldn't focus today, however. My birthday was on my mind. Caleb was on my mind. I could say I had a lot on my mind.

"Do pages 445-449. And, I believe I have a couple birthdays to wish."

That sentence caught my attention.

"Happy birthday, Sara and Cole."

Cole's voice came from the back of the room, "Thanks, Mrs. Hoffi."

"Yeah, thank you."

She smiled brightly, "You're certainly welcome."

In Chemistry, Toby was unusually happy. His was humming a tune I didn't know. He had a smile across his face.

"Happy birthday," he said as I sat down on my seat.

"Thanks," I said doubtfully.

"What have you gotten?"

Surprised, I answered as evenly as I could, "Jewelry."

He nodded and continued his work. At least he said happy birthday. He scribbled things into his notebook.

"What did you get for number three?"

I rummaged through my notes, "Carbon."

Then, the bell rang.

"Have a good day, Sara."

I sat in my seat, shocked, "Thanks." I could barely get the word out.

They announced who is crowned King, Queen, Prince, and Princess before lunch. Caleb had his arm draped across my shoulder as we waited for Lorii to announce who won. We were standing with Cameron and Cole in the hall.

"This year's King is," Lorii said pausing, "Cameron Young. Queen is," another pause, "Lauren Long." I wasn't shocked when they called a girl from senior class Queen but, I was shocked when Cameron won it. He's only been here for a month. Cole and Cameron gave each other a high five.

"Prince is," another pause, "Caleb Pierce." You could hear the clapping all around the school and they high fived again. "And, Princess is," another pause, longer than the rest, "Sara Young. Congratulations to all." When they called Caleb's name for Prince, I was prepared for it. Mine, I wasn't so prepared.

Caleb had the shocked look on his face with too much humor. "Whoa, California, congrats." Caleb's smile was almost too sarcastic to take. I glared at him and walked away.

Kali stopped me in the hallway, something unusual. "Happy birthday, Sara. And, congrats on Princess."

"Thanks."

She kept it short and walked off to class. It looked like she was in a rush to get away.

Senora Garcia quickly greeted me with "feliz cumpleanos," which means happy birthday.

Amazement fell over me as I walked into study hall, where I finally got peace and quiet. But Lorii interrupted it by saying over the intercom, "I like to wish a very happy birthday to Sara and Cole." Oh man, just perfect. My cheeks were on fire; thank God Caleb wasn't in the room. "Also, pre-season practice is cancelled for today, both girls' and boys'. While blushing, I managed to smile. Why was practice cancelled? And, when was this birthday going to end?

"Happy Birthday, Sara," Chris said to me in gym.

"Thank you."

He was shooting hoops. "What are you doing for your birthday?"

"Caleb told me he had a surprise for me."

"Ah, I see. That'll be good." He smiled. "Congratulation on Princess. Bet you didn't think you'd get it."

I nodded, "Never."

"Well, I'm glad you did. I voted for you."

"Thanks," I said.

After school, I walked down the hall to my locker and I saw Caleb leaning, arms crossed, against my locker, with a huge smile planted on his face.

"Happy birthday," he said. He grabbed my hand, and we walked to his car. "I heard Lorii announce your birthday on the intercom. I had to laugh. I know your cheeks were bright cherry red."

"That was so embarrassing. How did she know that it was today?"

He smiled a smug smile and opened the door with too much of a curtsy.

"You didn't!" I punched him. "You little...you...you knew I would get embarrassed."

"Oh, you know I had to. I could just picture your cheeks bright red." he laughed. I let go of his hand and stormed ahead of him. He followed me, smiling.

I walked to where I parked my car this morning, but it wasn't there. "Cole took it home," Caleb answered, wrapping his arms around my waist behind me and whispered in my ear after kissing it. "You're coming with me even if you're mad."

As we pulled up to my house, I noticed a strange car in the driveway, yet kind of looking familiar. Caleb just smiled.

"My birthday present?" I asked.

He nodded.

Before we reached the house's front door, he stopped me. He grabbed me from behind by the waist. He whispered in my ear, "Happy birthday." I turned around and kissed him. "I hope this is a good enough present. I want to see that amazing smile on your face."

"You didn't need to get me anything to see a smile on my face." I flashed him a smiled.

At that, the door flew open and out came Lili with the widest smile on her face.

"Oh! Happy birthday, Girl! You're looking great. Oh, I've missed you." She let go and looked at me and smiled. "Why, you look beautiful!" She grabbed me again and squealed.

Then, pulling back, she asked, "And, who's this?" She nudged my arm and whispered, "He's a hunk." I could see Caleb fighting a smile; she said it loud on purpose. We both giggled in unison.

"Caleb, this is Lili. Lili, this is Caleb." I could hardly keep a calm and smooth voice from the excitement of seeing Lili here.

"Nice to meet you, Caleb."

We all headed in doors, but I stopped Caleb, "Thank you. I don't know how you knew." He just smiled and kissed me gently.

Mom was sitting on the couch with a wide smile. I figured she'd be part of this. "Like your gift?"

"Do I ever! I can't believe I see her here. I love it!" I exclaimed.

Caleb moved closer to me, "There's one more gift. Can I borrow Sara for a moment?" Mom nodded and smiled.

He led me up the stairs with Lili following behind us and we made our way towards the game room. "Okay, close your eyes." He put his hands over my eyes to make sure I wasn't looking. "Okay," he said, removing his hands, "look."

Inside the room were seventeen balloons with a gift box in front of them. I walked over to them and grabbed the box. Inside were tickets to a Twins game and a sheet of paper that had, 'I love you. Happy Birthday' written on it.

I hugged Caleb and gave him a huge kiss on the cheek, "Caleb, this is way too much. I can't believe it. Thank you."

"Well," he shrugged, "believe it. Remember when you told me what you wanted in the whole wide world and you said a puppy and tickets? Well, your mom said no to the puppy but yes to the tickets. You deserve it." We both laughed at the puppy part.

"You mean you remembered?"

He smiled, "Of course I did. I gave you the world; you wanted a puppy." He laughed. "I have to admit, I was thinking something way different. I just hope that Lili is better than a puppy. And we'll have to wait until next year for the game."

I smiled, winking at Lili, "Much better."

I turned to go downstairs, but Caleb stopped me and grabbed me by the waist. "How about I start the seventeen kisses?" He kissed me ten times, telling me I'll get the rest later. Lili cleared her throat and smiled.

Cole and I opened gifts after cake. I later found out that Caleb had sweet-talked the coaches to cancel practices. Cole and I both got great gifts.

Later in the evening, Cole and I received a phone call from our Grandma Joanie. "I have an announcement to say," Gran explained in the conversation with me. "I'm moving to North Dakota in a week!"

"That's great, Grandma! Where?"

"In the little house across the street. It's perfect, just right for me. I've all ready packed all my things. They should be in North Dakota by the end of the week. I'll be there in a couple of days."

"Exciting!"

"Okay, well, I better go," she said quietly, "much more to do! Tell Cole happy birthday again! Love you all!"

As I hung up the receiver, I smiled slightly.

Caleb helped clean up and then, got ready to leave. He said his good-byes to everybody and we stepped outside.

I thanked him just once more, "Thank you for a great birthday. It was truly the best I've had since my dad." He wrapped his arms around me and we stood there in silence.

"How about the rest of the kisses?" he suggested.

"How many are left?" I asked.

"Seven." He kissed me once. "Six." He kissed me, again. "Five."

"Four."

"Three."

"Two."

"And, one." He smiled. "There, mission accomplished, but many more where they come from. Have a good night, California. Happy birthday and many more."

"Thank you."

"I love you."

"I love you, too. Good night." He walked down the steps so perfectly and turned around to flash a smile. I waved good bye and went in the house.

Lili and I sat on the couch for hours, drinking coffee and catching up on things.

Gran had explained to me on the phone earlier how her cancer was going. I tried hard not to cry. My gran always loved to talk about my boy troubles and relationships. You could say she was my older best friend. I don't know what I'd do if I ever lost her, too.

As we were getting ready for bed, I asked Lili, "I totally forgot to ask you. When do you leave?"

"Tomorrow," she frowned.

I sighed heavily and whined, "Really? Why?"

"School."

I nodded, "Forgot. I'm really glad you came. This has been the best birthday. Thank you."

She encouraged, "It's not over, yet."

She handed me a gift box. I took the cover off, and inside was the picture we took with Nadir Remerez. In the corner of the picture was a signature. His!

"Thank you! Where did you find this picture?"

"I found it in a scrapbook. And, like, the day after you left, Nadir was in Hollywood again and I had him sign the picture for us. I got a copy, too."

"Thank you."

"I've missed you so much."

I smiled, "I miss you, too. Tell me what I've missed."

"Okay, remember the big jock that made fun of you?"

I pursed my lips at the nightmare. "Yeah," I murmured.

"Well," she continued, "he has braces!" She let out a laugh.

I smiled and laughed, "No way!"

"Way! I had the biggest urge to go up to him and be like, bam! You know? I had to kick myself from that." Lili punched her fist into her hand gesturing her punching the jock.

That made me laugh more. "Do it."

"What?" she asked startled.

I punched my own fist into my other hand, "Do it!"

"Really?" her voice sounded relieved and ready and she smiled wide.

I had to laugh at our foolishness. "Yeah! He insulted me, insult him back! Do it! Please?" I begged.

She beamed with glory, "It'll be my pleasure!"

"What else?"

"Well," she thought, "a new boy that's absolutely dreamy came this fall. Man," she sighed, "is he p-o-pular!"

I laughed, cocking my head to one side and persisted, "You're crazy about him." It wasn't a question, either.

She blushed, but smiled, "Yeah! And, he talks to me. I think he likes me."

"Good. Name?"

"Drew."

"Cute." I thought a moment. "Cute."

She laughed and spoke after a moment, "Hot!"

We looked at each other in silence and after a few awkward moments, we burst into an uproar in laughter.

"I love you, Lili."

"Happy birthday, Sara. I love you, too."

"Thanks."

I reached over, grabbing my best friend and hugging her with no intention of letting go.

Lili always could get a smile on my face. I long waited for the next time I got to see her and now that his moment is finally came, it's already over. That quick. I gazed up at my almost asleep friend and smiled. I sure did miss Lili.

Last summer, we were the trouble-maker good girls, never getting caught. We did crazy things. I couldn't even control my laughter when I was with her. Most of the memories were dangerous, but they are the ones that are the best.

But I had a feeling that Lili and I would slowly drift apart, only for the fact that I'm not going to see her much. And, with my days getting so busy, I never had to time call her. I felt bad, but I had a new life here. Yes, I missed her and longed for our sleepovers, but I was tired of the reminder of my dad, day in and day out.

It's my new life.

My new beginning.

The next morning, I said sad goodbyes to Lili, along with Mom and the boys. When I left for school, she left for the airport. I knew I wouldn't see her for awhile.

Good-bye, Lili, I thought as I drove down the street, ready for a new day. I was seventeen. Seventeen!

Two days after my birthday marked the eighth anniversary of my dad's death. It wasn't the best feeling in the world to wake up on that dreadful morning. I didn't want to look at the time. I didn't want to go to school. I don't want to think about my dad today. Well, I did, but I wanted to be happy.

It was hard to give convincing smiles all day. Caleb was supportive because he knew. But the friendly faces were hard to look at.

I broke down after Chemistry. I quickly ran to the bathroom, hopefully hiding from everyone. But, I ran into Mr. Reynolds in the hallway.

"Sara!" His voice was more than concerned. "What's wrong?"

"Nothing." I tried to shove past him, but he gripped his hands around my arms.

"Come into my room."

I sighed but willingly followed.

He shut the door quietly behind me and came over to me and looked me in the eyes but remained quiet.

I moaned, "It's the eighth anniversary that my dad's been gone."

"Gone?"

"Dead."

He questioned with sympathy, "Dead?"

I nodded, "We were in an accident with a drunk. He was killed. I'm alive. The driver is alive. Dad's dead."

"Sara"—Mr. Reynolds moved closer to me, wrapping his arms around me—"I'm so sorry."

I didn't refuse a hug. Mr. Reynolds was like a big, short young grandpa. He was nice. And, obviously, he cared. As much as I didn't want to let go, I wanted to let go. It wasn't at all comfortable hugging my teacher.

I let go and stepped back and dried my eyes.

"I'm going to be late for class."

"I'll write you a note. I don't think you want to go back with red eyes."

I laughed, "Exactly my thought."

My eyes were beet red as I stood in the locker room. Luckily, I had my makeup for after practice.

"Sara?"

It sounded like Cole's voice.

"Yeah?"

"Can I come in?"

"Sure."

As Cole walked around the wall and into sight, he, too, was red-eyed.

"Are you okay? I met up with Mr. Reynolds. He told me where you were. Are you..."

I cut him off and fell into his arms. This was the person I wanted to be holding. I wanted to be holding my brother, the one who understood my pain today. I knew Caleb understood, but I didn't know where he was.

Cole didn't talk. I didn't want him to. I just wanted to stand there in his arms staring at myself in the mirror. I didn't cry. I didn't *want* to cry. My friends would ask too many dumb questions.

"Ready?" Cole said letting go.

I nodded and he handed me the note from Mr. Reynolds and I was off to history.

I found myself in the bathroom at lunch hour wiping tears, too. As I opened the door to leave the bathroom, Caleb was there.

I collapsed in a stupid sort of way into his arms.

"Are you okay?"

I sniffled, trying to hide the tears, "I'm fine."

"Are you sure?"

I nodded.

He shook his head and persisted, "Sara."

"I think I just want to go home."

He nodded with a smile and followed me to the office where I had to tell them the story. And, finally after ten minutes of explaining, they let me leave.

Caleb took the lead and I followed him out to his car. I held my tears down the blocks and up the stairs to the door. I stopped and finally let the tears come again and stream down my face.

"I miss him so much." Caleb grabbed me into his arms. "Why did he go?" His grip tightened around my waist. He smelled amazing. "It should've been me." I could feel Caleb shaking his head as I spoke that. "Why?" I felt dumb releasing all this on Caleb. "It's my fault. It's my fault."

Caleb kissed the top of my head and continued to hold me tight.

"I'm sorry."

He released his grip and stared me in the eyes. His lips were curved into a half smile, without showing teeth. "About what?"

I shook my head. "Let's go inside."

I walked up the stairs to my room, slowly, with Caleb's hand intertwined with mine. I sat on my bed, holding Dad's picture in my hands. I wiped away a tear. But I had to laugh. I was holding on to a picture of us drenched in water after a water fight.

"He just let me win. He faked he lost. But he said I won." I looked at Caleb. "This was the last picture we had together."

He draped his arm around my waist and pulled me closer to him. I looked up at his smile and the way it touched his beautiful green eyes.

"It's a hard day, but it's over."

"So will you put that smile back on your beautiful face?" I nodded with a smile.

He leaned in to kiss me. Some of my worries went away.

"I'm sorry I laid everything on you. It just"—I breathed in a gulp of air—"was too hard in school. You know. Nobody knows."

I could feel the tightness in my throat. The feeling where you *know* you want to cry, but can't. When you've cried so hard you can't cry anymore. It's when your eyes won't produce anymore tears.

"I know. It's okay."

I choked back the tears. I need to relax. "Want to go watch TV?"

He nodded and smiled, "I'd love to."

On the couch, Caleb's arm felt comforting. He didn't talk, which was nice. There wasn't anything I wanted to say. There wasn't anything I wanted to hear. I just wanted to be quiet and relax. Caleb knew when to be quiet.

I was preparing for Mom and the boys to come home and ask how the day was and to get into trouble that I skipped school because of Dad.

But, for now, I could only stare at Caleb when I had moments. What was it about him? Okay, it was his smile and his eyes. His hair perfectly shaped without any product. Leaning against his brawny chest, I smelled the cologne. Or, was it linen?

Mom came in quietly, lightly closing the door. I heard her sniffles, sounding like a long day of crying. She walked into the living room; eyes closed, and sat down on the chair. Her eyes shot open and she screamed. Making us scream.

"Oh! Gosh. Damn!" She held her hand to her heart. "You scared the crap out of me."

"Sorry, Mom."

"What are you doing here?" Her breathing was heavy and her eyes were bloodshot red.

"I couldn't take it."

Her face looked like she was exhausted. "Me either."

"Really?"

She nodded.

"I think," she began looking towards her room, "I'm going to take a nap. Hi, Caleb."

"Hello, Cadie."

"Wake me up, later. Okay?"

I nodded.

As she walked away, I looked at Caleb's serene face.

"Want to sleep?" I asked tired.

He nodded and laid his body on the couch scooting as far back on the back of the couch as possible, making a spot for me beside him. As I lay down, he slipped his arm around my waist. Before I knew it, I was drifting off to a dreamless sleep. My dad's anniversary was over.

CHAPTER EIGHT

too much too soon

Each morning, I let the water turn hot, just to wake me up, it became a repetition. Each day passed faster than the last one. I've realized that as I get older, the days get younger, shorter. I try my hardest to make them get slower, but it doesn't help.

September ended, along with the first quarter of school. School became simple. I had friends, I fit in with the crowds, and most importantly, Caleb and I were getting closer. I've become great friends with everyone in the school, especially Penny. I feel like I can always go to her if I have problems.

Penny is still head-over-heels about James. If Penny and I aren't hanging out, she and James sure are. Caleb is over often, either studying or just chilling. Half of October flew by like nothing. With pre-season ending, I was more than thrilled to go to school that Friday.

When I walked into math class every morning, it was awkward. I was uncomfortable around Mr. Reynolds. But, today, that feeling wasn't there. Maybe I was finally getting over the fact that I hugged my teacher.

Wade was antsy sitting in his chair. Caleb, Wade, and I have gotten to like this partner seating. Wade still never gave up on tutoring me, asking me numerous times to help out at my house in particular.

"Do you understand this?" Toby asked in chemistry.

"Yeah."

As the days went on, Toby talked to me more and more each day. Today, we were to watch a video. I've seen the video before.

Toby's eyes looked as if they were hooked on the screen. I laughed and tried to focus on the video.

"We made it through!" Penny exclaimed after practice on Friday.

"I can't believe it's over. It'll be nice to have this break," Sonya said. "What are your plans for tonight? I hear there's this party in the country. Sounds like fun."

"I heard about that," Penny added, "James and I might go. How about you, Sara?"

"I'll probably hang with Caleb."

"Figures," Penny laughed. "If you two get bored staring into each other's eyes, you should come to the party. I hear half the school will be there."

"Yeah, we probably will, but after the last party, I don't think I could handle it."

After practice, I walked to my locker, as usual. Every day Caleb would be there. Today, he wasn't. I got worried. I drove home and still no word of Caleb. I ate supper and waited for Caleb to call.

I wanted to talk to him, hold him, and know he was okay. I didn't let myself get too worked up over nothing. It wasn't worth it. Caleb was smart.

Finally, after dark, Caleb texted me.

It read, 'sorry babe...family emergency'

I replied, 'everything okay? i was worried'

His reply, 'yeah, it's okay. can i see you tonight?'

I replied, 'of course, you don't have to ask. when?'

His reply, 'asap. i need to hug you.'

I replied, 'okay. let me get ready'

His reply, 'you'll look beautiful either way.'

I replied, 'yeah yeah yeah. want me to drive out to your house?'

His reply, 'can you? that'd be good. i have a movie for us to watch.'

I replied, 'okay, i'll be out there in 30 mins'. I thought a moment.

His reply, 'k.'

I replied, 'scratch that, make it an hour.'

His reply, 'haha k bye.'

I got ready as fast as I could. I told Mom that'd I'd be home later and that'd it might be late. It took fifteen minutes to get out to Caleb's house. You wind your way through the country, way in the middle of nowhere. But that's how North Dakota roads are. Prairie roads everywhere!

Caleb was sitting on the steps when I pulled up, smiling. I parked and got out.

"Hey there," I said.

"Hello." He voice was low and sounding worried.

"Everything all right?"

"It's perfect." He didn't sound convincing.

"Oh really?"

"Yeah. I have an idea," he proposed, grabbing my hand, "how about you meet my parents? I've met your mom. My parents keep asking me to meet you, since I spend every waking moment with you." He smiled.

"Oh my. Why didn't you warn me?"

"Because I knew you would make a fuss about it and spend hours figuring out what to wear and what to say. I wanted to keep it simple."

I sighed; he only pushed me harder to the door.

When we walked through the door, his parents were standing there. They, too, had dark tan skin like Caleb and Penny's. For adoptive parents, they sure look like their adoptive children. Robert's dark hair was a mirror to Caleb's. They looked familiar, too. Then, I remembered. In the grocery store with the toilet paper.

Melanie screamed, "Oh! It's so good to meet you! You are just as pretty as Caleb tells us. We thought he was just bragging. I'm Melanie, his mom. Call me Melanie." She came over and hugged me. She was tall, skinny, and long, blonde silky hair. She was also very young. She was gorgeous.

Robert stepped up, "And I'm Mr. Pierce. You can call me, 'Sir'." I heard Caleb snicker behind me. Robert grew a smile, "I'm just messing with you. I'm Robert." We had an awkward hug. Awkward silence equals embarrassment. Robert was also tall and very muscular. He was young, too, and very good-looking.

"You know," Melanie said, putting her finger to her mouth, "you look familiar. Have we met?"

I chuckled, "Yes. In the grocery store. Remember?"

She nodded, "That's it. Ironic."

"Agreed."

Melanie smiled at me with perfect teeth.

"And, Caleb disappeared somewhere." Robert's laugh echoed.

I looked up to find Caleb *blushing*. Something I thought I'd never see him do. I smiled and he only nudged me.

I remember that day. We were new in town. I was hoping I'd meet someone my age that day at the store. I did, but I didn't get to meet him fully. It *was* ironic that it was Caleb and that I'm standing with him here, now.

Penny flew down the stairs, with an older version of her behind her. The woman behind her was flawless, beautiful in many ways. She looked like a mirror image of Penny, identical.

"Hey, Sara," Penny said. "Careful of Sir, he'll get you."

Everybody laughed.

Caleb spoke from behind me, "Sara, that's my other sister Chloe. Chloe, this is Sara."

Chloe smiled, "Finally nice to meet. I think you're all that Caleb talks about. Welcome."

I could only really smile. I was intimidated when Penny and Chloe came waltzing down the stairs side by side, each gorgeous.

Caleb was smiling, I knew it, "Sara gets a little shy."

I shook my head, "I do not," I deviated but smiled. "Maybe a little."

Chloe smiled and stuck out her hand, "Me, too." I couldn't help but notice the humongous rock on her left hand. I do recall Penny telling me that she was engaged.

"Are you hungry?" Melanie asked me.

"No, but thank you. I ate at home."

Caleb put his hand on my back, "Okay, well, we are going to go watch a movie, and then we'll be back up. Privacy please?"

"Of course, just tell us when you're done," Robert said smiling.

The air in the room seemed tense, like I was the only one out of the loop. Everybody smiled as we left.

Caleb led me down to the movie room. The movie room was down in their basement and resembled a small movie theatre seating ten. He had pop and popcorn sitting on the coffee table with a bouquet of tiger lilies on the table.

"Oh, how cute. Did you do all this?" I managed to hold back the laughing.

"Sure did. Don't you laugh."

"I'm not." I caught a smile before it showed.

"Pick a seat."

When the movie started, I noticed the familiar famous person Caleb reminded me of, Nadir Remerez. In fact, he looked more like Caleb than I thought. I thought back from when I met him in Hollywood with Lili.

"Okay. You look exactly like that guy. You should go on that one show. What's the name?"

"Look-a-like?"

Caleb slid hand fingers through my hand and held my fingers tight. His eyes moved from the screen to my face.

"Yeah, that'd be it."

As the movie went on, I noticed several facial features that bore a resemblance to Caleb's. And some of the movements that the actor had were similar to Caleb's. Then, it clicked. Caleb's eyes. Nadir's eyes.

Caleb was watching me study the actor throughout the whole movie. I hardly paid attention to the movie.

"Listen, Sara. We have to talk. You've been completely honest with me, but I haven't with you." His expression was in a half-smile, yet it looked like he was worried.

"What do you mean?"

He looked down. "I'm practically lying about my life."

"What?"

The words were sounding exactly like a break-up. Like when the other person says we need to talk and your heart skips a beat and you feel scared to death.

Caleb sighed, "You know Nadir Remerez?"

I sighed in relief, "Yeah." He wasn't breaking up. Yet.

"I noticed you looking at him in the movie."

I had a feeling where he was getting at, "He just looks familiar, and I've met him before. Lili and I went and got autographs. Why?"

He smiled and looked down, "Well, he's me. I mean, I'm him."

I knew it! And, yet, I didn't want to accept it. "I knew it!"

He nodded, "I'm sorry I haven't told you."

I shook my head. "Nah, it's okay. Wait, you're famous? What's your real name?"

"Yeah, you could say I'm famous. Caleb. Nadir is made up."

"So, which is the real you, Nadir or Caleb?"

"Caleb. Everything is Caleb." He looked down, looking ashamed. "Nadir is just the famous person."

I gasped, "I met you that one time. Do you remember? You probably don't. In California, you were signing autographs. You looked me in the eyes and stared and lost track of what you were doing. Remember?"

He laughed, "I remember. That's why I was worried, I was afraid *you* wouldn't remember. I scribbled all over the page. There wasn't enough room for my signature. I was surprised you didn't realize who it was right away."

He nodded and smiled a smug smile.

I smiled, too, "I noticed you as soon as I saw you, but I couldn't put my finger on it." Then, I remembered. "The picture!"

"What picture?" He looked confused.

"We took a picture that time with the autograph! That's what I remembered."

"Oh. I totally forgot about it."

I nodded. I didn't want Caleb to feel scared or ashamed or anything else since he told me. I wanted him to know how much I supported this.

"So, Nadir, you're this big secret in Edgemont?"

He looked up and smiled, "Pretty much. Now, about not being at the lockers. I felt horrible, but my manager called me and I had to go home and get flight tickets."

"Flight tickets? Where are you going?"

He sighed and looked down, "London. I've been asked to be in a movie."

"Soon?"

"In a month. We leave mid-November and don't get back until mid-January, at the latest."

I couldn't look at him. All that I could think of was, "That means you'll miss basketball. Are you really going to go?"

He mumbled quietly, "I have to, I have a contract."

We sat in silence for awhile, just looking at each other.

"How long have you been Nadir Remerez?" I asked breaking the silence.

"About five years. I was so surprised when you walked through the hall with Penny. I recognized you right away. I was afraid you'd be smart and recognize me, too. Luckily, you weren't smart." He grinned and I punched him. "What? Things could've been bad if you knew me. We would've had to move and transfer."

"But, in a way, I did know you. Just couldn't add it all up."

He started to laugh.

"Oh, no."

"What?" The smile was wiped off his face.

"I'm bringing trouble to your family, aren't I?"

He face turned to complete seriousness, "Don't say that. Never. Mom and I talked today to discuss how I was going to tell you. Please, don't think you're trouble." He held my chin and kissed me.

"How did you remember me? That was almost two years ago."

"You were so pretty and smiley. I dreamt about you for weeks. I was so depressed. I never looked at a girl again. Jordan was about ready to slap me. When I looked up from signing autographs, you almost made me faint. You looked wonderful. I felt sick. I had never felt that way before." He stopped and looked away. I tried not to laugh, but failed. "I told Penny the day of school that I saw you again. Oh, and remember in the park? I had to bite my tongue not to tell you. I felt so bad when I started to describe you."

I sighed, "It was *me*?" I felt relieved.

"Yeah."

"Small world, huh?"

He laughed, "Most definitely. I tried my hardest not to try too hard."

I smiled.

He stopped and looked down. "There's one dilemma."

"What's that?"

"I won't get to see you for those months."

"Wow. That's right."

"I wanted you to go along, but you'd miss basketball. See, I'll be able to play basketball over there, you probably won't."

I sighed heavily while shaking my head, "Caleb, I would go if I could. I really would, but basketball and Mom and Gran and my brothers. I couldn't leave them."

"Yeah, I know. My family is coming with me."

"What about school?"

He thought a moment, "We'll probably be sick again or something. We haven't thought that much about it."

"Like that time you were sick for three months?"

He looked shocked, "You know?"

I shrugged and looked down, "Small town." I laughed. Those were the same words Giselle told me when she explained the story.

He sighed and raised his eyebrows, "Who?"

"Giselle."

"Figures. Listen, I had to tell you because I didn't want you to think I had disappeared or something. I need you not to tell anybody. Promise?"

"With my whole heart. I promise. I just have one more question."

He sighed with a chuckle, "Shoot."

"Why Nadir?" I couldn't help but laugh.

"What do you mean?"

I had a wide smile going across my face. I mean, come on. Nadir? He could've done a lot better than that name. "The name."

Caleb only smiled, "Don't make fun. First thought that came to mind."

I just smiled and shook my head, "So this is what we needed to talk about?"

He nodded. I wiped my forehead as if I was relieved of something. He questioned me with a puzzled look.

I sighed, "I thought you were breaking up with me."

He laughed. Hard. He tried to breathe but couldn't without any air. I folded my arms and huffed, "It wasn't that funny."

"I would"—Caleb gulped for air—"never break up with you."

Caleb led me back up the stairs and went into the living room, where his family was waiting. I had a feeling that we were going to talk about Caleb.

"So," Robert began, "how was the movie?"

Caleb took my hand, "It was good. She handled it well. She promised."

"Your secret's safe with me. I promise."

"We're glad to hear that," Melanie said. "Caleb came home one day and talked only about you. After that autograph signing, he'd been miserable, thinking only of you. We kept telling him, "You'll find someone better,"0 but he never did. You came just in time; we were about to sell him to an asylum. I guess it was a prayer answered."

Everyone laughed.

"I know it was hard to tell me about his secret, but I, too, remember meeting Caleb. I had been waiting for months for the signing," I admitted. "Looks like we were crazy in love with each other and we didn't know it. When I saw Caleb the first time at school, I have to admit, I did pick him out of a group of boys." I paused to look at the faces of Caleb's family. "I will *never* tell anyone."

"Well," Chloe shrugged, "welcome to the secret."

"It's totally up to Caleb, but if you would like, we could get you a wig and you could be Nadir's girlfriend. Like, maybe, go to events with him?" Melanie asked with a smile and taking a glance at Penny.

"Oh, I don't know. Wouldn't they notice me?" I asked.

Robert shook his head, "If people haven't noticed Caleb by now, I don't think they'd figure you out. A good wig and some makeup should do it."

"What do you say, California?"

I thought a moment. It would be fun. "Sure, why not?"

So, the news shocked me a little, but I was happy they let me in the loop. Down in the basement while Caleb and I were watching another movie, my phone rang for a new message.

'Damn, I almost found you. Why did you leave California? So SO close! Beware, Sara. I'm coming for you.'

"Who was it?" Caleb asked.

"No one," I lied. "Forward."

He nodded.

Caleb's family was more than happy when we were upstairs. How do they expect me to keep this secret? No doubt I'll keep it. I would never tell a soul. Never.

Caleb slid his arm around my back. He had a smile plastered across his face. His long eyelashes fluttered when he tilted his head towards me. He leaned in and planted a kiss on my cheek.

"You missed," I said smiling.

He corrected himself and kissed me on the lips. It was nice.

For about a week, I was just in a daze. I couldn't believe that Caleb was Nadir Remerez. I had a poster of him in my room, and I couldn't believe that I didn't recognize who he was. It was hard to keep the secret from my family, but I managed.

Penny and I went shopping the next day for Caleb's trip to London. It really hadn't set in that I wouldn't see him or Penny for two months. I knew I would miss them terribly, although Caleb kept on saying he would text me and call me as often as he could. We also went to a wig store to get me a wig for when I appear with Caleb on special events. Penny and I took pictures with the weirdest wigs. It was fun; it felt like best friends shopping together. We finally found one that would disguise me to the point of no one knowing. The wig was dark and long, totally opposite of my hair.

It was scary, I'd admit it. To see myself disguised. It was confusing. In some ways, I didn't like it. I didn't like the fact I wasn't me.

I tried to keep busy with other things. Granny Joanie kept me busy helping her with the little odds and ends as she fully moved into her house. Her cancer was ever so slowly progressing. Her date for surgery was set for the end of November, which was rapidly approaching.

As the day of Caleb's leaving moved closer, it started to hit me. Sometimes I wouldn't let him leave the house without promising he'd come back. On one night, he left but only came back later to sneak in the house.

The Pierces came up with the idea of Penny and Caleb getting lost, but they soon figured that that would probably involve police and sooner or later they'd find them. They wanted to make them sick, but people would figure out one day. They finally decided on saying that they had a family member get sick from overseas. So sick that they had to take care of them.

On the night before he left, Melanie and Robert invited me over for a going away party. Melanie had supper ready when I got there. Caleb walked out the door as soon as I pulled in their driveway.

"Hey, California," Caleb said, giving me a hug.

"Hello. How are you?" I asked.

"I'm all right, you know I could be better, though." I gave him a hug. "All right, I'm a little better." I smiled. "Okay, so Mom has been cooking all day for this, she's been busier than you can imagine. I hope you like chicken." He winked. It's amazing of how much he'd remembered from when we played 20 questions.

Chloe and her fiancée, Casey Jenning, were standing in the doorway when we walked through the door.

Chloe smiled at me as we sat around the table, "Caleb talks and talks about you, Sara. I've never seen him smile like that."

I laughed, "So I've been told."

"But," Casey said, "he described you perfectly."

Knowing I was blushing, Caleb quickly added, "Okay, so dinner ready?"

The way the Pierces gathered around the table was comforting. Yes, my family sat together, but Melanie had everything on the table. They sat laughing and talking. They had a place set for me on the table. I almost felt part of the family.

"The food's great, Melanie."

"Thank you, Sara."

Melanie's smile could brighten a room. She and Robert were perfect for each other. They were both young, a cute couple. I remember when I first met them in the grocery store. How Caleb had been the boy sneaking around the aisle. It was weird how later I'd meet them again.

Robert explained to us the plans for London.

"When we get back, Sara, you'll probably be asked to appear on the Red Carpet with Caleb as Nadir's girlfriend. Sound all right?" Robert asked. "You can even make up your own name if you want to."

I replied, "Yeah, that'd be fun. Are you sure people won't recognize me?"

I poked at my food as I said this.

He shook his head, "The wig you guys picked out was good, you'll be fine. They'd have to be smart."

Caleb added, "But, this is all a choice for you. If it's too much, don't worry about it."

I shook my head, "No. I want to."

"All right then, what's your name?" Chloe asked.

"How about Elise?" Melanie suggested taking a momentary look at Penny with a smile.

"That sounds good. Nadir and Elise. I like it," Penny said. I nodded. "Honestly, Mom and I thought of it a while ago."

"Again, you don't have to do this," Caleb reminded me. "Once you've been introduced, you're practically as famous as me. They'll pull every little dirt they can on you. Of course, they won't find any. There will be cameras, photographers, paparazzi, you name it. It gets hectic. Sure about this?"

"I'm sure."

"Final answer?"

I thought a moment, "Final answer."

"Great," Melanie cheered.

Robert pushed a paper out from under the table, and asked me to sign it. Caleb explained that it was papers that said I wouldn't tell and if I did, I'd be sued. I gladly signed the papers, with no intentions of telling.

The family's plane left at five in the morning and I wanted to be sure I was there to say good-bye, so I spent the night. Penny cleared off a spot on the couch for me, with Caleb taking the other half. We talked all night long about how we are going miss each other, basketball, and school. Basketball was starting on Monday and it was going to be hard without Caleb there supporting me. Caleb promised me that he'd text or call me whenever possible, and if all else fails, he'd e-mail.

Caleb whispered occasional 'I love you' in my ear. He continued to kiss my neck every once in a while. His arm around me felt warm. It helped me relax. For those moments, I didn't want to let go of him. I buried my face into his sweet-smelling chest.

"Listen, Sara," Caleb whispered at one point so early I couldn't tell what time it was.

"Mhm?"

He paused. His silence scared me. I could tell he wanted to say something, but then again he didn't.

"What?" I looked into his green eyes and wondered what he was thinking.

He shook his head, "Sara, I was thinking."

I persisted. He was hesitating too much for this conversation to turn out good. "About?"

He mumbled quietly, "Us."

My anger flared quickly, "Why?"

Shaking his head once more, "Would it be better if we just left as friends? I mean London is far away and it's a different time zone..."

"Caleb?" I asked in awe my tone sounding surprised. My heart started to thump as he said those words.

"Sara, I'm just saying"—he paused and closed his eyes—"long distance relationships could fail."

"Ours won't."

He took a deep breath in and sighed letting it out. "I love you, Sara, I really do, but..."

I sat up and pushed him away, "Are you breaking up with me?"

Need to mind you, it was early in the morning and my mind wasn't where it should have been. I was shocked and stunned on top of tired and confused.

Moaning once more, he smiled, "No, just giving you the chance to make a decision."

"I'll wait for you."

When Robert came stomping down the stairs in the morning, I was shocked that'd we stayed up that late. Caleb said that he'd catch up on sleep later on the plane. Caleb went to pack his things and I helped. Robert and Melanie had asked me to drive their car back to their house after they boarded the plane.

The car ride to the airport to Fairview was short, almost too short. I had given all my hugs to his family, but I saved the best for last. Caleb came over and picked me up and swung me in the air, then gently setting me down for the last hug.

"I'm sorry about last night," Caleb apologized as he set me down.

I pounded my fist on his chest jokingly, "Just don't do it again!"

Of course, he smiled wide. "I'm not going to say good-bye," Caleb said, "So, I'm just going to leave it at see you later." Okay?" I nodded. He gently kissed me, too quick for me to catch the full effect and then whispered in my ear, "I love you."

"I love you, too, Caleb," I whispered back.

"Let's go, lovebirds," Chloe said.

"Please don't meet any cute Asian girls while you're there," I said.

Caleb laughed, "Hon, I'm not going to Asia, I'm going to Europe. And I promise I won't." We both heard his plane flight called. "See you later."

I looked down, "Later, alligator."

"After while, crocodile," he replied.

He waved and smiled, flashing his teeth as far as a smile could go, and turned around and left. I watched him all the way through the doors and out of sight.

I wasn't prepared for this outcome. I tried to calm down and focus on my driving. It was a long drive back to Edgemont. I was driving Caleb's Challenger. They didn't want to let it sit at the airport for two months.

As I pulled into the Pierces long driveway, I was calm. I saw my car sitting alone in where Caleb's Challenger should be. Melanie had given me a key to lock up everything after I was done gathering my things.

I went into Caleb's bedroom, neat and tidy as it was the first time I met him. The linen scent was strong. Figures why he always smells of linen.

A bookshelf in the corner had pictures on it. I picked up a frame of us at my birthday. I was happy. But I hadn't really looked at us together. I looked at him. Then I looked at me. I never looked at us together.

His skin was dark compared to mine. But Caleb wasn't dark. His skin flawless and soft. It was amazing how much Penny and Chloe resembled him. I set down our picture and picked up another one.

It was the three of them. In more ways than one, I was jealous. Chloe was tall, beautiful. Of course, her fiancée was something else, too. And, Penny was happy, always perky and ready for fun. Their love was compassionate.

My brothers and I have a strong relationship, too, I suppose. So, I'm not jealous of that. I guess, honestly, I don't know what I was jealous of.

I lay on his bed. I inhaled the sweet smell of him. I decided it was time to go. I walked out the room, glancing back. I smiled. Grabbing a pillow of his, I was satisfied. It would be a souvenir until he got back. He would never know.

Man, that pillow smelled good.

CHAPTER NINE

surprise!

When I woke up, it was past noon. I had to jog my memory of the events that had happened. My stomach sank when my phone read no new messages. Although I shouldn't have been so sad since I knew Caleb couldn't have his phone on the flight.

Knowing that Caleb would contact me when he reached London, I couldn't focus on anything. I just waited and waited to receiver his call. As soon as I heard his ringtone, I sprinted up the stairs, tripping up the stairs, catching myself, and continuing the rest of the way. We talked on the phone for hours. The time difference was going to get in the way. It was night there while it was day here. We called and texted each other daily, not missing a single day.

Real basketball season started the Monday after Caleb left. With every practice, I got to know Kali and Kori better. It almost scared me, Kali was nice. It seemed like the first practices she was chucking the ball at me on purpose, but I saw her do it to other girls.

"Sara?" Kali asked after practice. "Can I talk to you?"

I nodded and followed her.

"Okay, listen," she began, "I'm sorry about everything. I was selfish and dumb and..." she stopped. "I spoke without getting to know you. I apologize about that day with your butt." She looked down. "I know that was a long time ago, but I think about it every night. Kori told me just to apologize."

I had to stop her before she willed me her house, "Kali, it's okay. I judged you too fast, too. I was hurt that day, but I shook it off. You've proved to me that you're nice."

"Can we be friends?"

"Of course."

It was hard to answer all the questions that everybody had for me, asking how Caleb's sick family member was doing and when they would return. Not seeing Caleb in the hall after school brought tears to my eyes every day.

We celebrated Cameron's eighteenth birthday on November 23. It wasn't a big celebration, just big enough.

I also got the first taste of snow on Cameron's birthday. Caleb was right, it was very cold. It was weird; it was like water and ice together. I wasn't too happy about the thick coats we bought, although they were stylish.

My closet slowly became filled with sweaters and long sleeved shirts. In California, sweatshirts kept me warm, but in North Dakota, they were going to have to keep me from dying of cold.

"Be strong, gram."

I was hoping my words were encouraging to my grandma. Today was the date of her surgery. The strength in her eyes was amazing. The smile on her face told me she was okay.

"I will. I'll be strong. I love you, Sara."

"I love you, Gram. I'll see in awhile."

Her hug was strong. I didn't want to let go. I didn't want to see her leave. But I had to. She turned around and smiled.

Those iron doors would have slapped me in the face if they could have reached me. As they swung shut with each swing, I saw Grandma walking by the nurse heading towards the room.

The more I paced back and forth, the more anxious I got. I had skipped school for the day to be with Grandma. Mom was at work and the boys were in school. I was alone. Caleb was filming his movie, so I couldn't talk to him. It was nerve-racking to be alone.

An older man was also waiting in the room with me. He continually watched as I walked back and forth. After twenty minutes of walking, he spoke, but quietly.

"It goes faster when you read."

I stopped in my tracks, shocked by the noise.

"Trust me." He held up a magazine. A hunting one. I laughed but grabbed it.

"I'm Clark."

"Sara."

"I'm waiting on my wife."

"Surgery?"

He smiled, "Third one."

"What's wrong with her?"

"It's nothing really." He continued to flip pages.

"Three surgeries, it has to be big."

He just shrugged his shoulders and smiled.

A doctor walked in and said Clark's name. "Your wife is great. The lift on her butt went great." The old man nodded and laughed as he walked out the door.

"Clark?"

"Mhm?" He turned around and answered.

"Plastic surgery?"

He laughed, "77 years old and still looks like a star. Good luck with your grandma."

I had to smile. I sat and opened the hunting magazine. The article *was* intriguing. But it was sad to see hunter's holding up their big trophy deer with the gun hole dripping with blood. It made me sick to think they like killing animals. I pictured Caleb holding his prized possession for a photo.

"Sara Young?"

I looked up to a doctor wearing a mask and gown. Clark was right; it went faster when you read.

"Mhm? How's my grandma?"

"Perfectly fine. Everything went great. She just needs rest."

I sighed and tightly gripped the rosary around my neck and headed off to the recovery ward where my strong, cancer-free grandma lay.

My first encounter with ice was unpleasant. I was preparing for it, but it came so fast that I had no chance of a warning of some kind.

"Sara, go get the mail for me?" Mom asked.

As I walked down the steps, I slid, but didn't fall. It shook me up. I slowly walked to the mailbox. Finally reaching it, I grabbed on for support. With the mail securely in my hands, I turned around and headed for the house.

I stepped on the ice wrong and completely biffed it.

I screamed and fell flat on my butt. I jumped up, hoping no one saw me. But, to my dismay, I fell again, landing on my stomach.

"Are you okay?" I heard someone holler from far away. His voice was familiar; I just couldn't recognize it.

"Sara!" He had a hint of amusement in the way he said my name.

It was my neighbor, Toby, otherwise known as my chemistry partner.

"Are you okay?" he asked again once he reached me.

He let out his hand and I grabbed it. I was unsteady getting, more embarrassed than hurt. Laughing burst from my mouth. Toby was also laughing.

I stood, "Yeah. Thank you."

"Are you sure?"

I laughed, "Fine. Gosh, that's embarrassing."

He chuckled, "Don't worry."

I looked at him. He wasn't in his normal clothes. He didn't even have his glasses on. In a roundabout way, he was an okay looking guy. It shocked me.

"I just happened to see you fall, thought I'd come help."

"Thanks."

"No problem. Have a good day."

"You, too, Toby. Thanks."

He walked back with his head up, back into the little house next to me. I prepared myself for the long trip to the door. Step by step, I made it.

Caleb kept me well informed about the movie and how everything was going. We usually talked on the phone until one of us fell asleep at night, which was regularly me. He e-mailed me pictures of London and his new friends that he'd met.

Surprisingly, the school and everybody believed the family illness thing and frequently sent home cards with me to give his family.

At the first basketball game, I felt free. Basketball games let me free myself and push away all the stress. I scored basket after basket, scoring a total of 25 points. I had eight steals and three turnovers. We ended up winning by twenty points against our rival team LaVont. We had four basketball games, all of which we won by great amounts.

Mom and I went Christmas shopping in Jeffersontown on a Saturday a couple weeks before Christmas. For Caleb, I bought him a necklace and the DVD version of *The Grinch*. I wrapped it up and sent it off immediately when I got home.

Gran Joanie had completely settled into her home, frequently visiting us by walking across the street. She went to every basketball game, cheering all three of us on. Her surgery went well, the doctors removing everything they needed to. They also gave us the good news that she wouldn't need chemo, but she needed radiation.

Although she was getting stronger every day, every kiss, every smile, and every moment were precious. Who knew when the cancer would return and destroy our lives once again? I shook my head often to shake out those thoughts.

Chris and I became even closer. Without noticing, we hung out every time in gym. He never did, though, mention anything more than a friendship. And he never failed to make me laugh.

"How is your grandma doing?" Chris asked as we were sitting on the bleachers. Coach Hansen gave us the gym period off to study for finals. I had told him about my grandma one day when he asked about my family.

"Better. Much, actually."

"She's like your best friend, isn't she?"

"Uh-huh." Water filled up in my eyes, and one tear streamed down my face. Chris moved over and hugged me. "What am I going to do?"

"If what? She's fine."

"Just, what if?"

"You'd have to move on."

Like I did before, I thought.

I sniffled, leaning back, "I guess I'd have to."

He just smiled.

"Chris?"

"Mhm?" he answered.

"Have I told you about my dad?" He shook his head. "He was killed when I was nine..." His mouth opened and closed as I told the story of my father. It was hard to explain it to him, but I had to. I didn't want *him* to ask *me*.

"I'm so sorry, Sara. I had...no clue."

"Don't worry about it."

The bell rang and I was home.

On Christmas Eve, we all went to Granny Joanie's house. As we were opening presents, the doorbell rang. I ran over to open the door to a delivery man with a package.

"Package for a Miss Sara Young," the delivery man said.

"That'd be me. Who's it from?" I asked.

"I don't know. I believe it's from Europe." He smiled and handed me the package.

I smiled.

Caleb.

"Thank you. Merry Christmas."

He looked at me in sort of shocked look, "Thank you. Merry Christmas to you, too." He smiled and walked away.

I ripped open the package. Inside was a scarf from France, gift cards to my favorite clothing stores, and a jewelry box. Inside the jewelry box was a beautiful diamond ring with a note attached.

The note read,

Sara, I'm sorry I can't be there for Christmas. I hope you are having a very merry Christmas. I hope you like the snow, also. :) This is only a ring that I thought was almost as beautiful as you are. Be sure to tell Mama Bear that it's not an engagement ring. To let you know, I bought it in France. Thank you for the necklace and movie, we'll watch it when I get home. I love you. Merry Christmas and Happy New Year!   *Caleb*

"What do you have there?" Cole asked coming to see who was at the door.

"My Christmas present from Caleb. He sent it from London."

"What'd you get?"

"A scarf from France and gift cards."

I walked into the living room. Gran asked, "Who was at the door?"

"The delivery guy," I answered, "he had a package for me from Caleb."

Mom smiled, "What'd you get?" I showed her the scarf and the gift cards, then the note. "There's a ring? Let me see it." I held out my finger. "Oh, Sara, it's beautiful."

I got ample amount presents from the family. I kept looking at Caleb's ring on my ring finger on my right hand.

The bright morning sun woke me up. When I walked down the stairs, Cole was sitting in the chair dressed as Santa Claus.

"Ho, ho, ho. Merry Christmas, Sara. Have you been a good girl?" Cole chuckled.

I nodded and walked right by him, "Sure have, Santa. I have a question."

"And what is that, my dear?"

"I thought you were dead?" I ripped off his fake beard. He started chasing me and I ran around the couch. He caught me and threw me onto the couch, putting me into a chicken wing. "Okay! Okay! You're not dead!" He let me go and put his beard back on.

Mom was still sleeping when I awoke, so I thought I'd make her breakfast. I whipped together pancakes and sausage, the two things I *can* make. Mom came down the stairs just as I was getting done.

"Morning, Cadie," Cole greeted. "Merry Christmas. Have you been a good girl this year?"

"I sure have, Santa," Mom answered then turned to me. "This smells great. I wasn't expecting you to make this."

I smiled, "Let's just say it's part of your Christmas present."

"Speaking of that," she began, "when should we open gifts?"

"When Cameron wakes up and eats?"

142

"Sure. Why don't you go wake him up, Mr. Santa?"

"Oh, all right. Come on, Comet, let's go wake Cameron up," he joked.

We gathered around the tree with 'Santa' handing out the presents. Mom, of course, had the camera going, snapping pictures every minute someone moved.

The first present I opened was a new digital camera that I needed. I opened others, those being books, clothes, shoes, sports bras, and a hat. I gave Mom the ring that she wanted when we went shopping. Cole and Cameron both got a new pair of jeans from me, something I thought they didn't have much of.

Cameron gave me a fleece blanket and Cole gave me a gift card to a store. Cole and Cameron got numerous gifts as well.

I spent the mornings of the vacation with relaxation and talking to Caleb. He never mention when he was going to be finished with the movie, but I wasn't going to nag. Basketball practice would start this next week.

Courtney called me one night to discuss New Year's Eve.

"Hello?" I answered.

"Hi, Sara. It's Court. How's it going?"

"Good. You?"

"It's good. I was wondering what your plans were for New Year's tomorrow?"

"Don't really have one. What are you doing?"

"Well, there is this party at Josh's house. Of course, you're invited because of Caleb, but Josh asked me to come!" She screamed. "Can you believe it? Josh Ingles!"

"Man, you're lucky!" I tried to sound enthused since I did have a thing for Josh way back when, but now I didn't mind. I had Caleb and so far he was much better than Josh.

"I know, right? Okay, so you in?"

I chuckled, "Of course, better than being stuck with nobody. What time?"

She sighed into the phone, "Well, I don't know. Maybe nine?"

"Okay, just call me. We carpooling?" I asked.

"Yeah. Your car or mine?"

"Well, I suppose we could take mine," I suggested.

She sounded excited, "That'd be great, if that's okay?"

"Yeah, that's fine."

"Great. So, how's Caleb's uncle doing?" she asked.

I had to think of a lie and quickly. Of course the words just flew out of my mouth like nothing. "He's doing fine. Hopefully he'll make it. Caleb should be back by mid-January."

"That's good. Aren't you getting lonely?"

I nodded even though she couldn't see me nodding, "Most definitely, but we text every day and he calls me a lot."

"Well, that's always good."

"Yeah." I did miss him, though.

"Okay, well, I better go. I'll text you tomorrow. Are we dressing up like major?"

"That'd be fun. Let's!"

"Okay. See you later!"

"Later, Court."

"Bye."

As I hung up the phone, Cameron came up behind me, "Who was that?"

"Courtney. She wanted to talk about the New Year."

"I see."

Mom was up when I woke up. I could smell breakfast waiting. Cole came stomping up the stairs, his hair sticking straight up, Cameron right behind him.

"Okay. Listen, guys," Mom began with a smile, "I'm going out tonight with some friends from work. What are your plans?"

"There's a party at a guy's house from basketball," Cameron said. "Cole's going, too."

"Yeah, Courtney was invited to that and she invited me to go with," I added.

"Okay, we *all* come home, tonight," she demanded. "If you don't come home for any reason, you are in deep, and I mean deep trouble. Understand?"

"Understand," we agreed in unison.

Courtney came over and we picked out my outfit for the night. The party was crowded, tons of people there. It was in a barn, out at Josh's farm. Josh had a special DJ, his older brother, to play music. The music was loud and the strobe light was bright. There were drunk people all over the place. Beer cans and cups were scattered over the floor.

Brandon and Giselle were over in the corner flirting like crazy. I couldn't believe that the shy Brandon I knew is crazy about girls. I didn't see Cole or Cameron all night long. I just kept busy talking to everybody.

Since Caleb has been gone, I've had time to really get to know people. My attention was only on Caleb, now I could mingle. Although, I was sad that Caleb wasn't here for New Year's.

Giselle came over and grabbed me and pulled me into the dance area and we started to dance. I was having a good time. People started talking to me like we've known each other for a long time.

Giselle was drinking, but I said no to James when he asked me. I wasn't going to ruin my basketball career for being dumb and drinking.

I did happen to notice Cameron talking to a girl that I recognized. She was from the basketball team. Her name was Lauren. They were laughing. Good for Cameron, I thought, maybe he'd let off on me.

Then, a slow song came on. I felt my shoulder tapped. Turning around, Jordan, Caleb's other basketball buddy, was standing behind me.

"Would you like to dance, Cinderella?" he asked, remembering what Caleb had called me at the cafeteria one day.

"I would love to."

He reached out and bowed. I gently set my hand in his and he led me to the middle. There were other couples on the dance floor, so I wasn't totally uncomfortable. I noticed the song, one of my favorites. I just wished I was dancing with Caleb.

He wrapped his hands around my waist and I set mine on his shoulders.

"This is nice," he said.

"Yeah."

"Do you miss Caleb?"

I nodded, looking down, "More than you know. It's hard."

"But, now you have time for other people, right?"

"Most definitely. Example, you." I smiled.

"You know, when us boys are alone, you know, like me, Caleb, Josh, and Tyler, he only talks of you. Sara this, Sara that."

I looked down, "I'm sorry."

He lifted my chin, "Don't be. You brought a smile to his face."

"That's what everybody tells me. What was he like?"

The song continued as we talked.

"He was gloomy, never showed emotion. Except this one time, after he'd been sick for those three months, he'd come back to school all smiley. I asked him why but he just said he was happy to be alive. But, shortly after, he went back to being gloomy."

"Was he just as good in basketball?"

"Yeah, I think he took his frustration out in basketball. We went to the state championship two years in a row. Still hoping for one this year."

"My coach told me that, too."

"Yeah. I'm just happy he met you. Even though you do spend every waking minute with each other." He smiled and winked.

The song ended and he bowed again as he let go. He led me off the dance area and whispered, "Can I talk to you outside?"

I nodded. He walked in front of me and I followed.

"It's sort of warm outside for middle of winter," I said as we stepped outside the barn.

"Here, let's go in my car. It'll be warmer." He opened the door for me and flung around and got in. "Okay, I need to talk to you."

"What about?" I had hints of what it could be.

"Well, you know Caleb and I are close. I've known him since we were young. I live next door to him, about five miles."

"I didn't know that you lived that close."

He nodded, "Before Caleb left for his family member's illness, he told me to tell you everything." He put his fingers up as quotation marks around family member's illness.

"Everything?"

"Everything. I know about his secret."

"What secret?" I had to be sure he knew about it, and wasn't lying to get me to tell the truth.

"I know that he went over to London to make a movie." He told me the movie title, and I was shocked.

"When did he tell you?" I asked.

"Long ago, when he first got accepted to be in a movie. He came screaming to me. I had to sign a contract and swear not to tell. If I did, I could get into serious trouble. This doesn't count," he smirked.

"Wow."

I sat there, not knowing what to say.

"I know it's a shock, but he couldn't keep a secret without me knowing. We're two peas in a pod." He laughed. "So, yeah."

"So, you know about when he saw me at autograph signing?"

Jordan laughed, "Sure do. That's really funny, actually. We sat up all night talking about *that girl.* He couldn't get his mind off you. He wanted so badly to contact everybody just to get your number, know your name, and yeah, you get it."

"I can't believe it. I mean I can, I do. But, gosh, small world!"

"Sure is."

I looked at the clock; it read twenty minutes 'til midnight.

"We better go," I urged.

"Yeah."

We got in the barn and everybody was dancing, so we joined. Courtney and Sonya came over by us and started dancing. Kali and Kori were there in a corner drinking, both overly drunk.

They never really talked to me. Except that one time they pushed me out of their way, they haven't bugged me since. Mr. Field gave them one week suspension.

It got to be five minutes to midnight. There was a digital clock on the wall that had the countdown 'til midnight. Josh's brother played one last song before we started the countdown.

The clock read one minute left. The countdown began. I saw couples get near each other for the first kiss of the New Year. I was sad that I wouldn't have that kiss until later.

Ten.

Nine.

Eight.

Seven.

Six.

Five.

Then, someone's familiar voice whispered in my ear and wrapped their arms around me, "Four. Three. Two." I turned around just as everyone said 'Happy New Year.' And, then, I saw Caleb. "Happy New Year." His warm lips touched mine. I didn't want him to stop. He held on tight, as did I. He kissed me for what felt like hours, us standing with falling confetti around us. This was the best surprise ever.

Penny was behind him giving James the first kiss, those two looking just as happy as Caleb and I. I ran over to Penny and threw my arms around her. "I've missed you so much!" I screamed.

"I've missed you, too," she hollered as I let go. "Did you like your surprise?"

"Oh my, I had no idea! When did you guys get back?"

"Forty minutes ago. We sped all the way out here. He didn't think we'd make it."

"Well," I sighed, "I'm sure glad you did." Penny laughed.

The boys were talking to Caleb when I walked back over to him.

Jordan whispered in my ear, "You know how hard it was *not* to tell you he was coming home tonight?" I punched him. "What? Caleb told me to keep it a secret."

Caleb wrapped his arms around me, kissing my neck. "Oh, I've missed you. I've missed your face, eyes, hair, smell, and smile." He ran his fingers through my hair, touched my face and traced my lips. I smiled. "Well, that helps a lot."

"Please, don't leave me, again. That was torture."

"It's over, now. I won't have to for awhile. Besides, you and Jordan get to come next time. I am hoping that he told you."

I looked at Jordan and winked.

Jordan smiled, "I sure did. Shocked the hell out of her." He laughed.

"Where are you going next time?" I asked not wanting him to leave again.

"The premiere of the movie," he answered. "I'll explain later. Let's have some fun. I'll be right back."

As he left, Jordan said, "It's good to see him, isn't it?"

"Oh. Is it ever!"

Jordan gave me a hug and I hugged him back. I could feel our relationship as friends getting stronger. He was the only friend of Caleb's that actually understood my and Caleb's relationship.

Then, I recognized the song that played next, my favorite, ever. Caleb came over and grabbed my hand and led me out to the dance floor.

"You brat," I smirked.

"You're welcome. Now, dance with me!"

The songs played all night and we danced to everyone. Cole and Cameron came over as Caleb left to go get us drinks.

"I see Caleb's back," Cameron said. "Congrats."

"Yeah, and thank you," I said. "Cameron, I saw you with Lauren," I winked, "she's cute."

"Nah," he said shaking his head, "she's hot." He pranced his way back over to her.

Laughing, I turned to Cole, "Are you going to talk to Caleb?"

"Yeah," Cole nodded, "I'm going over there, now. Well," he said stretching his arms in front of him with a smirk on his face, "that was a nice break from my job, but I got to get back to work," Cole winked.

"Yeah, yeah, yeah, yeah."

We all—Cameron, Cole, Caleb, and I—went back to the house after the party had ended. Mom was already in bed when we got there. She had a note saying to wake her up when we got home. I ran up the stairs and woke her up and told her about Caleb, she only smiled and rolled back over.

Cole and Cameron went to bed as soon as they got home.

"So, how was the snow?" Caleb asked.

I could feel myself blushing, "Snow's okay. It's the damn ice that got me."

He started laughing.

"No!" I realized. Cole must've seen it and told Caleb about it.

He nodded, "Cole called my cell as soon as it happened. Did it hurt?"

I was too embarrassed and irritated to answer.

"Oh, come on. We've all slipped once or twice."

I nodded, "It hurt like none other."

"Can you do it again?"

I threw a pillow at him, but smiled, "If you're lucky."

Caleb and I talked on the couch for awhile, but then I'm guessing we fell asleep because we woke up to Mom coming on down the stairs.

Gosh, it was nice to wake up to Caleb's face and not his text message.

I rolled over and went back to sleep, dreaming about the sun.

The accident...

The bright lights...

My dad's killer...

CHAPTER TEN

the birds and the bees

"It's so good to see you, Caleb." I heard Mom's voice talking to Caleb. I opened my eyes to Mom and Caleb sitting by the kitchen counter.

"It's good to be back. Oh. I like this picture, it's the Eiffel Tower." He was obviously showing her pictures of his trip.

I started to walk over to them, but remembered morning breath. I held up my finger for a minute and ran upstairs and brushed my teeth and combed my hair through to get all the knots.

When I had got back down stairs, Cole and Cam were up, both sitting by Caleb and looking at the pictures.

"I'll let you see these later, Sara," Caleb said. I poured myself a cup of coffee and jumped on the coach. Caleb explained the other pictures and came and sat by me.

"I have to go home," Caleb said after we were alone. "My manager is coming today to review the movie."

"Okay," I sighed and looked away.

"It's good to see your blue eyes again, though," he said, putting his hand on my face and turning my head towards him. His eyes were soft, but fierce. He leaned in and kissed me gently.

"Get a room, you two," Cole said sitting on the couch next to us.

"We're done," Caleb said, "what's up, dude?"

"Nothing much. Meet any hot chicks up there?"

I threw a pillow at him.

"I meant for me," he defended throwing the pillow back.

Caleb just laughed, "Sorry, wasn't looking, too distracted." He smiled at me.

"Oh, gag me," Cole snickered.

Caleb just laughed. "I've got to go, hon," Caleb whispered.

"I'll walk you out. I'll be right back."

The morning air was crisp and it was snowing. "See," Caleb shrugged, "what'd I tell you about snow. It's cold and white."

"Yes, but you also told me I'd like it. So far, not so good." My teeth were chattering as the snow fell all around us.

He laughed, "You'll get used to it. Oh, and nice pillow." He smiled wide.

"I...I"

He smiled with a hint of sarcasm, "I must say that's hilarious! I looked all over for that pillow."

My cheeks became very warm. I wanted the subject to change. "When can I see you again?" I asked.

"As soon as you want. My manager will be gone by dark tonight. I'll come back as soon as he leaves."

I nodded, "That sounds good. I can go to your house, too, if you want me to?"

He shook his head, "We won't be able to be alone. Mom and Dad would bug us the whole time, saying how much they missed you and so on. We are better here."

"Okay. Sounds good. I'll talk to you soon, then?"

"Of course. Later, California."

His broad chest smelled of his sweet-smelling laundry soap. I looked up at him, still wrapped in his arms. I gave him a kiss as we parted and watched him drive off the driveway.

Inside the house, Mom was talking to Cole and Cameron. She motioned me over to the kitchen counter.

"I'm going on a date tonight," she began. "It's at seven thirty. I'll be home later, though."

"With who?" I asked.

"This guy I met last night. Gloria, James's mom, introduced me."

"Why?" I asked.

"She knew I was single and needed to have some fun."

"Okay, well, have fun." I tried to sound encouraging. I wasn't too happy that Mom wanted to start to date other people, but in a way, I had to be. Mom has been single for so long, how could I keep her from being happy.

"Really? That's all you have to say?" she asked, sounding surprised.

"Yeah, Mom. I want you to be happy. Not sad. If it's time, it's time."

"Well, thank you, Sara. And you know that I won't go any farther without asking you first."

"I know, Mom."

"I love you."

"I love you, too, Mom."

"Okay, so what are your plans tonight, boys?" Mom asked.

Cameron said cheerfully, "Well, Mother, since you so kindly asked," he started to laugh, "I have a date with a girl named Lauren whom I met at the party the other night."

"Oh really," she said.

He nodded.

"And, me, well, I'll be at home, watching TV, doing nothing, all alone, and sad," Cole sniffled.

"Caleb and I will be here," I added. "He told me he wants to come here. We'll hang out with you."

"Gee," he smirked, "thanks, sis."

I smiled, "No problem."

I wanted only to see Caleb at that very moment, but knew it wasn't going to happen. As I was finding things to keep me busy, Lili called me.

"Hey, there!" Her voice was more than excited.

"Hi, Lili. Gosh, it's good to hear your voice."

"Yours also. I miss you. How's everything going?"

"You know same old, same old."

I could hear her sigh in the background. "Yeah, I suppose."

"How's it going there?"

She sighed, "Boring without you."

I laughed, "I suppose. I wish I was there." I really didn't. I wouldn't want to leave this new life I've found.

"I wish you were, too," she said. "How is everything going nowadays?"

I paused to think of the right word to say. In reality, everything was terrific. Actually, everything is wonderful! "Good. Mom's dating someone."

"Really!" she shrieked.

"Yeah."

"That's good. And, how are the grandmas?"

"Both good. Don't really see them that often, you know?"

"Yeah."

"How's, uh, Drew?"

She shrieked, "Going steady for a few weeks now!"

"Wow, congratulations!"

I sighed, "I better go. I'll call you sometime soon, okay?"

"Okay. Bye, Sara." It sounded as though I crushed her.

"Later."

I counted down the hours until I got to see Caleb again. Mom started getting ready for her date, often coming out of the closet with different outfits on. I finally went in her closet and helped her pick one out. She never really liked what I picked for her, for we both have different styles, but she liked this one.

Cameron had left and wasn't expected home until late tonight.

I chose not to meet her secret date yet until it started to get a little more serious than the first date. He did drive up in a fancy sports car—must be a doctor, too.

I pulled out Caleb's pictures before he came. He had many pictures with his co-star, a girl. They looked happy. I could just imagine how he'd look if he had a different girlfriend. I was worried that someday he'd just forget about me.

Caleb arrived soon after, bringing a huge bouquet of flowers with him through the door.

"What's all this?" I asked.

"From all the days I missed at school." He just smiled and went over to the sink to find a vase and water.

We watched a new movie that he'd bought on his way home. It was funny, one of the funniest I've seen in a long time. Cole sat and watched it with us. He made us popcorn and joined right along.

Mom came through the door at about ten, jolly as can be.

"Hey, guys," she greeted, "how was your night? Oh, mine was great. Thanks for asking. I'm going to bed. I love you all."

"Yeah," I mumbled, "we love you, too."

Cole and I looked at each other and laughed. We were glad it went good for her.

"You know, Sara," Cole began, "I don't think I've seen her like that in a long time."

"Me either," I agreed. "She didn't even wait for our reply, this must be big."

We just laughed harder.

After I heard Cole snoring for sure, I asked Caleb in a whisper, "In your pictures, who is that girl?"

He smiled, "I thought you'd ask. My co-star."

"Oh"—I looked down so he couldn't see my expression of sadness—"she's really pretty."

Caleb shrugged his shoulders a little and smiled a half-smile.

"You know her?"

"Yeah, I've been doing movies with her since I started."

I nodded.

"Sara," Caleb whispered, kissing my ear as he spoke, "I love you and no one else."

That made me smile, to hear that was just what I needed.

"I love you, too."

"I missed you. I thought of nothing but you. You were on my mind constantly."

I smiled, but then thought of something, "Can I ask you a question?"

"Sure."

"Did you have to..." I paused, scared to ask him, "kiss her?"

He sat still for a moment, and looked down. He nodded.

"Can I just say this? It was horrible. Nothing like your sweet kisses." He leaned in and kissed me.

"What *are* my kisses like?"

He smiled, "Amazing."

"How?"

"The way your lips are so soft. Your breath is always sweet or smells of peppermint. And, you don't go too far. And you're so gentle." His facial expressions were so hilarious that I just had to laugh. He was serious in every way possible.

We must've fallen asleep during the movie. I woke up at seven and saw Caleb next to me along with Cole in the recliner.

I went over to make coffee for the morning.

Mom came down the stairs just as cheery as last night.

"Good morning, Mom," I whispered, trying not to wake the boys. "Care to elaborate on the date last night?"

"Oh, Sara. He is so nice. He laughs and smiles. He jokes around, but is serious. He's perfect."

"Perfect?" I looked down. I've never heard her say that before, except the mushy stories about my dad and her.

"Perfect."

"More perfect than Dad?"

She stopped, biting her tongue, realizing what she had just said. "Never. I guess we finally need to have this talk."

I shrugged.

"Sara, I will never love someone like I loved your dad. We were opposites, that's for sure, but we connected. If it wasn't for the accident, we'd still be in love. I will always love your dad, always. I'm tired of being alone, though."

"I know, Mom. You do need someone by you, supporting you and what not."

"Exactly."

Moment of silence.

"So, what's his name?" I asked encouragingly.

"Andrew or Andy." The way she smiled when she said his name made me realize this was real. "He's an oncologist, too. He's really smart."

"Well, that's certainly good."

"Yeah, we are meeting again tonight. Do you want to meet him, yet?"

I shook my head, "Too soon."

"That's okay. You choose. Okay, well, he's taking to me lunch. He truly wants to meet you guys. He'll be here at noon." Mom's expression never changed from complete happiness. It was amazing how one special someone could change your whole attitude.

Andy pulled up at noon and Mom ran out the door. I could see him, but faintly. By the look of his car, you could definitely tell he had money.

Wednesday morning, I had to press the snooze button more than once. It was hard to adjust to waking up early when I've been sleeping in late.

At school, Penny and Caleb were surrounded by people asking how the family member was. Melanie had told me that their plan was it was Melanie's uncle and that he was perfectly fine.

It was harder than I thought to keep a secret—like when you know the truth and it accidentally slips.

Brandon talked to me at lunch like usual, with Caleb noticing, although he didn't seem to be jealous.

"While you were gone," I whispered to Caleb, "I started to meet new people and become great friends."

"More than me?" He planted a wide grin on his face, already knowing the answer.

I shook my head and turned back to Brandon. Caleb quickly got comfortable and joined the conversation with ease.

"Caleb? How was London?" Brandon asked.

"Well, once my uncle got better, I enjoyed it."

The boys separated from the group and it was just us girls—Courtney, Sonya, Penny, and me.

"So, are you going to prom?" Sonya asked me.

"I don't know. Caleb hasn't mentioned it and I haven't been brave enough to ask him.

"You really should go," Penny urged. "It's so much fun. Royalty is asked to be there. That's where you're recognized. You sit in fancy chairs and all."

"When is it?" I asked.

Courtney answered, "Beginning of April. Like April 5, maybe?"

"I'll ask him if he doesn't ask me soon. That would be fun to go. All the dressing up. Are you guys going?"

Courtney shrugged while playing with the peas on her tray. She showed a hint of smile.

"Court," I persisted.

"What?" she smiled denying all possibilities she'd be going to the prom.

I smiled at her, "Who is it?"

She looked around at the excited faces of her friends, "Josh asked me."

"What?" Penny shrieked. She clapped excitedly.

"Really!" I exclaimed. "That's great! How cute."

She changed the subject, "How about you, Sonya? Penny, I'm guessing you're with James?"

Penny nodded.

"Well, Cole asked me," Sonya admitted, looking at me worried.

"Are you serious? That's good!" I exclaimed. He needed to find a good friend, maybe more. "You two would have fun."

I winked at Courtney one last time. It didn't really set in that Cole had asked Sonya.

Surprisingly, Caleb continued to be at my locker with a single flower in his hand every day. He never mentioned the prom. The days went by like nothing. January passed, with February following.

For Valentine's Day, Caleb had plans to take me out for supper to Jeffersontown. It was a Saturday morning and I was tired.

"Good morning, Sara."

Caleb's soft voice near my ear scared me.

I jumped as I opened my eyes to Caleb's face inches away.

"Happy Valentine's Day," he whispered.

"Happy Valentine's Day."

I sat up and stretched. I remembered morning breath. As Caleb leaned in for a kiss, I moved away, causing him to fall. I sprinted to the bathroom to brush my teeth and comb my hair.

When I walked into the room, Caleb was laying on my bed with his hand propping his head up. His grin was wide across his face. He had a giant stuffed bear sitting beside him. Life-size.

"Wow."

He smiled, "Not exactly the name I thought you'd name him, but okay."

"That's what I call a big bear."

"I have to give my girl a big bear."

Caleb left, letting me get dressed for our date tonight. As I got dressed, memories flipped through of past Valentine's Days. I had no one except for Lili. It was sad, but we were single together.

I glanced down at the ring Caleb had gotten me for Christmas. It was just as radiant as it was the first time I got it. It was safely secured on my right hand on my ring finger. I caught myself playing with it more than once.

"Why aren't you eating?" Caleb asked while I was picking at the food in the restaurant.

I couldn't stop thinking of being single.

"I am."

"You've eaten two bites. What's up?"

I sighed, "Last Valentine's Day, I was sitting at home eating ice cream. I didn't know that one year later, I'd be sitting here with you."

He smiled, "Well, you are. So, smile!"

That only made me smile wider. I made Caleb promise me he wouldn't get me flowers for the fact my room was filled the way it was. He promised saying he'd find something better.

Caleb's smile never left his face throughout the dinner and the ride home. I finally wondered so much that I had to ask.

"Why are you so smiley?"

"Your gift waiting at home."

"That's why you've been so jumpy and jittery?"

He nodded.

As I walked through the door of my room, my giant teddy bear was holding a pink gift bag. As I lifted the tissue paper, inside was a jewelry box. In the box, was a beautiful pink heart bracelet.

Caleb wrapped his arms around me and whispered, "It was my mom's."

"What?"

"She wanted me to give it to someone special. I chose you." His smile grew wider. "Happy Valentine's Day, hon."

"I love you, Caleb."

"I love you, Sara."

The feeling in my heart got to be strong as Caleb's eyes kept looking at my lips then back at my eyes. I knew what he wanted as I laid on the bed. Our legs were intertwined and his hands were around my back. As we lay on the bed kissing, I knew he wanted to go further.

I didn't, though.

This was the most we had done before. His lips harmonized with mine and his eyes stared into mine. I could feel his lips curve into a smile as he reached for the bottom of my shirt.

He started to yank it off.

I let him in the beginning but realized that he wanted to see me in my bra. As much as I loved him, I wasn't ready for it yet.

All awhile, he continued to kiss me in the most incredible way. My mind went from, "Yes, you can do this" to "No, don't take it off!" It sucked. It really did.

Inches away from nakedness, I stopped, "Caleb."

He kissed my neck and sat up. His ripped off his shirt and I saw his breathtaking, ripped body. Those abs must have taken hours to sculpt and frame. Hard work.

He came back down and kissed me again. Realizing how much this meant to him and now me, I let him get his way. I thought it would be uncomfortable to be just in my bra, but it wasn't bad. Not what I preferred, but it was what Caleb wanted.

Can I just say it was wonderful?

And the best part, he supported me and my intentions. We didn't go any further than I wanted him to.

One Friday night in March, Caleb had texted me that he wanted to hang out. He told me it was a surprise, and that I should get dressed up. Most of his dates are surprises.

The snow for the most part had melted. It didn't snow as much as it had in past years Caleb had told me. To me, it snowed a lot. The weather, too, was cooperating. It was surprisingly warm, if you would say that. It wasn't hot by any means, but you know 40 degrees was warm.

Dressed in a silky black dress, I ran down the stairs when the doorbell rang. Caleb was dressed in a black suit.

"Ready?" he asked with a smile.

"More than you know."

We drove through Jeffersontown down a familiar road. It was the road to his father's lake area. He hadn't taken me there since the day I told him about my dad. I guessed this had to be serious. He parked the truck and opened my door. The cool breezy air sent a shiver down my back. I saw two chairs sitting on the sandy part of the lake.

He grabbed for my hand as we walked down to the sand. I would never reject his hand.

"Sara?" he said in a whisper.

"Yeah."

He paused a moment and smiled, "Will you please be my escort for my sister's wedding?"

I nodded with excitement. "Are you kidding? I would love to!"

"By the way, you look beautiful tonight."

"Thank you."

I could hear music going when we got closer to the chairs. I couldn't figure out where it was coming from. As we grew nearer, I saw an iHome sitting on one of the chairs.

"What's this?"

His lips curved into a perfect smile, "I thought we'd practice our dancing."

He wrapped his arms around my waist. I gently set my hands on his shoulder. As we swayed back and forth listening to the music, we were silent. I could hear his heart beating. I could smell his cologne.

I looked up into the sky just at the right moment. A shooting star went across the sky. I haven't seen many shooting stars in my life, but when I *do* see them, I make I wish for something extra special. When you wish upon a star, it has to mean something.

I wish for nothing. I have it all.

Though it wasn't much that he'd asked me, I was ecstatic. In a way, I was hoping he would ask me to prom. But he didn't.

Cameron took his senior pictures and we sent out the announcements. It was sad to think about Cameron leaving and it just being Cole and me.

Basketball games came and went. Our team looked good. We had only lost three games. We made it all the way to State. March 1, 2, and 3 were the best days of my life. We soared through the first and second games. The third game was a nail-bitter, neck and neck the whole time. We won the game by six points towards the end. It was the most exciting experience. I never stopped giving it my all. I wanted that trophy more than anything. And yet, I was in shock that we were the state champions.

Mom was seeing Andy more often, but I still chose not to meet him, just wasn't comfortable enough. It was mid-March; spring time was coming around.

On one occasion of their dates, it had been their three-month anniversary. Mom was dressed in a nice purple dress, one I had never seen before. It was a cool, Friday night.

"Wow, Mom," I exclaimed as she came walking into the kitchen.

"Is it all right?"

"More than all right. You look...! I'd claim you."

"Well, thank you, Sara."

She went to the fridge to rummage for her diet Coke. Diet Coke has been in her hands for weeks now; it's become a habit.

"Mom?"

"Mhm?" she answered, her nose still in the fridge.

"Can I meet Andy?" She shot straight up from the fridge and came over to me.

"Oh, Sara." She grabbed me in her arms and hugged me tight.

The middle of March isn't what you'd say would be the warmest month in North Dakota. There wasn't, however, snow on the ground. That night had also been a night Caleb and I set aside to be alone; as if we've never been alone. We had hung out every weekend that was available.

I had gotten all dressed up for Caleb, not sure what the night had held. He told me he had something important to tell me.

I heard a horn beep outside, just guessing it was Andy.

"Mom!" I hollered.

"Coming," she replied walking into the kitchen. "Are you sure you want to meet him?"

"Yeah, it's time." She smiled.

"I'll be right back."

My heart kept going crazy. They were times like these that I'd wish Caleb was standing behind me with his arms wrapped behind me, whispering that everything will be okay.

I shuffled my way to the kitchen and plopped myself on the stool. I heard the door open and voices.

First I heard Mom's, "Come this way. Sara? Cameron? Cole?"

"In here," I answered.

I kept my back at the doorway as Andy walked through it.

"There's my girl," Mom said. I turned around slowly.

Andy was not as I pictured him. He was tall, dark, and may I say *handsome*. He walked in an Armani suit and his hair gelled back. I was shocked. He had a smile on his face, his teeth perfectly straight. I could smell his cologne over where I stood, not that it smelled bad. It smelled wonderful. I guessed his age at mid-thirties.

"Hello." His voice startled me. He smiled and held out his hand. "I'm Andrew. Call me Andy. Sara?"

"Hi, nice to meet you." I struggled to put my hand out but managed to reach out and shake his hand. His hand was soft.

Cameron and Cole came strolling into the kitchen, "Well, hello there, Mr., uh, what's your last name?" Cole asked.

"Benson. Andrew Benson." He stuck out his hand for both of them.

"I'm Cole."

"Cameron."

"Nice to finally meet you all. Cadie only talks of you guys." He turned to Mom and smiled. Mom was right, he was dreamy. I'd admit, I'd claim him, too.

We all got comfortable around the counter.

I began the conversation, "So, Andrew, you have kids?"

He shook his head, "I've never had time to settle down. I've never been married before."

"Really?" Cameron asked.

He nodded.

Well, that's a plus, I thought.

"Didn't I tell you guys that?" Mom asked.

"No. You sort of left that out," Cole said.

"Sorry, didn't mean to."

"Where do you live?" Cameron asked.

Andy smiled, "In the country, only five miles out. I have cattle and I like to farm a lot."

"You have time to farm?" I asked.

"Sure do. That's my main priority. My brother lives a mile away from me. We share everything. He, on the other hand, is married and has children." He looked at his watch. "We better go, Cadie, our reservations are for eight."

"Okay. I'll be back later. Sara, leave me a note if you go anywhere. Okay?"

I nodded, "Have fun."

"Good to meet you, Andrew," Cameron said, waving good-bye. "Nice guy," he added once they'd left.

As soon as Andy and Mom pulled away, Caleb spun in pulled into the spot right where Andy had once been. I sprinted up the stairs to finish getting ready for the date. Caleb was so used to coming, he just walked right in.

"Oh, Miss Young!"

"Coming," I hollered from my bathroom. "I'm almost ready. Come upstairs."

"I'll wait down here; surprise me with your beauty."

I could hear the boys making conversation downstairs as I finished up my hair. Caleb and I had been going out for seven months and I've become so close to him. The closer that prom came, the more worried I got that I wasn't going to go. Mom and I had picked a long, purple, silky dress out for my part as Princess, for they wanted Royalty to be there at prom.

Caleb was the only one who, here in Edgemont besides Chris, I had told about my dad. I hadn't told Penny yet, although she was beginning to notice that I don't ever talk about him. She hadn't ask yet either. I had planned to tell her soon, before she put two and two together.

I was wearing my favorite blue dress, one that ended just above the knee. I matched high heels and a clutch. My hair was in curls, the hairdo Caleb most liked.

Each stepped I took on the stairs made a noise. The boys came around the corner, with each of their mouths open.

Cameron was the first one to speak, "Wow. You look..."

"Gorgeous!" Caleb finished with a smile.

"Well, I was going to say sexy, but that works, too." Cameron winked at me.

I reached the bottom, "So, I wasn't expecting *that* much feedback, but thank you guys."

Cole still hadn't spoken when I got to the bottom.

"Cole?" He was only staring at me with a shocked look.

"Sara. You look—words can't even describe how you look."

"Okay. Okay. Enough, I'll go change." I winked at Cole. I mouthed 'thank you' to him.

Caleb said, "We'll be home later. I'm taking her out to lunch and then somewhere special."

In the car, Caleb wouldn't stop fidgeting. He has never acted like this before. I wasn't sure what was bugging him. When we walked out of the restaurant, it was breezy, but still a nice night. I had just adjusted to the snow, but finally it melted and spring was popping through the cracks.

He took me to their father's lake. We walked along the beach, hand in hand. The stars were bright and it all felt right. The moon was full and shined high above us. We hadn't said a word since he told me where we were going.

Then, he spoke, "Elise?"

CHAPTER ELEVEN

secrets are out

Elise shocked me. That wasn't my name. I couldn't register why he'd call me Elise. Then, I remembered.

I stopped, but smiled, "Nadir?"

"Good. You caught on."

"What was this *all* about?"

Caleb looked down and loosened his hand and walked on. I followed reaching for his hand and the opposite one, turning him to face me. He smiled and kissed me. I pulled back, "What's wrong?"

"First," he started, "you look amazing, as always."

"Thank you. As do you."

I couldn't read the look in his eyes. It was almost fear, but also excitement.

"I didn't ask you to get all dressed up just to walk on the beach. I really wanted to ask you—" he started to stutter. He grabbed me by the waist, and turned me around. How I missed them was beyond me.

In the sand, I saw hundreds of flowers. From far away, they looked like they were scattered all over. As we moved closer, I saw they spelled out 'PROM?' I could only cover my mouth in awe.

"I'm sorry it took so long for me to ask, but, will you go to prom with me?" he asked with a smile.

I could only nod. I was speechless. "Of course."

He lifted my chin and kissed me.

It was a perfect ending for the perfect evening. I could smell all the flowers, which I found out were real. I grabbed a handful as a keepsake. I snapped a photo of it for memories.

My head was in the clouds all the way home. No one had ever done anything as special as that. As soon as I walked through the doors, I hollered to mom, "Mom!"

"In here, Sara." Her voice came from the living room.

"Mom! You'll never what Caleb asked me!"

"What's that?" she asked, turning the TV on mute. Her eyes looked tired and her hair was a mess.

I screamed, "Prom!"

She smiled but slightly; I could tell how tired she was.

"Yeah. What are you doing up so late?" The clock read past one.

She mumbled turning the television volume back on, "Just watching TV."

"Mhm, I see that," I chuckled to myself walking up the stairs. "Okay, well good night."

I stayed in my room, sometimes pacing, sometimes sitting and reading. I couldn't keep my mind off those flowers and how long that probably took. It took my breath away.

Saturday morning, I woke up to my phone vibrating. The screen read one new message from Chris. Chris has never talked to me outside of gym class. I had given him my number, though, remembering he'd ask to hang out sometime soon.

It read, 'hey whats up.'

I laid the phone down, thinking what to say.

I replied, 'morning. nothin much. u?'

His reply, 'same. what are you doing tonight?'

I thought a minute, did I have a date with Caleb?

I replied, 'nothing as of yet.'

His reply, 'would you like to hang out?'

I was prepared for his reply. Maybe I should ask Caleb? I shook my head. If I hung out with Chris, it'd just be as friends.

I replied, 'that'd be fun. what'd you have in mind?'

His reply, 'well it might be lame to u, but my friends are going bowling in jeffersontown.'

I replied, 'fun!'

His reply, 'i'll pick u up at eight?'

I replied, 'sure thing. c ya then.'

When Caleb texted me, I refused to tell him my plans. My plan would work if he wouldn't bring up the subject. Surprisingly, though, he never mentioned that he wanted to see me. Shocking. I prepared myself for hanging out with Chris.

My phone vibrated.

New text message.

'Sara. Man oh man. you people move on me! how could you!? when i find you, the punishment will be harsh. HARSH!'

I set down the phone after deleting the message quickly.

Mom had gone out with Andy and Cameron with Lauren. Cole went and hung out with his friends from school.

I was peeking out the window when Chris swung into the driveway with a Chevy pickup. He jumped out the door, and I quickly jumped back and acted casual.

When Chris knocked on the door, I ran straight to it. I couldn't help but notice his clothing. I haven't seen him out of sweaty gym clothes. He looked nice. His hair was gelled gently around his curls. He smelled of cologne, absolutely amazing. He wore a polo shirt with jeans. When I'd climbed into his pick up, it smelled fresh.

"New pickup?" I asked.

He nodded, "Birthday present." He smiled and started the engine.

"It's nice. But," I stopped and smiled. I looked at him with a huge grin planted on my face.

"But, what?" He looked confused.

"I prefer Dodge."

I chuckled while making noises, "Please. Dodge. Please." He chuckled again. I looked at him with a questionable humorous face. "Okay. Dodge makes nice vehicles. That's all I'm saying."

I raised my hands, "Truce."

He nodded and grinned.

On the way, he sang along with the radio to songs I haven't heard. He never excluded me, though. He never talked too much, or sang too loud. It was just comfortable, and fun.

As we pulled up to the bowling alley, I saw cars lined up all along the road.

"Big party?" I asked.

"Maybe." He just grinned.

As soon as he opened the door, everyone screamed, "Happy birthday, Chris!"

I looked at him, "It's your birthday? Why didn't you tell me?"

"I just wanted to have fun."

"Well, happy birthday." Then, I thought. "Wait, you just got that pickup today?"

He nodded.

He smiled and introduced me to all his friends. I wouldn't have guessed I was hanging out with sophomores. Chris and I bowled against each other in a separate lane. Even with all his friends there, he didn't forget about me.

I was embarrassed after the seventh gutter in a row. I was getting frustrated and about ready to give up.

"Here," Chris said, "let me show you."

He grabbed a ball, put it in my hand, and showed me how to hold it. His placed his hand around my waist and his other hand around the ball and threw the ball down the lane. Strike!

"Man!" I sighed, "How do you do that?"

"Just try," he urged.

I concentrated. I breathed in deeply and flung the ball down the lane. I managed to knock down three. My next trip down, though, was, of course, a gutter.

When the announcer said that it was midnight bowling time, it startled me. I hadn't realized how late it'd been. I reached into my pocket for my cell, but it wasn't there. I must've forgotten it at home. It didn't bother me, and I kept on bowling.

"Happy birthday, Chris," I said again on the ride home. The clock on his radio read 2:34 a.m.

"Thank you. Did you have fun?"

"Of course! But," I sighed, "I didn't think I would suck *that* much at bowling."

He laughed, "You weren't that bad."

It was 3:41 a.m. by the time we pulled into the driveway. Parked along the road were four different cars. I could only recognize Caleb's and Andy's.

"Thank you for the fun, again."

He smiled, "Anytime. See you on Monday."

As I walked through the door, I heard a lot of loud voices coming from the living room. Then, I heard Mom's voice, crying.

"Where is she?" she sounded panicked.

I ran into the room, worried, "Where's who, Mom?"

When I said that, everybody in the room, turned and looked at me, like I was crazy. In the room were Andy, Caleb, Penny and their parents, my brothers, and two policemen. The loud room suddenly turned quiet, with every eye on me. All eyes were bloodshot red, tears soaked their faces.

"Sara!" Mom screamed and ran up and hugged me. Her hug was powerful, like I'd been gone for years.

"What? What's wrong?"

"You're all right," she sighed. Cameron and Cole came up behind her, each hugging me.

"Yeah, I'm all right. Where's who? Who's missing?"

She looked confused, "You. You didn't call. You didn't answer. No note."

I gasped, realizing, "Mom! I'm sorry. I didn't..."

The police officer cut me off, "It's okay. Are you okay?"

I nodded, "I just forgot to tell someone where I was."

"Okay," he nodded, "just as long as you're okay."

Mom went and led the officers out the door. I felt foolish. I couldn't believe that they thought I was missing.

Caleb and I were left alone in the living room. He walked up slowly. I'd thought I would've gotten yelled at by him, but he just embraced me. His arms were tight and warm. He had tears on his cheeks.

"Are you crying?" I asked.

170

He smiled, "No. I just...yawned." He still had me in his arms. "You scared the hell out of me!"

"Sorry."

"Don't apologize. Explain. Where were you?"

"I went to hang out with friends." Caleb smelled of fresh linen, as always, as I inhaled deeply.

He let go and looked me in the eyes, his green eyes full of fear, "Where?"

"Jeffersontown."

"With?"

I just shrugged.

He'd find out sooner or later. I chose later.

After things calmed down and we were all together, I wanted to explain things.

"Sara," Mom began, "I was so worried." Andy was still there, his arm around her. It made me queasy. But his face was just as horrified, which astounded me. I didn't think he'd care.

Caleb had his hand on my knee, his body close to me.

"I know." I looked down to avoid her deathly gaze.

"Where were you?" she asked.

"I went out with friends," I looked at Caleb, again his eyes full of fear. "Have I told you about Chris?"

Mom shook her head, "Sounds like a trouble maker."

"Oh! Shut up! You don't even know him." Without thinking, I slammed my fist down on the table. I quickly put my hands in my lap feeling ashamed. I met Caleb's hand and grabbed it. "He's a sophomore. We have gym together. He asked me if I wanted to hang out tonight."

Caleb's head was down; I could tell he wasn't happy.

"He didn't tell me at first, but it was his birthday. He just needed a friend to go with him to his surprise party."

"Surprise?" Andy asked.

I laughed, "He sort of knew about it. But we've been friends since the first day of school. Friends," I said it louder with more emphasis. Caleb just nodded his head, but his smile never came on his face.

It was 5 o'clock, far too late for Andy to drive home, so Mom showed him the guest bedroom. Caleb wanted to talk to me still. He shut the door quietly of my room and made his way over to my desk chair and avoided coming over to me.

"Did I mention I was sorry?"

He nodded.

"Are you going to talk?"

He nodded.

"Soon?"

He nodded.

"Can you come sit by me at least?"

He got up slowly but made his way over to the bed. He wrapped his arms around me and set his head on top of mine.

But he didn't talk for awhile. We lay on my bed, holding hands, in the dark and silence. Occasionally, he'd kiss the top of my head. I tilted my head up for a better one, but he just looked away.

"Caleb."

"Mhm?"

"Got you to talk."

He breathed deeply, "I'm just thinking." I'd really wish I could have seen his face.

"About?"

"Chris?" It wasn't a statement. It was a question of revulsion.

I sighed, "What about him?"

His sounded truly upset, "Why would you go out with him?"

"He's a good friend." I rose my voice is defense for Chris. They were angry when they didn't even know him.

"Too good you couldn't have told me?"

I shrugged, "Didn't think I needed to."

Caleb forcefully shoved me off of him as he stepped up. He was pacing back and forth rapidly as if he was so angry. And I didn't know why he was so mad.

"I'm not in this relationship to play games, Sara."

I was stunned at his angry voice. I had never heard it before. I quietly whispered, "Neither am I."

"Then don't play games!"

I tried to look at him but his face was too horrific to look at, "I'm not!"

"You know how lucky you are to have me?"

I questioned his response. He sounded smug and immature right now and I didn't want to be around him when he was like this.

"Leave," I murmured harshly.

"What?" he questioned in disbelief.

"You're acting like you're five. I don't want to be around you when you're like this. Leave!"

He slammed his fists together and raged out the door. Something told me this wasn't just a joking around fight. But why would Caleb have to get so worked up over nothing? I didn't touch Chris in any way that would hurt my relationship with Caleb.

I was confused.

I looked out the window and saw Caleb just sitting in his car. I wanted to look away in case he saw me, but then I saw Caleb get *out* of the car. He paused ran his fingers through his perfect hair and got back *in* his car. This made me laugh considering how mad I was.

Finally, he pulled out of the driveway slowly but soon stepped on the pedal as he zoomed down the street.

Caleb didn't text me for a couple of hours. I was too awake from the fight to go to sleep even though it was almost eight in the morning. I thought he would call or text or something. I just lay there on the bed until I heard a knock at my door. It was quiet and as the door creaked open, I saw Caleb's hair pop in.

He asked in his sweet, apologetic voice, "Can I come in?"

"Have you grown up yet?"

He gently nodded and came in slowly sitting across from me.

"How come you haven't told me about him?"

I shrugged my shoulders but didn't talk to him. I wasn't ready quite yet. I looked up to his smile—well half of it—and I couldn't resist smiling.

"I didn't think you'd approve."

He snickered, "Why wouldn't I approve?" I could hear his soft laugh, finally. He moved from the chair and joined me on the bed. Although we didn't touch, we lay there side by side.

I smiled, "I don't know."

"We don't have to talk about him. If he's your friend, he's your friend."

I leaned over and turned on my lamp. Caleb's face was tired, but still handsome. He had the smile I've been waiting for. I reached over and kissed him.

"Please, don't leave me again," he said.

"I won't."

He whispered quietly into my ear an apology so magnificent I couldn't be mad at him forever.

He smiled and reached to the lamp and shut it off. My eyes were fighting me to stay open. I just remember falling asleep with Caleb's arm around me.

Cole was sitting on the couch when I came walking down the stairs, it was late in the afternoon and it was just Cole and me. We had, though, missed church. I ran behind him and hugged him. I sat down beside him. I could see him trying his hardest not to smile. "So, what happened last night?"

He turned the TV on mute and sighed, "I got home at ten. Nobody was home yet, so it didn't bug me. I thought you'd left a note. When I saw no note, I was curious, but not worried. Then, Cameron got home. Mom walked in at midnight. She'd asked if we've talked to you. When you came home the police had only been there for a half hour. Mom was hysterical. And, when she found your phone, she freaked.

"When you came through the door, all the worries were gone. I had to smile when you had the worried look on your face. It was funny, you were clueless. When I hugged you, to feel you, oh." He paused and shivered.

"You should have seen Caleb. He was just as worried, but he stayed calm. He never talked, just stayed quiet." He looked at me. "Please, don't do this again."

I laughed, "Caleb already told me that."

"Please?" His face was more than serious.

"I won't."

I'd planned that night to tell Penny about my dad. It was time to let her know why my family was so shaken up about me gone.

Mom was more composed than I thought she would be. She acted as though nothing happened, which I hoped she had.

"Mom?"

"Yes."

"Uh. Can I go out with Caleb and Penny?"

She looked at me fiercely, but she turned soft, "Only if you take your cell phone." She smiled and continued cleaning. Saturday was her day to clean, and I wasn't about to mess that up.

Caleb and Penny were, as always, right on time. I said good bye to all and ran out the door. Penny came out of the car, while Caleb stayed inside. Penny ran up to me and hugged me.

"Don't you ever do that to me again!" she demanded. "I couldn't handle it."

"Like I haven't heard people say that today. I'm fine. Let's go have fun." I smiled, hoping the mood would lighten.

She climbed into the back seat of Caleb's Challenger and I in the front. Caleb grabbed my hand immediately and held it tight. He turned his head and smiled.

"Where's James?" I asked.

"I told him I wanted to spend time with you tonight. He said it was okay."

"So where are we going?"

Caleb smiled, "Now, we're having fun. The lake? Nothing special, just supper and some talking."

Penny laughed.

The lake was just as stunning as the first time I'd seen it. Only this time, fresh flowers were blooming, and the water was just beginning to thaw. Penny had prepared sandwiches in a picnic basket. It was breezy and chilly. Caleb started a fire and we huddled close to it. The flames flickered and sent up ashes; all in all, it was peaceful.

As we finished up, Caleb whispered, "You should tell her now."

I nodded, "Penny?"

"Yes, Miss Sara." She looked up and smiled.

"I need to talk to you."

"About?"

"My dad."

Her face turned puzzled, "What's wrong?"

"Nothing. I just haven't told you the truth." I could feel Caleb's arm sliding around me, holding me close. I looked at him, he just smiled. "Okay," I breathed, "he's dead."

She covered her mouth with her hands and gasped, "What?"

I smiled and tried to reinsure her that it was all right. I failed. Miserably. "He was killed a long time ago."

"What?" She looked dumbfounded, her mouth still covered.

"When I was nine, we were on our way to auditions for me. A drunk driver hit us on the way." My story continued with Penny nodding and just sitting there taking in the news.

Silence fell over us. The fire crackled as we sat there.

"Why didn't you tell me?" she asked finally.

"It was my secret."

She just nodded.

"Are you mad?"

She shook her head, "No! Don't think that! I just feel so sorry for you."

I shook my head, "That's the response I was trying to avoid. Everyone in California felt sorry for me."

"Sorry," she said again.

"It's okay. Can we have fun, now?"

"Of course. Just one question. Who was that guy with your mom then last night?"

"Andy, her—boyfriend." I had to spit out the last word.

Boyfriend.

Eh.

"Oh." Penny simply said staring at the fire. She looked at Caleb and smiled with a nod. Something was up, but I didn't know what.

Caleb said, "Okay, now, Sara, we have something to tell *you*."

"Well, I've talked about it with Mom and Dad," Penny began, "and they give Caleb full permission. They think it's the perfect time to tell your family about Caleb."

"Tell Mom, Cole, and Cam?" I asked

Caleb nodded smiling.

Penny giggled, "Think of it. When the premiere comes around, we can all go to California!"

I looked at Caleb, his green eyes were perfect. He was just sitting there smiling.

"Are you sure?"

He nodded once more. "Do it. I'll be right there. Heck, I'll even tell them."

"What about Melanie and Robert?"

"What about them?" Caleb asked.

"Will they be there?"

"They can be."

I looked at my phone. I remembered school tomorrow. We packed up things, while Caleb put the fire out. We'd plan to tell them about Caleb next week, when all of us could meet.

I took a long, hot shower when I got home and finished up my Spanish homework and fell asleep, without a dream.

School was busy as we were now decorating for prom. We spent every moment we could getting ready for it. Because prom would be in the gym, we didn't have gym class; we had a study hall.

Chris was his normal self, talking up a storm. Every day that I'd seen Chris in gym, he'd always been happy. Not once have I seen him angry.

"Did you have fun?"

"Most definitely."

"Good."

We were in study hall without a teacher. Chris looked down and fiddled with his pencil.

He gazed up at me, "Are you going to prom?"

I nodded, "Caleb asked me."

He almost looked upset, but not too obvious. He only mumbled a bit, "That's good. Excited?" I could tell by the sound of his voice he tried to sound interested.

"Oh! Yes. I can't wait."

All week long, the juniors were busy creating the perfect scenery for prom. It was nice when Friday rolled around and relaxation time was ahead.

I invited Melanie and Robert to come over on Saturday for supper and to discuss Caleb. Mom wasn't the least bit suspicious of something unusual. Cooking supper was unusual for me, Mom normally cooked it. When Melanie and Robert came through the door, with Cole welcoming them, I was more than overwhelmed. I was too into the chicken, that I didn't even hear Caleb come up behind me.

He slid his arms around me and whispered, "Hello, beautiful."

The spoon that was in my hands hit the floor with little noise. "Man, you can scare a girl to death."

He smiled, "Sorry. Ready?"

"Never."

I heard Mom talking to Melanie, making their way into the kitchen. "Ready or not, here they come."

I sighed as I heard Caleb's soft chuckle from behind me.

Melanie's smile soothed me somewhat, but my heart was still out of rhythm. Melanie came over, hugged me and asked, "Are you ready? Everything smells good."

I nodded, catching my breath, "Thank you."

The conversation was casual, with Mom, Melanie, and Robert talking. I could see Caleb getting antsy, so I rushed the dishes through the dishwater, leaving ample amounts of food left on them.

I sat down by Caleb and grabbed his hand underneath the table and quieted the voices.

"Mom. Cameron. Cole," I started, "Caleb and I have something important to tell you guys tonight." When I realized what I'd said, I wished I hadn't. It sounded like I was about to say I was pregnant or getting engaged.

The room turned so quiet that you could hear a pin drop. Mom's face turned pale white, with Caleb trying to hold in a laugh. My face got heated.

"Now, Cadie, it's nothing like what you're thinking," Melanie corrected me, laughing.

Sighing, I said, "Yeah, I worded that wrong. Sorry."

Mom relaxed, as did my brothers.

I figured I would have to tell her anyways, so I just began, "Okay, well, do you remember when Lili and I went to get Nadir Remerez's autograph?" She nodded. "And how I came home worried because I didn't get his autograph, I just got scribbles?" She nodded again.

"And how I talked constantly about his green eyes, how beautiful they were?" She nodded.

Caleb continued, telling *his* side, "And I went home telling my parents about how I met *the* most gorgeous girl I've seen ever."

Mom's jaw dropped when Caleb spoke, "What?"

"When she left the autograph table, I was speechless. I wanted to follow her, but I couldn't. I couldn't talk, walk, or move."

Mom looked confused, "You were at the signing when she was there?"

"Technically," Caleb said.

"Did you get his autograph, too?" Cole asked.

Caleb shook his head.

"Then, why were you there?" Cameron asked.

"I was the one signing autographs."

Cameron smiled, Cole was in awe, and Mom, well, was in a daze.

"Mom?" I asked.

She looked at me, "So, are you telling me that Caleb, our Caleb, is Nadir Remerez?"

I nodded worryingly. I was preparing myself for an outrage. But, Mom's face suddenly turned happy and she let out a piercing scream. She got up and hugged Caleb.

"Are you serious!" she screamed with excitement.

When Mom controlled herself, she spoke, "I'm sorry. I wasn't expecting *that*. I thought you were going to say that you were pregnant or something. Gosh, Sara, you scared me."

"That was quite funny, though," Cole said. "The look on your face." He started laughing.

I could tell Robert was thinking hard. When I looked over, he looked up and smiled.

"Cadie and boys," Robert began, "we let Sara into the secret when we first met her. She took it well, better than you." He chuckled. "But can we have your promises that you won't tell anyone?" The room turned serious. "We only told you because the premiere of the movie..." he stopped. "Do they know?"

I shook my head, "One more thing. Remember when Caleb went to London for family." I shook my head, "Well, he went there to be in a movie."

"Now it makes sense," Mom said.

Robert continued, "Can we trust you?" He laid the papers out that I had signed. I could see my signature at the bottom beside Caleb's. Mom signed the paper quickly, pushing it to Cole who scribbled his name. Cameron, though, sat for a moment, flipping the pen around.

"What are you waiting for?" I asked.

He shook his head, "Nothing." He signed his name, looked up, and smiled, a reaction I was expecting. "This is going to be sweet." He chuckled.

When Melanie and Robert left, things quieted down. Caleb and I finished all the dirty dishes I avoided earlier. I realized that Penny wasn't there.

"Oh! Where's Penny?" I asked.

"James wasn't feeling good. They took him up to the hospital. Penny went with. You know, they've been dating for three years."

I gasped, "Really? Is he okay?"

Caleb shrugged, "I'm sure he'll be all right."

"Yeah."

When I laid my head on my pillow after that busy night, I was exhausted from telling Penny about my dad to telling Mom about Caleb. It was good not to have any secrets with Caleb's family and with my family. I was clean. All secrets were out. I fell asleep, dreamless.

I had the house to myself one Saturday. Caleb was working around his house doing chores and things but planned to meet me later. The boys went to Jeffersontown for a movie and Mom was with Andy.

I decided to rummage through some old home videos, ones of dad and us when we were younger. One caught my eye. It was when Dad first taught me to ride my bike.

As I put it in, I took a deep breath. Was I strong enough to watch this?

Yes.

The 'play' button was beneath my finger and as I pressed it, I immediately tuned in back to that time. Like I was actually there.

Flashback.

Tears.

"Get back on, Princess." Dad's voice echoed off from the speakers of the screen.

"I can't, Daddy. It hurts to fall."

"Once you've mastered it, you'll be fine, Sara," Mom said from behind the camera, her voice sounding the same.

I huffed but climbed back on the bike.

"Bug! You're doing it!"

I was! I was riding a bike! I was seven years old and I was riding a bike!

Mom was screaming from the background and Dad's smile couldn't have been bigger. Cole and Cameron were sitting on the porch steps. I saw Lili standing next to them.

"Cole's turn!" I said jumping off my bike.

Cole jumped up and grabbed his bike. Dad quickly ran beside him as he took his turns falling off. Mom frequently shot the camera to me, and I smiled whenever she did.

"I'm done!" Cole said, coming inches away from the lens of the camera.

"You guys did great."

As I looked at the TV, I saw how happy we were when my dad was alive. But, I realized, we are just as happy now. Nothing was different. Well, except for no dad.

Dry-eyed, I turned the TV off as I heard Caleb knock and walk through the door.

"Oh babe!" Caleb said hollering through the doorway, dragging on the ending with emphasis.

"In here," I said from the living room.

Caleb came walking into the living and threw himself on top of me. He smiled and kissed my neck. Then, kissed me on lips.

"Aren't you in a good mood," I said.

He nodded and continued.

"Caleb?"

"Yeah."

He had all his weight on me. "You're squishing me!"

He leaned over and fell off unto the floor, laughing.

"What were you watching?"

"Nothing."

He got up and turned on the TV. It was Dad and I chasing each other in a game of tag. Mom was laughing her beautiful laugh; it rang through the speakers on the television. I could see Cole sitting on the stairs angry that he'd gotten out. His bottom lip stuck out further than his top one.

"I got you, Daddy," I said into the camera, catching my dad.

I grabbed the remote and shut it off.

"Come on! You were so cute!" Caleb whined as I shut off the TV.

"May we do something else?"

"Sure," he said, climbing back on the couch kissing me.

He slipped his arm around my back. I threw my hands up unto his neck. But I couldn't concentrate. As I kissed him, I thought of the video and how alive I was. How happy I was as I ran around the yard chasing my dad. To hear his voice was amazing. My dad's voice. I hadn't realized how long ago that I had watched these movies. Really, all I needed to do to be closer to my dad was watch these videos.

Caleb had started to kiss my neck.

"Caleb?"

"Mhm?" he responded kissing my lips, making me unable to talk.

"I love you."

CHAPTER TWELVE

goodbye

I felt glamorous being all dolled up for prom. I slipped on my silky, purple dress and strapped the heels on. I've waited for this night for weeks after Caleb asked me. My hair was curled loosely and tied to one side of my head. The date was April 5, prom night.

There was a knock at my door, "Sara?" It was Mom.

"Come in."

When I looked at her, she had tears in her eyes. "You look just amazing."

"Thanks, Mom."

"Are you ready?" she asked excitedly.

"As ready as I'll ever be. Did Cole and Cameron leave?"

She nodded, "They went to get Lauren and Sonya."

I heard the door bell ring. I turned around and smiled. Caleb was here. I was ready for a fun time.

Mom smiled, "Let's go."

She left the room first as I fixed my hair one more time. I opened the door, hearing Caleb's parents patiently waiting.

As I walked through the doors and down the stairs, I could feel all eyes on me. The room grew quiet. I could see Caleb dressed in his white tux with a purple vest. His smile was wider than the room.

"Sara, you look gorgeous!" Melanie screamed. Robert was just smiling.

As I reached the end of the stairs, Melanie reached out and hugged me. I walked towards Caleb who hadn't lost his smile. His took the corsage out of the box and placed it on my wrist.

"Wow," he whispered as he hugged me.

I could see nothing but white as we finished the pictures. I sighed knowing there'd be more. Before I climbed into his car, Caleb spun me around and held me in his arms.

"You look..." he paused and looked up at the sky then twirled me around like we were dancing. When he looked down, he smiled, "...hot."

I grinned, "You look pretty hot yourself. I really like that purple."

He held my head in his hands and kissed me.

"Let's go have fun," I said pulling back. "We don't want to be late."

"Oh, yes, we do," he said kissing me again.

"Caleb," I said with him kissing my neck.

He sighed, "One more?"

And, before I could answer, he got his one more kiss. "Okay. Now, let's roll."

When we walked through the doors, it was surreal. Lights lined up the ceiling and the black tent was full of balloons. 'Forever in Your Arms,' the prom theme, was hanging on the black tent. I spied the Royalty chairs sitting in the middle of the walkway. Couples were spread out taking pictures all around me. Family members were hurrying to catch their time for a photo with their beautiful woman or handsome man.

I could see Penny and James sitting over by the tables. Cameron and Lauren came up to us and started talking. Cole and Sonya were over with Courtney and Josh. I also saw, in amazement, Jordan with Hannah, the senior from basketball. Brandon and Giselle were over getting their picture taken.

I glanced over at Penny again, who happened to look at me and she smiled and waved. Before a second could pass, she was on her way over with James following.

"Oh my gosh! Sara, you look amazing!" she screamed.

"As do you! Your dress is beautiful."

"Thanks!"

"How's James?" I whispered before James got over to hear us.

"Good."

James came up smiling, "Hey guys, you two look spiffy."

Caleb shook his hand, "How are you doing?"

All I heard James say was good. I turned to Penny to get the whole story.

"Penny, what happen to James?"

She sighed, looking back, "He got a really bad headache. He was screaming in pain. Just awful. Horrible!" She shook her head. "Anyways, they gave him medicine, and within about an hour, they controlled the headache and sent him home. They said if it happens again to rush him up as soon as possible."

"When Caleb told me about him, gosh, I was scared."

She nodded, "It was scary. But, he's fine now."

"That's good."

"Yeah, let's have some fun."

Lorii called over Royalty and for all couples to line up for Grand March. She placed a crown on my head along with Lauren's. People had arrived and the audience was packed. Royalty was first in line. Lauren and Cameron got a loud applause. When they announced my name, I felt good. Nerves set in, though.

As I walked side by side with Caleb, I could feel his warmth. I looked at him and he smiled. We, too, got a loud applause. We took our place on our chairs and watched the couples go through. Penny was smiling bigger than I've ever seen. Cole and Sonya were smiling and talking all the way through it.

I was in a daze as I watched the couples go by. All were beautiful in their own way. Prom was the night that all girls should feel glamorous about themselves, and all did.

The dance started after all the audience had left. The first was a slow song for Royalty, with people joining in at the end. Every girl in the building was extremely beautiful. Any boy would be lucky to have any one of them.

We had a group going; even Cam and Cole were dancing with their dates. And, I will admit, Caleb was a good dancer. He had the moves that most boys wish they did. It wasn't cocky, it was nice.

When a slow song came on, Caleb came over to me and put his hand in front of me.

"May I have this dance?"

I nodded sheepishly, embarrassed in a way by his gesture that he made, one of which I see in the movies. He moved with grace, leading me out to the floor.

I was exhausted by the time prom was over with. My hair was a mess and my dress had footprints all over the bottom. Not to mention, my feet hurt worse than you could imagine.

Caleb cut the engine of his car as we sat in my driveway.

"You looked amazing tonight," Caleb said.

"You've told me that, more than once."

He laughed quietly, "I know. I guess you could say I'm speechless."

"You clean up pretty good yourself." I yawned.

"Thank you for a great night."

He shook his head and smiled, "Thank *you*." He kissed me. His lips were warm against mine with his breath smelling of peppermint. I could smell his cologne coming off his body. He turned his head and started kissing me again. His hand slid around my back with the other one on my face. I couldn't, however, breathe correctly.

"Good night," I said finally regaining my breath.

"I'll walk you to the door."

He took hold of my hand and held it tight. The moon was out, shining brightly on us.

"'Night, Sara." He kissed me one more time before he turned his back. I heard the roar of his engine and the sound of tired squealing on the street.

I rested my back on the door when it shut and tried to breathe evenly. As I looked up, I smiled.

"Thank you," I said out loud to my dad in heaven.

I thought I was alone, but Cole answered, "For what?"

I jumped, startled by my company. "Not ruining the moment."

"Sure thing," he mumbled turning back to the TV.

"What are you still doing up?" I looked at a clock that read 4:16a.m.

"Waiting for you. Remember last time you didn't come home?"

"Yeah, I remember." I recalled the last time that I'd forgotten to take my cell phone; everybody thought I was lost when I was really hanging out with Chris. The police were even involved. Everybody was scared for me. "How was your night?"

"Good. Sonya's really nice. Just, uh," he paused.

"What?"

"Not my type."

"Why?" I felt bad for Sonya. My brother was so picky.

"S'just not."

I shrugged and walked up the stairs. In my room, I dug for all the bobby pins that were in my hair. And, when the bobby pins were out, my hair stayed the way it was because of all the hairspray.

After a while, Cole knocked on my door, "Sara?"

"Come in."

"I forgot to ask, how was your night?"

I smiled, "Good. I had fun."

He hesitated, as if he had something else to say.

"What are you trying to get at, Cole?"

He was playing with a ball with his feet. I could see him thinking hard.

"I was just thinking tonight, when you didn't come home 'til now. Everything ran through my head. Like nightmares." He shook his head. "I wasn't worried tonight; I knew you'd be late because of prom. But I told myself that I wasn't going to bed until you got home.

"You may not know it, but I love you." He wasn't looking at me when he said that. I've never heard Cole say that before. He just smiled and nodded whenever I said it to him. "If I ever lost you." He shook his head. "Sara, you're my other half. I know when you're sad, lying, happy, anything. I know." He looked up at me with frightened eyes.

"Cole..." I started.

"Just, promise me, promise!" He almost screamed the last word. "Promise, you'll never leave." His eyes turned red and his bottom lip started to quiver.

"Promise."

I was expecting him to just say okay and leave, but he came over to the bed and hugged me. Tight. I could feel all the anger or fear, whatever made him like this, in his hug. I was up on my tiptoes to reach over his shoulders for a hug. I looked over at a picture of Cole and me sitting with our dad. We were smiling bigger than the sky.

"Cole? What sparked this?"

He shrugged, "That night. I thought I lost you."

"Don't worry. You won't lose me."

"And, *you* won't lose *me*." He chuckled a little.

"Are you okay?" His big, brown eyes looked better; they had a smile in them.

He nodded, "Get some sleep."

"'Night."

In gym class the following Friday, Chris was acting strange, more than usual. He still wore a smile, but it was awkward. It wasn't the one that I looked for every day. I wasn't going to beat it out of him, but something was definitely wrong. Maybe it was the hint of him missing four three-pointers in a row. Or, how he tripped over his own feet. He was more athletic than I thought, but today, it wasn't showing.

The teacher took him out of the game, and I, voluntarily, wanted out, too.

"Hey, Chris."

He looked at me like it was a shock that I was talking to him, "Oh, hey."

"What's up?"

"Nothing."

"Yeah—me either."

He stared into space for awhile, without recognizing me sitting two inches away from him.

"Chris?" He didn't answer. It was almost like he was staring into space. "Chris!"

"Huh?"

"What's wrong?"

He looked confused, "What do you mean?"

"Coach? Can we be excused?" The coach nodded and turned his back. I grabbed Chris by the sleeve and dragged him into the locker room, not caring that it was the girls.

"What?" he said offensively.

"I've never seen you like this before. What's wrong?"

He looked down, and a drop of water hit the floor. Was he crying? "Are you crying?"

He glanced up, and yes, with tears rolling down his face he was crying. "Sara! It's so bad. It's all I can think about. I know you were strong, but, gosh."

"What?"

"Mom has cancer. Bad! They don't think she's going to live."

I grabbed him, and held on until he let go.

"I'm sorry." I repeated that in his ear many times.

We stood in the girl's locker room, hugging, until we heard the bell ring. Chris wiped his eyes.

"Are you busy, tonight?" he asked.

"No. Want to hang out?"

He nodded, "I want you to meet my mom. I've told her plenty about you."

I agreed to meet her. Maybe it might help Chris out more. I can't imagine the news that your parent is going to die. Check that. Actually, I can. It happened to me.

When I saw Caleb, waiting by my locker, I nearly ducked and headed the opposite way. But the other half of me said stay and tell him about tonight. I had told Caleb that he didn't need to buy me flowers anymore. My room was far too packed. He only laughed, but agreed.

He welcomed me with a smile and a quick hug with a kiss on the cheek.

"If I get in trouble, I'm blaming you," I said.

He just smiled, and leaned in for another kiss but I ducked. He leaned back and laughed.

"Okay," he spoke while walking towards the door, "on the agenda for tonight, I think..."

I interrupted him before anymore was said, "I have plans."

"With?"

"Chris." By this time, we were at my car.

He crinkled his nose, "Why?" he asked, whining, but with a smile on his face.

"His mom..." I began, but Caleb cut me short.

"I heard. I figured you'd be hanging with him, but I thought I'd give it a whirl."

I laughed, "He needs me."

"I know. It's sad."

"Okay. If I'm home later tonight, is the agenda still good?"

He shook his head, "We *were* going to watch the sunset by the lake. But we could just watch the sunset tomorrow night."

I nodded, "Sounds good." He kissed me and walked off to his car.

Chris' house was just a few blocks from mine; something I didn't know. I guess I never really asked him about it.

Chris came and picked me up to explain his family members.

"Okay, so my mom and dad, of course. And I have a sister. That's pretty much it."

I nodded, easy enough.

Chris parked his car and turned the engine off. "Thanks for doing this."

"Anything for you."

"Are you ready?"

I nodded.

The inside of his house was bright and very homey. Chris's Mom and sister were standing in the kitchen when we walked in. I couldn't recognize his sister from behind, but her hair and her height looked familiar. As she turned around, it was Giselle.

"Sara?" she looked confused.

"Giselle? You're Chris' sister?"

She nodded, "You're his best friend?"

I blushed, but nodded.

"Do you two know each other?" Chris asked just as surprised as us.

We laughed in unison, "Yeah, from gym. Weird, I know both of you from gym."

Chris' Mom walked from the counter and into view. Her hair was wrapped in a scarf with strands hanging down. She looked anorexic, obviously losing weight from the chemotherapy. But her smile was more than welcoming.

"Hello, Sara. I'm Pam." She reached out and hugged me. "I'm glad you could come. Chris talks of nothing but you. Sounds like you two have become great friends."

"We have."

"Are you hungry? We just finished up supper."

I shook my head, "I'm fine, thank you."

"Dad?" Chris called.

A short, heavy-set, smiling man came walking into the room. "Is the girl here?" he asked walking in.

Chris cleared his throat.

"Oh, excuse me. I'm Chris." That's cute, they have the same name. His stuck out his hand and sat himself on the chair. "Have a seat." He gestured me to a seat near him.

Chris came and sat with me along with Giselle and his mom following. I could see the fear in each of their eyes. The look of not knowing when their mom would, well, *die*. Thinking that word made me shiver in fear. I felt sorry for all their worries that they had.

"Okay, I guess this is the best time to tell you guys, even you, Sara. I'm happy you're here." Chris' mom gave me a smile, and I gave her a convincing one back.

His dad cleared his throat, "Giselle and Chris, we went to the doctor today like always." He cleared it again and his lip started to quiver. "And"—he glanced over at his wife—"the doctors said that they've done what they can." But his once worried look turned into excitement, almost humor. "The cancer is gone!"

Giselle jumped up and screamed. She had tears running down her face as she hugged her mom. I felt overwhelmed. Chris turned and smiled and hugged me with force. He let go, rushing over to his mom and grabbing her frail body into his brawny arms.

His dad came over to me and hugged me, his belly hard against mine. I laughed. His mom quickly followed his hug, rejoicing again in my arms. The way they treated me made me feel like family. The celebrating in the room was unbelievable. They had tears streaming down their faces.

"So, what now?" Giselle asked in the noise.

"She's in remission," Chris's dad said with a smile. "It's good. She's going to be okay as long as she stays in remission."

Chris took me into the living room and we watched TV. His attitude was different. Different from this afternoon in gym class. We laughed and talked on the couch for hours, forgetting about anything else.

I only remember being woken up by his dad, telling me we've fallen asleep. Man, I was horrible at falling asleep without knowing how or when. I said my good-byes and headed towards my car.

By my car was Caleb. He was leaning against my driver door with an irritated look on his face. I still didn't know what time it was, all I knew was that I was in trouble.

"Hi," I said.

"Hello," he murmured.

He opened my door and knelt beside it when I got in my car.

"I'm sorry. I fell asleep. Is Mom mad?"

He shook his head and smiled. I breathed in relief that he wasn't angry.

"We called at midnight and Chris's father had said you two had fallen asleep. We said to just let you sleep."

I sighed, "Okay. I'm sorry. What time is it?"

"Three."

"In the morning?"

He nodded, "I'll follow you."

Mom and Cole had gone to bed when we got home. Cameron was watching TV on the couch. His graduation was weeks away, and *I* was the one who was counting down the days. I didn't want to lose Cameron. I didn't want him to move. I didn't want him to leave.

Caleb went to the guest bedroom to change, and I jumped on the couch with Cameron.

"Hey there, Bug."

"Why are you still up?"

"I just couldn't sleep, and I wasn't tired."

"How was your night?"

His face turned into a smile, "Great. Lauren came over and we hung out."

I just nodded and looked down.

"What's on your mind, Bug?"

"Graduation."

He chuckled, "That's not for another year. You have nothing to worry about."

"I meant yours."

He smiled and cocked his head sideways, "Why?"

"I'm going to miss you."

"I'll be two hours away."

That shocked me; I hadn't realized that Cameron had chosen Britton, a school two hours away.

"You chose Britton?"

He nodded beaming his teeth. I hugged him. This did make me feel a little better.

"You know, Bug," Cameron began in a serious tone, "the day that Dad died, you looked awful. And, I know you had a close relationship with him, but that day was horrid. The way you looked as if you were going to pass out at any minute. The way you cried whenever we spoke.

"It was the look in your eye when they carried him out of the room. It was when I hugged you that you screamed and kicked until you couldn't breathe. I had to shake you." He looked at me with his eyes full of fear. I wondered what brought this on.

"I can't imagine what you had to see or hear with the accident. I accepted that Dad was gone, but I could only look at you and smile, knowing you were okay. That one day we didn't know where you were, I could only think of the worst."

"Cameron..." I started but was quickly cut off by him.

"No, it's okay. Just promise me you'll never get lost. You are more precious to me than..."—he paused but only for a split second—"than any other girl I know. I love you."

He looked at me and smiled. This must have really bothered him that I didn't have my cell phone. I hadn't realized that our dad's death scared him so much.

193

"I've had to promise that to a lot of people, but I've meant it each time. I will *try* not to get lost."

He got up and hugged me, "'Night, Bug."

"'Night."

I reached for the remote and lay down on the couch. The TV was on low volume. My eyes were slowly drifting shut. It seemed like I was alone on the couch forever. But then I overheard Cameron talking to Caleb.

"Hey, man," Cameron said.

"Is Sara sleeping again?"

Cameron laughed, "I think so."

"That girl can sleep."

"Yeah," Cameron said in his serious voice. "Hey, will you take care of her once I'm in college. I mean, I can't be here and there. I need to know that she'll be safe."

"I will *always* take care of Sara. Always."

"Thanks. 'Night."

"'Night."

I felt Caleb slide behind me on the couch, laying his body beside me. He wrapped his arm around my stomach and kissed the top of my head. I turned around and opened my eyes.

"Sorry," he whispered, "did I wake you?"

"No." I cuddled up to his warm body. My toes were at his shins. He kissed me and smiled. I wrapped my arms around him and kissed him more. I locked my hands around his soft, black hair. I've never felt his hair before. It felt amazing, silky and smooth. I smiled while he kept kissing me.

He pulled back, "What are you smiling at?"

"Your *hair*," I exclaimed feeling it more. "It's amazing."

He laughed, grasping my face with his hands and kissing me again. My hands went around his stomach, pulling us closer together.

He loosened his lips, "Having fun?" I could hear him chuckle.

I nodded and reached up to play with his hair again. I could hear him laugh as I played with it. He was wearing sweats, but he still looked amazing. His cologne was drifting into the air, almost freshening it. I only wished I could've seen his eyes. Those brilliant green eyes would melt my heart if they could. To hear him say those words to Cameron made my heart that much more in love with him.

I heard a noise. I couldn't figure out what it was, but then I realized it was Caleb snoring. I tried my hardest not to laugh. I've never heard him snore before. Maybe that's because I always fall asleep before he does. The laughter couldn't stay in. Laughing a little too loud, I caused Caleb to jerk awake.

I pretended to be asleep, hiding my noises with my hand as he rolled back over to continue snoring. My hand over my month smelled great from his hair. I couldn't believe I hadn't even recognized or realized how luscious his hair was. I rolled over smiling, cuddling closer to *my* boyfriend.

With finals two days away and Cameron's graduation a week away, who could blame me if I was moody? I could only think of how much I was going to miss seeing Cameron every day. The talk he had with me a few weeks ago stayed in my mind. He wasn't the least bit worried, however. He was thrilled to get to college. Especially since Lauren would be there.

"I give up!" I hollered throwing my math final study guide on the ground.

"Come on," Wade said picking it up. Wade insisted on helping me with studying for the math final. I didn't object; I needed all the help I could get. We were sitting in the living room with the TV off and the house quiet. Everybody had left; Mom with Andy, Cole to Grandma's house, and Cameron with Lauren.

"I just don't understand. How can you square something that's already been squared?"

He laughed but pointed out how to do it.

"Maybe you should pay more attention," he suggested.

"Maybe," I mocked him silently. I paid plenty attention to Mr. Reynolds; I just don't understand.

Wade showed me a different way to look at it, and it finally clicked. So when I did it the way Mr. Reynolds taught, it made sense!

I offered for Wade to stay over and watch a movie with me. He smiled and nodded. I chose the shortest movie of all, so it wouldn't be awkward. Caleb frequently texted me, bugging me if Wade had left yet. Finally, when the movie ended, Wade said he had better go. I grabbed my phone and quickly texted Caleb.

"Thank you, Wade!" I said goodbye as he walked out the door. Caleb promised he'd be over right away after Wade left. It was a Saturday afternoon and I was home alone.

I played my guitar without singing.

"I thought he'd never leave," Caleb said, startling me as he walked into my room. "New song?"

I nodded, but didn't sit up, "I didn't hear you come in."

"I let myself in. Sara, that sounds really good."

"Thank you." I kept strumming the tune of it.

"Will I ever hear it?"

I shook my head, "Probably not." I continued humming the song.

"Ah, Sara."

"What?" I said smiling.

Caleb jumped on top of me, grabbed my guitar and placed it on the floor. I was extremely ticklish. My dad used to lay me on the floor and rub his foot against my stomach. He would make me laugh until I wet my pants.

Caleb tickled me but paused and came close to my face. He smiled. I thought he wanted a kiss. I went in for a kiss, but he moved his head and continued to tickle me. I pleaded him to stop and he paused. This time, he leaned in for a kiss, but I turned my head when he was close, and he kissed me on ear instead.

"Now, that's not fair!" he whined.

I smiled, "Sure is! You did the same thing to me!"

He laughed, "Truce?"

"Truce." Little did he know I had my fingers crossed. When his head came down for another one, I locked my lips together. His lips curved into a smile against my skin.

"I thought we had a truce?"

I put up my fingers, "Crossed."

"Please?" he whined with the puppy dog lips.

I smiled, uncrossed my fingers, and kissed him.

He wrapped one arm around my stomach and one was behind my head. The scent of his cologne was moving up to me and it smelled wonderful. We stopped with a jerk when we heard Cole slam the door and call for us.

On the day of Cameron's graduation, everybody was at our house. I had passed the finals with flying colors thanks to Wade. Cameron wasn't the least bit nervous about graduating. It seemed like I was the only one who was.

It was a beautiful May day. It was finally the beginning of summer. The flowers were blooming and the sun was hot and high in the sky.

Our seats were front row. My grandmas were sitting on both sides of me. Andy was trying to calm Mom down before the ceremony even started.

The speech in the beginning was too practiced and sounded phony; as if the valedictorian practiced and researched so long it didn't mean a thing anymore. As Mr. Field handed out the scholarships, I drifted off into space. Cameron looked so happy up there, sitting by his friends, smiling about being close to graduation.

He sure does look like you, Dad, I thought. And he did. I was wearing my dad's rosary around my neck. Caleb was sitting by my grandma Marion.

James was also graduating so Penny was down the aisle sitting with her parents. Usually, she was bubbly and happy, but I could see the sadness on her face. James never had another headache after the last one. Doctors had told him that one more headache like that and he would die instantly.

My focus returned when I heard Mr. Field starting the call of names. I clapped when Hannah received her diploma. Lauren was all smiles when she crossed the stage.

"Cameron Luke Young."

"Woo! Go Cameron!" I hollered while snapping a picture. Cameron gave me two thumbs up as he walked to his spot.

"I present to you the class of 2011!" Mr. Field's voice was full of excitement.

The class tossed up their hats into the air with hollering and clapping.

Cameron's graduation party was small. We combined it with James's. Both of the grandmas were there. James's mom, Gloria, brought a delicious fruit salad.

After the celebrating was over and things quieted down, it was just us. Caleb's parents had gone home along with my grandmas. James and Gloria helped clean up, but left shortly after.

"I can't believe you're graduated," I said to Cameron.

"I know. It seems like just yesterday we were playing Barbie dolls." He laughed.

I said goodbye to Caleb and Penny and went up to my room. Soon after, Cameron knocked on the door.

"How you holding up, Bug?"

"I'm good," I lied.

He chuckled, "I can tell when you're lying. You're horrible at lying."

I smiled, but sighed, "I'm acting so childish. I just don't want to..."

He frowned, "Lose me?" I nodded. "Oh, Bug, don't worry about that."

"But we've become so close."

"And we still will be! Nothing changes; you just won't see me every day. I have a phone, we'll text when we can."

"I know."

"So, then"—he lifted my chin so I would have to look at him—"where's my smile at?"

I gave him a smile and hugged him. "When do you leave?"

"Next week. How about we spend one day together, us four? I'll be back throughout the summer. You think I'm really going to miss out on things here?"

I laughed, "I guess not."

"Okay. So, let's hang out and go to dinner and a movie: you, Mom, Cole and me."

"Sounds fun."

"'Night, Bug. Sleep well."

"You also. And, Cameron," I said, stopping him on his way out.

"Mhm?" He turned around with a smile.

"Congratulations."

"Thank you." He smiled and vanished down the hallway.

The week passed by without notice. Cameron packed up his room in a matter of hours. I couldn't believe how bare it looked without anything in there. We chose the night before he left to have our special day together.

We headed to up Jeffersontown. We were laughing like we always had. We cracked jokes. We bonded like there was nothing different happening. When, in fact, there really wasn't. I just made it a big deal.

The weather in North Dakota was finally like California's. It was hot, and the sun was out. The occasional rain showers weren't fun, but the sun shined most of the days. I was ready for the community pool to open up. I hated having to wait to go to the water.

In California, it was open. I could go whenever. Wherever. It was nice.

Penny asked me to go swimsuit shopping with her. It would get my mind off Cameron leaving tomorrow.

"This one, or this one?" Penny asked rotating two back and forth. Both would be stunning on her, so how could I choose?

"The purple. You'd look great in purple."

She smiled, "I like that one, too. Are you going with the white one?"

I had chosen a white one with black and blue leopard print spots. I liked it. I went for funky stuff like that. I wanted to be different.

"Yeah, I like it."

She giggled, "Caleb would, too." She flashed me her white teeth at me. "I like it, too. Gosh, isn't May just a wonderful month?"

Yeah, I'm losing my big brother. Just wonderful.

"Better than winter," I laughed.

"That's for sure. Let's go pay."

That night, I tossed and turned in my sleep, only thinking of saying goodbye to Cameron the next day. I looked at the clock periodically, each hour passing slowly. I gave up sleeping at three and went downstairs.

I found the TV on and Cameron sitting on the couch with a bag of potato chips sitting in his lap. He looked at me and smiled and patted a spot for me on the couch. He handed me the chips and placed one arm over my shoulder.

"Can't sleep either?" I asked.

He shook his head, "We haven't been here long, but I'm sure going to miss it." I could hear his voice crack.

I smiled, "I knew I'd get it out of you."

He laughed and ate more chips.

"Do you remember that one time you fell and you cracked your head open?"

I shook my head.

"Yeah, probably not. There was blood everywhere"—he laughed and nudged me—"I almost had to laugh. You were crying your head off. Dad came rushing in and blamed it on me. I swore to him that I didn't do it.

"He just said go get your mother. We rushed you to the hospital." His face was smiling the whole time and his big arm around me was comfortable. "And, because of you falling, you have a percent mark on your forehead." He laughed and pointed to my scar on my forehead. I had the chicken pox when I was younger and scratched them to scars. I have one on the side of my eyebrow and two on my forehead. They have a line in between them to make them a percent mark.

We quieted down and munched on chips. The TV was quiet, almost making no sound.

"Do *you* remember the time I broke a window and blamed it on you?" I asked laughing.

He frowned but chuckled, "I'll never get that money back for paying for a new window."

I laughed harder, "And the time that Mom fell into a suitcase when we were going on vacation."

He burst into laughter.

"She couldn't"—he breathed but laughed harder—"couldn't even walk!"

I had tears streaming down my face, "And that big black and blue mark right on her butt!"

"Oh, man!" He continued to laugh. We quieted down, but soon looked at each other and roared some more. We were going to go on vacation and Mom had just gotten the mail. She thought her suitcase was a chair and bam! She fell into the suitcase, half crying and half laughing. At the hotel, she couldn't walk without our help. We laughed the whole time.

"How about the time that we went to Valley Fair?" he asked.

"I don't really remember, but portions I do. It was fun."

"You and Dad went on the roller coaster like five times in a row. Then, you were too short for one, so Dad stayed back while Cole and I went on it."

"Yeah. I was scared his glasses would fall off his shirt because we went upside down."

"Yeah. It was our first and last family vacation."

I looked down, "I wish I could remember."

He tightened his grip around my shoulder.

"Remember when you and I went for a bike ride, with you sitting on the handle bars? And, you fell off!" He laughed, "You just got up and laughed."

"I don't remember that, either." I laughed, though. He's told me that story before.

"I'm leaving tomorrow, Bug."

I sniffled, "I know." I looked down, but Cam lifted my chin up.

"Does someone need a hug?"

I laughed and nodded.

Cameron squeezed me hard.

"Can't"—I pretended to *not* breathe—"breathe!"

He chuckled and let go.

We sat in silence watching TV. Cameron's arm stayed around me until he jerked it off. I hadn't realized that we had fallen asleep. Cameron's arm moving was him waking up in the morning. I sighed and slumped off the couch and fell to the floor with a thump.

The heat from the shower felt great and woke me up. I took as long as I could, to avoid saying goodbye to Cameron. The mirror was fogged up by the heat of the shower. Mom hollered up the stair to warn me that Cameron was leaving in a little bit.

As I walked down the stairs, I saw his suitcase and boxes near the door. I told myself not to cry, I would see him often.

"There she is," I heard Cameron say. "I'm going to go, Bug. Ready?"

I nodded.

"Help me carry out?"

I nodded. Cameron said his goodbyes to Mom and Cole and saved mine for last. I grabbed his suitcase and put it into the car. His face was tight, his bottom lip quivering.

"Okay, Bug, I saved yours for last."

I ran over and jumped into his arms.

"You know what?" he asked. "You really need to eat a sandwich. You're looking small and light."

"Oh, Cameron. I'll miss you."

"I'll be a phone call away and two hours from that. Don't worry." He smiled and grabbed me into his arms with force.

"I love you, Bug," he whispered.

"I love you, Cameron."

I couldn't help it, but tears were coming. Maybe I was overreacting, but I couldn't handle Cameron leaving. I sniffled and let go.

"Drive carefully."

"You know it."

He climbed in and waved goodbye as his pickup pulled away. Cameron was off to college. But, I smiled, it was summer and school was out!

Goodbye Cameron, I thought.

CHAPTER THIRTEEN

bad mistake

The morning sun was bright coming through my window.

Hearing my phone go off, I stretched my arms and leaned over and grabbed it.

The message read, 'Why don't you ever reply? I have paid my fines and you have caused me hell since you put me in prison about your daddy. Reply or regret!'

I gasped. I covered my mouth, shaking my head. Water swelled up in my eyes as I realized who had been sending me these messages.

Dad's killer.

Cameron had been gone for a week now and summer vacation was wonderful. Just this morning, I had made plans to spend the evening with Caleb at a party.

Running down the stairs screaming, I couldn't focus. I couldn't get myself to calm down.

"Mom!"

"Mom!"

I needed her and she wasn't answering.

"Mom!" I screamed at the top of my lungs.

She came running from her room with a frantic look upon her face. "What! What?" Her face was worried.

"It's..." I couldn't get the words out. "It's..."

"What?"

I collapsed on the couch as soon as Cole came running in. I heard a scream. Then, it all went black.

"She just collapsed on the couch. I couldn't wake her." I heard my mom's voice in terror.

Something was stoking my face, and then, coldness on my forehead.

"She has a fever." It was Cole's voice.

"Why was she screaming?" Caleb.

"I don't know, she..."

I opened my eyes to Caleb sitting by me, arms securely around me. I was lying down. My head hurt. What more?

Mom sighed, "...she's awake!"

It became clearer. I remembered the text message.

"Oh, Mom. It's awful!" I screamed, trying to sit up. Caleb kept me down.

"Stay down," he whispered gently.

"It's Dad."

They looked at me like I was crazy.

I shook my head and finished, "Dad's killer. The guy who rammed into us. He's out!"

"I don't understand," Mom said shaking her head.

"He's out! He's mad! He keeps sending me threatening messages. I've been deleting them thinking they were just dumb forwards." I looked around at the confused faces.

"How did he get your number?"

I shook my head and fear suddenly swept over me.

"He kept on texting that I was a good hider, but that he'd find me. And that I should reply, or I'll regret."

Caleb let me sit up, slowly. I wasn't sick, I wasn't hurt. I was furious! They didn't understand.

"Mom! Listen!"

"I'm listening."

"Take this seriously! He said he's going to do to me what he did to Dad. Help!"

"Okay." She took a deep breath and closed her eyes. "We need to just stay calm. When was the last text message?"

"Right before all this happened."

"Next time he texts you, let me know. This might get police involved."

I nodded.

Caleb promised to stay with me for as long as I wanted. The memories of the crash came floating back. I tried my hardest not to think about them. They were just too painful.

Andy arrived as soon as Mom called him and asked him to come in.

Andy.

Gee, what can I say?

He's a saint. He has patience that I never knew existed. He is so caring. Mom spends most of her time with him. He doesn't have one bad bone in his body.

Mom explained the situation to Andy as calmly as she could. Dad's death is a touchy subject with Andy and Mom. Mom doesn't want Andy to think anything bad or good.

Caleb kept stroking my hair, kissing the top of my head at occasions.

"Sara?"

We were lying on the couch watching TV, trying to keep my mind off things.

"Mhm?"

"Let's go to that party. It'll get you distracted."

I shot straight up, "I totally forgot!"

Caleb smiled.

The party at Josh's house was packed. Everybody was there; all our friends. The music was loud and every room was smoke filled. It was dark, musty, and maybe moldy. I grabbed what *I* thought was my Gatorade bottle. I took a drink; it tasted strong. Didn't cross my mind, though. I danced with my friends, letting my worries fade away. The text message didn't faze me, I never thought of it.

My head was spinning and it hurt, and I was sweating. I couldn't see straight. Caleb came over and asked for a drink. He took a sip and looked at me funny.

Over the music, he hollered, "What did you put in here?"

"Huh?"

Caleb grabbed my arm, with force, and pulled me out the doors into the cool crisp night.

"What did you put in here?" His voice was stern. I've never heard his voice get that loud around me. He had four eyes! Four! But, all were the beautiful shade of green that I liked...

"I doon't kkkknooww what you're talkinnn abboutt." My speech was slurred. My head was spinning. Knots were in my stomach.

"Sara." His face, it was full of anger. He's never looked at me like this before.

Disappointment.

"What?"

And yet, he still smirked, "You're drunk."

I shook my head, too quickly, and stumbled to the ground. Caleb's warm arm grabbed me by the waist and started to lead me to his car. My legs wanted to collapse.

"Sara," he murmured with his voice half upset and half comical.

I didn't feel good, my stomach going around and around. I leaned over, and the food that was once in my stomach was now on the ground below me. I could only hear Caleb's soft laugh.

Then, I started to fly...

The room was spinning when I woke up. Only it wasn't my room. I blinked to focus the room.

Caleb's room.

His clock read noon. I tried to sit up, but failed. The beating on my head was like someone pounding a hammer on my head. I wanted so badly for Caleb to be sitting next to me, but he wasn't. Calling for him seemed bleak; any noise would make the hammer worse.

I lay in his bed for awhile, trying to remember why I was here. What happened last night?

Right when I was about to get up and find Caleb, he came walking in.

I quickly turned over and pretended to sleep. The bed moved and soon enough I felt Caleb's arm slip around my waist.

"I saw those blue eyes," he whispered, kissing my neck. I turned over to him smiling, but the smile was gone in a split second. "What were you thinking?"

I was confused, "I have no idea what you're talking about."

He pursed his lips and his forehead wrinkled up.

"Sara," he sighed, "you were drunk last night."

With my head still spinning, I shook it.

"What were you drinking in the Gatorade?"

"Gatorade. But," I thought a moment, remembering the funky taste, "now that I think of it, it tasted funny."

His eyes were curious, "When I drank it, it tasted like alcohol."

"What?"

"You didn't put alcohol in your drink, did you?" he persisted like I was on trial.

"Never!"

He cocked his head.

"You know me! I hate drinking and anything to do with alcohol!" I shook my head. "You mean someone put alcohol in my drink?"

He nodded, "Must've."

I sighed and rolled over so he couldn't see the tears. I tried my hardest not to breathe different. Who would want to put something in my drink?

"California, don't cry."

I sniffled quietly, "I'm not."

He chuckled, "You're a horrible liar. I hear you crying."

I turned over to face him, "Why aren't you as worried as I am?"

He shrugged, "It's probably just someone dumb, thinking it was their drink. There were so many drunken people there."

I sighed. "What did you tell my mom?"

"I called Cole, told him to write your mom a note saying it got late. She called this morning, I just told her you were still sleeping."

He paused, now playing with my hair.

"And?" I urged.

His mouth was near my ear, "I'm a good liar. I'm getting it from you."

I smiled. I turned my face to look into his eyes. I told myself I would never forget those green eyes of his. The way they were pure green. His eyes looked down at my lips and back to my eyes. He smiled, his lips curving and little dimples coming up. His smile made me forget.

The warmth of his lips against mine was soothing. The way he kissed me gentle enough but with force. He was in control. His fingers ran through my hair and I tightened my grip around his waist. I pulled myself closer to his body, lessening the space between us.

I could feel his lips curve into a grin, stopping the kissing.

"Hungry?"

My smile wasn't helping my urge to be angry. I wanted to be frowning.

"Am I hungry?" I huffed angrily. "You stopped to ask if I was *hungry*?"

He just smiled and propped his head up with his hand.

"If I say no, can we continue?"

He sat up, and got off the bed. I had forgotten about my headache. Then, the nausea kicked in. Food was the *last* thing on my mind.

Drinking was evil to me. I couldn't believe *I* got *drunk*. It was mind boggling. I wanted so badly for this to be a dream. My goal was to *never* drink. Obviously, that will not be happening. If Mom ever found out, I'd be dead, more than dead, grounded.

Caleb's head popped back through the door with a smile.

"I'm taking it you're not in the mood for food, so how about Tylenol and water?"

"Please!"

Penny pranced through the door after him, "I hope I'm not disturbing anything."

I shook my head, "Nope. What you need?"I threw the drugs into my mouth and sucked down the water fast.

"See if you're all right."

"Headache. Nausea. Can't be better."

Penny laughed, "Sorry, had to ask." She sat beside me on the bed. "I saw who put the alcohol in your drink."

"Who?" I mumbled not really caring.

"I'm sorry, but Josh said that you needed to loosen up a bit."

I frowned and murmured, "Jerk." I sighed loudly as I laid my throbbing head on the pillow. "I hate dumb boys who think drinking improves their live." I grabbed a pillow and screamed my loudest right into it which only made the headache worse.

Caleb persisted, "Babe."

I set the pillow down.

"I'm all right."

"Are you sure?" Penny asked.

I nodded. "How long do hangovers last?"

Caleb laughed, "All day."

I sighed and tucked myself back into Caleb's bed.

"What am I going to tell my mom when I go home and I feel like this?"

"The flu?" Penny suggested after a moment.

I nodded reluctantly.

As I lay in bed, my head was pounding. Penny left me to peace and quiet. I closed the blinds which made the room completely dark. My eyes fought to be open as I lay in the dark. As they closed the last time, I felt the bed moved.

I turned to see a figure in bed with me. I screamed. But I heard Caleb's laugh.

I punched him, "You scared the crap out of me!"

He whispered with a hint of humor in his voice, "Sorry."

"I'm trying to sleep."

"Me, too," he quietly laughed.

I could hear his light breathing. I threw my arm over his stomach giving the hint of me wanting his arm around me. He got the hint and wrapped his arm around me. I buried my face into his chest, warm and smelling amazing.

"What did my mom say?"

"To feel better and come home when you can."

And as we lay under the covers together, Caleb kissed me. He didn't seem like he wanted to stop. He kept on going. I didn't care. I liked it more than I could express. His hand kept moving up and down my back.

The next day, my head felt much better. Mom didn't believe that I felt better, but I convinced her. She kept giving me the 'look.' It wasn't good. Caleb found it humorous.

As I sat watching TV alone on morning, my phone beeped. It wasn't a ringtone from anyone I knew. My heart raced as I walked to my phone on the counter.

It read, 'Not in California, huh? The US isn't that big.'

I was home alone. My heart raced, and I panicked. I didn't know who to call. Or what to do. I screamed. I dialed Caleb's number, the first thing that popped into my head.

I jumped and paced as it rang.

Finally, "Hello, my love. How can I..."

I couldn't take it, I interrupted, "Caleb!" I screamed into the receiver.

"What's wrong?" His voice suddenly more intense.

"It's him! He texted me back!"

I could hear him gasp. "What did he say?"

I tried to calm my breathing, "He knows we aren't in California."

"Did you tell your mom?"

"No, she's not home!"

"I'm coming. Lock the doors. And, babe?" He paused.

"Yeah?"

"It's okay. I love you."

"Love you, too. Hurry!"

I listened until I heard the line go dead. What did he want with me? I didn't do anything to him. He should be happy, he's out of jail. What did I do?

Quickly running to each door, I locked them, twice. I knew there wasn't that great of a chance of him being here in North Dakota. I cuddled up into a ball and waited for Caleb to come.

As the door bell rang, I jumped, along with my heart. I walked slowly towards the door and then shook my head.

This is crazy. It's Caleb, I thought.

I unlocked the door and Caleb came rushing through.

"Did you call your mom?"

I shook my head.

"Why?" he hollered like he was angry. It shocked me.

"She's at work," I mumbled.

I looked down.

"Hon, I'm sorry." He walked over to me and put his arms around my waist. "I didn't mean to yell. I'm just, well, worried."

I looked up at his green eyes full of worry.

"It's okay. Can we wait to call Mom until she's off of work?"

He nodded, grabbed my hand, and led me over to the couch. As we were lying on the couch, I could hear his heart beat fast. Faster than normal. I didn't want Caleb to be scared for me. I grabbed the remote and flipped the channels to SpongeBob.

I could hear Caleb quietly chuckle behind me. I turned my body so I was facing him. The smile on his face was cute.

"SpongeBob?" He grinned wider. "Are you kidding me?"

I shook my head, "He's the only thing that can make me smile."

Caleb's face turned to a frown.

"Thing." Still no smile. "You're a person. SpongeBob is a thing."

He nodded and I turned over to watch the yellow sponge. Something about SpongeBob made me laugh endlessly.

Thoughts ran through my head. I couldn't imagine having to involve police with something dumb like this. Although, it's not dumb. Some guy out there wants to come and kill me. Why?

I could hear Caleb's laugh from behind me. His arm slid around my stomach and squeezed me tight. His continued to laugh at the sponge on the TV.

What does Dad's killer want? *I* didn't do anything. *He* did. *He* killed my dad. *He* injured me. *He's* the one that was drunk and decided to drive. It was *him*. It was *his* fault. Not mine. And, yet, *he* wants revenge. I just don't understand.

"Why aren't you laughing? This episode is hilarious." Caleb's sweet voice behind me rang in quietly in my ear. His warm lips were against my neck, kissing me gently.

"I've seen it before. I'm laughing on the inside."

The living room was quiet except for the voices of SpongeBob and Patrick. Any small noise made my heart jump. Honestly, I wanted Mom to come home to get things over with.

"Sara?"

The door opened and Mom's voice rang through the hallway. I jumped to my feet, not too rushed though. I didn't want to scare her too much. I hoped my face wouldn't give away the fear.

"Mom?"

"Mhm?"

She was rummaging through the mail, not really listening to me. She did this often, and more times than one I needed to raise my voice for her to listen.

"Mom?"

"Mhm?"

The second time it was fainter and less meaningful. I smiled, but knew what I had to do.

"Mom!" I screamed at the top of my lungs.

"Yes, Sara?" She looked up from the mail.

"Finally. Okay, I got another text message."

She set down the mail and looked up at me with fury. I could tell this was the last thing she wanted to hear when she got home.

"When?" she asked quietly.

Caleb answered before I did, "About an hour ago. Sara didn't want to call you. That's why I'm here."

She nodded and mumbled, "We have to get the police involved. What if he finds us? God only knows what could happen. The boys. I hope they're okay."

She walked over to the phone still rambling on about things, but she spoke so swiftly you couldn't understand, but she paused.

"Who do I call?"

"Not 911," Caleb began walking over to her, assisting her by rummaging around for a phone book. They were talking, but I blocked it out. I headed up to my room in search of my phone.

I needed Cole.

I needed Cole!

My hands were trembling as I flipped opened my phone. The buttons looked smaller than ever. My attempt to type took forever. I had to keep backspacing.

My text read, 'cole, come homme. he texed me back. i need uu.'

I read it again and even with the spelling errors, it was somewhat legible. A smile slid across my face. Waiting for Cole to reply seemed endless.

Finally, he replied, 'i'm coming! five minutes.'

I didn't know exactly where he was but all I wanted was him here. I wanted to feel his hug. I walked down the stairs slowly. I could hear nothing. It was quiet. Mom and Caleb were sitting near the counter in the kitchen. They both turned around as I walked into the room. Their faces weren't smiling, but they weren't horrified, either.

"How did it go?" I asked breaking the silence.

Caleb answered quietly, "A cop is on his way over."

Mom added, "I asked if this was serious. He said yes."

As I sat on the counter looking at the faces of my mom and boyfriend, I realized how serious this really was. Mom's face was more than concerned and Caleb's mouth, I hadn't seen it shaped like that since I got home that night that they thought I was missing.

Cole came running through the door minutes later, rushing into the kitchen.

"I'm here! What's going on?" He was out of breath and looked worn-out.

I ran over to him and gave him a hug.

"Mom called the police," I explained. "They are sending people over now."

The silence in the room was too much to handle. I walked into the living room and sat down on the couch and continued to watch TV. I could hear quiet words in the kitchen. But they were too quiet for me to understand them.

I heard a door slam and talking outside. Then, the doorbell rang and everybody went to the door. I continued to sit on the couch, preferring not to greet the officers.

"Good evening, everyone. I'm Detective Elliot Smith and this is my partner Lia Benson."

I could hear Mom greeting everyone and introducing Caleb and Cole.

"And I'm Deputy Moser. Is there a place we can sit and talk?"

"Yes. Let's, um, go in the kitchen around the table." Mom's voice sounded calm. "Sara, bring your phone and come in here please."

I grabbed my phone and dragged myself in to the kitchen. The detectives weren't old, maybe middle age. Deputy Moser had a little too many donuts in his life time. But his smile was more than welcoming as I walked in.

"Hello," I murmured to the crowd of people staring at me as walked through.

"Miss Young, I'm Detective Smith, and this is Benson." Detective Smith threw out his hand for me to shake and I did.

"All right, let's get down to business," Detective Benson said. "Now, what's going on? Cadie, you said that your daughter is receiving threatening text messages from someone you know? Am I right?"

Mom and I nodded while giving each other convincing glances. There was part of me that didn't want to talk but, I knew I had to. I needed to stop this.

"My dad and I were in a car accident when I was nine. Eight years ago. Dad was killed"—I choked on that word—"and I was only injured a bit." I had to look down as I continued on. The gaze of the people around me wasn't what I wanted to see. "The drunk driver walked away. He was put into prison and released recently. He texted me telling me he is coming for me.

"He won't stop. I get one at least every month since, if not more. He says he wants to kill me. He wants revenge. I didn't know it was him at first. I thought it was just forwards like I always get. So I deleted them. But one message finally clicked."

The detectives scribbled down words as I told them the story.

Caleb placed his hand on my knee, tightly holding onto it.

"Okay," Detective Smith started, "did he give you any clues where he might be?"

I shook my head and willingly handed the phone to the officer. He scrolled through the phone, with the occasional 'oos' and 'ahs'. I couldn't take it. If he said it one more time, Caleb would certainly have to hold me down.

"Well," he looked up, "we can track the number and where it is from, but who knows where he is. We will be putting a tracking machine on your phone. We'll get every text message that you do, but we'll only read the ones from him."

I nodded.

"Cadie, we are willing to place a cop outside every night, somewhat hiding, not obviously sitting in your driveway, of course." Detective Smith's voice sounded too concerned. It had firmness.

Mom shook her head and looked down. Andy had joined us shortly before the cops arrive and was sitting uncomfortably close to Mom. I could see Andy gently stroking Mom's back.

"I can't believe he'd come back like this," she finally said while shaking her head. Her voice sounded defeated.

"We can protect you," Detective Benson promised. "We'll do our best."

"Cadie, if it's the safest thing, we might as well," Andy persisted.

"Mom?" Cole asked frightened.

As we stared at our mother looking frantically down on the table, I gazed up at Cole and the fear on his face was unbearable. I didn't want to cry. I didn't want to cry. I didn't want to cry! I had to stay strong.

"Yes," she mumbled still looking down. "I want to be safe. I want my kids safe." She looked up. Her eyes filled with water and one tear trickled down her cheek. "Please do what you can to help my kids."

Caleb never released his hand on my knee. I couldn't get myself to look at him. I just couldn't. Too many things were going through my head. My heart didn't feel the same. There was a lump in my throat that just needed to be swallowed, but I couldn't swallow it.

"Cadie. Sara. Cole. Caleb," Deputy Moser said, "Please, don't worry. We'll find him. You'll be all right."

Mom nodded, and I was speechless.

"Who's the first to be outside?" I asked. It was a dumb question, but I needed to hear that I could still talk.

"Our sheriff," Deputy Moser answered. "You won't even be able to tell that he's here."

After the house had quieted down and with the darkness of the night and the creaking of the rocker, I didn't hear him pull up, but Caleb whispered in my ear that the sheriff was sitting in the trees across the road. Andy was with Mom upstairs while Cole, Caleb, and I sat on the couch. Caleb had his arm across my shoulder and Cole was rocking rapidly in the recliner.

I could just feel myself about ready to yell at Cole for the constant creaking of the recliner.

I plopped myself down on Cole's lap trying to stop the rocking. He looked at me as if I was on crack. I smiled, making Cole smile. I reached down to hug my Cole.

"If that recliner creaked one more time, I would have shot you."

He smiled, "Sorry, Bug."

Caleb's soft breathing woke me up. I kissed him lightly on the cheek. The sun was shining brightly through my window. As I peered through my window, I could see the cop car sitting in the trees, but faintly. I shivered remembering *why* it was there. Detective Benson told us to get on with our lives as if this had never happened. She said we'll be fine. I wish I could believe her.

Caleb handed me a white envelope as we were sitting in his basement, one of the many occasions that we hung out in his movie theatre. It was quiet. Penny had left with Courtney and his parents had gone out on a date.

As I opened the envelope, I realized what was inside: two first class tickets to California. The date read July 3.

"What's this for?" I asked.

He smiled, "Plane tickets to California for the premiere."

My jaw dropped, "Really?"

He nodded.

I screamed, "I can't wait!"

He wrapped his arm around me, gazing deeply into my eyes. I've known him for months and his green eyes still take my breath away.

"I don't think I've said this to you, but your eyes are amazing."

He chuckled, "You *do* stare at them an awful lot." I could tell that he was biting his lip trying not to smile.

I tried to loosen my body from his grip but failed and started to laugh.

"So!" I hollered. "It's not my fault. Those things are mesmerizing."

His soft laugh rang through my ears.

"It's called looking! I'm not a stalker!"

He smiled and inch by inch moved closer to me. His lips turned into a small grin as he pressed his lips against mine. His warmth soothed all my fears. I didn't want to stop this moment. Caleb started to laugh as I kissed him.

I pulled back, "What?"

He shook his head and leaned in for a kiss. I ducked out of the way.

I didn't want to smile, but my lips quickly won and curved into a smile.

I lay on my bed after I got home from Caleb's. There's something about going over to his house that makes my stomach full of butterflies. Caleb seems perfect and I don't have anything to believe that he's not.

I was laying sideways on my bed with my head looking touching the floor and my feet up in the air on the other side. Looking under the bed I found a familiar looking box. It was my birthday present from Caleb.

Twins tickets.

I opened the box. Inside were the tickets for the Twins. I cannot believe I forgot about these. One of the tickets read for a game coming in two weeks. I smiled knowing there was a chance that we could go. I looked and *all* the tickets were for the game in two weeks against the Yankees.

Quickly finding my phone, I texted Caleb.

I said, 'hey babe, guess what i just found.'

I had to twiddle my thumbs waiting for Caleb to text back. The seconds ticked by as I waited.

And waited.

And waited.

Finally, he replied, 'what's that?'

I replied, 'twins tickets for the game in two weeks.'

His reply, 'i thought i would have to remind you. want to still go?'

I replied, 'of course! nuffin stoppin me! nuffin!'

His reply, 'haha okay. family going too?'

There were seven tickets.

I replied, 'ya i spose, there's seven tickets'

His reply, 'well, there's you, me, cole, cam, your mom, andy, and a surprise person :)'

I replied, 'tell me?'

His reply, 'nope. it's a surprise.'
I replied, 'fine:) be that way;)'
His reply, 'you'll like it'
I replied, 'i always like your surprises'
His reply, 'i know...can i see you?'
I replied, 'i'm home alone'
His reply, 'i'm halfway there:)'
I replied, 'o really.'
His reply, 'nah, can i see you?'
I replied, 'of course'
His reply, 'on my way! see you in 15'

I laughed, I could just imagine him leaving what he was doing and getting into his car and coming. I looked out the window and saw the sun high in the sky. The green grass needed to be cut but smelled great as I walked out the front door. In my arms I held a lounging towel. It was humid, but the sky was blue. The birds were chirping.

I could see Grandma Joanie across the street busily cooking away at her stove. As she glanced up, she smiled and waved. Her wave was priceless, using her whole hand. Her head went right back down as she went back to work.

Caleb's music could be heard as he pulled unto the block. His Challenger looked sharp pulling up and coming to a stop.

"What's this?" he asked getting out of his car.

"It's so nice outside; I didn't want to waste the niceness."

He smiled and sat down beside me, "Niceness? Is that a word?"

I shrugged, "Maybe."

He looked up in the sky, "The news said we're getting a bad storm tonight, possible tornado. Ever seen a tornado?"

I glared at him, "I lived in California, not Antarctica."

He looked at me with those green eyes. Am I ever going to get used to them? I couldn't take it anymore. What do I have to do to get used to them?

"Are you looking at my eyes again?"

I blushed and looked away.

"Sara, you know, your blue eyes are just as breathtaking. Just look in the mirror."

I let myself fall unto the blanket, hitting the ground with a bang. I laughed as I held my head with the quick sting of the pain. Caleb snickered beside me only to join me lying down.

"I would play that game where you guess the figures with the clouds, but there aren't any clouds to play with."

"That would be difficult to play," I jested.

Caleb threw his arm over my stomach and held it tight. He was now in an upright position looking into my eyes.

"Are you"—he smiled while holding me tighter—"*mocking me?*"

"No!"

He grabbed my leg and held me tight. He had my leg and arm in a cradle.

"Are you sure about that?"

I couldn't help but smile, "Yes!"

He tightened his grip. It was tight before, but now, it was tighter!

"How come I have a feeling you're lying?"

"Maybe because I *am*."

"Oh-h," he sneered, "that's what I thought."

He let go of my leg and loosened his grip around my arm. He put both of his hands behind his head and looked up at the sky. He closed his eyes with a smile on his face.

The heat wasn't too overpowering, it was just right for me. I had my shorts on with a tank-top. Perfect weather for wearing summer clothes. North Dakota weather is definitely different than California's. I'd say summer would be my favorite season. I wasn't a fan of the storms, but that was Mother Nature at her best. I'd just have to get past them.

I was going to say something but his head moved too quickly and before I knew it, Caleb was kissing me. I wanted to warn him about the neighbors watching and my grandma in the window. PDA (public display of affection) was not something I was a fan of.

"Caleb?" I whispered when I could.

"Mhm?"

"My"—breathe—"grandma."

He quickly took his head away and smiled and positioned himself on the grass once more looking at the sky.

When Caleb and I talked now, it was easy. Words just flew out of our mouths. We understood what each other was saying. We knew what the right and wrong words were.

Caleb lay there smiling at occasional stories that I had to tell him. Every once in a while, we'd feel a cool June breeze. We lay there for hours, just talking and staring.

Clouds rolled in as Mom pulled into the driveway just getting home from Grandma Marion's house.

"Hello, guys," she greeted us with a quiet voice.

Andy shortly pulled up behind her getting out of his car with a bag. He looked at the clouds in the sky and shook his head.

His smile was the first thing I saw. "Howdy, kids. Storm's a coming."

"Hey, Andy," Caleb answered. "Yeah, I heard that, too."

He shook Caleb's hand as he reached us. He was young. My mom's in-love eyes for him never changed.

I was scared. I didn't want my mom to forget about Dad. If she did, what would I do? Could I still love her? I shook my head. Not possible. I'll forever and always love my mom.

"Where's your brother?" Mom asked as we sat around the kitchen counter.

I answered, "With Tyler. Swimming."

"I better call him. This storm doesn't sound good."

The thunder sounded like a bomb dropping on our house. Suddenly, hail the size of golf balls smashed against the sidewalk. The rain fell like snow in winter blizzard. Warnings flashed across the TV screen for every county around us, except us.

We sat in the basement, hearing only the loudest of thunder. I waited for the man on the screen to say that our county was now under a tornado warning. Yet, he never did.

I heard the front door slam and footsteps.

"Man, it's cold out there."

Cole came walking down the stairs, his hair soaked.

"There was a tornado spotted fourteen miles out. Are we in a warning yet?"

"Really?" Andy asked, "No, they haven't said anything."

The lights went on and off and the lightning struck the poles. Mom lit some candles. The best part was that we played games in the candlelight. It was a family night. When we should be worried about the weather, we were laughing and having fun.

I woke up to the light pitter patter of the rain on the basement windows on the floor. Caleb was snoring three feet away from me. I gently kissed his cheek and looked around. Mom and Andy were curled up on the couch sleeping in the sitting up position. How comfortable. I walked by Cole's room and he was tucked tightly in his bed.

I climbed into his queen size bed and covered up. Cole yawned and turned over. I swore he saw a ghost. The way he jumped into the air when he saw me was funny.

"Sara!" he screamed in a whisper, "you scared the crap out of me!"

"Go back to bed."

I smiled and drifted off to sleep listening to the rhythmic falling of the light rain.

CHAPTER FOURTEEN

twins

I couldn't sit still as we crossed the North Dakota/Minnesota border. Everything was the same on Interstate. Our bags were packed and we were on our way to cheer on my team. We were off to Minneapolis.

The Twins.

The early morning sun was bright. Two weeks ago, the cops were over at my house. Two weeks ago, I found my birthday present for Caleb. And now, two weeks later, we were off for our vacation.

The purr of Caleb's engine made me smile. Caleb's posture was comfortable with one arm draped over the steering wheel, the other hand holding tight of my fingers. Cameron was asleep in the backseat, softly snoring.

I turned around to see Cole driving the pickup behind us with Mom and Andy.

"Can you *please* tell me who the surprise is?" I whispered as quietly as I could.

Caleb just shook his head and smiled and turned up the volume of the music. I wasn't going to start to complain with Cameron in the car.

Six hours in a car isn't bad. Especially since I've been waiting years to see the Twins play. I longed for the sound of their bats smashing into a slider. You know, when the announcer says 'GRAND SLAM'! Yeah, I couldn't wait for that either. And my surprise.

Surprises.

There's one thing I like about surprises and one thing I don't. First, I like to be surprised. It shows someone cares about my emotions. But I don't like it when they *tell* you that there will *be* a surprise. You can surprise me, just don't tell me. Simple enough. Or else it'll bug the crap out of me!

It was a nice morning. The sun was up, barely any traffic, and the thermometer read 78 degrees. Perfect day for a family vacation.

My phone vibrated in my purse. It was the dreaded text message as I looked on the screen and read *his* number.

'Okay, I'll admit, I don't know where you are currently living, it'd be a help if you'd just text me back! I'll find you Sara Young. I didn't get thrown in jail for nothing! Watch your back!'

I shut the phone and handed it to Caleb, whose forehead wrinkled up when he read it. His grip around the steering wheel tightened.

"It's okay." I tried to calm him down, but my effort was worthless.

"Let's just get to Minneapolis," he murmured under his breath.

"Caleb, look at me."

His eyes once furious were now soft with fear.

"The cops just read that message. They are going to find him before he finds me. Don't worry. Let's have fun."

His smile was soothing and I could finally relax. We passed the 'Welcome to Minneapolis' sign and my heart raced.

"Cameron, wake up." I couldn't help but scream it. "We're here!"

He sat up and groaned, "She's acting as if she's never been out of state before."

Caleb chuckled, "It's humorous, let's let her continue."

At the hotel, the man at the front desk instructed us to our room. We still had a few hours until the game and the seven tickets in my purse seemed to be moving. They just wanted to be used! But who was the seventh one for?

The room decision was tough, but we decided on the boys having their own room and the girls having their own room, with Andy maybe joining us later.

The hotel was amazing, best I've ever seen. In the lobby was a stream that flowed throughout the hotel with live fish. The pool had a slide. The elevator was glass. And every room was a suite.

Caleb couldn't help but smile all the way up to our rooms. Luckily, our rooms were side-by-side. His hands felt sweaty in my hands. I could feel him shaking.

"All right, this is it," Caleb said nervously, "Room 345 and 344."

I pushed opened the door and I couldn't believe my eyes. My luggage dropped to the floor. I wanted to cry. The person in front of me wasn't the surprise I was expecting.

"Lili!" I screamed at the top of my lungs. "You're here!"

Her smile spread across her face. "Isn't it time that *you* surprise *me*?"

I laughed and flung my arms around her.

"Are you ready for some fun?" she asked.

"Most definitely!"

I turned around to Caleb's smile. His green eyes weren't full of fear anymore but excitement. Vacation, here we come!

I wanted to go to the mall before we went to the game. No way was I missing the Mall of America. With my best friend at one side and my mom at the other, I felt free.

We went to every store. I could slowly feel my wallet getting thinner and thinner.

I heard my phone ringing—Caleb's ringtone.

"*Yes.*" I added emphasis to sound like I was annoyed with him calling and interrupting my shopping trip.

He laughed, "Are you three almost ready? Game starts in a half hour."

I looked at the time, "Shoot, yeah we're ready. Totally lost track of time."

With my T-shirt and Dad's cap on, I couldn't sit still in my seat *above* the Twins dugout. I never thought I'd be right above their dugout. Full view of them warming up was a dream come true!

The excitement of the game continued. Caleb to my left and Lili at my right and the rest of my family there with me, I couldn't have been happier. My favorite player, Joe, was having a fantastic game.

"Lili," I said, "I can't believe you're here!" I had to holler over the noise.

"Me either. Once again, you can thank Caleb. He really likes you."

I looked over at Caleb hollering for the Twins.

"I know. And I really like him, too."

"Enough for marriage?" Her smile was wide with curiosity with a little bit of humor in it.

I shook my head, "I'm 17. Don't plan to get married for a *long* time."

I heard the smack of the bat and loud cheering.

"Grand slam!" the announcer sang out to the crowd.

"How long are you staying?" I asked her.

"Well," she thought, "we are going back to your house tomorrow. I can stay for however long, really. Until I get a plane ticket, I'm staying with you."

I screamed. Loud. Lili giggled and continued to watch the game.

"Lili?"

When she turned her head, she was smiling. I didn't want to ruin it with the news of the man that was wishing to kill me. Wanting to end my life. Maybe at home.

"The Twins are going to win!"

The volume of the people was loud. Louder than I've ever heard. The rush of feelings was overpowering. I've never felt like this before. This was my dream ever since my dad introduced me to the Twins.

Top of the ninth.

Two out.

Two on.

Twins up by one.

Best batter for the Yankees batting.

Three balls and two strikes.

Joe Nathan pitching.

And, the pitch.

Strike three!

Batter out!

Twins won!

"And, the Twins win it! Joe Nathan did it again!" The announcer was screaming into the microphone. "Thanks for coming."

After the game, we sat in the boys' room munching on snacks and watching the newest movie. Caleb's arm around me was comforting. He was smiling and every now and then he would lean down and kiss my neck. Cameron and Cole were catching up with Lili. Mom and Andy went to a bar on a date. Their dates have become lame from my point of view. I had to laugh to myself.

"What are you laughing at?"

"Mom and Andy."

He had a confused looked but I just shrugged and gave him the 'inside joke' look.

"I've made you leave your home twice now and I don't even know you," Caleb said to Lili.

She laughed, "I know. Well, I'm Lili."

Caleb smiled, "How long have you two known each other?"

"Forever," I answered.

"...and always!" she replied.

When Lili continued to talk to the boys, I whispered in Caleb's ear, "Can I steal her and talk to her about this whole situation?"

"Of course. Take her to the pool or something."

He leaned down and gently kissed my lips and helped me up.

"Lili? Want to go swimming?"

We sat in our bikinis with our feet dangling over the edge of the hot tub. We were the only ones in there except for the male lifeguard reading his magazine at the other edge.

"How's life?" Lili asked splashing her feet in the hot water.

"It's all right."

"All right? Sara, look at your boy toy."

I smiled and thought of Caleb. But then I thought of the killer.

"It isn't all that glamorous. We are having some troubles."

"What do you mean?"

I kept my head down to avoid the scared eyes of my friend.

"Remember my dad?"

"Of course I do."

I looked up, "Remember the accident."

She nodded, "I'll never forget."

"It's been bad. The guy who killed my dad, he..."

"What?" I didn't answer her "what" for a second or two trying to figure out the correct wording for the situation. I thought a little too long. Lili got restless and I could tell by her expression that she was frightened. "What? Sara!"

So, I just spit it out. "He wants to kill me. He's been threatening me with text messages." She looked away shaking her head. "We got the police involved."

"What?" She questioned me in disbelief.

I continued, "There's a cop sitting outside our door in the trees monitoring our house 24/7."

She shook her head and was speechless. She looked away from me and stared at the wall.

I ended, "He texted me on the way up here. They're scary, the messages. The way he talks, it's as if he just wants to slaughter me. It's scary. But the cops now receive every message that I get and send. They get every message and read it."

Lili laughed, "Now, that sucks."

"I know, but they promised"—she tilted her head in disbelief with a crooked smile—"not to read them. Hey, if they promised, they promised."

"So," she said worried, "you're safe?"

I shrugged my shoulders, "Apparently."

"Okay, then"—she stood up and took off her tank top, striping down to just her bikini—"let's have some fun with the lifeguard. He couldn't take his eyes off us." She smiled and walked over to the main pool and dived in. I took off my clothing, still in my bikini and jumped in right after Lili.

We glanced up at the lifeguard, whose nose was now not currently looking at the book, and giggled. He quickly put the magazine back up.

"Let's get out and go down the slide," Lili whispered in a laugh.

I got out first with Lili being the lookout. I didn't look at the lifeguard, only at Lili, who was giving me two thumbs up.

The slide was fun, I'll admit, the rushing water and the little part that went outside the hotel.

Lili was antsy when I came back, hurrying me up for her chance. As she got out, no doubt the lifeguard's eye watched her all the way up the ladder.

Gross.

But I had to laugh knowing he'd just done the same to me. I, too, gave Lili two thumbs up as she went down the water slide.

The clock on the wall read after midnight. The sign on the door says the pool closes at 11:00. Time for some more fun.

"Watch this," I said to Lili, trying my hardest not to laugh.

I got out of the water, grabbed a towel, and made my way over to the guard.

"Excuse me, sir?" I said in my best accent. I kept my composure better than I thought.

His eyes wanted to pop out of his head, "Yes?"

"Will you be too kind as to tell me what time this fine facility closes?"

He scratched his head and pushed his glasses up with his nose. His skin was snow white and his face was covered in acne. I felt bad about what I had just done.

"Yes," he spoke quietly looking at his watch, "well, it was supposed to close an hour ago. You ladies finished?"

"We are. Thank you."

"No problem."

I walked back to Lili, silently motioned her to get out, and walked out the door. Lili looked like a blowfish ready to pop. I could tell she wanted to laugh but was holding it in with all her might.

As soon as the door closed, she popped.

"That was hilarious!"

I shrugged, "I feel bad now."

"Oh, don't. He's been through that many times." She nudged me and headed for the elevator.

I shrugged and looked back through the window. Poor guy. He was cleaning up after us, all our water spills. I looked away before I went back *in* and helped him.

Caleb's worried face as I walked into our hallway for our room scared me.

"What's wrong, Caleb?"

He shook his head, "Lili, may we have a moment?" It wasn't his sweet caring voice he normally had around Lili. It startled me. Lili hesitantly nodded and walked into the room.

As the door shut, Caleb handed me my phone.

The text message read, 'go twins. glad you got to see that game?'

I couldn't blink. Move. Breathe. Focus. I couldn't register the message. My legs felt like Jell-O.

"Sara?"

Caleb's soft, scared voice rang close to my ear. I hadn't realized he had me in his arms. I looked up at his face and I kissed him. I thought it would help. But, the way he kissed me told me it wasn't one of our special kisses. "How did he...find...me?" I could feel my throat tightened.

Caleb shook his head, "I don't know."

"What do we do?"

He cleared his throat, "The police called. The phone is from California. But when they checked his house, it was empty."

I dug my face into his chest. The aroma was phenomenal. I inhaled a whiff of his scent before unburying my face.

"And?" I cried out.

"And what?"

"Are we safe here?"

He nodded, "I didn't want to tell you, but there are police outside our window. They'll be in the lobby. We are being watched. We'll be fine. They don't think he's in Minneapolis." I looked down. Caleb lifted my chin.

"Sara, it's been eight years, he won't remember what you look like. You'll be fine. I'm not going to let anything happen to you. I promise."

Caleb's warm lips are what brought the tears to my eyes. I wanted so badly to believe him, but I couldn't stop picturing Dad's killer opening our door during the night and...

I shivered.

"It'll be all right. It'll be all right."

Every sound I heard in the night became 'the guy.' My eyes didn't stay closed for more than a minute. When I saw shadows, I saw *him*. But it never was. Our door was locked in three places, no one was getting in. The moon was high and it was late in the night, past midnight.

Mom and Andy were in one bed and Lili and I were in another. I had the boys' key to their room in my hand burning, wanting to be used and curl up against Caleb's warm, soothing body. I had the biggest urge.

I didn't want to wake up the others, but I needed Caleb. I told Mom that I might move in with the boys if I need to.

Her reaction to the text message was hysterical. She immediately called the detectives and asked a million questions. She wanted to leave, but they told her just to stay and relax.

I was thankful for the door connecting our rooms. I wouldn't have thought *twice* about stepping outside of the room to go into their room. My luck would have been that the key didn't work and I would be stuck in the hallway.

I slid the key into the slot and pushed the door as quietly as possible. Cole was snoring on the pullout couch in the corner. Cam was spread out on one bed. And, Caleb. He was all alone. He looked lonely. But, I realized I was the one that was lonely.

The bed squeaked as I climbed in. I didn't want to wake him up and yet again, I did. I wanted him to stay awake with me. As I slipped my arm over his stomach, he jerked. His face was puzzled, like he was dreaming. He opened his eyes and smiled, wrapping his arms around me. Not long after, he was sleeping. So much for that. But, at least I was in his arms.

I wasn't letting him let go. I wasn't going to sleep.

There was no way...

"She came in here at like five, wide-eyed. Poor girl." Caleb's voice was quiet, or at least trying to be.

"I'd be scared, too," Cameron said with a chuckle.

Caleb sighed, "I've trying to do everything I can, but I'm only human. I think I'm as scared as she is. I can't let her know that, though. I just"—silence with breathing—"don't want to lose her."

What? I was hurting Caleb? I never thought of that. I didn't think of *his* pain through all this. I only thought of mine. How selfish! He was hurting because of me!

"No, dude, you're doing great. She came to be with *you* last night."

Cole.

"It's not getting to be too much, is it?" Cameron asked.

There was a moment of silence. Then I felt his warm lips against my cheek. I was praying I didn't smile.

He sighed, "Never."

I opened my eyes. Caleb's kiss would've woke me up anyways, that would have been time to wake up anyways.

"Good morning, Miss Sleep Walker," Cole said as I sat up and yawned. "No girls allowed in this room."

I gave him the 'very funny' look and kissed Caleb.

"Sorry, I didn't think I'd wake you up."

"It's okay. It's"—I looked at the clock with read past noon—"definitely time to wake up."

Lili popped her head through the door with a smile, "Shopping?"

I quickly got off the bed, "Yes!"

Shopping is my middle name.

It was heartbreaking to pull out of the Cities. But at least I had the experience. Cameron and Caleb sat in the front while Lili and I sat in the back. Even after I told her about the guy, she still wanted to come to our house.

It was a long drive and no doubt, I fell asleep to the sound of Caleb's engine purr. I woke up drooling on Caleb's coat just as we were pulling into Edgemont. I flipped his coat over so he wouldn't see. It was dark out.

"Look who's up," Caleb said as soon as I sat up.

I glanced towards the trees where there was supposed to be a cop. I studied it carefully through the darkness. Sure enough, the white car was sitting far into the trees. The person inside, however, could not be seen.

The smell of our house was welcoming. I was glad to be home. Lili wanted the grand tour of our house. She saw it briefly on my birthday, but not enough to really recognize anything.

Later that night in my room, I paced back and forth in my SpongeBob lounging pants as the clock ticked and Lili quietly slept. I glanced out my window and saw the cops changing duties. From my view, it looked like Detective Smith coming now and a deputy leaving.

There was a feeling in my stomach that wouldn't leave. I made my decision.

The coffee pot was silent as I brewed enough for two. I grabbed two coffee cups, my jacket and shoes, and headed out the door with the cups in my hands.

I wasn't scared as I headed into the night. I knew Detective Smith could see me. The moon and stars lit my way as I entered the trees. Soon, the detective's car came into view. I heard the door open and squinted as a light flashed in my eyes.

"Sara?"

Detective Smith's voice wasn't convincing.

"It's me. I thought you could use some company. And coffee."

I walked closer now seeing his face. He walked around the car and opened the door for me. He ran around the front of the car and got in. I handed him the cup of coffee and he inhaled the aroma.

"Smells good. Thank you."

I only nodded with a smile.

The only sound was the slurping of the coffee from both of us.

"Aren't you too young to drink coffee?" he asked breaking the silence.

"Nah, I've been drinking for years. You can thank my dad."

"I see."

We sat in silence for minutes just looking into the trees and then back to the house. I didn't come here to just sit and stare. I needed answers. I needed the truth. Was I safe? Should I be scared?

I looked at him, "I didn't come out here to sit in quiet. I came to get the truth."

His expression was confused, "The truth?"

I nodded, "About my dad's killer."

"Don't you know his name?"

I shook my head.

"It's..."

I quickly interrupted him. I didn't want to know it. "No! Don't tell me. I don't want to know."

Detective Smith paused and looked down.

"Sorry."

"It's just been hard on me. Do you know the story?"

He shook his head, "The brief part. Care to elaborate for me?"

I breathed in deeply, "I used to love to sing. I always acted around my family. Daddy would call me his 'bug'. He was my best friend. He was there for me. He taught me everything I know about basketball.

"He was handsome." I laughed, "I'd claimed him. He had a smile that lit up the room and melted my heart. He was just...amazing. For my ninth birthday, he got me auditions for a musical or play. I was excited. It was just me and him, our special day. He was always a careful driver.

"It was a red light. An intersection. Bad timings. Then, it all went black. At the hospital, I stayed by his side until he died. My mom and brothers made it just in time. I'm alive and healthy and my dad's dead. How does that work? And his killer, free in the world. Free!"

"I feel your anger. I really do."

"No," I shook my head, "you don't! I don't get to see my daddy..."

"Listen, my dad died when I was young, too. Been dead since I was fifteen. Nothing I could do about it."

"How?"

I felt bad as I listen to him pour out his life to a stranger who had just blown up at him. He never looked at me. His face kept straight and his voice even. He explained how his dad had overdosed with pain killers due to cancer. How awful it would be to die from drugs!

A person can't say what kind of dying is worse. Whether it's unexpected or expected, it's just bad! Losing someone from cancer or from an accident to losing someone from a heart attack or from old age, all death is bad and cannot be easily forgotten. Grieving is the best you can do in any case.

No one can cope easily. I didn't. It took years for me to accept that my daddy wasn't going to walk through that door every night. He was buried eight feet below the ground visiting the Great Man up above.

Detective Smith's voice stopped as we were staring out the window in silence. The sky was clear and all stars were visible. As he looked at me, he smiled.

He spoke, "We both have a story to tell. We both survived deaths of a loved one. We can do anything now."

I laughed, "Maybe not jump off a bridge."

His soft laugh made me smile.

"Now the truth?" I asked.

He sighed, "He's on the move. We went to his house. That's how he knew you were in Minneapolis. He had a note sitting there for us. We don't think he knows you're in North Dakota." He looked at me with his eyes worried, "But I promise, nothing will happen to you. Or your family."

I questioned his promise, "Promise?"

"We'll do our best. It's us against him and the whole United States of America."

"Thank you for everything. Really. This can't be...easy."

He chuckled, "It's not. But when I saw that smile across your face for the first time, you touched me. The first rule of being assigned a case is that you're not supposed to get personally involved."

"I'm guessing you're personally involved."

He smiled, "You remind me of my daughter."

We sat in silence some more keeping still only drinking coffee at moments. My coffee turned warm. Sleep suddenly dropped over me as I let my eyelids close without a fight. I slept...hard...

I felt comfortable. The sun was in my eyes. I swatted my arm at my alarm clock which was ringing like crazy. But I quickly sat up. Wasn't I in a car last night when I fell asleep? I was in the detective's car. How did I get here? I got out of bed quickly and ran down the stairs. Cole was eating at the counter and Mom was busily working at the stove. The smell of bacon floated through the air.

"Smells good." I inhaled the sweet aroma.

"You've been sleeping walking quite a bit lately," Cole said with sarcasm.

"Morning," Lili smiled.

"Mornin'," I replied.

Mom smiled and grabbed a plate and plopped down bacon and eggs on it. "Detective Smith brought you in early this morning. Four, I think it was. You were out cold."

I ate the eggs, not realizing how hungry I had been.

"He said you brought him coffee." I nodded, taking a break from eating but quickly returning. "He said you two bonded."

I sighed and glared up at her the 'leave it alone' look.

She laughed and continued to wash the dishes.

"I think it's cute."

"Mom!" I moaned and lifted my plate off the counter and sat in peace and quiet up in my room. I looked at my phone and decided to call Penny. It's been weeks since I've talked to her. The phone seemed to ring forever. Then I got her voicemail. So I tried again.

"Hello?" Penny answered, sounding as if she was rushing.

"Hey, Penny! I haven't talked to you in a long time."

"O-M-G! I know. How are things going?"

"Good."

"Is my brother there?"

"No?"

She laughed, "Oh, yeah, he's upstairs sleeping. Forgot."

I chuckled, "So how's the dress looking?"

"Amazing. Want to come over to try it on?" Her voice sounded too enthused.

"Sure, I suppose I should since the wedding is like, what? Four days away?"

"Yeah," she said with a sigh. "Being the maid of honor is hard. I'll be happy when it's done."

"I bet."

"Okay, so come over later?"

"Sounds good."

"Caleb will be here," she said enticingly.

"Very funny, Penny. I'll be over soon." I said in a dry, sarcastic tone.

"Bye," she said laughing.

"Bye."

Lili willingly stayed home with Cole and Cameron. She missed them. Besides, she'd be bored with everything. She didn't know the Pierces and it'd be too long of an introduction.

The road to Caleb's house was burned in my brain. It was nice to know where to go. Remembering back, it had taken me weeks to memorize where to go. When Caleb took me out the first time, I was completely lost. I enjoyed the ride out to the house. Like Caleb, I just walked right in.

"Pierces!" I hollered into the emptiness.

I could hear talking and laughing in the kitchen.

"Oh, hello everyone," I said, seeing all the laughing faces as I walked through the door. The room suddenly fell quiet.

"Hi, Sara!" Penny screamed as she saw me. The room went into a busy constant sound of mumbling. She came over and hugged me.

Casey was there sitting beside Chloe and flashed me a wide grin but went straight back to all the smiling faces. Robert and Melanie looked as if they haven't gotten sleep in weeks. Dark black circles were under their eyes. There were women in the room whom I hadn't seen before and men that looked bored out of their mind. Wedding party, maybe? But I couldn't see Caleb in the room.

"Where's Caleb?" I asked over the noise.

"Upstairs sleeping. Come with me. Let's try on that dress!" She smiled and bounced up the stairs to Melanie and Robert's room.

As she opened the door, I saw why she took me there. There was a 240 degree mirror in the middle of the room with a stool in the middle to stand on and twirl around in your dress.

Penny came out with a long white bag meant for dresses. I squealed as I ran over to it.

"Ah! Just wait. Close your eyes!"

I heard a zipper and rustling of the bag.

"Okay, open!"

The dress *was* absolutely gorgeous! I'm sure it wasn't going to be as beautiful as Chloe's, but this sky blue dress was good enough for me.

"Get it on me! Get it on me!"

The dress fit perfectly. Penny was impressed, as was I.

"All right," Penny sighed in relief, "I am done and the dress is finished. It is ready for you when you walk down that aisle! You may now go see your love bug." She laughed and unzipped me.

By this time, it was close to midnight. The moon was high in the sky and peeked through the window as I walked down the hallway to Caleb's room. I peeked into the dark room where my boyfriend lay snoring. I had to laugh. Caleb was a snorer. That just cracked me up.

Tiptoeing to his bed as softly as I could, I climbed in under the covers. I slipped my arm over his stomach. I was facing his face. As I watched his face, his mouth turned into a smile. Then he stuck out his lips.

I kissed him.

For a long time.

He wasn't asleep anymore. As his lips synchronized with mine, I felt like I was flying. His breath was sweet and his lips were soft. And, he slipped his arms around me pulling me closer to him.

"Caleb." I said trying to catch air and say a few words.

"Hm?"

He wasn't letting me talk. I did the only thing that I could that would grab his attention. I laughed and stopped kissing him. I lifted my lips in a smile and let *him* figure out that I wanted to talk.

He sighed and finally opened his eyes. Man, it was good to see those green eyes.

"Yes, Princess?"

"How are you?"

He frowned with a smile, "You stopped me for *that*? Come on!"

"*Well*," I asserted, "I haven't seen you in what, 24 hours?"

He laughed and tightened his hold around me. We lay in silence listening to the noise going on down there. I really hadn't planned it, but we fell asleep. Penny opening the door woke me and I checked the time. Caleb's clock read past four. I sighed and rolled back over and fell asleep...again...

"Sara."

Someone whispered in my ear.

Then I felt lips against my cheek.

My wake-up call.

I sighed and opened my eyes to Caleb smiling, showing his teeth. His green eyes twinkled in the bright sun light.

"Mom mad?" I asked.

"Not too bad, I just explained about the little 'party' that my parents had. Told her it got late."

I smiled, "Thanks. You're getting to be a good liar for me."

He moved closer and kissed my lips, "No problem."

Lili!

I totally forgot that Lili was waiting for me at our house!

His lips were amazing but I had to stop, "Caleb, we've got to go! Lili!"

Lili was laughing with Cole when we stepped through the doorway. She smiled at me and continued to talk with Cole. At least she wasn't mad that I didn't come home last night.

"Big party last night, Sara?" Mom persisted as I walked in.

"Yeah, sorry."

With Lili here, I didn't have time for Caleb. I planned to devote the last two days that Lili was here all to her. Not a text or call from Caleb, although I did sneak one in without her noticing. And the day she left, I didn't want her to go, but she'd already been here for a week and she was ready to go.

"Thanks for coming," I said holding the tears.

"Anytime. It was fun. But it's your turn to surprise me, right?"

I laughed, "Right."

"I've got to go," Lili said as her flight was called.

"I love you. Forever..."

"...and always!"

CHAPTER FIFTEEN

robert and ross

I let out a deep breath as I looked at the nervous bride standing in front of the doors that will open up to her future. Chloe was keeping it cool, but I could tell she was nervous about this. Who wouldn't be? She's getting married.

It was a perfect June day. The middle-of-June breeze was going through the windows of the packed church. The sun was high in the sky. It wasn't too hot or too cold. It was perfect.

Caleb's birthday was days away. This probably wasn't the time to think about it, though.

I heard the wedding march and the doors flung open. Caleb and I were the first couple to walk down the aisle. We had practiced our walk at the wedding rehearsal last night, but suddenly I forgot my footing.

When I met Caleb halfway, I immediately calmed down. I get worked up so easily. I slid my arm into his. He looked even better in the tuxedo.

"Breathe," he whispered in my ear as we started to walk.

I could see the priest standing at the altar and Melanie and Robert smiling in the front pew. Casey's parents were sitting on the other side. All eyes were on Caleb and me. Then they all focused to the couple walking behind us.

I reached my place at the altar and looked down the aisle at Penny and the best man walking up. She was beaming in that beautiful dress. Penny could look beautiful in anything.

Casey took his spot on the altar, adjusting his tie and nervously looking towards the doors that his wife-to-be would walk through. I couldn't tell whether he was about to cry or fall over. When his eyes filled with water, I realized he was crying.

The ceremony was beautiful. I felt bad that I was up there instead of one of Chloe's friends. But, I couldn't help but think of the dance that Caleb and I were about to have at the reception.

Mom and Andy were sitting in the pew holding hands. Gag me. Andy was nice, but, *please*, keep the touching to a minimum in front of me! The way she smiled at him and the way he got those eyes around her told me it was coming soon, too. The day that would be her wedding and with me the maid of honor. It's not that I didn't like Andy; it's just that I wasn't ready for him to come into our lives on a more permanent basis. He was nice. He was handsome. He was... everything she needed.

"You may now kiss your bride!"

There were loud cheers while Chloe and Casey were lip-locking on the altar with Casey dipping Chloe. They were all smiles as they walked down the aisle as man and wife.

I thought the pictures would never end. First, the wedding party. Fifty shots later, it was the bride and her bridesmaids. After that, the groom and his groomsmen.

The bride and groom.

The family.

The siblings.

Finally, it ended and we were off to the reception and dance. People stopped Caleb as he walked by saying "hi" or "you've grown up so fast." He'd introduce me to each one and each one ended up in me getting a hug from them.

I'm sure I'll be happy when it's my wedding and I hear the guests tapping the sides of the wine glasses, but at others' weddings, the fifteenth time is too much for me. But I never stopped smiling and joining in on the tapping of the glasses.

When the DJ announced for the first dance as husband and wife, I literary jumped out of my seat to wait our turn for Caleb to dance with me.

I felt Caleb's arm wrap around me from behind and I could feel his soft breathing.

"We are almost up."

"I know," I whispered back.

The DJ interrupted our moment, "Would the wedding party please come and join these two *lovely* people?"

Caleb slipped his hand into mine and led me out to the dance floor. The feel of his arms on my back made me smile. His tuxedo smelled just like he did always, fresh linen. Pictures were snapping all around the place. In my mind, it was Caleb and me, dancing to the music, *alone.*

Towards the end of the night, my head hurt from the loud music and from the dance. The bottom of my dress was covered with spilled alcohol and other drinks. My beautiful hairdo for the wedding was falling out. The makeup once on my face was not there anymore. And I was tired. But I had a blast. Caleb is surprisingly a good dancer.

The dance had ended and only the family was left at the dance hall. The DJ was packing up and only Casey and Chloe looked fired-up. Caleb sat down by a chair beside me.

"Let's go," he said in a tired tone.

"Are you sure?"

He nodded, "I'm tired. There's no music. And you look horrible." I dropped my jaw as if I was offended but I knew exactly what he meant. "Kidding."

"I know."

I didn't know what happened, but one minute I was sitting in the chair the next I was in Caleb's arm and out the door. I couldn't control my laughter.

"See you later guys," he said as we walked out the door.

"Congrats!" I tried to scream back to them. I faintly heard a "Thank you" come from Chloe.

Caleb plopped me in the front seat of his Challenger after planting a kiss and smiling as if he'd defeated an army. He jogged around the front side of the vehicle and got into the car.

He leaned his head and flashed me another smile.

"What are you so happy about?"

He laughed and only kept driving.

"So, are we going to my house, or yours? I'm tired. I need a bed."

"Well," he thought, "yours. Mine is going to be quiet. Is that guest bed ready for me?"

"Sure is. And my bed is screaming my name."

He laughed and tightened the grip around my fingers.

The house seemed quiet for a Monday. Too quiet. Mom was at work. Andy was out at his farm. Both of my grandma's are in a thing called Bible Study. The boys, including Caleb, were at baseball practice, getting ready for the first big game tomorrow night.

It was a beautiful June day. The kind of day that I love to lay out and tan. With the house too quiet and me being all alone, I changed into my swimsuit and headed out to the back yard to tan. I had my phone in hand and the towel in the other.

My phone vibrated like any other time it would have. But this particular time, it was the killer.

'All right, so it's so much easier with GPS. You're lucky that I don't have the money right now and/or a car! And, with the cops looking for me at every state line. Damn you're good. You've got three weeks. I'm COMING FOR YOU!'

I sighed and shut my phone; the police got the message.

The sun was hot, and the breeze was humid. I felt good in my new swimsuit.

"Haven't talk to you in forever."

I jumped at the sound of the voice coming from beside me. I looked over at Toby walking over across his backyard and into ours.

"Toby?" He wasn't wearing his glasses and his acne cleared up. His hair was gelled and he looked good! The whole ripped and faded jeans and the polo matched!

"What's up?"

"Just sun tanning." I was speechless.

"Where are your boys?" He sat down feet away from me. I was uncomfortable, so I grabbed my tank top and pulled it on.

"Baseball practice."

He nodded, "I see. How's your summer going?"

"Slow. But fun. What's better than no school?"

He was silent, "Nothing."

"Honestly, sometimes I forget you're over there."

"Yeah, I usually stay in the house. I saw you guys leave. Where'd you go?"

"Minneapolis. Caleb got me Twins tickets and we went to one of their games. Then we went shopping. It was fun."

"Sounds like it."

We lay on the grass looking at the sky.

"Honestly," he said in the silence, "I miss you in Chemistry. Before you came, I was quiet. You could probably tell."

"Yeah."

"Anyways"—he smiled as I've never seen before—"there's this girl."

"Toby!" I screamed with a smile. "Can I tell you this?"

"Sure."

"When you walked over, I had no idea you'd look like *that*. Toby, you look *hot*! I'm serious!"

He started to laugh, "My sister came to town. Said I needed a makeover."

"Well, you look good. So," I inched closer to him, "who's the girl?"

He shook his head, "From another town. But she's gorgeous. Nice. Smart, too. When she laughs...man, she takes my breath away..."

I couldn't help but smile. The look in his eyes was unbelievable. He wasn't the Toby I met in Chemistry class. No. He was much, much more. His personality came out, finally.

"...and her eyes, they are gorgeous. Her voice. Am I boring you?"

I hadn't realized that I had drifted off.

"No, I was just thinking. When do you get to see her next?"

"Soon, hopefully." I heard a voice calling for Toby. "I better go. Good to see you again."

"You, too. Good luck with, um?"

"Abby."

"Abby," I repeated.

"Bye."

I watched him until he crossed the yard and disappeared into his house. Seeing Toby reminded me of another friend I hadn't seen in awhile.

Chris.

I threw on my shorts and put on my tennis shoes and decided to go for a little walk. I knew exactly where I was going. But, didn't really know the exact way. I hadn't been to Chris' house since the night with his mom. This would be interesting.

I noticed the familiar features of his house. Prior to ringing the door bell, I froze. Just as my finger was about to press the button, the door swung open. Chris' smile was wider than I've ever seen it.

"Sara! What a surprise! What are you doing here?"

"I was just thinking of you and I was home alone, thought I'd pay you a visit."

"Well, come in."

I remembered the features of his house. It all seemed familiar. It seemed as if we were alone.

"How are you doing?" I asked.

"Hanging in there. You?"

"I'm good. How's your mom doing?"

"Good, actually. Doctors are pleased with her progress."

I sat down on their couch.

"That's good."

"Yeah."

We sat in silence for awhile, my eyes wondering around the room.

"How have you been?" he asked. "You look great as always."

I looked down sure I was blushing, "Thanks. I'm good."

"We should hang out sometime soon before this summer ends."

I laughed. He was the same old Chris. His dimples showed and his curly hair was gelled.

"Of course. But I better go."

"Okay," he sounded glum, "I'd ask you to say hi to Mom but she's sleeping."

"Be sure to tell her I say hi, though, okay?"

He nodded and as he stood up, I felt myself wanting to hug him, which I did. He smelled the same. He felt the same. He *was* the same.

"It's been too long since I've seen your smile, Chris. I'm really happy I came over."

"Yeah, too long. I'll call you soon then, when I'm not busy. First sign of free time I'm calling you."

I looked back one last time before I took off jogging down the street.

"Bye, Sara!" he yelled down the road.

"See you!"

Caleb's birthday was days away and I was still scrambling for a gift idea. It was hard to find something for him. Whenever I'd ask, he'd always say he had everything he needed. I'd have to surprise him. He'd never see what hit him.

Then I remembered.

With his birthday in a week, I had a lot to do. I made some phone calls and ordered off the internet. I was positive he'd like it.

His present arrived right on time. I wrapped it up in a pretty box and put a bow on it. I laughed at my present for him.

I prayed that Caleb's birthday present would a success. I had backup if it wasn't, but I was sure that Caleb would like anything that I got him.

"Mom?" I hollered down the stairs the night before Caleb's birthday.

As I walked into the kitchen, she wasn't there. I proceeded into living room and into her room. She wasn't in either of those. I looked outside and found her digging into the ground in the backyard. A garden? Mom planting a garden? Strange.

"Mom?"

"Yes, my dear?"

She wouldn't take her nose from the dirt and her hands kept on busily working.

"I burned my hand on the stove."

"Well, that's good. What's new?"

"Mom."

"Yes?"

"Mom!" I screamed.

"What?" she said smiling finally looking at me.

"Did you hear me?"

"Yes, you said you bought sand colored gloves."

"What?" I laughed.

"I'm sorry, dear. I'm just busy with this garden. I thought we could use fresh vegetables for this fall. I'm all ears."

"Okay. Caleb's and Penny's birthday present? All things set and ready to go?"

She smiled knowing what I was talking about and nodded.

"All right, I'm going out to their house as soon as I talk to Caleb tonight. When he's on his way, I'll be on *my* way."

"Sure thing."

'caleb robert pierce?'

I waited for the phone to beep that the message had been sent. Then, when it did, all I could do was wait.

His reply, 'what's up?'

I replied, 'can i see you tonight?'

His reply, 'most certainly. my house or yours?'

I replied, 'mine please.'

His reply, 'okeedokee. i'll be there in fifteen.'

I replied, 'okay.'

So far so good. My plan was working. When ten minutes was up, I would take the opposite route to Caleb's house, the back roads, and go talk to his parents about his present. I had already warned them about it.

It was nerve racking to walk up those steps not to see Caleb, but to see his parents. And for a reason I had a hunch would upset them in a way. I knocked on the door as lightly as I could.

Melanie answered with a smile, "Come in. We've been waiting."

"Thank you."

I twiddled with my thumbs while we sat around the table in silence.

"Sara?" Robert asked. "What's on your mind?"

I looked up to their curious faces full of anxiety wanting to know what I had on my mind. I had to get it over with. I had to tell them. It was for Caleb.

"Okay," I sighed with a deep breath, "for Caleb's birthday I have a little surprise for him. But, I needed your permission. And, believe me this is wild. But, do you know where..."—Robert's gaze made me stop—"...where..."

"Where?" Melanie asked still patient waiting for my answer.

"Where their parents are?"

"Whose?"

"Caleb, Penny, and Chloe's."

Melanie looked at Robert and a hint of a smile showed on her face. But I couldn't tell whether she was happy or sad. I wanted to go back in time right then and there. I realized what I had said hurt them to an extreme.

Robert looked at me and nodded. It was the first time since I've met him that I had noticed his eyes. They were green! Pure green. Resemblance to Caleb's.

"Robert, your eyes..."

Robert looked away as soon as I said that and looked down.

"Maybe, this isn't right. I shouldn't have said anything. It's just that Caleb said that if he wanted anything in the world he wanted his parents, or at least find them. And I thought I could help, but this isn't any of my business."

I started to get up and I heard the little whispers from Melanie and Robert.

"Sara," Robert said stopping me.

"Caleb really said that?" Melanie asked with curiosity in her voice. I nodded. "Then we can tell you. We wanted to wait until they were older. We didn't think they minded it. But,"

Robert finished for her, "Since Caleb brought it up, seems like it'd be the best time."

"I don't understand."

Melanie laughed, "I'm 38 years old. *That's* old to me." Her soft chuckle was funny. "I made a mistake when I was younger. My mom hated me. *Hated* me. It was awful. But there was nothing I could do."

"We were in love," Robert said with a smile. "I'm 41 so I was out of school and well into my first year of college. I invited Mel to a college party. She wanted to go." He looked at her like he was looking at a million dollars.

"Man, college parties. What a difference from high school parties! They just don't slow down." She shook her as if trying to stop the memory, but then she laughed. "Robert introduced me to some wicked stuff. We were young and thinking back, I shouldn't have done it."

"But looking back," he said directed for her, "we made the right choice and look what we have now! I wouldn't trade them for the world."

"We got married before I graduated high school. The look on my mother's face wasn't good. And, oh, Robert and I wanted kids. We tried, but the doctors said it wasn't possible."

I didn't understand. That means, "They aren't your kids," I said out loud realizing.

Robert shook his head, "My younger brother looks just like me. He had a beautiful wife."

"Gorgeous," Melanie added.

"He was a bad kid. Always doing something to get in trouble with. One night he woke me up late by calling me in college. He kept saying he made a mistake. He said he had sex."

Melanie said, "He was a senior in high school. This was after Robert and I got married. So we were living together and attending college. Robert was a senior in college. Ross cried to Robert on the phone saying how his reputation was ruined and how he couldn't keep this 'thing.'"

"That's when Chloe came along. Madison, their mother, didn't want to keep Chloe, and since we couldn't have kids we wanted her. We were happy with Chloe. She was a perfect baby. I was so proud to be a dad. Then..."

"...then, Ross, Robert's brother, called *again*. She was pregnant again. And, when the babies were born, I knew I wanted them, too. Caleb and Penny. Poor Madison, she didn't know what to do. She didn't want kids, yet. She loved all three of her kids, but she didn't want them because of mistakes."

"Melanie and I talked about it for hours and decided we could very well take them in, too. Ross was beside himself. He had three kids and he couldn't help it. He was ashamed, embarrassed. Mother wasn't happy, but she still loved him. And, when she heard we took them in, she was ecstatic.

"Ross and Madison got married years after their graduation but moved away from us. They were scared. I really haven't talked to them since."

Silence fell over the room. I didn't think this would be the outcome of his birthday present. Now thinking of everything, I didn't want to tell him. What if he were to be angry with Melanie and Robert and it would be my fault?

"I'm sorry," I whispered.

"For what?" Robert asked sounding shocked.

"For this," I looked up at their curious faces. His eyes were so, *so* green! "I'm sorry." I hung my head low again.

"Sara," Melanie said quietly moving closer to me, "you would have found out sooner or later. We were going to tell them. We couldn't pretend to not know where their parents are. It's okay."

"Are you sure?"

Robert chuckled, "Of course."

"Then, can I ask a question?"

"Shoot," Melanie smiled as she spoke.

"Robert, tell me where you two got those beautiful green eyes from."

He smiled, "It's a family thing. Our grandfather, father, and now my brother and I and Caleb. It's in our genes."

"So, Caleb's dad has them, too?"

"Sure does."

"I'm thinking I'll just go with plan B for his present."

"Plan B?" Melanie asked.

I took out the gift box. "He *also* said he wanted one of those expensive watches. I hope he likes it."

"He'll love it."

"One more thing, so, you are their aunt and uncle?"

They smiled and nodded.

As we said our goodbyes, I knew Caleb was waiting for me at my house wondering where I was. For all he knew, I went to get groceries for my mother.

"So, with all that information, Sara, what do you plan to do now?" Robert asked in the doorway.

I shook my head, "It didn't turn out like I thought it would. I don't want to tell him. You guys tell them when *you* want to. They're your kids. And, once again, I'm sorry."

All Melanie could do was smile and shake her head, "Don't be."

"One more question?" They both nodded with smiles.

"Will they ever meet their parents?"

Robert answered before Melanie, "When they are ready to."

"Thanks, guys."

"No problem," Melanie answered, "Now, go have fun with Caleb."

Caleb's Challenger was sitting in the driveway along with Andy's car on the other side. Who are they to think they can take my spot? The sun wasn't as high as it was when I had left for the Pierces. The temperature wasn't 90 degrees anymore either. I walked into the house without a trace of what news I had just gotten. I would have to keep that one to myself.

"...July 3. I have plane tickets for everyone. I want you all to come." Caleb's voice came from the kitchen. It sounded like they were talking about the premiere.

"Hey, everybody," I said entering the kitchen.

"Hey, doll," Mom said.

"Hello, Sara," Andy said in the most dreamy voice. *Good for Mom,* I thought. Andy was perfect for Mom.

"Anyway, Cadie, you are all welcome. Obviously not on the Red Carpet with Sara and me, but to the movie."

"Thank you, Caleb. I think we all need a vacation."

Cole laughed, "Definitely, I'm in!"

Mom laughed, "Okay, so I'll just have to book tickets for..."

Caleb shook his head, "I've got that under control. Your hotel, plane, everything is ready for you. We are also staying at Topanga Beach. I thought it'd be a nice welcome home gift. We leave bright and early July 3. The premiere is July 5. That should give us enough time for things."

Mom sighed, "Can I *seriously* let you *do* this?"

A soft chuckle came from Caleb, "Of course."

"Okay, then, we'll talk about it more when we get closer to the date."

"Of course. And besides, *I* have a date right about now."

Andy chuckled, "Have fun."

The smirk on Caleb's face told me to run. I took off up the stairs as fast as I could, but I could hear Caleb coming behind me. I screamed and ran into the game room but realized I was trapped.

"You can run, but you can't hide." He blocked the doorway with a grin across his face.

I could only let out a scream as he grabbed me and picked me up. He was headed for my room. He threw me on my bed with a thump, harder than he planned. He laughed.

"Sorry, did I hurt you?" he asked between breaths and continued to laugh.

"Nah, just a few cracked ribs and a broken foot."

He chuckled, "Oh *I'm sorry*." And he tickled me.

When my laugh attack was over and Caleb controlled himself, things calmed down.

"All right, Caleb, it's your birthday tomorrow."

"What? It *is!* Why didn't anyone tell me?" He said jestingly slamming his fist into the bed.

I gave him my best fake annoyed smile, "Anyway, I have a surprise for you. If it's nice out, can we go swimming at your dad's lake?"

"Sure," he said with a nod and smile running his fingers through his hair. "That would be nice. I could bring the jet skis out, too. I have two of them. It should be nice outside."

"Okay, so noon?"

"Absolutely," he agreed with a smile. He leaned down and kissed me. He laughed and stopped.

"What are you laughing about?" I reached up for another kiss before he could answer.

"The way you screamed."

I punched him in the arm with force, "I had the fear of someone chasing after me!"

"You sure do," he laughed continuing to kiss me.

"As much as I would love to stay," he said in between kisses, "I better go hang with the family."

"Okay, don't forget tomorrow."

"Of course not."

As soon as Caleb stepped out the door, I had to act quickly. I had a plan to surprise Caleb with all his friends at the private lake with a fire and barbeque. I called Melanie and Robert first to ask permission.

As soon as they said yes everything, I texted all our friends from school inviting them out to the beach tomorrow. I invited around forty people. Everything was set.

Andy was glad to let me use his grill. He even offered to cook the food. With everything going as planned, I was more than awake on his birthday. Although my first birthday present for him didn't go as planned, I had something else he wanted.

When Melanie and Robert told me about Caleb's mom and dad, I couldn't stop thinking about it. If and when Chloe, Caleb, and Penny found out, who would they love? Melanie and Robert or Madison and Ross? It would be hard for me to choose. I couldn't imagine what it would be like.

I texted him as soon as I woke up.

'Happy birthday, my love!'

His reply, 'thank you!'

When the time was for the party to begin, Mom and Andy headed out to the lake with all of Caleb's friends and waited for us to join them.

Penny was busy with James this morning, so I thought just a simple happy birthday would be good enough. The surprise in some ways could be for both of them, but it was mainly for Caleb.

'happy birthday penny. don't forget the lake this afternoon.'

She replied, 'thanks! we'll be there.'

I texted Caleb when I was ready.

'are you almost ready?'

His reply, 'sure am. my vehicle?'

I replied, 'please.'

His reply, 'i'll be there soon. i'm leaving now.'

I jogged out the door as his Challenger pulled up. I tried my hardest to keep my composure clear so Caleb won't figure it out. I had my bikini on and a tight tank top with shorts. I was ready for a day in the sun with my best man.

"You look great." He smiled wide and sped down the road while grabbing my hand and placing his fingers in between mine.

"Ready for some fun?"

"Of course. I took the skis out there yesterday afternoon. It's all ready for us."

"Happy birthday." I leaned over the middle counsel and kissed him on the cheek.

"Thank you. And you missed."

"I'll aim better next time."

"Can't wait."

I got a little jumpy as we went on the windy curves into the part of the lake. Vehicles were lined up the rest of the way. Caleb's expression was priceless. He was more than confused. I could only keep a smile on my face. I couldn't help but wonder what was going through his head.

"What the—?" he said when he saw all the people standing by the lake. A smile spread across his face as he parked the car.

"Surprise!" I exclaimed before more words were said and got out of the car.

"Surprise!" Everyone shouted as Caleb stepped out of the car. His expression was adorable. He couldn't help but smile.

His basketball buddies came up and high-fived him. They headed towards the water all running. Caleb stepped back and grabbed me and flung me around and around in the air in his arms. I could tell he was happy.

"Thank you, Sara." His kissed me on the lips with happiness. "Nice aim." His ripped off his shirt and headed toward his friends. His six pack of abs was amazing. His hair blew in the wind as he jogged down to the water. A perfect picture which made my mind go wild. He was *hot* and he was mine.

I could see Melanie and Robert were dressed for the sun as they walked over to me.

"Good party, Sara," Robert complimented.

"Thank you, Robert."

"The smile on Caleb's face is priceless," Melanie said with joy.

"My thoughts exactly."

I saw Jordan pull up. I hadn't noticed that he wasn't part of the group with the other boys.

"Hey, Jordan, what's up?"

He smiled and shrugged, "Nothing much. Hanging around." He, too, was dressed in just his swim trunks.

"Ready for some fun?"

He smiled wide, "Of course." He looked at the empty jet skis. "Race you to the skis."

And I took off before we settled it. I quickly jumped on one with Jordan jumping on the other.

"I think I beat you," I smirked.

"Yeah, you did. How have you been?"

I sighed, "I'm all right. In all honesty though, I've been getting threatening text messages from the guy who ran into us and killed my dad. He's angry."

"Really?"

"Yeah, but I'm good. How are you?"

"I'm all right. I went to the doctor's office..."

"Hey, Jordan!" Caleb said interrupting Jordan's sentence. "What's up, man?"

"Nothing much."

They exchanged looks and smiled. By the smirks on their faces, I could tell this wasn't going to be a nice easy ride.

"Sara, you riding with me or Jordan?" Caleb asked getting onto the Jet Ski I was on.

"I'll stay with you, just don't dump me off!"

He laughed but didn't say anything. Before I knew it, we were splashing through the waves. I grasped my arms tightly around Caleb's strong stomach. But Caleb stopped with a jerk.

"I forgot life jackets."

He spun the ski around and headed towards land. With the life jackets securely on, he took off once more. But with the life jacket wet, my hands were slipping. I couldn't get a grip on his life jacket.

And, without a notice, I was feeling all wet. And cold. I was in the water with the waves pulling me every other way. Caleb and Jordan were zooming out of sight, so I started to swim after the shock. But then I saw the skis come back for me.

Caleb cut the engine when he got near.

"I'm so sorry, babe!" He jumped off the ski and swam over to me.

I could only laugh. "I'm okay. That was fun."

Caleb helped me onto the ski and sat *behind* me this time. But, he controlled the speed and everything else. I could hear him laugh when the Jet Ski would jump too high and turn sharp. I saw Andy waving us down.

"Are you hungry?" he whispered in my ear while kissing my neck.

"Starving." I turned around and saw him smile and I kissed him.

"Let's go, lovebirds," Jordan said as he splashed towards the ski.

Caleb grasped the wheel again, but I wanted to drive. I turned around and smiled gesturing towards the wheel. He willingly took his hands and moved them to be around my waist. I grabbed on to the wheel the pushed the throttle in too quickly. Both Caleb and I jerked back.

But with Caleb's help we made it safely to the shore where food awaited us.

Everything was going well. Caleb was mingling with his family members and friends. I sat down by the shore and dangled my feet in the water. I thought I was alone but realized I was soon joined by Penny.

"Hey, girl," she said sitting down next to me. "What a party you have here."

"Thanks. He looks like he's having fun. Happy birthday, Penny."

"He is. Thank you." She paused and looked back at Caleb talking and looked at me. "I miss you, Sara. What has summer done to our friendship?"

I laughed, "I guess lessened it. We'll have a lot of time to hang out at the premiere. But I miss you, too, Penny."

She looked down, "Caleb told me about the guy who keeps threatening you. That's scary."

"Yeah."

"Well, you know I'm here when you need me."

"I know, and I miss our nights. By the way, where's James?"

She gestured toward the crowd, "Talking with the boys."

Melanie yelled from the other end of the dock, "Girls! Cake!"

"We better go wish the birthday boy happy birthday," she sighed and got up while helping me up.

"Penny?" I asked as she turned around.

She turned around and I flung my arms around her and whispered, "Thank you."

"For what?"

"Still being my friend. I love you, you know?"

She laughed, "I'll always be your friend. And I love you, too. Now, let's go eat cake."

"...Happy birthday tooooo you! And mmannyy morre!"

The sky grew dark and the fire was started. Some people left but most stayed. Andy had brought marshmallows for roasting. Caleb talked with people but never forgot about me. He always had the time to come find me and plant a kiss.

When everyone but his parents, Penny, James, Mom and Andy, and Cole had left, we sat around the fire reminiscing.

When everyone was quiet, I thought it was the perfect time to give my present.

"First off, I want to wish Caleb and Penny a happy birthday. For my birthday, Caleb got me Minnesota Twins tickets and brought me my friend my California. When I first met him, he asked me what I wanted more than anything in this world.

"I said in my mind my dad, but I knew that was impossible. So I said Twins tickets. Then I asked him and he told me what he wanted."

I handed him the wrapped present. His eyes lit up as he saw the expensive watch.

I smiled, "He wanted a watch. Armani to be exact."

"Sara," he said speechless, "this is too much."

"No problem."

"Thank you so much!"

When the fire was out and everybody left but Caleb and me, that's when I had him alone. We were cleaning up the last bits of paper when he came over and hugged me.

"I can't believe you remembered. But," he stopped turning to face me, "it's too much. I didn't mean it literally."

"I know, but it's what you wanted. I thought you deserved it. You've done nothing but continue to make me smile and laugh day after day. What more could I want?"

He smiled and kissed me, "Sara, you're everything *I* want."

And, standing there in the moonlight, I knew he meant it. I knew he truly loved me. Because in all honesty, I truly loved *him*.

And, as I kissed him in the moonlight, I couldn't help but smile. His arms wrapped around my waist. Our feet buried in the sand. My knees feeling weak. What more?

Why did I ask? My phone vibrated the dreaded ringtone.

I reluctantly took out my phone and read the message. Worst one yet.

'You chose north dakota? edgemont? well i'll be there soon. i hate you and your family. you'll regret this. you shouldn't have sued me, you couldve just accepted that your daddy is D-E-A-D. DEAD!'

I sighed and shut the phone which was taken from me by Caleb. Caleb read the message and put the phone in my pocket and continued to kiss me. For some reason, I wanted to kiss Caleb to forget the message. It was a perfect day and a perfect night. Why did he have to text again?

Would these messages ever end?

CHAPTER SIXTEEN

the street

"He's never going to stop!" I found yelling got my rage out faster than anything else.

Mom's eyes were droopy and disappointed.

"Sara, you know there's a cop out there watching us. He's not going to find you!"

"Ah, Mom," I mumbled as the tears started to come down my cheeks, "I dream about him. I think constantly of his messages. What did I ever do? It was *his* fault! He killed him!"

"Sara," Cole whispered softly and took me in his arms.

I couldn't take it. I fought against the hug. I broke. I exploded. But Cole only held on stronger. I punched until I couldn't punch anymore. Cole was still holding me with his strength he had.

"I'm sorry," I whispered when I could regain my focus.

He just shook his head.

"I miss Dad so much," I cried. "I miss him so much."

I heard Mom break, too. I was hurting her. I needed to pull it together to help my mom. She was hurting. Because of me! Everyone was hurting because of me! And, yet, there was nothing I could do! This man was ruining our lives!

"I'm sorry, Mom," I looked up at Cole and looked at Mom. He nodded and let go. I headed over to Mom and wrapped my hands around her. "I'm sorry I'm hurting everyone. If I hadn't..."

"Sara, you didn't do anything. This man, this man is doing it all. Don't think you did anything wrong."

"Mom, he knows we are in Edgemont. We have to leave."

She shook her head, "We'll be leaving soon for California. We won't be here long. Sara, there are cops out there 24/7. Don't worry." She sighed, "Don't worry."

I needed my guitar. I needed it now. I didn't care whether they could hear me or not. This was the only way I could let my feelings out. It wasn't even a song. It just came out.

There was a knock on the door and in walked Penny. I was surprised to see her here. My face was drenched with tears when she walked in. I quickly put the guitar down and under my bed.

"You play?" her voice sounding surprised.

"A little."

"And that song? Yours?"

I shrugged.

"It's beautiful and your voice. It's...amazing!"

I shrugged, "It's nothing."

"Nothing!" she huffed disagreeing, "It was beautiful!"

"Aw, Penny, thanks but," I stopped, "it's just a way to release myself." I still didn't look at her and my voice was dry.

"Okay. How are you doing?" Penny asked.

I shook my head and remained silent.

"Caleb is at baseball practice along with Cole and James. I'm the best that'll do, I guess, for right now."

I had to laugh, "Sorry, Penny. I didn't want you to think that I didn't want you. I do, trust me. It's just...hard."

She sat down beside me and fell back on the bed.

"I know."

"But I don't want to be sad. What's up?"

"Well, Nadir has been asked to be on a TV show. They want him to go to California early. Early as in two days. Can you guys still come?"

I was shocked but excited. "Of course. Actually, the sooner the better. I need to get out of Edgemont. He said that he's coming here soon." I screamed into the pillow. "I didn't do anything."

"He's just stupid. Of course you didn't."

I sighed, "Is Nadir's co-star going to be there?"

She smiled, "Lie or no?"

"No," I mumbled.

"Yes. She's going to be there the whole time. But they'll be looking at you, the fresh meat." She giggled and rolled over. Rolling a little too far, she fell with a *thump!*

Laughter fell over both of us. I couldn't control my laughing. It was just too funny not to laugh. Penny was laughing her hardest down on the floor and had troubles getting up.

"Ouch," she said getting up and laughing some more.

I calmed my breathing as well as I could.

"Penny, would you like to spend the night?"

She grinned, "I thought you would never ask." She got up and walked towards the door.

"Do you have to go..." and before I could finish, Penny had her bag for sleeping over in her hand. I laughed and shook my head at my brilliant friend.

"Penny, do you want to find your real parents?"

She looked at me with wondering eyes.

"Yes and no. If they didn't want us, they didn't want us. I love my mom and dad. Why you ask?"

"Well," I hesitated, "Caleb told me a long time ago that he would like to know who his real parents are. It shocked me."

"Oh."

"I'm sorry."

She shook his head, "Don't be. Don't you think I think about finding them every night? But what if I found them and I loved them more than Mom and Dad? I just couldn't do that to them."

There was silence as Penny was rummaging through my nail polishes.

"Penny, how did Caleb get to be Nadir?"

She stopped and sat up straight on got comfortable.

"He always had a thing for acting. He was so annoying when we were little. Dad got him an audition and they loved him. But Dad was worried about his life being too glamorous. They came up with Nadir."

"I guess we both had the same thing on our minds."

"Yeah. Ever since then, he's been famous. I've never really gotten jealous. The way girls flock over him." She smirked at me. "The way wherever he goes he can't help being hounded by the photographers and girls. I don't want that. Maybe the boys, though."

"Yeah," I chuckled, "the boys would be nice."

"Anyways, yeah, Caleb was thrilled about it. But he enjoys being just Caleb, too."

"I still can't believe no one's recognized him yet."

"Well, you didn't recognize him when he walked in with that wig."

I smiled, "Yeah. I'm just a blonde though."

She paused and glanced up at me with wondering eyes. Worried, almost. Full of curiosity.

"What about you and your dad?"

"It was so long ago. I'm not saying that I don't miss him. I miss him more than ever. But I'm used to it. You know, no dad around. I would give anything back to have *him* back. You don't know the feeling. It's empty. Like there's a hole in my body that left when he did.

"He was my best friend. He'd sit with me when I was sick. Maybe because I was his only girl. Whatever it was, it was strong. Gosh, I loved him. His smile. And his eyes. Not as bright as Caleb's but they were blue. Man, they were blue.

"The look in his eye before we crashed. He was about to say that I'll do great. That's when, well, you know the rest. I guess I've survived by my mom's love. And Cole and Cameron's, of course. But his love will never be quite there. I know he's here, of course. But, yeah, I'm good otherwise."

She was speechless, just shaking her head as if in shock.

"How do you do it?"

"Time goes on. And I never give up."

She smiled, "That's a good reason."

We didn't sleep until well into the morning. It took awhile to catch up on the things that we've missed out while we both were busy. We continued to laugh all through the night. Penny kept the same smile on her face all night long.

I woke up to Penny still sleeping. I heard loud murmurs down in the kitchen. As I walked down the stairs into the kitchen, I saw the detectives and Deputy Smith sitting around the table with concerned faces. One unfamiliar faces was there, too.

"There she is," I heard Mom say as I walked into the kitchen. Her eyes looked beet red and her hair was a mess.

"What's going on?" I asked.

Detective Smith turned around and gave me a weak smile. He motioned me to sit in the empty seat next to him. I hesitantly sat in the chair with all eyes on me.

"Sara," Detective Smith sighed with a big exhale, "he's in North Dakota."

My heart skipped a beat. I couldn't speak. I just shook my head.

"In Edgemont to be exact," Detective Benson corrected.

I buried my face into my hands. Warm hands were around my back rubbing it. I kept shaking my head. I didn't want to cry because Penny was upstairs. I had to stay strong for Penny.

"We want you guys out of here as soon as possible. We'll watch your house when you're gone, but you guys need to leave." I looked up at the unfamiliar voice.

It was a man wearing a much too expensive suit to be working in Edgemont. As much as he tried to hide that bald spot, he couldn't with his hair pulled over it.

"I'm Captain Morgan. Head of this whole scheme. This guy has shown what he can do. He's very smart. He got away once, he won't get away again. We promise."

I continued to shake my head.

"She's in shock," Cole whispered behind me. He was the one who put his hand on my back. "Will we be okay for a few hours?"

He nodded, "We are going to triple the cops. There will be three surrounding your house. We will be watching. Nothing will happen. Just leave."

"What about Penny?" I asked finally with my voice low.

They looked at me in confusion.

"Penny. How will she get home? Get her home safe!"

"Penny is her friend," Mom added. "She's sleeping upstairs."

Detective Benson answered, "I'll take her home."

"Take me with. I need to talk to Caleb."

I tried to act as calmly as I could when I walked into the room. Everybody downstairs had left, but when I looked out the window, the cop cars were still surrounding the house. Penny was still asleep on the floor when I walked in.

"Penny? Wake up."

She twisted and turned before sitting up and stretching. "What a night!" she exclaimed.

I tried to force a smile on my face, but with all my effort I couldn't. Penny obviously noticed because her once happy expression turned into complete fear.

"What's wrong?" she cried. "What?"

"He's here."

She shook her head, "Who?"

"My dad's killer."

"Where?" she quickly asked and sat up.

"In Edgemont."

She sat there in silence.

"He's driving around looking for our house. He doesn't know where it is. We are to leave immediately. So Detective Benson, or was it Smith, I can't remember, said they'd take you home." I shook my head. "I'm sorry this turned out this way."

"Don't worry," she said while packing up her stuff. "Let's get you packed."

We threw in clothes that would last a month, and I threw in some important things. My hair products, makeup, toiletries, and many other things were stuffed into my gym bag.

My suitcase was filled to the brim when I was done with everything. I put in important pictures of family and friends. I had to laugh at the two large suitcases and one large gym bag. I am a girl, what can I say?

Penny was more than ready to go when we walked into the kitchen. Detective Benson was very anxious to leave and get back.

"I just got off the phone with Melanie," Mom said as we approached her. "They are getting packed and we are all going to California early. I think they said Hollywood. Or they said they'd be more than willing to stay in Topanga Beach where Caleb usually stays."

"Even them, too. Caleb?"

Mom nodded, but her face remained worried.

"Andy is coming, too."

I heard a car door slam and as I looked out the window, I saw Andy carrying luggage with him.

The car was silent on the ride to Penny's house. The only time I spoke was telling the detective when to turn. I didn't want to talk. This wasn't the time.

I wiped the tear that fell from my eye and squeezed my eyes right to keep the other tears in. I couldn't break now. Not when I would be seeing Caleb and his family in minutes. I didn't look the best, but I didn't care. Caleb would accept me either way.

"I'll wait out here," Detective Benson said with a smile.

The sun was shining high in the sky. It was hot out. In the police car, the thermometer read about 95 degrees out. I was dressed in shorts and a tank. The blue sky was endless with no clouds anywhere.

I paused and looked at Caleb's house. I hadn't realized how homey it was. Melanie had flowers on the steps and a 'Welcome' mat outside the door.

Frozen, Penny startled me, "Are you staying outside?"

I shook my head and walked through the door I've walked through many times before. The scent of fresh linen was there just like it was every time I hugged Caleb. I could hear voices coming from the living room.

"Home!" Penny hollered loud enough it could be heard throughout the house.

I heard the footsteps and laughing as Caleb walked into view. When he saw me with Penny, his smile was wide.

"Didn't know you were here," he said puzzled.

"Thought I'd come to see how you all were doing. And," I stopped to look at the faces, "to apologize."

"Apologize?" Robert asked. "For what?"

I sighed and looked down at the floor and fiddled with my shoe as I mumbled, "All this. Making you guys leave early."

"Sara," Robert whispered with a chuckle, "we want your safety more than we feel the need to stay home."

"Of course," Melanie added. "This is a bonus—to leave early."

I looked up to all the Pierces smiling. The mood softened and Robert and Melanie were back to talking again, heading up the stairs towards their room.

"I better go pack," Penny said, going after them.

I stood in the door way feeling somewhat ashamed to have Caleb's family suffering for me. I couldn't look at Caleb's expression. I didn't have to know what it looked like.

But then he laughed, "You should have heard Mom. She was excited to get out of here early." I heard his footsteps grow nearer and then I saw his black socks in my view. He wrapped one arm around my waist and with the other lifted my chin up so we were looking at each other.

Then his warm lips soothed me.

"I'm so scared," I cried, stopping him. "He's in Edgemont! He's within a mile of me! I just can't stop thinking that he could hurt my grandmas. Or he could have sneaked in the back yard and got in somehow and finished..."

"Sara," Caleb whispered.

I continued, ignoring him completely"...the job right then and there. He could've done whatever he wanted to. He's where he wants to be. He's here. I wonder..."

"Sara," Caleb whispered a little louder, tightening his grip around me.

"...what kind of weapons he has. What if he looks up my grandmas? Ah, I couldn't handle myself if he killed *them* and not me. Horrible."

"Sara!"

He had the hint of smile in his eyes. I sighed and breathed in his scent of linen.

"Are you done?" he chuckled. I nodded. "Everything will be okay. It will be *okay*. The police aren't going to let him hurt your grandmas. We are leaving in a matter of hours. We'll be okay!"

I moaned, "How can you always make everything better?"

His soft laughter made me smile. He shrugged his shoulders and kissed me again.

"Okay, are you calm yet?"

I smiled and knew what I wanted. I shook my head and he kissed me again. I willingly wrapped my arms around him and kept kissing him.

Everything went away. Even though we were standing in the doorway, I was happy. I was comfortable. I didn't want him to stop. And I didn't want him to let go. I wanted to stay like this forever.

But as we heard his parent's voices get nearer, he stopped and I settled for holding his hand. All three had large suitcases in their hands but all were also smiling. I thought they'd be angry about all this. Obviously, they were not.

"Why can't we stay in our usual?" Penny whined as they walked down the stairs.

Robert looked as if he was thinking about it. "I suppose we could ask for two extras."

Caleb said behind me, "I could easily get us two extras. I'll just have to make some calls before we leave."

I was still confused. I had no idea what they were talking about.

"Wouldn't you have to be Nadir the *whole* time then?" Melanie added. "Do you really want to do that, dear?"

"Well, they wouldn't notice me if I didn't wear my wig the whole time."

"What about Sara, though?" Penny asked. "If you two were lovey-dovey and they saw you when you were wearing your wig, and then they saw you and Elise? It could get bad."

"She'll just have to only appear at the premiere. She'll be Sara the rest of the time." Silence fell over the room as I continued to take in the previous conversation. "But," Caleb continued, "Nadir *could* have his own room, then I'll just sleep with you guys."

Melanie nodded, "That's what I was thinking."

Speechless, I added laughing, "Can anyone tell me this conversation?"

They all laughed in harmony with Caleb telling me, "Where we should stay. I go to the same hotel every time because I get a discount and they know me. Oh, wait, I did make reservations at Topanga Beach," his attention turned to his family. "Forgot, sorry,"

"Well," Robert cleared his throat, "we are ready, then. We don't want to hold you guys back."

I smiled, "Let's go, then."

Andy was loading up his car, which was a four door, when we pulled up in Caleb's Challenger. I didn't want to sit for two hours on the way to Fairview to the airport with my mom and her oh-so-dreamy-too-good-looking-of-person-to-be-that-old boyfriend.

Melanie, Robert and Penny went ahead already to arrange the flight plans. I was to ride with Caleb while Mom, Andy, and Cole rode together. I had a feeling though, Cole would get his way and ride with us.

"Please?" he begged as I gathered my things and put them in the trunk.

"If you don't mind squeezing in the back."

"Oh! Thank you!" He walked up behind me and picked me up and swung me around and around.

"Cole! Put me down!"

I could hear Caleb laughing in the background.

"All right," Detective Smith said walking from his car in the trees, "you guys better go before he drives by and sees you guys leaving. Have fun."

Before I got into the car, I had to do one last thing. I ran over to Detective Smith and hugged him.

"Thank you," I whispered.

I looked up and he smiled, "No, thank you. Be safe."

"I will. Watch my house for me."

"I will."

"Later alligator."

He smiled, "After while crocodile."

I laughed and got into Caleb's car and waved good bye to my detective friend. I blasted the music for the first couple minutes, but Caleb's hand turned it down.

"Are you okay?"

"Yeah," I sighed. "It's hard to leave the house behind. But I have faith in Detective Smith."

I could hear Cole laugh, "Can you relax and just have fun, Bug?"

I nodded and closed my eyes.

Cole and Caleb talked about the baseball team and how "angry" they are about leaving. I wanted to apologize for it, but I bit my tongue realizing they wouldn't have been so willing to leave. Boys. They can have the most pointless conversations for what seems to last for hours. My phone lured me into curiosity. I wanted to text Lili, but I wanted it to be a surprise. She's surprised me now more than once and she deserve to be surprised.

I decided to text Penny.

'boys and their sports. how are things going?'

Her reply, 'haha good we have 9 tickets, is that enough?'

I replied, 'yeah, that's just right.'

Her reply, 'first class, too.'

I counted on my fingers that there were eight of us going. One extra ticket. Not another surprise for me.

I replied, 'oh penny you guys shouldn't have done that. but there's one extra'

Her reply, 'it's okay. i like first class:) that's a surprise for your whole family'

I replied, 'really? what would that be?

Her reply, 'can't tell you, but ur going to thank me.'

I replied, 'okay. well we are about 15 minutes away.'

Her reply, 'did cole come with u to?'

I replied, 'yes, they are talking only about sports!'

Her reply, 'haha hang in there. you're almost here!'

I replied, 'i will see you soon. i'm sitting by you!'

Her reply, 'my thoughts exactly!'

"...Did you see the opener?" Caleb asked Cole.

"Yeah, that was wicked. Poor guys. Get their butts kicked."

Caleb chuckled in disgust almost, "That was pathetic."

"Yeah."

"But, they're doing better," he quickly added.

"Yeah," Cole huffed, "after how many years of us waiting on them."

Caleb laughed, "Yeah, even through all that though, they are still hanging on."

"Better be."

Typical boys. I stared at the billboards and remembered the games we'd play. Get through the alphabet with all the billboards before you run out. Usually, we won.

"'A'," Cole said from the backseat.

I turned around and smiled.

"'B, C, D, E.'"

"'F!'" Caleb yelled.

"'G, H, I!'" I screamed.

Cole laughed, "'J.'"

Caleb added, "'K, L, M, N, O.'"

"'Q!'" I screamed.

Caleb and Cole broke into laughter.

"What?"

"It's supposed to be 'p,'" Caleb said laughing.

"I knew that," I said blushing, "'P, Q, R, S, T.'"

Cole chuckled, "Sure. 'U.'"

"'V.'"

I smirked, "'W, X, and Y.'"

"'Z!'" we all screamed as we saw the billboard reading 'You'll surely catch your z's!' I laughed at their excitement.

"Cole, I was just thinking back when we used to play that with Dad. We'd always win."

"You'd cheat."

I blushed, "Only sometimes."

Caleb chuckled.

"Only because you were daddy's little princess."

"Yes, and you were daddy's little prince."

He smiled, "And Cameron was his little king. I know."

Fairview was big. The shopping mall was the biggest in North Dakota. Fairview has around 91,000 people. That's big for North

Dakota. I've only been here to get my prom dress and even then the city was too big for me.

I was anxious to go back to Topanga Beach and see everything that was my home. I had so many things that I wanted to do. First thing on my list was to see my dad's grave. I wanted to buy flowers, balloons and everything else for a welcome back. I wanted to see his grave so badly.

I would sit by the tombstone and cry with the flowers for him in hand. There were days where I would sit and cry no matter who was staring at me. There was nothing else I *could* do. That was how I was close to my dad. I'd get up after hours of crying and bounce back and return smiling when I got home.

I visited his grave daily, whenever I had time to start the engine of my car and drive. I would talk to him. People probably thought I was losing it. But, I talked anyways.

I recall one moment when a stranger came up to me.

He was about my age...

"Who are you talking to?" he asked in an almost disgusted tone.

I looked up at him teary-eyed, "My dad. He just doesn't reply."

He sat down beside me, "What happened?"

"Drunk driver accident."

He nodded, "My sister, too." He motioned to the headstone two feet away from my dad's.

"I'm sorry."

He shrugged, "She chose to drink."

"My dad didn't have a choice."

"Sorry about that, too."

I shrugged, "I'm still alive."

He got up, "I have to go. I'm Bobby by the way. I'm sorry about your dad."

"Sara, and sorry about your sister."

I clicked back to reality as Caleb pulled the car to a stop in front of the airport. I heard Cole talking to Mom in the backseat explaining that we were already there.

"Penny is waiting inside with Mom and Dad," Caleb said, "but she told me to have you guys wait out here for your mom and Andy. She doesn't want to ruin the surprise for you."

I sighed, "Why am *I* the only one always getting surprised?"

He laughed, "That's not true. You are about to surprise Lili. And my birthday, you sure surprised me."

"Well," I protested, "lately I've been surprised."

He laughed, "You like it."

I could only blush and kiss my boyfriend.

I had to blink again just to focus who was really standing beside Penny. I didn't think he'd be able to come. He lied and said that he had to work.

Cameron.

Cameron was standing next to Penny with a wide smile on his face. I ran into his arms.

"I can't believe you're here!"

His soft laugh echoed in my ear. "Hey, Bug."

"Ready for fun?"

"You betcha."

"I'm happy you're here, Cameron."

He smiled and headed towards the plane.

I hadn't flown before. We've driven everywhere. Mom isn't much into flying, but somehow we got her onto the plane without a fight. First class was luxurious. The hours weren't that bad in the plane. Penny kept me pretty occupied with her chatting the whole time. Caleb was lazy and slept in the seat next to me, along with Cole and Cameron next to him.

"Please stay seated as we are landing in just minutes." The lady over the intercom was too perky for this time of day. It was afternoon and I was tired and hungry. I didn't show my attitude to Penny, though. She didn't seem crabby at all.

Penny leaned over and whispered in my ear, "You slap Caleb and I'll slap Cole. This'll be fun!"

"On my count. One. Two. Three!"

Caleb sprung awake, eyes wide open. And Cole flinched but didn't wake.

"Hit him harder," I instructed trying to hold in my laugh.

As Penny was going in for another one, Cole's arm shot straight up and caught it. His large hand squeezed Penny's tiny wrist.

His eyes opened wide and his smile was a smirk, "Did you think I wasn't awake after the first hit?" He laughed and released her. He yawned and stretched, lightly punching Penny in the face as he did. "Oops, *sorry*."

Caleb was laughing on the other side of me.

"Sorry, hon," I said feeling bad.

He just laughed, "I'm sure you are."

"Same old Sara," Cameron chimed in with a deep laugh.

The welcome sign at the edge of Topanga Beach felt like home. I was home. The stretch limo that carried us all caused a little distraction, but it was nice to be all together. Everything looked the same. I saw the tree that I ran into when I first got my license. I saw our old Grandma's house still up for sale.

Then, my heart stopped.

"Stop!" I screamed without a warning. The limo slowed down and down came the window from inside.

"What's wrong, Mr. Pierce?"

Caleb looked at me with confused eyes, "I don't know, just pull over please."

The window went back up.

"Mom. Don't you remember?"

They looked at each other and shook their heads.

"It's the road!"

Silence fell over the limo. I looked out the window and avoided a major breakdown. The stares were too much.

"Honey, maybe it's better if we drive through there. It's been eight years..."

"Mom, I'm just not ready."

"Okay. Caleb?" Mom said, obviously gesturing to Caleb to have the driver turn around.

"Driver? Please turn around and take a the long route to the hotel."

I could see everyone's confused faces all staring at me. But I could only look out the window and look down the street where my dad and I once lain not knowing the outcome. This was the street I was driving down to get my auditions. This was my life. This is where it all started. My home was my nightmare. Now I realized why we moved.

Caleb tightened his grip with my hands. As I looked out the window again, this next street looked familiar. When I saw it, I was happy. It was my street. Where my house was. The limo stopped outside my house and parked in the driveway.

"Why are we stopping here?" I asked.

Melanie smiled, "We thought you could use some happiness for a little bit."

"It's still for sale?"

Mom nodded with a smile. She held up familiar looking keys and dangled them in front of my face.

"After you," she said with a smile.

Excitement ran through me. I jumped out of the limo and sprinted to the house. The key slid into the lock with ease and the door opened with a creek. The blast of the scent startled me. It smelled the same. It smelled like my home.

I noticed everything. The stairs. Kitchen. Living room. Up the stairs and into my room. My room. It was nice to see it again. The marks from Lili and me were still there. It was just how I left it. But then I wondered.

How come it still wasn't sold?

This house was beautiful, beach side view. It wasn't too expensive and with the ocean and beach behind it, who could resist?

I inhaled the sweet scent of my home. I heard the quiet sounds coming from the kitchen. All were waiting for me as I walked down the stairs.

I exhaled, "I'm ready."

"Are you sure?" Mom asked.

"It's nice to be back, but this isn't my home anymore."

She smiled and nodded.

"I miss it," she admitting pausing while leaving.

"Yeah."

Cameron nodded, "My room. Dad's room."

"All the memories," Cole added. "The night we came home without him."

"That was awful," I answered with remembrance. It was quiet and lonely. We slept on the couch and all were snuggled close together that night.

Mom smiled, "We made it, though. Look at us now!"

"Happy as can be," I agreed.

"You guys are a wonderful family," Melanie said quietly over in the corner. Robert and Penny were smiling with tears in their eyes.

I nodded with a smile.

"Everything you guys been though. It's amazing."

"Yeah," Penny nodded, "I don't know what I would do without my dad."

Everything was familiar. And I had to laugh as we passed Lili's house as she was standing outside staring at the stretch limo passing her. Little did she know her best friend was riding in there. I knew I'd see her soon.

The hotel was one that I'd stayed at before. But I had never stayed in the suites. They're for 'famous' people only. Nadir Remerez would be part of that. It was weird to think that *he,* Caleb, was more than likely to be staying at the same hotel with me.

Andy and Mom were flirting in the corner of the limo. He had his arm casually around her shoulders and they were laughing. They were enjoying each other. I just couldn't get used to it. The googly eyes that they made me sick. But to know that she was happy was all that mattered.

I knew I wouldn't be leaving the limo being Sara, I would leave as Elise. And, in ways I was excited. But, in others, I was scared. The thought in the back of my head was the fear of someone noticing me.

My daydreaming stopped when I heard rummaging around. Caleb was fiddling with his wig as he pulled it out of the suitcase. Melanie sitting near him was swiftly applying his makeup. I was astounded by how fast *my* Caleb turned into the mysterious Nadir. I honestly couldn't speak.

"Sara?" Robert said grabbing my attention.

I turned my awareness to him and noticed he was holding up the wig I had chosen. It was dark, brown, and long. I smiled as he offered the wig my way. I switched spots with Penny and in a matter of seconds, I was Elise. Melanie had finished with Caleb's makeup and moved onto me. I didn't know what I looked like, but, as I stared at the looks of my family, I knew I didn't look like Sara.

Melanie smiled and nodded as the limo lurched to a stop. I heard a door slam outside and then the door open beside me. Caleb stepped out and I scooted towards him.

"Hold on," Penny shrieked with a smile holding up a mirror, "I want you to see how wonderful you look. No one will recognize you, I promise."

I didn't know *who* was in the mirror, but all I knew it wasn't me. The wig had bangs, which covered up my scar. The long locks of hair fell well past my mid-back. It didn't look like a wig at all. And my makeup wasn't at all what I would normally wear.

Melanie was smiling and nodded. Cole and Cameron looked speechless. Penny had a smirk on her face, as if she knew this is what I would look like at this whole time. Andy was just smiling in the corner of the limo.

"Wow," I found myself expressing without thought. My words were wrong, though. I didn't want to sound smug, because it was the opposite feeling. I was in shock.

"Ready, Elise?" Caleb smiled outside the limo door in the bright sun light of California. I could see the flashes of cameras and hear the hollers of the paparazzi.

"Just don't talk and be sure to smile!" Melanie instructed me as I started to get out.

I nodded at Caleb's prompt and was on my way to the first appearance as Elise.

CHAPTER SEVENTEEN

facing the fear

"Elise! Smile!"

The shouts of the men with the cameras were annoying and the flashes hurt my eyes. Caleb's arm was wrapped around my waist leading me into the hotel main lobby. However, I couldn't help but smile. This is what I was waiting for!

"Nadir! Your woman is *hot!*"

I didn't lift my head as I heard that comment. But I had to smile when the doors of the entrance closed and we were finally alone.

"Ca—Nadir, is it always like that?" I asked as quietly as I could.

He nodded and smiled.

People watched us cross the lobby and the quiet murmurs surprised me. It was weird. People were talking about *me.* Me! I couldn't register it in my brain when they were smiling and pointing at Nadir and me.

"Welcome, Mr. Remerez. Good to see you back."

The woman at the front desk was too friendly and too welcoming. Her smile wasn't a welcoming one, it was one of flirting. But with Caleb's hand firmly in mine, I knew he was *mine.*

"Good to be back. I have reservations." Caleb's voice was dreamy, welcoming, and pleasing.

"Yes, three rooms?"

"Mhm."

My mind wandered. Caleb was sweet talking the front desk and with all the eyes on us, how could I not wish to be invisible? Did I look that different that no one recognized me? I just couldn't believe it.

Is this what Caleb did every time he went out in public? How could he handle this? This was not something that I would want to do for a living. I can see *why* he would want to be two different people. Famous life was too stressful.

There was a boy with his eyes popping out of his head staring directly at me. He was squirming around in his seat while his dad read the paper. I turned around to focus on Caleb. But I felt a tugging on my pants.

I looked down to the boy whose eyes once were far away. He couldn't be more than ten years old.

"Can I have your autograph?"

I could only stare at him in disbelief.

"You *are* Elise, right?"

I nodded and picked up the pen his held in his hand and scribbled my name on the paper. His smile was broad as I handed him the paper.

"Thank you."

I smiled, "You're welcome."

He pranced over to his seat, his eyes glued to the sheet of paper with ink on it.

"Good job," Caleb whispered in my ear tugging on my waist towards the door. He opened the door into the flashes and hollers and slid his fingers between mine.

"Cute couple!"

"She's a keeper!"

"Thanks for bringing her out of the cage!"

The limo door was opened waiting for us to climb in. I almost leaped in to get away from the hollering paparazzi. And when I heard the door slam, I relaxed.

"How was it?" Mom asked before I could regain my thoughts.

I sighed with a smile throwing my back against the seat, "Amazing."

Caleb's soft chuckle confused me. And, yet, I knew why he was laughing. I couldn't talk. I froze inside and just did what Caleb told me to do.

"Okay, Mom, I have these two rooms set aside. I called them in. You should be able to get the discount that I did. And I have a connecting room with you guys. It'll be easier. We'll just have to be sure that only Elise and Nadir walk out that room."

The words went in one ear and out the other. I was on cloud nine. Even though the comments were rude and some were okay, I still *wanted* to go back out there. It was exhilarating. There was a rush of excitement. It couldn't be better than this. It was nothing what I thought it was going to be.

"Elise?"

Caleb's voice interrupted my thoughts and I looked at him standing outside the limo patiently waiting for me to respond to him.

"Ready? Round two," he said with a smile.

I took his hand and once again was blinded with the immediate flashes of the photographers. I blocked out the comments this time, not hearing a single word. I only heard the hum of Caleb's happiness. So this is what Caleb is like when he is famous. The same. He is himself.

He's not cocky. Smug. Quiet. Loud. Anything. He's the same Caleb that I've known all along. And to think I had thoughts he would be different.

"There," he said once we were inside the hotel again. "You did it."

I sighed, "I can't believe it."

Caleb looked confused.

"You're you!"

He tilted his head in more confusion and raised his eyebrows.

"You're the same. I expected you to be, well, a *snob*."

He chuckled with his whole body. He couldn't control his laughter. I couldn't believe it. He snorted! And then he laughed more!

"What are you laughing at?"

He couldn't breathe. He couldn't contain himself. So I just took off up the stairs. But soon I felt his arms around my waist and his warm, soft lips against my neck.

"Can we get to the room before we...?" Caleb's lips stopped me from finishing the sentence. I released my lips and started to walk up the stairs. Caleb's fingers interlocked with mine until we reached the room.

With the door securely shut, Caleb's lips were immediately on mine. I thought back to the first time he'd kissed me and said it was his first kiss, too. Which was hard to believe since his kiss was perfect and getting better every time he kissed me.

I reached to yank off my wig but Caleb's hand stopped me. His lips stopped and he shook his head.

"Not yet."

He continued to kiss me with passion, almost. His arms were around me, his hands moving with his lips. In ways, I didn't want to do this. I wasn't ready. I knew he wouldn't go too far, absolutely not. But was more than making out okay? I felt good when we kissed, but when it became more, I didn't know *how* I felt.

And yet, with everything telling me to stop, I didn't want to. The darkness in the room, his sweet smelling breath, the cologne coming off of him, and his arms around me. And then I realized. I wasn't kissing Caleb. I was kissing Nadir. And I was Elise. Why couldn't I take the wig off?

And I was in awe again. My mind wandered from us kissing. It was unbelievable how fast Caleb changed. He didn't look like him. He was, of course, still beautiful, hot, handsome and any other adjective you can think of. But, in my opinion, he was hotter in his regular hair.

I laughed out loud to my last thought.

Caleb released me and looked at me with a smirk on his face. "You stopped me with your laughing. Humor me."

I chuckled, "You look hotter without the wig."

He smiled and continued to kiss me. After a moment, he added, "You look gorgeous either way." He started to move towards the bed. "Although, I do miss your blonde hair." We inched closer and closer to the bed. I tried my hardest to fight against him pulling me down to lie on the bed.

But he got his way. Within seconds, we were on the bed. Caleb reached down and wrapped his hand around my waist, reaching underneath my shirt to rest on my skin. His hand was smooth and wonderful in many ways, but his touch made my heart jump.

But, luckily, a knock sounded at the door. I jumped up a little too eagerly and headed for the door.

The gang was standing in the hall as I peered through the peep hole.

"It's the rest. I thought they couldn't use this door."

"They can't. I'll let them in the other door." He smiled and kissed me on his way out, "I'll be back."

Finally in privacy, I darted for the bathroom. Again, I was in disbelief staring into the mirror at the girl who wasn't me. She was gorgeous. And yet it was me with layers of makeup on and a totally different hair-do.

I played with it for a moment. The wig easily went into a pony tail. And it felt like real hair. My makeup was different in so many ways. The eyeliner was thicker. I had bright eye shadow on, not to mention the mountain of cover-up.

I jumped at the knock on the door. Penny came waltzing in with a smile on her face.

"Mind-boggling, huh?" Her voice was just as impressed as I was.

"Yeah." Again, I didn't want to sound smug. I just wanted to sound shocked. "It's incredible. I mean, in a matter of minutes I turned into her. Me. *Whoever* I am. Thank you."

She laughed and tugged my arm. "Sit, I'll help you take it off."

"But Caleb..."

"Do you want to be Elise all day?"

I shook my head with a smile.

"Okay, sit still. Then you, and only you, have a special place to go."

Where? Penny took off my wig and put it on a mannequin face on the bathroom counter. I hated surprises. I have been surprised one too many times. She wiped my face clean of makeup and allowed me to put my own on.

When I looked in the mirror again, it was me. Sara. It was good to be back.

"Now, we'll have to change your clothes. You and Elise cannot wear the same thing. I packed an extra suitcase for her. But we'll have to get you a stunning dress for the premiere."

I just nodded and followed her out of the bathroom. She threw jeans and a T-shirt at me and I quickly put them on.

"There is a car outside waiting for you. Use the front lobby doors. Go! Before Caleb can sneak in and steal you again. It's a pink car. You won't miss it."

I was hesitant, but with Penny's help, I was pushed out the door. I jogged down the hallway and pushed the elevator button. The elevator was empty so I jumped in. The top floor of a five story hotel wasn't the most convenient.

Sure enough, a bright pink car stood out in the parking lot. A new Charger. Thanks, Penny. I jumped in with people immediately staring at me. I started the car quickly and knew exactly where I was going.

Driving past Lili's house, I zoomed down the street. I passed my house without a glance back at it.

Barbara's Flowers was still open from when we lived here before. She was a sweet old lady who became my best friend in my years of living here. We had become quite close. When I left, it was a sad good bye. I knew she'd recognize me. Actually, I hoped she would. I had shopped there for all my flower needs. The familiar bell on the door rang when I stepped through the door.

And I saw her.

Barbara's eyes lit up. Her smile couldn't have been bigger. She dropped the flowers in her hand and started to walk towards me. Man, she hadn't changed. She was still as short and as wonderful as can be.

"Sara, my dear!" she screamed while tears streamed down her face. "You came back!"

"Of course, Miss Barbara. I've missed you!"

She wrapped her arms around my waist and squeezed the air right out of me.

"Oh, darling, I've missed you, too. You look just beautiful."

"Thank you, Miss Barbara. As do you."

"Well dear, what can I help you with?"

"Flowers, Miss Barbara. Biggest bouquet you have. I need to pay a visit to someone special."

She smiled and disappeared behind the wall. Her little shop was the same. Smelled like roses. All the little antiques and knick-knacks were still on the wall.

"Here you go, Sara. It's good to see you. Please come visit again before you leave. How long are you staying in town?"

"About a month."

"Really? Well, be sure to stop by again."

"I will, but Miss Barbara, how much for the flowers?"

She shook her head with a smile, "On the house, child. God bless. And, say hi to your father for me."

I smiled, "I will, Miss Barbara. Thank you."

Same old Miss Barbara.

I knew the road like the back of my hand. It was burned into my brain. I knew I was right when I reached the 'Memorial Graveyard' sign. I stopped the car and reached for my cell phone to turn it off. I didn't need anyone right now except my daddy.

Luke Robert Young

November 24, 1958-September 24, 2003

Loving father to Cameron, Cole, and Sara

Loving husband to Cadie

I set the flowers down in my usual spot and made myself comfortable. I prepared myself for the waterworks.

"I've missed you. I hope these flowers are good enough. Balloons are overrated, right? Isn't that what you've always said? North Dakota is good. Colder than here but good. You know Caleb, he's amazing. I miss you. Terribly. I think about you constantly. I love you. I always will."

I looked at my name carved in the stone along with my brothers' and mom's. If people only knew who we were. I shook my head, knowing that my talking like this was crazy.

"Still talking to yourself, I see."

The voice I couldn't recognize, but that line made me wonder. I turned around to a boy my age smiling. I couldn't recall who he was however.

"Don't remember?"

I shook my head, "Sorry."

"It's all right. It's Sara, right?"

I nodded.

"Bobby, remember? My sister is dead over there with the drunk driving?"

He pointed to the headstone feet away. It came back clearer now. I remembered perfectly who he was. He thought I was crazy the day I first met him and started to talk with my dad.

"Yeah," I chuckled, nodding, "I'm still talking to myself."

He laughed and sat down beside me. "I haven't seen you here in a long time."

I mumbled looking down at the headstone again, "I moved to North Dakota."

He nodded in understanding, "That makes sense."

"How are you doing?"

He was nodding his head and gave me the look 'I'm all right with having a dead sibling'. He was picking the grass and throwing it in every direction. "You know, life goes on. I miss her more each day."

I looked at my dad's grave and repeated in agreement, "Life goes on."

"You look different."

I laughed, "Thank you?"

He smiled, "In a good way."

I wiped my forehead as if to be in relief that he meant in a good way. Bobby only smiled and stared into the sky.

The minutes seemed to tick by because I don't know how long we were there. We didn't talk. And, we were the only ones in the cemetery. My gaze went from Dad's tombstone to Bobby's sister's.

The sun was high and hot. I had almost regretted slipping into jeans before I left.

What would life be like without alcohol? Well, of course, Dad and Bobby's sister would be alive. Plus many of the others who were killed from alcohol, whether they did it or if they had no choice. What would the teenagers think about that? They shouldn't have it in the first place.

And, yet, life might not be good without alcohol. But I sure wouldn't mind. I'd give anything to have Dad back and in my arms. It'd be nice to know that he was there when I needed one of his famous bear hugs.

I didn't notice that the tears were streaming down my face. I could picture his bloody face in my mind. I saw what he looked like the last time I saw him. I remembered.

I remembered.

I'm alive.

"I better go," I mumbled looking back at Bobby.

He smiled and nodded, "Me too."

We sat there for a couple of awkward seconds. I jumped up too fast and stumbled, but laughed as Bobby caught me. I needed to leave immediately. I realized how late I had stayed out. People were probably freaking.

I spoke unclearly afraid to ask, "I have to go. But can I have your number?"

Shocked as I was, Bobby nodded, handed me his phone, and I typed my phone number in his phone. I gave him my phone and he typed his number into my phone.

"Keep in touch. Tell me how your life is, okay?" His look of confusion was priceless, but I had to go.

He nodded, "I will. Good to see you. And Sara?" He asked quietly as I was walking towards the car. "Take care. Life goes on!"

I smiled and repeated, "Life goes on."

My phone had two messages when I turned it on. One from Caleb and one from the guy. Would he ever stop? He had my house, what else did he want?

Caleb's read, 'I see Penny let you out without me. haha. be safe. love you!'

The killer's read, 'this is very disappointing, Sara. i came all the way to see you and you go back to california. hm. well, at least i know where you are. hows home? don't worry, i've been keepin tabs on your dad's grave. he's still there. dead.'

My finger went straight to the lock button without thinking. I quickly turned the car on and headed for the hotel. My makeup was ruined and I was warm. Too warm. And eyes were all on the bright pink car that zoomed past them.

Thoughts ran through my head like shooting stars. Fast. All the days I went to go see Dad in the past came down to this. I didn't see my dad's grave for months but someone else had. And he didn't even like my dad. Why would he do this to me? I wonder if he went into my old house and rummaged around. What kind of person is he? Doesn't he have a family?

All the paparazzi were still there with the cameras glued to their faces. I was preparing myself for them but realized I wasn't Elise. I smiled and got out of the car and literally jogged into the lobby. They didn't even glance my way. I sighed in relief.

Caleb was sitting in the lobby when I got in. He didn't look happy. He had his head resting on his hand and his eyes closed.

I sat down beside him hesitantly and gently placed my hand on his knee. He jerked his head up and smiled when he saw me. Then he grabbed me in his arms like he was worried about me or something.

"Sara," he sighed still holding onto me. "He's not in North Dakota anymore."

I nodded.

"What? You know?"

I nodded again.

"Did you see him?"

I shook my head and showed him the message. He mouthed a swear word and I could only imagine what was running through his head. He pounded his fist into the chair.

"Caleb," I whispered, "if this is too much for you, then you can..."

He raised his voice louder than I expected, "Can what? Let him get you and lose you forever?"

I looked up to his eyes and for once I couldn't tell his emotion whether his was scared or angry. It wasn't readable. "Caleb, this is scaring me! Isn't it scaring you?"

"Of course it is," he mumbled with a sigh.

I cried out, "I'm putting you through so much hell!"

He got up, grabbed my hand, and headed for the elevator. When the doors finally shut, he finally talked. He wrapped his arms around my waist and smiled.

"You *are* putting me through hell…"

I had to interrupt. He had just answered me truthfully. "Then why are you still with me?"

"…but it's worth it! To see you smile. To see your eyes. That's what I live for! I love you, Sara. We're young, but I love you! I'd do anything for you. I'm not some super hero that will never get hurt and can protect you from all evil, but I'll do my best.

"If I ever lost you, I don't know what I'd do. I'd lose it. Sara, you are what I want! Always. Those little dumb but precious moments are what I live for."

I couldn't help but feel stupid. Caleb was pouring his heart out to me even after I yelled at him. I felt foolish. Ashamed. And the sad part was all that he was saying was the truth. We *were* young, but we loved each other. And he wasn't a superhero. He was human. And he finally cracked.

"You are my love. When I first saw you, I knew. That's what I'm talking about. I love you. Always."

I had to laugh, "You said that already. And forever?"

He tightened his wrapped arms around my waist and nodded, "Well, I really, really do. I'm going to stick by your side until this guy is locked up for good."

My mind told me not to, but my heart was screaming. I kissed him. And as I did, the elevator opened to Melanie and Robert standing there. They started to laugh as my cheeks changed from a classic ivory colored into a bright red cherry tomato.

"Hi," I said sheepishly.

"Did we interrupt anything?" Robert asked laughing.

Caleb shook his head, "The end of a stupid fight. The guy is back and is still after her."

Melanie gasped, "I'm so sorry, Sara!"

"It's all right. I'm used to it."

I hadn't slept well after the excitement that we'd been through. From the photographers to the grave and the message. We went to the mall and to a movie. Surprisingly, days flew by made plans to see Lili. Time just went by too fast.

I didn't think all the sights in California could keep my mind off of *him*. But surprisingly they did. I had plans to surprise Lili at the beach where I first met her when she first moved in. That was a lot of years ago and I'd hope that she'd remember.

The day was beautiful. I had it all planned out. I ordered more flowers from Miss Barbara. She'd received a bouquet of flowers with a note. The note said to meet someone special down at the beach.

I could hardly hold still as I waited for Lili to come. I knew it'd be any minute now that she'd come waltzing down the beach and scream because she saw me sitting there in our spot. The look on her face would be priceless.

This was the beach that I spent my life on. I sat in this same spot with my dad. I used to splash in those waves with him. This was the life. It was perfect.

Then, in the blink of an eye, it was gone.

Forever.

I could hear the little kids screaming as they got splashed with the waves. And I could hear the waves as they splashed the little children. This sound was familiar. And then I heard her.

"You surprised me this time!"

Lili was jogging down the beach, sand kicking up from her heels. She didn't have to think twice about tackling me as she hugged me with force. And I knew what that smile was for.

"Are you surprised?"

She laughed, "Of course I am! You're back!"

"Good, it's about time I surprise you."

"What do you want to do first?" She practically screamed the words.

"Sleepover?"

She shrieked, "You know me *so* well! Are you at a hotel?"

I nodded.

"So we sleep there or my house?"

"Your house. It's a girls' night!"

From when I left, Lili's house hadn't change one bit. In a way, I was happy. But, then again, it seemed like I was just here yesterday. The pictures on the way were still there from when I left her house almost a year ago. And her mom hadn't changed one bit. But I could start to see the bald spot on top of her dad's head.

Then there's Drew. I sat and painted my nails over and over again while they talked on the phone for two hours. Aside from that, it was a blast. But there was something different. Maybe it was the way Lili seemed to talk *only* about Drew and nothing else. She had never done this before. I didn't think my Lili could turn into one of those girls that can't shut up about a boy once they meet one.

And Lili sure was one of those girls.

But I still love her.

She *did* make me laugh all night long with her sappy stories about her and Drew. But the look in her eyes told me she was happy with him. More than happy. Ecstatic.

Then again, it was like I never left. Everything seemed so routine of how it was a year ago. The stories we told were us just reminiscing about the past. We did that every time we had a sleepover, though.

She gasped and covered her mouth with a smirk on her face.

"What?" I persisted. *"Lili!"*

She laughed, "Want to go on a mission tonight?" She went into her closet and pulled out black sweaters, pants, and gloves.

"What are you talking about?"

She smiled, "The guy that made fun of you. I know where he lives."

"Lili..."

"Oh, come on! You know you want to! We won't do anything, I promise. Just, you know, spy a little."

I sighed, "That does sound fun and *illegal!*"

She flashed me a smile and flung clothes towards me. I reluctantly put on the pitch black clothes with the 'I can't believe you're making me do this' look. She only smiled and got dressed. We sneaked down the stairs without a problem. I headed towards the door while Lili headed towards the kitchen. She opened the refrigerator and pulled out eggs.

"No! Put them back!"

"Shh! You're going to wake up my parents!"

I whispered in an angry matter, "Put the eggs back!"

She sighed and placed them back in the fridge. Before I knew it, we were standing in front of the guy's house. The light was on the second floor. I couldn't help but smile. Then, I heard something like a rock hitting a window. I looked to find Lili throwing rocks at his window. I quickly stopped her.

"Lili!"

She laughed quietly, "Shh! Here he comes."

As the window opened, we ducked behind the bushes and I couldn't control my laughter. Lili threw her hand over my face which made me laugh more.

"Who's out there?" His voice was divine, something I didn't think it would be.

We heard the window close and continued to burst out in laughter.

"That was—great!" Lili screamed when she was sure we were okay. But then we heard the front door open.

"Just come out. I heard a girl laughing."

"Lili, I just want to talk to him. See what he thinks of me, now!"

She nodded and laughed as she stepped out of the bush. I took in one breath and then followed her. And, there he was.

Man, what more to say? He was...well, can I say not hot? He totally changed since I'd seen him last. I mean, he wasn't in any way ugly, but he wasn't the jock he was before. From my view he had put on weight and the braces shined in the light.

He was the first to speak, but he sounded disappointed. "Lili?"

"Hey, Brett."

"Who's your friend?"

Lili and I looked at each other and smiled. I walked closer to him giving him the smile of a lifetime. He looked at me. He *stared* at me. Then his eyes lit up.

"Brace face?"

"Me, brace face? Yeah, who's the one with the wire on his teeth?"

He smiled, "I'm sorry."

"Do you even know my name?"

He shook his head.

"It's Sara."

"Well, Sara," he said gesturing his hands towards me, "you look hot. There I said it. I'm sorry."

I laughed, "Apology might be accepted but," and I winked at Lili and walked towards him, "I think you got something in your braces. Better go clean it." And, yes, I bumped into his shoulder! I've wanted to do that for *so* long.

He chuckled, "I guess I deserved that. Good to see you, Sara. You've definitely grown into a beautiful girl. You're going to make some guy really lucky."

"See you, Brett."

It was nice to get that off my chest. Lili caught up to me, laughing. She high-fived me and we ran the rest of the way home. Mission accomplished!

I could hear Lili rustling with something noisy in the morning. I yawned and stretched. But it wasn't Lili I saw when I woke up. It looked like Caleb from behind, but yet it wasn't his luscious hair. I looked to my side and there was Lili still sleeping. Why would Caleb be here? And, what was he doing?

"Lili," I whispered a little too loud and the good-looking hair guy turned around.

"Did I wake you?" he asked smiling.

"No, I mean, er, who are you?"

He whispered, "Drew."

That makes sense. Lili *did* say he was dreamy. Just not *this* dreamy!

"Sara."

He smiled, "I know. Coffee?"

I nodded and he pointed towards the door.

"Let me just say you scared the crap out of me," I said once we were alone in the kitchen.

"Sorry, Lili said she wanted me to be here this morning when she wakes up."

I nodded in understanding.

"You're all she talks about," he said sheepishly. "I only wished she'd talk more about me." He laughed as he took a sip of coffee.

"Oh, but she does! I couldn't get her to shut up last night."

"Really?"

"Yeah."

His eyes lit up and just stared into the room with a smile. I'm glad Lili has someone like this to take my spot while I'm gone. She needs this. She's beautiful. Her short curly hair is shoulder length now. She's still sparkly pretty.

My phone vibrated. It was Caleb.

'morning hope you had fun. but, we must get ready for the premiere darling. i'm having the charger be brought to you and we'll get dressed. see you soon!'

I totally forgot about the premiere today. We'd left without thinking about it. We were so preoccupied about dad's killer that I didn't think twice about the premiere. I looked up at Drew still smiling into nothing.

"Will you tell Lili that I had to leave and that I had a blast? I'll call her later tonight."

"Something wrong?"

I shook my head, "Family vacation."

"See you later."

And when I stepped out the door, there sat the pink Charger that catches everyone's eyes. I jogged to the car and saw Caleb's driver sitting there.

"Good morning, Miss Young." He smiled at me like we've known each other for months. "Mr. Pierce wants me to swing by and get your gown. Melanie and Penny thought you'd like it."

I nodded.

The driver pulled in front of a store that I'd passed so many times back when but never thought twice about it. For the fact that half of the items cost more than the car I'm driving in, it's scary. But the driver just tipped his hat and smiled as he walked through the door. In the minutes that he was in there, I stared into nothing.

First thought, what would I wear? This 'gown' that they'd bought me I'm sure was stunning. So that was out of the question. Then, my hair. It was a wig, what could they possibly do with that? Penny probably had the wig all ready for the premiere. Finally, talking or even smiling. There would be photographers and other stars there along with a 'nobody'. Caleb's costar would also be there. With my whole heart, I didn't want to meet her. I didn't want to see her. She was beautiful. And Caleb and she had so much chemistry during the making of the movie. And need I say that the movie is anticipated throughout the United States.

The car door opened, startling me. The gown was covered in a black bag. My eyes were curious.

"It's a surprise!" the driver warned as I hesitantly reached for the zipper.

"Don't move!" Penny screamed in my ear as she was curling my 'hair'. I could smell burning hair, and I saw the steam roll out from the curling iron.

"Are you almost *done*?"

"Stop whining."

"I'm not whining," I countered, "I'm just impatient."

Penny smiled, "Fine, you're done. What do you think?"

And once again, as I looked in the mirror, it wasn't me who was looking back. It was Elise. With Penny's hairdo, it was breathtaking. And, I really don't want to sound smug, but with all this happening to me, I couldn't help but be happy.

"The dress! The dress!"

Penny unzipped the bag and inside was the dress of my dreams. Deep, dark purple was lying in front of me. It was silky. And, as I slipped into it, it was form fitting. Exactly what I pictured, only better. I could tell by the smile on Penny's face that she was just as pleased. Now she *did* look smug. But in a good way.

There was a quiet knock on the door. Penny smiled at me and nodded, "Are you ready?"

"Definitely."

"Come in, Caleb, er, Nadir."

As Caleb appeared around the corner, his eyes sparkled. He smiled my favorite smile. I had been waiting long just to see that face.

"You look beautiful, Sara," he whispered as he hugged me.

"It's Elise."

He shook his head, "No, Sara, *you* look beautiful. Elise looks good." He smiled and pulled out the bouquet of flowers from behind his back. "Technically these aren't for the premiere, but they are for afterwards. Are you ready? I want you to meet someone."

Now, I didn't mean it, but my eyes rolled to the back of my head. I sighed and did the whole 'do I have to?' thing to him. He smiled and grabbed my waist with his free hand.

"She looks like a dog next to you."

As he whispered those words, I couldn't stop staring at his truthful eyes. Those exquisite green eyes took my breath away every time. He kissed me gently and pulled back.

"Be nice to her. She's willing to meet you. I bet she's just as happy as you are." He smirked and pulled me forcefully towards the door. I gave him the puppy-dog lip. He shook his head and continued towards the door.

He kissed me again, "Do it for me?"

I sighed, *"Fine."*

He pushed opened the door and there stood the dreaded co-star. The beautiful long, black hair was in ringlets that bounced as she turned around with a smile. She was just as beautiful as she was in the picture. And, I felt that knot in my stomach that I knew I'd get.

"Elise! I can't believe I'm meeting you! I'm Tonia." Her voice was much too fake to like. I wanted to gag. "You are even more gorgeous in person!"

I managed to spit out, "Nice to meet you, too, Tonia." I felt Caleb grab me tighter, a sign to be a little nicer. "You are pretty, too."

"Thank you. Are you ready for the premiere?"

"As ready as I'll ever be."

She smiled and winked at Caleb, "Well, I'm meeting you two there! Toodles!"

As she pounced down the hallway, I seriously wanted to gag. And, the wink she flashed Caleb. Hello! Wasn't I standing *right* there?

Caleb whispered in my ear, "Behave a *little* better next time, but not bad." He smiled and led me down the hall and into his famous-person life.

I managed to pull out a smile when the photographers flashed us at the hotel, but if that was mediocre, what was the premiere like? The limo was different than the one we first had. But the same smiley driver opened our door for us. I wonder if he had to sign the contract. I mean, he did know that Caleb was Nadir and that I was Sara and Elise.

Caleb grabbed my hand and held it tight. He didn't let go, although he didn't seem nervous. This was totally opposite of me, who was freaking out. I'm sure if it hadn't been for Penny reminding me to use special deodorant that I would have sweat a river. Which is disgusting for me. Then I looked over and Caleb, and he was just smiling.

As the cars started to pile up down the sides of the street, I knew we were close. It was a long drive from Topanga Beach to Hollywood, but it was worth it. The moment came down to this.

"Ready?" is all I heard before the door flung open and more cameras flashed. And that was the last time I would talk to Caleb until the movie actually started.

He seemed to be a pro at this. He stopped and smiled and waved at the photographers screaming his name and mine. I did my best to follow him and copy what he was doing. I smiled as much as I could, but soon it began to hurt. And Caleb never took his arm from around my waist, as if it was glued there.

Everybody screamed my name; I didn't know which way to look. It was a beautiful day. To explain everything would be hard, I would lose my breath. I was surrounded by famous people and stars. Some would say hi to Caleb and me, but others just walked by. I had to smile because these were the people I only dreamed about meeting and now I was walking on the same carpet as them.

Tonia, looking as radiant as she was, was smiling on the other side of Caleb. But I only heard her name a few times. I'd have to say that I heard mine more. Which surprised me. Tonia has been doing this for years. How could she just be ignored?

It seemed like we were there for just minutes, but it was longer than I thought. Caleb was leading me into the building before I wanted to go. He was smiling as we stepped through the door.

"How was that?" he asked, sounding a little worried.

I sighed and shook my head.

"You didn't like it. I'm sorry. I should have..."

"Stop. I loved it!"

He looked dumbfounded.

"I really did. It was more than I was expecting. It ended too soon!"

He laughed softly and made his way through the crowd. With the help of two men dressed in black suits, we made our way through the busy cinema. It was packed with people trying to find spots to sit. We were led to the balcony area. I recognized the familiar faces of stars that I dreamed of meeting. They smiled at me as if we've known each other for a long time.

And, then the movie started...

"...and the stars there just swarmed around us. And I was next to my favorite actor! Can you believe it! I mean, man, it was a rush." I couldn't help but scream the entire event to everybody. Mom and Andy were smiling and both happy. Cole and Cameron seemed annoyed, but I didn't care.

I ripped my wig off and fell back onto the bed with a *thud*. I smiled, "And the movie! Caleb was amazing. I've seen movies before, but this one was good. He did warn me when they were about to kiss, and I covered my eyes." I winked at Caleb sitting over in the corner still dressed in his tuxedo. He smirked while closing his eyes.

"And when the movie ended, it was the same. Flashes and screams and people. The people! I've never seen that many people in one spot. It was all incredible. Nothing I've seen before. I'd do it again without thinking."

Melanie laughed, "Well, it's a better response than you had right, Caleb?"

He laughed quietly and agreed.

Knock. Knock. Knock.

Penny grabbed me and yanked me into the bathroom. It all went by so fast. One minute I was lying on the bed, the next I was in the bathroom. She was fiddling with my wig. I heard whispers and doors in the room while Penny fixed my wig.

"Sorry I took it off."

She shrugged, "It's okay. Go ahead, get out. I'm staying in here."

"...she was there. She looked right at home." Tonia's voice was irritating as I could overhear that she was talking about me. "She looked..." She paused as she heard my footsteps.

"Hello, Elise, we were just talking about you."

I forced a smile on my face I as walked out of the bathroom nervous.

"I was just about to say how stunning you looked tonight."

"Thank you," I messed with my hair nervously, "I had a little help."

Caleb snickered behind Tonia and as she turned around I shot him the 'talk one more time and you won't like it' look. He smiled and nodded, "You both looked beautiful."

Tonia sighed, "Well, big day today. I'm beat. Good night, you two." She walked towards the door but whipped around with her locks of hair flipped through the air, "Nice to meet you, Elise."

"You, too," I said through my teeth with little enthusiasm.

As the door shut and as soon as we were alone, Penny burst through the bathroom door.

"That was close."

Caleb sighed, "Too close."

Once again, I flung myself on the bed and my wig fell off by itself. I let out one big sigh that went on and on. Caleb and Penny laughed in unison in the corner of the room.

"Penny, let's go swimming."

"It's late."

"Well, would one call from Nadir help that?" I smiled at Caleb who had a smirk on his face.

He sighed, "Of course."

The hotel gladly kept the pool open for Nadir's guests. He just requested that the pool stayed open for a while because he heard that guests were complaining that they wanted to keep swimming.

"I'll be back later."

Caleb kissed me and smiled, "Go have fun."

I started to leave, Caleb grabbed me by the waist and kissed me again. I didn't want to let go, but Penny was waiting for me.

"Thank you for all this. I know you didn't have to, but I'm glad you came."

I shook my head, "I wouldn't miss this for the world."

"I love you, Sara."

I kissed him again, "I love you, too."

"I'll be back later."

He smiled and nodded, "Oh, and get some towels for me. We're running low."

The feeling of tranquility I get when I sit in a hot tub was there while Penny and I reclined in the pool's hot tub. We weren't talking, just relaxing. But after an hour of in the hot tub, we were as shriveled up as prunes.

In the elevator, I remembered that Caleb needed towels.

"Caleb needed towels; I better go back and get them for him. I'll ride the elevator down again. Tell him I'll be right back."

Penny smiled, "Okay, see you."

And when the elevator beeped for the door to open on a different floor, I didn't realize that that would be the beep of my fate.

CHAPTER EIGHTEEN

missing in action

"Going to the lobby?"

The man asked with a warm, welcoming smile before stepping into the elevator. Well-mannered and pleasant, he smiled politely. Although well-built, he had worn-out over-alls on with one hook broken and his shirt was ragged with holes all over it. He had shaggy brown hair and a big nose. It looked as if he hadn't shaved in days. And he smelled terrible. But he smiled.

I nodded and moved as far away as possible.

I was uncomfortable wearing my bikini with a tight, wet tank top on and shorts. And the numbers seemed to beeped slowly. Within seconds, I felt something cool against my neck and his hand against my mouth forcefully.

"Scream or anything and I'll shoot you and others. Walk out with me and you'll live."

I tried my hardest not to panic, but my heart would have given it away. His grip was painful. The nose of the gun was pressed hard against my neck. And his once welcoming voice turned into a harsh, low growl.

"Walk out the front door."

I nodded and kept my cool. I couldn't break down and plead with him; I'd give him what he wanted. I could only pray that he wouldn't hurt me. I glanced up at the camera in the corner of the elevator and prayed that they saw him.

When the door opened for the lobby, he turned off the malicious expression and put on the nice-guy face. He put the gun into his overall pocket which completely covered up the gun. He smiled at the people who switched spots with us in the elevator.

He didn't seem to switch back to the evil side until we were completely alone in the parking lot. It was dark out and the stars were bright and high in the sky. But with his strong hand pushing against my back, I couldn't focus on the beauty of the night. I could only think about the pain and suffering that my family would soon be in when I didn't come back.

I felt the gun against my back, again. He pushed me into a compact black car. I couldn't tell the make. I guessed Ford because Dodge wouldn't have made something that square. And as he forced me in, I inhaled the scent of smoke.

I couldn't control my thoughts.

Just obey him, Sara.

Run!

No, he has a gun.

Maybe you can sweet talk him.

Be safe!

I had to laugh at telling myself to be safe. How could I control if I was safe or not? That was up to him. And who was he? I've never seen him before. Who could he possibly be? No one is mad at...

Oh, no.

It can't be.

I shook my head and counted out the days that we were in California. A little less than two weeks. That gave him more than enough time to get from North Dakota to California and still plan out how he was going to find me. And, well, he did it.

As he got in, I sighed, "I had a hunch."

He turned around with a shocked face, like he wasn't expecting my voice to be that calm and collected. He turned around to face the front only to turn towards me again.

"About?" He almost smirked, but caught it and frowned like he was angry. I had to laugh which made him even madder. "What are you laughing about? You just got kidnapped."

"The look on your face."

He turned serious and shouted, "Shut up! Talk again and you're done."

I sighed and slumped in my backseat. And, in a way, my heart was thumping louder than the bass drum in a band. But I had to stay calm. I didn't know what to do otherwise. My plan was to act cool, maybe he'd let me go.

I just couldn't believe that he got to me. I couldn't believe that he *actually* found me. Everybody tried their hardest to keep him away from me, but he did it. He got away from the police and kidnapped me.

I had to smile because I could easily unlock the door and jump out, but he was driving at least 70 mph on the highway now and I didn't feel like hurting my chances for next season's basketball. So I sat smiling in the back seat. I wouldn't be gone for long. Two hours tops. The elevator camera would see and I'd be safe and sound snuggled up to Caleb in no time.

"You know how hard it was to find you?" He sounded smug, as if he was proud of his accomplishment. "And why didn't you reply to my text messages?"

"Why *would* I? You killed my father!"

I could hear him grip the steering wheel tighter, "I did not. That was *not* my fault."

"Then whose was it?"

"His fault, he was at the intersection when it was my turn!" The anger in his voice scared me. He actually *blamed* my dad for dying, as if it was his fault. We were innocent.

I huffed, "Are you *kidding* me?"

He shook his head and took out a cigarette and lighter. Smoking is disgusting to me. Secondhand smoke smells and looks disgusting.

"Can you not smoke? I'm allergic," I lied. I kept my face smooth; I didn't want to inhale smoke just as much as I didn't want to be stolen.

"Oh, sorry." He put out the cigarette.

I sat there frozen. I could not believe he had listened to me! He respectfully put the cigarettes down and kept driving. Awe swept over me. A smile went across my face, but I immediately removed it before he could see it.

"Are we there, yet?"

"Shut up."

I sighed, "I just asked."

"And I just answered. Shut up," he growled.

So I sat there. It seemed like he was just driving around Topanga Beach for hours. He just went up and down the streets. In reality, though, we were gone for an hour. He parked the car alongside of the curb by an unfamiliar house.

But a familiar street.

The accident street.

"Remember this?" he asked satisfied.

He yanked me out of the car with the gun pressed heavily at my side. He had his hand securely tight around my arm. He led me to the grass past the marks on the street. There, the spot I was standing was the place I stood as I watch the firemen removed my dad from the car. There, feet away from me, was the sign with a big red X on it which marked the spot of the accident and where my dad had lain. There were all the memories that ruined my life.

He snickered, "Is it coming back?"

"It never left," I murmured with water swelling up in my eyes.

"Is that right?" He laughed to himself. "So you never forgot about the accident. And how I walked away. And your poor daddy died!" He laughed again so smug that I could feel the anger quickly boiling up. The tables finally turned. The wicked side of him came out, and I totally forgot the way he put the cigarette out.

"He suffered the last hours while I sat in prison. Isn't that wonderful?" I couldn't handle his chuckle anymore.

"Shut up," I whispered under my breath.

"What? What did you say? Shut up?" he asked egotistically. "*You* want *me* to shut up?" He chuckled one last time before he turned serious. He wrapped his arm tightly around my neck with the gun pressed up against my temples. "Talk to me like that again and your brains will be blown out and you'll lay right where you did eight years ago."

His arm was so tight around my neck. I couldn't get air. I gasped, trying to get air, but he was just too strong. My lungs wanted to collapse. *I* wanted to collapse. I could feel my knees getting weak and the stars came closer and closer...

When I opened my eyes, everything was all fuzzy. My head pounded with each breath I took. I couldn't keep my eyes open. I struggled for each breath as I forced it out. But soon I began to feel my fingers and toes move. I opened my eyes once more to make sure I was still alive. My throat was sore and I couldn't feel my neck with all the pain that I had.

I couldn't tell what I was lying on, but it was soft. I tried to move my body, but it was too sore and painful. The piercing pain up my back told me something wasn't right. It was too much pain to be normal.

I opened my eyes fully and finally saw everything clearer. The room was bright, one I've never seen before. I was lying on a soft bed. The curtains were pulled down past the window, but the sun was shining through.

But then I remembered. I wasn't in the hotel anymore. Dad's killer kidnapped me. He had wrapped his arm around my neck so tightly that he cut off my air supply and I had collapsed.

I jerked in the bed and tried to sit up, but I was tied down. Literally. My hands were tied up to the head board with duct tape, over and over again. My body was tied down with a rope. I struggled to break free but failed. There had to be a whole roll of duct tape on each of my wrists trying to hold me down. I sighed and stopped knowing my effort was pointless.

I was still in my bikini and shorts. At least he hadn't done anything with that. I was worried that, well, he did bad things to me.

I searched the room for him, but he was not there. The door was shut and that was the only escape except for the window. But since I was a little tied up, my chances of escaping were slim. And then I had another sensation.

My bladder.

It was telling me it was time to use the bathroom. It was all I could think about as I lay there helplessly. I wanted to scream, but he'd only be more furious. So I sang a song in my head. And I thought about my family. I was gone for a day now. They had to be going bananas. I couldn't imagine what my mom was like, let alone Caleb.

Then I heard footsteps coming up the stairs. The feet were heavy on the wood stairs. I just guessed it was wood by the sound of each foot hitting the step. They were coming nearer and nearer. Then, they stopped.

My heart thudded with each step and stopped beating when they stopped thudding. The suspense was killing me. And then my heart began again beating faster than it has ever gone before. There was no way of controlling it.

The footsteps continued until right outside the door. The doorknob turned and the door opened. I debated whether to keep my eyes open or shut. I couldn't choose so I just let them stay open.

"I see you're finally awake," he mumbled softly. It wasn't his killer voice he had used last night. It was depressed, almost too sad. Sounding like he had been defeated. But, he hadn't! I'm the one tied up! Why should he be so sad?

He slumped into a chair near the opposite wall of the bed beside the window. He held his head up with his hand and didn't look up at me for the longest time. And, as dumbfounded as I was, I couldn't find the words to speak.

He just shook his head and finally looked up. His eyes were beet red and drowning with tears. I blinked to make sure I was seeing right.

"I prayed each night that I didn't kill you. Each night. But I just couldn't get myself to untie you. The first night, I could have killed you right then and there where you were just lying." He looked back down, but continued, "My finger was on the trigger and ready to pull it. But I looked at your long blonde hair and I just couldn't. I couldn't."

I thought. Did he say each night? I've been sleeping for more than one night! What did he do to me that kept me unconscious for more than one night?

He continued to shake his head, "The next day I prayed that you'd wake up, but you never did. And, this afternoon when I heard the bed move against the floor, I nearly broke down with tears at the table downstairs."

He looked up at me once more and stared deeply into my eyes with concentration. "Why aren't you screaming? Or, crying. Or, reacting in any way?"

I shrugged my shoulders.

"I don't have any feeling right now. I'm too..."—I paused and gestured towards the ropes and duct tape—"a little preoccupied at the moment."

And for the first time since the time in the car, I saw him smile. Again, his evil side was put away and here came the nice-guy act. Damn, he was a good actor.

"I thought I killed you. I didn't mean to. I truly didn't mean to. But my anger that night was stronger than it's ever been. You standing there in the same spot you were eight years ago when I watched you from the police car. Your memories were just as bad as mine.

"I just wanted to torture you. I wanted to watch you suffer. I wanted to see you lie there and die in pain like I had to sit in jail and pain. You needed to feel what I felt all those years in prison. You needed to!"

I shuddered at the volume of his voice which suddenly rose. His temper obviously was flaring again.

"Listen..." I started but was interrupted by him putting his hand up in the air.

"Sara, you've been gone for days. I just can't..."

"Please, I can't take it anymore. What is your name?"

He looked at me with confused eyes, "What?"

"I've known you for a long time and I've never known your name. I walked out the door before my mom could tell me the day my dad died. What's your name?"

He looked down, "Dave."

"Dave, can I ask you a favor?"

He looked up, not with a smile, but more of a pout, and nodded wearily.

"Can you untie me and please let me use the bathroom? It's killing me!"

He jumped up without a second of hesitation. He began taking off the ropes tied around my stomach. After that, he worked with the tape. Layers of tape aren't the easiest thing to take off. Finally, when he was done, I could let my arms down and move them. But I couldn't help but notice the big, bright red marks that completely surrounded my wrists. I looked up at Dave who shrugged with sadness in his eyes.

I jumped off the bed without a thought and ran out the door.

"Next door on your left!" Dave yelled.

As I shut the door, I locked it. I ran straight to the window to see if I could see where I was at. But I sighed as I looked out and saw nothing but another building and grass. I was also two stories up.

I hesitated as I looked in the mirror. I found myself gasping at the sight of my neck. There were marks where he held my neck. They were deep and bright red. And, when I touched them, they throbbed with pain. Also I realized that my back pain was real, probably from lying in the bed for days.

How many days?

Dave had never really said.

I scanned the rest of my body to make sure he hadn't done anything to me when I was out. If he had—and I had to choke out the word, but it was quite possible—raped me. I could only pray that he hadn't.

My hand reached for the door but jerked away as I decided to stay in the bathroom. But then I realized he'd get furious and do anything possible to hurt me. I unlocked the door hesitantly and walked out the room.

He was leaning against the railing, his arms crossed and his head down.

"In the room," he murmured in a low breath.

I paused and didn't register why he was so sweet in the room and now his killer voice was back. Again, it scared me. His different moods.

"Now!" he hollered looking up. "Why the stand still?"

I frowned at him, "Your moods."

He sighed and just pointed to the bed room. I walked slowly into the bedroom, letting my feet drag behind me. He gave me one final shove. I thought he was following me, I heard the door slam louder than I've ever slammed it before in my life. Then I heard him fiddle with the lock.

My heart raced. I panicked. My mind couldn't register fast enough but I ran straight to the door. I jerked with the handle. The door was locked.

"Don't even try to get out the window. That's locked, too." I could hear him sigh. "I'm sorry for all this, Sara. But," he paused, "I'll be back later with supper."

"Don't leave me alone too long. I need some answers!"

He sighed again and I heard his footsteps hit each step.

"And Dave?"

I heard the footsteps stop.

"Can you get me some decent clothes?"

I heard him sigh, almost reluctantly, "In the dresser. They were my, well, you can just use them." He stuttered but continued to walk down the stairs.

The dresser was full of teenage girl clothes. Beautiful. Who could they possibly belong to? It did make me shiver at the thought that these were clothes from previous girls he had here. I shook my head. There's no way he could have had girls here before. Nope.

The shirt was too big, but that's the way I wanted it and the pants looked like they were pajama pants. I opened the drawer full of bras and panties and found a bra that looked my size. This would be much more comfortable than that bikini.

The bed to me looked like the most comfortable, but I couldn't help my curious glance to wander over to the window. And my hands were itching to actually see if the window was locked. Trial and error. It was locked.

I sighed and slumped onto the bed. My stomach growled, telling me I was way past due for food. Dave did say that he would be back with supper. Hopefully not too late. He's starving me to death.

Then my eyes spotted something that would help me in more ways than I could count.

Dave's cell phone.

I jumped up as softly as I could. I grabbed and wanted to place it in my pocket but thought he would easily find that. I thought about putting it in my sock, which sounded like a good plan, but what if it would make noise?

I thought of the only place that it would be hidden. It looked like a perfect place on the TV screen when all the actresses did it. I've seen it done in movies so it must work. It's why girls wear them, right? So I stuck the phone in my bra. And I made sure that it wasn't noticeable. My heart thudded again as I heard his footsteps against the wood again.

As he opened the door, I could smell the macaroni and cheese. It made my stomach grumble louder. I was sure I was blushing as he set it down in front of me.

"Best I can do. Hope it's good enough." He had a hint of smile on his face.

I laughed, "It's just fine." I hesitated before I grabbed the fork, but my stomach told me to eat it. The first bite was amazing. I hadn't realized how thirsty I was. I grabbed the cup of water sitting next to the plate and drank it down without catching air.

Dave laughed and went to refill my cup. I had the plate clean when he came back minutes later. He laughed once again and reached for my plate.

"I'm full." I gestured him towards the chair near the window. "I need answers."

He sighed as he sat down and his face looked defeated and tired, "I'll give you what I can."

His look on his face was too depressing, I had to look down. I fiddled with my fingers before I spat out the first question.

"Where am I?"

He huffed, "I planned on *not* telling you but might as well. You can't do anything about that. You're in Jeffersontown." My eyes must have given away the shock. "Couldn't keep you in California. Authorities were all over my house."

I sighed, "Where at in Jeffersontown?"

He shook his head, "An old friend's house. He's, er, out of town."

"You mean to tell me I'm *minutes* away from my family!"

He shrugged.

"I bet they are in pain!"

He smiled with a hint of smug in his smirk, "They are. Want to watch on the TV?"

I nodded and unwillingly followed him down the stairs. He pointed towards the couch, gesturing me where to sit. He flipped on the TV and immediately turned on the news.

"She's been gone for 10 days, now." The news lady was serious with compassion. She almost showed tears. "But, the family isn't giving up. Sara Raquel Young has been missing since the night of July 5 in the hotel in Topanga Beach. There is only one suspect and his name is not being released at the moment.

"There's a number to call scrolling at the bottom of your screen if you see her,"— recent a picture of me—that I might add looked horrible—showed up on the TV—"or if you see him." A picture of Dave appeared. "Please call authorities immediately."

He switched the channel more times than once and every channel was the same thing. All for me. They were really looking for me! I couldn't believe how national it got. I was on CBS! But, how could I be gloating when I'm minutes away from my family and they don't even know it. They must be going bananas. I could only think of their pain.

"There's one more thing you have to see." He left and headed out the door only to return with a milk carton.

"Milk? I *know* what milk is."

He glared at me, "Look on the back."

And there in my hands, was a picture and information of me on the back of the carton. I couldn't believe it. I was truly gone. People were scared. People cared! They actually cared about me! But, again, I found myself angry and disappointed that I was happy that I was missing and hurting the ones who care about me. I felt foolish.

He just sat there still.

"When can I go home?" I asked, finally breaking the silence. My voice cracked as the tears streamed down my face.

He shook his head, "I don't know. I just don't know." He looked at me with serious eyes. "I don't want to go back to jail," he admitted with a defeated tone. "I just can't. Do you have any idea what I lost?"

I shook my head.

"My family. My wife and daughter...abandoned me. They left me when I was in jail. I never got a visit." His fists rolled up into balls. "I never got phone calls. Anything. They were ashamed of me! Their own husband and father!" He held his head in shame.

"The only reason I didn't shoot you was because you looked so much like her. My daughter. She was beautiful, just like you. Her smile would light up the room when she'd walk in. And one dumb mistake changed that all.

"I didn't mean to run into you. I really didn't. It was dumb to be drunk. But that day was a bad day for me. I got laid off my job. Said they had too many workers. Pissed me off! I went to the bar as early as I could. I had to get home so I drove.

"That day is hazy for me. I don't remember much, only seeing you standing there helpless watching your...father...laying there." He paused and looked up again. "Did he die at the scene or at the hospital?"

I choked it out, "Hospital."

"When I saw you guys walk into that hotel, my heart raced. It took everything in me not to shoot you all then. I was so mad. I blamed you for everything. My wife leaving me. My beautiful daughter. Both gone. It just," he slammed his fist into the sofa arm, "shocked me." He looked at me again with teary eyes, "I miss them so much. And now I'll go away for longer. They've got to hate me even more now."

There was a knot in my throat, "I don't know what to say."

He laughed dryly, "Me either." He paused and smiled, "Someone texted me from your phone. Called me a dirty person."

"Who?"

He shrugged his shoulders and didn't look at me for a long time. He turned the TV up and we sat there watching the news lady talk about the girl from North Dakota that has been gone for almost two weeks.

He yawned and demanded, "I'm tired. Up the stairs."

I took my time up the stairs and paused before the door, "May I go to the bathroom?"

He nodded reluctantly and leaned against the railing as he did before. I sighed and went into the bathroom and locked the door again.

This was the time I could finally panic in peace. My heart thudded louder than it has ever before and I couldn't stop it. But Dave said I reminded him of his daughter. There's no way he would kill his own daughter.

I stared in the mirror. It must've been weeks, technically almost two, since I washed my face. I gave it a good wash and dried it with a towel. I rinsed my mouth out a good amount of times. There was a taste of left-over Mac-and-cheese.

I didn't want to but I went out of the bathroom and met the evil glare of Dave. I smiled and didn't look back as I went into the room again. With softer bang than before, he slammed the door, locked it tight, and I heard his footsteps go down the stairs again.

I waited until I was sure he was asleep that I pulled out the phone and made sure it was on with no volume. I tucked myself deep into the bed. My hands were shaking as I opened the phone. My mind went blank. I couldn't remember Caleb's number.

But my fingers dialed a number before I could remember. I don't know why I called it, it just happened. I had called the police. When the lady answered, I whispered as loudly as I thought I could without his hearing me.

"911 operator."

"Please help me."

"What's wrong, dear?"

"I've been kidnapped."

She almost sounded as if she didn't believe me. "Why are you whispering?"

I sighed, "He can hear me if I talk too loud. Please help me."

"Okay. What's your name?"

"Sara Young."

I heard the lady gasp on the other line and scream in the receiver that she's talking to the missing girl from North Dakota.

"Sara, police are on their way. Where are you?"

"Jeffersontown."

"Do you know specifically?"

"No."

"Okay, don't panic. We'll be there soon. Did he hurt you?"

"No." I looked at the marks on my wrists and felt my neck. "A little. I'm fine, though."

"Okay, don't panic," she repeated with a deep breath.

"I have to go, please tell my family I'm okay and that I love them."

"I will," she sighed, "Be strong."

I flipped the phone shut and breathed a sigh in relief. I stuck the phone back in my bra where it would be safe and sound. His footsteps started to move again and grew nearer and nearer. I turned over quietly in my bed and pretended to snore and be asleep. The door creaked open and my scheme must have worked because he huffed and shut the door again, fiddled with the locks, and went back down the stairs.

I smiled a wide smile and shut my eyes drifting off into a deep, deep sleep...

CALEB'S VIEW

CHAPTER NINETEEN

until it's gone

I took off my wig and scratched my head. I waited for Sara and Penny to return from the swimming pool. Nadir was going away for awhile while I had fun with Sara. Sara and I had just gone to our first premiere together. It was amazing. And she actually liked it! I was so worried she wouldn't like it. I relaxed as I waited for Sara to arrive.

"Caleb!"

Penny's voice rang through the room as she came in alone. She was humming to herself, but my question still remained.

"Where's Sara?"

"She went back down to get towels? I think that's what she said."

I pondered that for a moment and then realized I'd asked her to get me some while she was down there. I couldn't wait to see her again. To hold her close to me and to smell her sweet perfume. To look into those deep blue eyes and smile at her when she smiled.

I can't handle her in this much pain. The pain that she has to be hiding the whole time. She has to be in fear for her life. She blew her top more than once. I can't believe that she thinks that I would end what we have because of *him*. In reality, there was nothing I could do to help her except love her and comfort her.

In ways, I felt like I could protect her and keep her safe. But I wasn't supernatural. I didn't have super powers. Thoughts went through my mind like what if he actually got her? Or what if she was hurt because of me.

I made myself comfortable on the bed after I got out of the shower. The spot next to me lay empty for Sara to sleep in when she was to get back.

The minutes ticked by and I grew antsy when she didn't return in a half an hour. I walked into the other room to see if maybe she went in there.

"Is Sara in here?" I asked over the noise of the family in the next room.

The room suddenly grew quiet and the happy faces turned into worried faces.

Cadie stood up and shook her head, "No. Why?"

I looked at Penny who was just as worried as I was, "She never came back from getting towels."

"What?" Cadie gasped, throwing her hand up over her heart.

Penny shook her head, "Let's not panic. Caleb and I will go down to the lobby to see if she's still there. Someone call her phone. We'll see what happens when we get back."

Penny's eyes were soaked with tears as we got to the elevator. "Caleb, I'm so sorry."

I shook my head, "It's okay. It's not your fault." I lowered my head and all the anger was building up. My fists wanted to slam right into the elevator door, but I settled for squeezing them really tight.

Now all I really wanted to do was hold her tightly. I needed to hold my girlfriend in my arms and embrace her. Penny would have to do for now.

But the time the elevator beeped to the lobby, Penny was frantic. I wrapped one arm around her holding her close into my arms. She looked up at me with the eyes of pain and walked out into lobby.

The two men at the front desk didn't seem to be paying attention to anything. We would probably be the only action they had all night. My eyes scanned the lobby, but Sara was nowhere in sight. My heart sank as the lobby came up empty except for us and the two people at the counter.

"Excuse me, Sir?" I didn't want to sound scared but I couldn't help it my voice cracked.

"Can I help you?"

I spit out the words as clearly as I could, "Have you seen a girl with blonde hair down here lately? Long blonde hair. Short. Maybe escorted by a man?"

He thought a moment and asked his partner. His eyes lit up in a matter of a second. "Yes! She left about 30 minutes ago. The man was smiling though. What's wrong?"

I hung my head and closed my eyes.

Sara was gone.

"Sara's missing," I whispered with my head still down talking to Penny, not the men. "She's *gone.*"

I felt Penny's hand against my back. She started to talk to the man, but I tuned her out. It didn't make sense. I thought he was in North Dakota. I thought he'd leave her alone. And I thought I could protect her! I was wrong! I failed!

I just wanted to punch something and not stop. There was an empty feeling that I had inside me, the feeling of someone missing. I looked at the two at the counter with their concerned faces. One had the phone close to his ear and the other watched a computer screen.

Anger boiled up. "This isn't time to check email," I mumbled with my head still down.

Penny whispered, "He's looking at security cameras. Calm."

I could hear the other guy talk to the police on the phone describing the situation. I couldn't believe that he was talking about Sara. *My* Sara.

I shook my head, "The love of my life is gone! How can I stay calm?" I looked at the man with the name tag reading Rob. "Rob," I whispered as softly as I could. "Do you see her in the cameras?"

Rob looked up and nodded his head. "She's right here in the elevator. The guy," he paused and swallowed and looked at us, "has a gun."

I couldn't take it. I slammed my fists into the counter. I stormed away from the counter and headed towards the elevator. I didn't go in, but I stood there and wished I could have been there to prevent this.

The guy preventing me from seeing Sara needed to be punished. And if I ever got the chance, he wouldn't see the light of day again. He has put Sara through hell; now he needs to go through hell.

Penny came up behind me, "Police are on their way. He can't be too far."

The rest of the family came down after we paged them. Cadie's eyes were streaked with tears. Cameron and Cole also had red eyes, first time I've ever seen them like that. This wasn't easy on any of us. Melanie and Robert were also down here, eyes puffy with tears. Melanie came over to me and wrapped her arms around me,

Penny ran to Melanie, "Mom, I can't help but think this is my fault."

She shook her head, "Don't think that! We'll find her."

My voice cracked, "I need to find her."

Robert softly spoke, "We will."

Cadie's cries were heard from the lobby. I was sitting in the coffee room a good distance from the lobby. It killed me to hear her cry that hard. And to think it was my fault. To know that that *person* has her somewhere. Hurting her. Torturing her!

I sat in the dark room alone for what seemed like hours waiting for the police to arrive. The sadness out in the lobby was too much for me to handle. Although sitting in a dark room isn't much better.

I jumped up as I heard Melanie call my name. A dozen officers were standing in the lobby with more entering the building. I made myself sit near the group of people as the officers questioned us, as well as the two men at the counter.

Sara's family was too speechless to speak and I was in shock. But I couldn't have Penny describe Sara, I'd regret it later.

"She's about 5'4", blonde...," Penny started but I quickly stopped her.

"...*beautiful*, long blonde hair. Deep blue eyes. Her smile will melt you away."

I looked up at the officer who had a smirk on his face. Steam would have been blowing out of my ears if I was a character in a book.

"Are you finding this humorous?" I asked with a tone that was threatening.

The smile was quickly gone and he shook his head. He scribbled more in his small notebook and walked over to the counter to talk with the other men.

Half my body said go look for her. The other half said stay here and wait. I went with my instincts. My eyes didn't look at the people surrounding me. I just walked by.

"Where are you going?" Cadie said finally watching me leave.

I turned around to her eyes and had to look away, "I'm going to find her."

"Caleb," she began but I just walked out and didn't pause as I stalked out of the hotel. I went straight to the bright pink Charger. As I got in, I inhaled her perfume from the last time she'd driven it. The seat was as far forward as it could be. I had to laugh. She was so short.

I had a place in my mind where I would go first. It wasn't quite where Sara would be, but I needed to feel peace for a few minutes.

The stars were out and I thought back to the time I first took Sara on the roof and watched the stars. She was radiantly beautiful that night. Then she had asked me what my worst fear was. And, though it took me awhile to answer, I told the truth. The fear was that I was lost and I didn't know where I was. Or that someone was lost and I didn't know where to look. What to do. To think that someone I knew was lost. Every time I started to think about that, I shivered.

Now my fear was coming true.

My eyes were glued to Sara's house as I drove by. Turning down the next street and seeing the familiar house, I could see Lili in her house up in her room near the window. How would I tell her about Sara? How much would she care? But, I didn't stop the car. I kept driving until I drove under the 'Memorial Graveyard' sign. I didn't know where he was, but I needed to find him.

His grave stood out. Maybe it was the height of the tombstone or the bright flowers that stood out in the dark. Although I've never had anyone special in my life die, I knew exactly what to say.

"Luke, find your daughter. Help us. If you were here, would you want her missing? Please, keep her safe. Keep her alive. Bring her to us."

I stopped. I realized how crazy I sounded. This is what it feels like to talk to someone who doesn't respond. Sara's name was carved into the stone. I traced my fingers over the letters and stood up.

"You guys have a crazy family."

His voice startled me. I didn't know who it was. In the pit of my stomach I had a feeling that it was *him*. But then there was the part of how his voice was too young.

I turned around to a teenage boy.

"Excuse me?"

He smiled, "Your sister talks to herself every time she comes here."

I sighed, "Sara. She's not my, er, sister. She's my, um, girlfriend."

"She's quite something. I'm Bobby."

"Caleb."

"Where is she?"

This would be the first time I would have to admit she was gone. I sighed, "She's missing."

"What?"

I couldn't get his expression out of my head on the way back to the hotel. He had stood there with his hand over his mouth for the longest time. He took it harder than I ever thought.

I drove past the street where her father was killed. I paused when I saw a small, dark-colored car speed away from the curb. Sara was right; you could still see the marks from the accident. It had been eight years; wouldn't the city have cleaned it up by now?

I parked the car in front of her best friend's house, waiting to get up my nerve to go and talk to Lili about it. But with all my might, I just couldn't. I couldn't go and tell her that her best friend was missing. There wasn't anything in me that told me to. But I had to.

My body wanted to turn around as I knocked on the door, but Lili answered it before I could react. I'm sure my face gave away the misery because she was smiling before and now it was just plain painful to look at her face. Her mouth had dropped into an oval shape and she shook her head frantically.

"What's wrong?"

I shook my head, "Can I come in?" My voice was low and full of fear.

I followed her into the living room and sat down on the couch.

"Sara's missing."

She gasped, "What? Is it that guy?"

I had to mumbled, it's all I had left, "We think so."

"Oh, my. I can't believe"—she kept shaking her head frantically—"he actually got her? I thought the police..."

"I thought so too."

"Are we going to look for her?"

I shrugged my shoulders, "Police are."

"We aren't."

I shook my head, "No, but I better go. I didn't say where I was going."

She nodded, "Keep in touch. Tell me as soon as you find her."

"I will."

As the time passed, I dreamt of her small soft fingers in between mine holding on tight. Her smile was as real as if she was feet away from me. I was holding her. Holding her tight. But it turned out to just be a dream and I'd wake up sweating and alone in the darkness of my room.

I could hear the highway still buzzing with cars, one of them possibly contained Sara, but who was to know?

I held my head in disappointment. I didn't care about anything anymore. I was done. I needed Sara and I needed her now.

My body was covered in sweat as I lay back down on the bed breathing each breath more desperately than the last one. I couldn't resist slamming my fist into the pillow harder each time I did. I was a man, but was nothing without her. I cried. I didn't care.

California wasn't the same without her. Police were searching every house they possibly could to make sure he wasn't here. They raided his house and found nothing. Sara's old house was also a target but turned up empty.

After a week, the nation was alerted and WANTED signs were up around the states. Andy and Cadie had T-shirts made with a picture of Sara, need I mention she looked beautiful. On the back of every milk carton was her face along with *his* face. I kept the picture of my beautiful Sara next to me each night, wishing that it was her and not just a picture.

And when the day finally came that the police had an idea where she was; I couldn't believe where they thought.

The policeman stood with his hat in his hand and his eyes full of sincerity. "We've tracked his phone. They aren't in California."

I wasn't the only one who was frozen. Everyone in the small hotel room was in shock. Sara was on the move while we sat here and searched around California.

"We don't think he's hurt her. We've searched everywhere here. They've got to be in Edgemont. There's nowhere else. They are either in Edgemont or on the move to Edgemont."

I wanted to smile and yet with all the sadness that has come this week, I couldn't. My lips wouldn't form into the smile that would brighten up Sara's eyes every time.

Everyone stood still. I was the first to speak. My words were harsh. "What are we waiting for?"

The policeman looked surprised that my tone was that harsh.

He just coughed with the shocked look on their faces, "I have tickets for you all."

We found Sara's phone in the room the night she went missing. Hundreds of text messages came from her friends intended for me saying how sorry they were. There was only one number I was looking for on here and it was *his*. I wanted to say the worst possible things to *him*. He needed to know the anger and the fury I had towards him.

'you dirty person.'

My eyes were locked unto the phone waiting for it to vibrate. I wanted him to reply so the police could track his number. They needed to know exactly where he was. But I realized he wouldn't text me back. And, in all honesty, I didn't care. I just wanted him to read it. To know that I hated him.

I didn't care whether we were first class or riding with the monkeys down below; I just wanted to get home. But the plane seemed to take forever and a year. I couldn't get up and walk around without getting yelled at. I settled for listening to Sara's iPod. I had to laugh at all her country music.

After we got off the plane in Fairview, I rode alone in my Challenger looking frequently towards the passenger seat where Sara should be. She should be riding home with me. Men don't cry, but I broke down. I pounded the steering wheel plenty of times before my hands registered the pain. Sara's rosary that she wore on occasions was around my neck.

I slammed on the brakes as a deer made its way over the road. My heart raced faster than it has ever before. The deer trotted away like nothing happen as I sat stunned in the car. The tears rolled down my face. I guess I gave up at the moment. Sara wasn't here and *he* had her. There was nothing I could do. It was me against the whole United States. How could she be so close and then in minutes she's gone?

You could say I felt sorry for myself. I sat in the middle of the gravel road for hours watching the sunset. Melanie and Robert were probably flipping out that I didn't come home, but I didn't care. I couldn't look at their faces. I didn't feel like talking.

The car behind me with lights is what made me move. I reluctantly pulled into the driveway and put the car in park. In the window, I could see my parents sitting by the table with their heads down low. I slammed the car door and they immediately put their heads up and saw me. Melanie got up. My brain told me she was headed towards the door.

She beat me to it.

"Why didn't you call?" she yelled frantically out the door.

I just mumbled, "I'm sorry."

Edgemont was, you could probably say, decorated in signs of WANTED and HAVE YOU SEEN ME?. Sara's pictures were up on every tree and post. Flowers were constantly arriving at her house. Cadie didn't know what to do with all the flowers. She donated most of the bouquets to the neighbors and other friends, but the house was still full of flowers.

It was a repetition. Every day on the news, there would be a good portion about Sara and the family. They didn't release anything major except that she was still missing. Every channel had it on. And I couldn't get myself to drink the milk that had her face on the back of the carton.

"I miss her so much."

Cole and Cameron came over late on the ninth day she was missing.

"I know, man, me too," Cole sniffled with the thought. "I regret the times that I didn't say I love you back to her."

Cameron laughed, "Bug."

"We'll see her again, guys," I assured them. "We will."

Every night I didn't sleep. I just stared at the picture of us at her birthday party. Her smile was wide. A smile grew across my face whenever I saw the picture. I tossed and turned until the sun was rising in the distance. I walked outside in the fresh air for miles until I couldn't walk anymore. By then, the sun had fully risen and my family would be awake.

Penny wasn't herself either. I hadn't seen her laugh since she came in smiling at the hotel. She blames herself since she didn't offer to go with her.

"It's my fault," she pleaded, "it's my fault that she's gone."

I could only shake my head, "It's not."

She screamed, "Yes! I should have..."

"I shouldn't have asked for towels then!" I raised my voice too loudly and stunned my sister. She stared at me with water swelling up in her eyes. Melanie and Robert quietly joined us in her room. I shook my head and grabbed Penny in my arms.

"I'm sorry. It's *his* fault."

I heard Melanie's cries and saw Robert's saddened face as I held my sister in my arms.

Each day, my family and I moped around the house each taking our turn beside the phone. Whenever it would ring, it would be Cadie keeping us updated. I kept marking on the calendar how many days she had been gone. We were in California for seven days. There were ten X marks on the calendar. Ten days she'd been gone. It was repetition now until we found her.

Today marked the eleventh day she was gone. As I paced back and forth in my room, my mind went blank. The wall in front of me became the person who took my Sara. I wasn't thinking as I forced my fist into a ball and hammered it through the wall. I quickly pulled it back. The pain piercing through my hand was more than I could handle.

The hole matching the size of my fist in the wall made me want to punch it again. I cursed at myself for letting this happen to her.

A knock on the door startled me.

"Caleb?" Penny's voice came from behind the door.

"What?" I said more angrily than I had planned. I wasn't in the mood to talk to her.

She walked in slowly, seeing the hole in the wall.

"I heard a noise," she said as she gestured to the wall, implying she figured it out.

I hadn't realized I was holding my hand. As I glanced down, I saw blood. I sighed and cursed.

"Are you okay?" Penny came over to me grabbing my hand.

Pulling back was my first intention.

"Sorry," she replied angrily walking out the door.

"Penny," I sighed. "I'm sorry."

She turned around, eyes tear-streaked. She ran over to me and buried her face into my chest. I wrapped my arms around my sister, hoping to not let go. There was this empty feeling inside me not knowing where Sara was.

The police promised!

Promised!

And he got her!

My rage was far too much inside. I was about to explode. By the looks on my wall, I already had.

"I miss her so much." Penny loved Sara just as I much as I did. Sara is like a second sister to Penny.

"Me, too. Me, too."

She let go and sniffled, "Let's go get your hand fixed, okay?"

I nodded.

"Caleb!" Melanie screamed as I walked through the door.

"I'm all right, Mom. Anger got the best of me."

She quickly ran to my side. I hated to be babied especially when Sara needed us the most. Melanie laughed. I was shocked she had humor left.

"Your father's anger got to the best of him, too," she laughed and pointed to the hole in the kitchen wall. "This has been hard on all of us. Sara was so—" she choked back the tears as she fiddled with my hand, quickly changing the wording, "—*is* nice and beautiful." She looked up at me with her worried eyes, "She's coming home."

I nodded and grasped my mom in my arms. Tears swelled up in my eyes. Penny was standing beside us, wiping her own tears away.

Robert came around the corner with a bag of peas over his hand. He stopped when he saw us all together and turned around and headed out the door.

"Dad," I stopped him, "don't leave. We have the same problem. We'll fix our walls together." I showed him my swelled hand and he smiled. I let my lips curve into a smile.

"When she gets back," he mumbled, "she'll help us." He looked down as he said the words. "When she gets back." He shook his head.

"Okay, when Sara gets back."

As I sat in my room looking at the photos of her and me, I only wanted to hug her. To smell the lotion she puts on constantly, I wanted to smell her scent. I needed to see those blue eyes. I need to see her long, luscious blonde hair. The long for her tiny fingers in between mine is there.

I need her.

I want her.

I'm going to find her.

I jumped as I heard my phone go off. With every ring of the phone, I believe it's the news she's back. But it was only Jordan. No one mattered to me now. Only Sara.

"Hello?" I didn't want to sound angry or anything, but I couldn't help it.

"It's Jordan, how are you?"

I sighed. He knew the answer. "I'm fine."

"Doesn't sound like it."

"Did you only call to interrogate me?"

"No, sorry, man. Just wanted to check. She grew on me."

I murmured harshly, "She grew on everybody."

"I'm sorry. I didn't mean to make you mad." I now could hear the frustration in his voice with the tone of *my* voice.

I breathed deeply, "Sorry, Jord. It's so frustrating. I can't handle it."

"Want me to come over? Or do you need a guy's night?"

It has been almost two weeks since Sara had been gone. It seemed like forever ago when I had laughed.

"Dude, you need to get out. She'll come back. She'll come back!"

"Really, I'm okay. I just need"—I paused because my voice cracked—"Sara."

Jordan sighed and I knew he wasn't happy with the ending of this conversation. "If you need me, man, I'm here."

I smiled, "I know. You, me, and Sara will hang out soon, okay?"

There was a long pause before Jordan answered again. "Most definitely. Get some sleep, you sound awful."

I laughed, "Will do."

"Later, Caleb."

"Later."

The twelfth day.

Everyday got harder and harder.

It was excruciating pain to watch the news every night and see Sara's face along with the man who took her. I honestly couldn't bear it every time and ended up leaving even angrier than when I began to watch the TV.

"Today marks the twelfth day Sara Young of Edgemont, North Dakota, has been missing. Police say there's a good chance she might still be alive and in the area. If you have any news or information, please contact the police."

Melanie quickly flipped the television to a different channel and sure enough. Breaking news scrolled across the bottom about Sara.

If only she was famous for a good reason.

And yet she could be dead in a ditch. Or tortured in the basement of some house in Mexico. She could be in London for all I know.

And that's the part that hurts the worst.

"Caleb?" Robert's voice broke through the voices on the screen.

I only nodded. It's all I could do.

"You need to eat something."

He was right. I had barely eaten since we got home from California. Just a simple glass of juice or some crackers. I didn't have an appetite. I did, however, drink water like crazy. Crying so much left me thirsty.

I shook my head and grinded my teeth together to keep me from exploding.

"Honey," Melanie pleaded, "you have to!"

"Mom," I gritted, "I can't."

She sighed understanding why I wasn't eating. But I could feel her pain I was causing. But I was in so much more pain.

The stars were high in the sky on the thirteenth night. I lay on the same spot I had taken Sara to many, many nights ago. There, she lay in my arms. There, I told her I loved her. There, I told her my biggest fear. And it was the first time we fell asleep together. Now my biggest fear was coming true.

But I was alone tonight.

There was that one star that shone so bright made me smile. It wasn't Sara. It was her dad. I wanted so badly for him to talk to me. I wanted him to tell me it was going to be okay and that she was coming back tonight. I wanted him to just say that Sara would be in my arms soon. Very soon.

I closed my eyes and wished on the shooting star that ran across the sky. It is obvious what I wished for.

In the middle of July, it is always likely to storm. But, tonight, however, was a beautiful night with not a cloud in the sky and just the tiny hint of the northwestern breeze. I ran my fingers through my hair and remembered all the times that Sara played with it, telling me how great it was. I had to laugh.

"Caleb!"

Penny's scream was coming from the open window in my room. It wasn't the scream of fear or anguish. It was excitement. As if she was jubilant. I shot straight up without thinking. My feet reacted before my brain could and I was running down the ladder and into my window.

She was standing in my room and her face was lit up just as the stars were. A smile slid across her face that touched her tear-streaked eyes.

"Caleb! They," she sighed happily, "found her."

epilogue

Anger rushed over Caleb faster than anything else. He, along with everybody, had to keep praying in order to stay somewhat sane. But he couldn't stop thinking about Sara every waking moment. Sara didn't know, but although he fell for her fast, he knew her before.

At the autograph signing that Lili and Sara attending, Nadir remembered Sara and immediately fell in love with her there. Nadir looked terribly hard for the beautiful blonde haired girl from the signing but failed.

And when he saw her walking down the hallway with Penny, Caleb immediately freaked and couldn't control his love and passion for her. Creepy at first, their love turned real. Sara fell for Caleb and Caleb fell for Sara.

Even though Penny came screaming in that they found her, that doesn't mean that Sara is alive and well.

That's where our story ends, for now. But what will happen next? Their trials and struggles aren't over quite yet!

Made in the USA
Lexington, KY
13 August 2011